Marius' Mules V:
Hades' Gate

by S. J. A. Turney

1st Edition

'Marius' Mules: nickname acquired by the legions after the general Marius made it standard practice for the soldier to carry all of his kit about his person.'

For Garry & Agnieszka.

I would like to thank those people instrumental in bringing Marius' Mules 5 to fruition and making it the book it is. Jenny and Lilian for their initial editing, Tracey for putting up with me. Leni and Barry for their proofing skills. Garry, Paul and Dave for the cover work. Paul B, Prue, Gordon, Robin, Nick, Kate, Mike and innumerable other fab folk for their support, and Ben Kane, Tony Riches, Angus Donald and Doug Jackson for constant words of encouragement.

Cover photos courtesy of Paul and Garry of the Deva Victrix Legio XX. Visit http://www.romantoursuk.com/ to see their excellent work.

Cover design by Dave Slaney.

Many thanks to all three for their skill and generosity.

Published in this format 2013 by Victrix Books

First Edition

Also by S. J. A. Turney:

Continuing the Marius' Mules Series

Marius' Mules I: The Invasion of Gaul (2009)
Marius' Mules II: The Belgae (2010)
Marius' Mules III: Gallia Invicta (2011)
Marius' Mules IV: Conspiracy of Eagles (2012)
Marius' Mules VI: Caesar's Vow (2014)
Marius' Mules: Prelude to War (2014)
Marius' Mules VII: The Great Revolt (2014)
Marius' Mules VIII: Sons of Taranis (2015)
Marius' Mules IX: Pax Gallica (2016)

The Praetorian Series

The Great Game (2015)
The Price of Treason (2015)
Eagles of Dacia (Autumn 2017)

The Ottoman Cycle

The Thief's Tale (2013)
The Priest's Tale (2013)
The Assassin's Tale (2014)
The Pasha's Tale (2015)

Tales of the Empire

Interregnum (2009)
Ironroot (2010)
Dark Empress (2011)
Insurgency (2016)
Invasion (2017)

Roman Adventures (Children's Roman fiction with Dave Slaney)

Crocodile Legion (2016)

Pirate Legion (Summer 2017)

Short story compilations & contributions:

Tales of Ancient Rome vol. 1 - S.J.A. Turney (2011)
Tortured Hearts vol 1 - Various (2012)
Tortured Hearts vol 2 - Various (2012)
Temporal Tales - Various (2013)
A Year of Ravens - Various (2015)
A Song of War – Various (Oct 2016)

For more information visit http://www.sjaturney.co.uk/
or http://www.facebook.com/SJATurney
or follow Simon on Twitter @SJATurney

Dramatis Personae at the outset of the tale

The Command Staff:

Gaius Julius Caesar: Politician, general and governor.
Aulus Ingenuus: Commander of Caesar's Praetorian Cohort.
Quintus Atius Varus: Commander of the Cavalry.
Quintus Titurius Sabinus: Lieutenant of Caesar.
Lucius Aurunculeius Cotta: Lieutenant of Caesar
Titus Labienus: Lieutenant of Caesar.
Gnaeus Vinicius Priscus: Former primus pilus of the Tenth, now camp prefect of the army.

Seventh Legion:

Quintus Tullius Cicero: Legate and brother of the great orator.
Lucius Fabius: Senior centurion
Tullus Furius: Primus pilus

Eighth Legion:

Decimus Brutus: Legate and favourite of Caesar's family.
Titus Balventius: Primus pilus & veteran of several terms.

Ninth Legion:

Publius Sulpicius Rufus: Young Legate of the Ninth.
Grattius: primus pilus, once in sole command of the Ninth.

Tenth Legion:

Servius Fabricius Carbo: Primus Pilus.
Atenos: Centurion and chief training officer, former Gaulish mercenary
Petrosidius: Chief Signifer of the first cohort.

Eleventh Legion:

Aulus Crispus: Legate, former civil servant in Rome.
Quintus Velanius: Senior Tribune.
Titus Silius: Junior Tribune.

'Felix': Primus Pilus, accounted an unlucky man.

<u>Twelfth Legion:</u>

Publius Sextius Baculus: Primus pilus. A distinguished veteran.

<u>Thirteenth Legion:</u>

Lucius Roscius: Legate and native of Illyricum.

<u>Fourteenth Legion:</u>

Lucius Munatius Plancus: Legate
Titus Pullo: Primus Pilus
Lucius Vorenum: Senior centurion

<u>Other characters:</u>

Marcus Falerius Fronto: Former legate of the Tenth.
Quintus Balbus: Former Legate of the Eighth, now retired. Close friend of Fronto.
Servius Galba: Former Legate of Twelfth. Now Praetor in Rome.
Faleria the elder: Mother of Fronto and matriarch of the Falerii.
Faleria the younger: sister of Fronto.
Corvinia: Wife of Balbus.
Lucilia: Elder daughter of Balbus & betrothed of Fronto.
Balbina: Younger daughter of Balbus.
Galronus: Belgic officer, commanding Caesar's auxiliary cavalry.
Publius Clodius Pulcher: Powerful man in Rome, client of Caesar and conspirator.
Paetus: Former officer, presumed dead, but fled to Rome.

The maps of Marius' Mules V

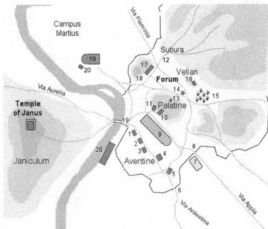

	South & Central Rome
1	Temple of Luna
2	Temple of Minerva
3	Temple of Diana
4	House of the Falerii
5	Temple of Bona Dea
6	Porta Naevia
7	Piscina Publica
8	Porta Capena
9	Circus Maximus
10	Temple of Apollo Palatinus
11	Temple of the Magna Mater
12	Balbus' favourite tavern
13	Ruined Porta Mugonia
14	Shrine of Jupiter
15	Marshes
16	Temple of the Penates
17	Tabularium
18	Tarpeian Rock
19	Pompey's theatre complex
20	House of Pompey

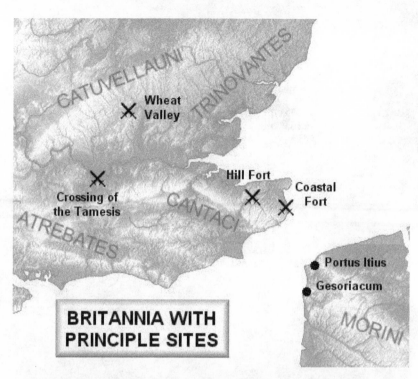

Wheat
Valley

CATUVELLAUNI

TRINOVANTES

Hill Fort

Coastal
Fort

Crossing of
the Tamesis

CANTACI

ATREBATES

Portus Itius

Gesoriacum

MORINI

**BRITANNIA WITH
PRINCIPLE SITES**

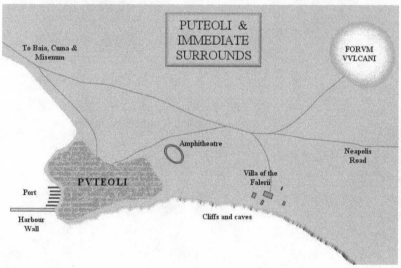

PUTEOLI &
IMMEDIATE
SURROUNDS

To Baia, Cuma &
Misenun

FORVM
VVLCANI

Amphitheatre

Neapolis
Road

Villa of the
Falerii

Port

PVTEOLI

Harbour
Wall

Cliffs and caves

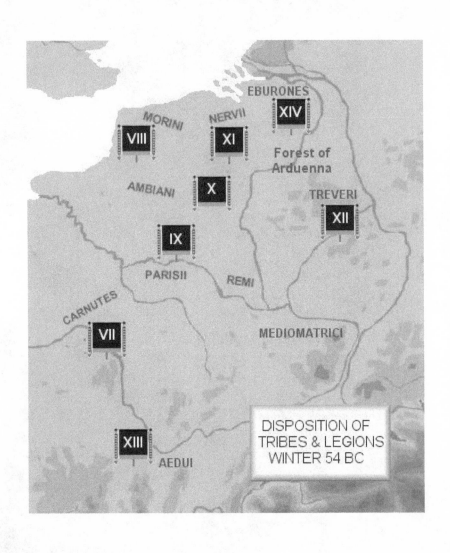

MORINI

NERVII

EBURONES

XIV
I

VIII
I

XI
I

Forest of
Arduenna

AMBIANI

X

TREVERI

XII
I

IX

PARISII

REMI

CARNUTES

MEDIOMATRICI

VII
I

XIII
I

AEDUI

DISPOSITION OF
TRIBES & LEGIONS
WINTER 54 BC

Prologue

Cold toes in sodden boots heaved wearily through the deep snow, long soaked trousers clinging to the young man's shins as he stumbled and staggered, one hand on the hilt of the eating knife that was his only armament, the other gripping the pouch on the thong around his neck. A trail of footprints betrayed his passage, but better that than a trail of blood. Silently - silence was a prerequisite of the hunted - the young man cursed his decision to travel without a sword. When two heavily armed bodyguards travelled with you, where was the need?

Botovios was no warrior, though, anyway. He had been chosen by the ageing Druid of Durocatalauno as an initiate into the ancient and sacred ways; chosen for his mind, his subtlety and his honour. But that had been before the Romans came; before *Caesar* came. Little could he have seen four years ago that instead of reading the Greek scrolls old Obaldos kept in his house he would be running for his life in the all-consuming blizzard, pursued by dogged legionaries and gripping the hope of all Gaul tightly to his chest.

It had been an uneventful ride from the Matrona River - the river of the Protecting Goddess - all the way deep into the territory of the Belgae, and Botovios and his two escorts had felt as though their journey was all but complete once they entered the great dark and comforting confines of the forest of Arduenna. But the ancient Goddess that sheltered the people of the Treveri tribe seemed not to be extending her gifts to the young adept and his guards.

The first he had realised that something was wrong had been when the rope suddenly tautened across the forest trail, unhorsing him and sending him onto his back in the two-foot-deep snow, knocking the wind and the sense from him.

By the time he had struggled out of the white grave that had claimed him and peered through the thick, drifting flakes trying to take stock of what had happened, his horse had gone, charging off down the trail ahead, screaming with the pain of some unseen wound.

Spinning round, he had desperately sought his companions.

'Tarvos? Icorix?'

But as his vision resolved the shapes through the snow, he knew they wouldn't answer. The shapes of thrashing horse's legs rose

1

above the white blanket that covered the world, attesting the violent and crippling wounding of the poor noble beasts. The bulky, heavy shape of Tarvos he could just make out, the big, bull-like warrior clutching his throat with both hands as a jet of dark liquid sprayed out to melt the snow. Icorix was in similar trouble, staggering backward through the snow, gripping the shaft of the pilum that jutted from his chest, the point faintly visible as a needle projecting from between his shoulder blades.

Both were as good as dead already.

Panic had gripped Botovios then: panic on so many levels. Panic that he was alone and virtually unarmed. Panic that unless he could flee to somewhere safe he was almost certainly about to die. Panic that his vital message would not get through to the chieftains gathered at Trebeto. Panic that that very message would find its way into the hands of the beast-spawn, whore-son that was Caesar of the Romans.

Panic.

Botovios had fled, but not before he had seen the shapes of two armoured nightmares emerging from the treelines, growing as they closed on the scene like demons from some childhood tale.

Everything was eerily silent in the blizzard. The only sound was the gentle flutter of the flakes falling around him, the occasional creak of a groaning branch sagging under the weight of the snow and the rhythmic crunch of his soaked boots in the calf-deep drifts.

Winter had not been kind to northern Gaul and the lands of the Belgae, and the snowfall had been disastrous to many. Here in the hills and endless woodland of Arduenna's forest even the trees had not managed to save the ground from its white shroud, such had been the regularity and severity of the snowfall. Botovios had ducked beneath the boughs of the forest proper as he had moved off the open track, hoping that the going would be easier but if anything it was more dangerous. The snow was perhaps a foot shallower beneath the branches than in the open, but it concealed the myriad dangers of tangled thorns, fallen branches and animal warrens.

Several times the young adept had fallen, tripped or become entangled. His shins were bruised and scratched, his trousers torn and bloodied, tiny pink spots melting into the snow in his deep footprints. But his pace never let up.

Despite the fact that he had seen or heard nothing of his pursuers, he knew they were there, and close. Old Obaldos had chosen him to the calling partially for his uncanny foresight and his strange kenning of things unseen. By much the same token, he knew that there were only two men following him, and not a cohort of the cursed Romans. But he also knew that those two men were every bit as deadly as a full cohort.

What he didn't understand, and could only put down to the displeasure of Arduenna, was why his uncanny sight had not warned him of the danger in the first place. Could it be that the Goddess disapproved of his mission? Of the whole plan? If she did, why would she? How could she favour the steel and bronze clad armies of the invader over her own sacred folk?

Once again, Botovios' shin struck a hidden branch in his desperate flight and he found himself pitched into the air and hurtling forward into the snow.

His eyes widened.

Desperately, his arms and legs flailed as he saw where he was falling. Beyond the hidden branch and a few more boles the ground slipped away into a short, steep slope that then dropped into a ravine. Far below, the icy, deep and fast river that thundered along the gorge was the first sound that cut through the eerie muffling snowfall.

Botovios' heart pounded at an alarming rate as he slid, his hands grasping desperately at slippery, frozen bark. Suddenly he had a grip, one hand deep into a hole burrowed in the slope by a hibernating animal, one foot jammed against a protruding stone.

Slowly, painfully, he pulled himself back up the slope, making sure of the sturdiness of everything he gripped before putting all his weight upon it. After what felt like an hour, he reached the flat once more and located the now-protruding branch that had felled him. He was safe - from nature and the whims of Arduenna anyway. Not from the armoured shapes that he could just make out stomping inexorably through the forest.

Botovios pulled himself up and stood, almost collapsing again into the snow. His ankle had twisted in his dangerous descent and he could barely walk, let alone run.

It was over. He could no more evade and outrun these impossible steel demons than he could fly across the gorge like a graceful hawk. His hand dropped to his belt and with a sinking heart he discovered he had even lost his eating knife in the fall and slide.

What had he or his people done to anger Arduenna so? Could it be that even she, one of the most potent spirits among the Celtic people and here in her very centre of power, was actually afeared of the gods these Romans brought with them? He knew their names. Anyone who dealt with the Romans or studied them did. Jupiter. Mars. Minerva. Neptune. And while the sacred people of Gaul devoted themselves to their deities and the druids bridged the gap between man and god, the cursed Romans seemed to treat their own gods as an everyday inconvenience - more like furniture than the powers that controlled all things from beyond the veil of the seen. Something has gone wrong? Spill some wine on an altar and the Goddess Minerva will put it right. Going into a battle? Promise a shrine to Mars and he'll keep you safe. All practicality and reason. No faith. No love. No service to the unseen purely because that was what they deserved.

A horrible people.

And if their gods were that mechanical and intertwined with the mundane, how could one such as Arduenna fear them?

But something had made the Goddess withdraw her protection, for the forest might as well be trying to kill him without even the intervention of the two murderous shadows moving through the white downfall.

In a last effort to test the will of the gods, he tried to turn and wade through the snow. His ankle screamed at him and sent white fire lancing up his leg and straight into his brain.

He fell again.

By the time he had pulled himself up to his feet once more, the two shapes had resolved into far too much detail for his liking. Officers. He knew the signs. While in other eras he would be learning the signs of nature and the ways to please the gods, the past four years had been filled with lessons on how the enemy worked, how their army was organised and how their commanders planned campaigns. The transverse crests on the helmets of these two nightmares labelled them: centurions. Commanders of units of eighty men plus lesser officers. The backbone of the legions and the most experienced and dangerous men Rome could field.

But why two officers here with no soldiers to command?

Close enough now to make out the details. He would run if he could, but there was no chance.

The demon to the left was shorter than Botovios - like all his kind - shorter than any Gaul really, but his body was clearly muscular and lithe. His skin tone was weathered and tanned, enhanced by a growth of stubble that covered much of it and which made his one piercing ice-blue eye almost shine. The patch of recently scarred skin that sat in place of the other made it all the more disturbing.

The one to the right was slightly shorter than his companion, but wider in the shoulder and emanating an aura of the kind of power one would usually associate with a wild bull. His stubble was every bit as face-consuming as his friend's, but was a grey that almost blended with the snow around him, his eyes dark and intense as they scanned the forest.

Both men wore exactly the sort of equipment that he had seen on other centurions: a mail shirt with extra flaps at the shoulders for added protection; a helmet that almost entirely covered the man's head with a crimson crest from side to side that stood out like blood in the snow; a red tunic and kirtle of studded straps to protect the groin. And on both men a harness across the chest hung with numerous medals, discs and torcs that looked irritatingly Gaulish. They were apparently highly experienced and well-decorated men.

The only oddity was the fact that they appeared to be wearing Gaulish long trousers after the same fashion as his own and their tunic bore long sleeves, albeit both dyed red. It appeared that the invaders were assimilating facets of his own culture to aid them in their systematic destruction of all things Celtic. He could have laughed in other circumstances.

Both men had swords drawn: the short, stabbing sword - the gladius.

Both blades glistened faintly pink. Both had been blooded with the innards of Tarvos and Icorix and their horses and had been dipped in the snow not quite thoroughly enough to completely clean them.

'Stand!' one of the centurions shouted, gesturing at him with the sword.

Botovios wondered for a moment whether to feign a lack of comprehension of this unpleasant southern language, but it seemed pointless. Latin was one of the first things the druids had begun to teach their trusted ones after the fall of the Helvetii and the suppression of the Belgae, and he had a good grasp of both it and of Greek.

'What do you want with me?' he asked nervously - he knew the answer.

'Yes... I'd like to know that.' This reply came, surprisingly, from somewhere off to the left and Botovios' head shot round to see two more centurions clambering through the snow beneath the heavily-laden branches. To his small satisfaction, he realised that the new arrivals had surprised his pursuers as much as him. Irritated them too, by the looks on their faces.

'Who in Hades are you?' snapped the shorter pursuer to the newcomers.

It was farcical. Botovios had a sudden thrill as he realised there was just the faintest chance that he might get out of this alive.

'Pullo - primus pilus of the Fourteenth, and Vorenus, pilus prior in the same legion. And who the hell are *you*, *soldier*?' the man stressed the last word. Botovios found himself nodding. The primus pilus was the top officer in the legion's centurionate. The chances of his hunters outranking the newcomer were tiny.

'Centurions Furius and Fabius of the Seventh.' A defiant note, almost daring the others to challenge over seniority.

The air almost crackled with tension. For a moment both pairs of Roman officers locked their gaze on one another and had his ankle been stronger, Botovios would have risked running for it. Instead he stood silent, waiting to see if there was any possibility that these soldiers might just fall on each other in bloodshed. The tension suggested it as a possibility.

'We've been tracking a small party of Gauls down here that we spotted on the road from the south' the Fourteenth's senior centurion said. 'You would be the pair who left the two bodies back on the forest path, then?'

Suddenly the balance changed in their favour as Botovios saw the figures of numerous soldiers emerging like ghosts from the depths of the forest, armed and ready. Unlike his two original pursuers, these two officers were not without their men.

'What's your business with him?' the bull-shouldered centurion from the Seventh demanded without an ounce of the respect Botovios would expect from a junior officer to a senior.

'Our legate,' something about the tone of the word 'legate' suggested that it left a sour taste in the senior man's mouth, 'Lucius Munatius Plancus, has a standing brief for his patrolling centuries to apprehend and execute any Gaul we find under arms without the permission of the general or his staff.'

The two centurions from the Seventh exchanged a look and the stockier one turned back to their counterparts from the Fourteenth.

'That's ridiculous! You'll have to execute the whole Godsforsaken nation. Anyway, this lad's unarmed, so you can leave him be. Go bother the local fauna somewhere, sir.'

Primus Pilus Titus Pullo bridled. He may not be happy with his orders, but to be spoken to in such a manner by a junior from another legion was pushing the bounds of acceptability.

'Unless you have a damn good reason to be after this man yourself, Centurion, you'll want to still that tongue when speaking to a senior officer unless you want to find yourself being lashed within a finger width of your life back in camp.'

Botovios watched, fascinated. After four years of studying the Roman military machine from a distance and through texts he was finally getting to see it operating first hand and it seemed to be nowhere near as organised and efficient as he had been led to believe. Perhaps there was a chance for Gaul after all.

The stocky centurion ripped something - a small baton or scroll case - from a pouch and tossed it over to the senior officer, who caught it deftly and turned it over to examine it.

'That's the seal of the camp prefect, Priscus.'

'Yes. We're on a job for him. So I suspect we take precedence over your witch-hunt for pitchfork-wielding peasants. Listen, sir: no disrespect, but we've been waiting for this one for weeks, spent time setting up an ambush and plenty of effort tracing him in the first place. He's important, and I'm not about to relinquish him to you because you happened to drop by, regardless of rank.'

'By Juno, Centurion, your impudence knows no bounds. Take the lad, then, but I'll be reporting this incident to the camp prefect when we return.'

Even as the primus pilus tossed the sealed object back to Furius and he and the accompanying 'Vorenus' turned back to their approaching units and waved them on, heading away into the woods, Botovios realised with an air of sad finality that it was truly over. The original pursuers were starting toward him again and any moment now, he would be in their hands. Then, doubtless, he would be broken, burned and cut until he screamed everything he knew through shattered teeth and bloodied lips. Such a thing must not happen.

His ankle would not carry him any further and he was unarmed.

Calmly, his thoughts going out to the Goddess of the woods, Arduenna, begging her for the strength to do what must be done, he turned his back on the centurions. They came on - he could tell from the crunching of their approaching footsteps - but he had not turned his back to protect himself or to take flight. He had done so to conceal his actions as he hurriedly untied the strings on the tiny pouch at his neck and fished around in it, ripping out its contents. For a moment he stared at the vellum and the characters scrawled across it. He knew not what it said exactly - hadn't risked reading it - though he had the gist and knew it must not fall into the Romans' hands, even if they couldn't initially decipher it. With a deep breath, he opened his mouth and stuffed the small piece of vellum inside, starting to chew rapidly as though on tough meat. The maceration mixed with the saliva should serve to clear the writing from the piece before it could ever be found. But just in case...

A last glance across his shoulder confirmed that the two centurions were almost on him now, climbing over the now-uncovered branch that had initially tripped him. He gave them a confident smile and threw himself down the slope and slid into the ravine.

* * * * *

Centurion Furius, the bear-shouldered centurion of the Second century, First cohort of the Seventh Legion, dropped the last seven feet from the rocky gulley to the grassy floor of the ravine, mere paces from the fast flowing icy river.

'Sometimes I think we should have stayed in Puteoli with Fronto. It'd have been warmer and filled with fewer arseholes.'

The taller of the pair, already standing on the grass and dusting the muck of the climb from his hands, grinned.

'You got bored after a week. I managed a month. Neither of us can keep up with the old bastard's wine habit, and those women are more demanding than any bloody senior officer. Our place is with the army and you know it.'

'Even if we spend all our time out on our own knee deep in snow hunting boys not old enough to grow a beard?'

'Even if. Besides, what we're doing is important. You know that. Priscus isn't a man to sod around on wild chicken hunts. A man after my own heart, that one.'

8

Furius nodded. There were perhaps three or four men in Caesar's army that had a pedigree that outstripped their own, and Priscus was one - probably the best.

'He's not going to be happy if we've spent three weeks chasing around Gaul unravelling all this crap only to let the miserable little runt throw himself off a cliff without an interrogation. We'll be right back at the start, having to locate another contact.'

'Let's just have a look at the bugger first. Come on.'

The pair waded through the knee deep white toward the river's edge.

'You should have told that knob from the Fourteenth that you were the primus pilus, you know' Fabius said, shaking his head as he trudged toward the water. 'You had more authority than him and you know it, yet you let him go on assuming you were a junior.'

'I'm not wearing the crest or the tunic with the gold embroidery, and he couldn't see my cloak pin insignia that far away. I could be any centurion. And anyway, I'm imagining what Priscus is going to say to him when he accuses a 'junior' of getting in the way of his own duty. The prefect'll tear him a second arsehole.'

'He *had* a second arsehole standing next to him!'

Snorting his agreement, Furius peered into the river.

The Gaul, whose name was unknown to them, but who they had bribed, cajoled, threatened and even tortured numerous of his countrymen just to locate, lay on the rocks close to the bank. He was a shattered thing: a broken mass of flesh and muscle with sharp white bone protruding through the skin in numerous places. He had landed flat on his back and had probably died that very instant. The blood had all run out now, washed clean from body and rocks by the fast flow, leaving him grey and clean, the water lapping at his legs and arms where they dangled from the rocks. The back of his head appeared to have gone entirely, the sharp rock that it had hit now protruding half way through his brain. It was a mess.

Both centurions had seen - and caused - worse.

'Fucking typical that he land there' Fabius grumbled. 'I call dry. *You* go in that cold water and search him.'

'If I do, you buy the drinks when we get back to camp.'

'Deal.'

Furius took a deep breath and clenched his jaw, stepping cautiously from the snowy bank into the freezing cold water. He felt instantly as though his skin had shrunk on his leg. His toes were

9

numb before they had even touched the pebbles at the bottom, a foot beneath the surface. He realised he was shivering and his teeth were clicking together rhythmically, and forced himself to stop. It was all in the mind. Shivering actually made you colder rather than helping deal with it.

With another deep breath of apprehension, the veteran plunged his other foot into the icy flow, squeezing his eyes shut for a moment. Though he could not feel his feet, he could see them and they were still theoretically working. Grumbling, he took three steps through the water out to the rocks where the body lay.

'Hurry up.'

Furius cast a sour look back at his companion as though Fabius had said something stupid which, clearly, he had. Bending over the body, he started rifling through the Gaul's belt pouch, lifting it from the water as he did so. Glancing only momentarily at the coins, he cast them into the water to help appease any local water spirits that might take all life from his toes. He had seen men serving in places like this lose their appendages, black and brittle.

'Nothing in his purse but shitty Gaul coins and a broken brooch pin. Worth shit.'

'Go through his tunic.'

'Lucius, I am not an idiot!' Ignoring the chuckle and the sarcastic comments from the bank, Furius rifled through the tunic and trousers down to the waterline, finding nothing. One of the submerged hands was tightly clasped shut and he spent precious moments snapping off the frozen fingers so he could check its contents only to find it empty. Silently, he cursed the nameless courier for wasting his time.

'Nothing.'

'There has to be something. He's a young 'un. Those twisted bastard druids wouldn't trust such things to a youth's memory.'

'There's a pouch on a neck thong' Furius said quickly, moving frozen, numb feet to get a closer look. 'It's empty, but it's open, so he's only just taken something from it!'

'Trying to dispose of the evidence. It's either in his mouth or his arse or he threw it in the river.'

'Can't search the river, and I ain't searching his arse.'

Again, Fabius laughed from the bank.

'A *lot* of wine!' Furius snapped. 'For this, you owe me a *lot* of wine. And the pick of recruits at the next draft. And preference with equipment.'

'Fine, so long as you have something to show for all of this.'

'I think...' Furius wrenched the lower jaw down until it cracked, peering inside. 'Yes. There's something. Vellum I think.'

As Fabius offered obvious suggestions and unhelpful advice, Furius drew the scrap from the mouth and began to stumble on numb feet back to the bank, where his companion helped him up.

'Give me your scarf.'

'Piss off.'

'My feet are cold-bitten. I might lose my toes. Give me your damn scarf!'

As Fabius reluctantly removed the thick russet-coloured wool garment from his neck and passed it over, Furius unlaced his Gaulish-design enclosed boots and lifted blue-purple feet from them. His socks had become so sodden they had stayed inside as his feet came out accompanied by a sucking sound. With a grimace, he drew the soggy wool socks from the boots and cast them into the river. Ridiculously, standing barefoot in the snow seemed warmer than the water he had been in. Life was starting to return to his feet. As his companion handed the scarf over, Furius bit down on the edge and tore it into two strips.

'Hey, that's my scarf!'

'And these are my feet. Shut up.'

Bending, he fashioned a makeshift sock from half the scarf and wrapped it round his left foot, plunging it into the sodden boot and lacing it up. Despite the fact that it would soon become cold and wet again, temporarily his foot felt blissfully warm. It would save his toes and that was, right now, all that mattered. Hurriedly, he repeated the process on his right foot and then stomped around.

'Well?' Fabius was holding out a hand.

Furius grumbled and passed over the scrap of vellum as he stomped in circles, returning life to his limbs. The snow was settling heavily on his shoulders.

'Half of its gone. I reckon he swallowed it.'

'I'm not gutting him and searching his innards either.'

'There's still faint writing on this part though. I think it's Greek. Yes, definitely Greek. You want to look? Your Greek's better than mine.'

11

Furius glared at his companion as he took the vellum and peered at it. 'It's beyond me how you can spend so many years serving out in the east and not pick up the lingo, Lucius.'

'Greek's the language of bum bandits. I learned enough to get by - no more.'

'It's almost illegible. I can't really make out what most of the words say, and I don't think anyone else will. But there's three names here I can see that look a little familiar.'

'What? Come on!'

'Treveri I think? Yes, got to be Treveri. That's one of the tribes near here, yes?'

'All around us. They're the ones who live at Trebeto and all over this forest. No shock that they're involved, given where the little prick was heading.'

'And Suevi. I know that name from last year.'

'Germanic bastards across the Rhenus. Juno, we don't want the Germanic tribes getting their blood up and throwing in their lot. Bad enough with the argumentative Gauls, Aquitani and Belgae. Priscus is going to have to make some pretty tough decisions in the coming weeks, I'd say. Anything else?'

'Couple of fragments. Nothing concrete. Sporadic verbs and appeals? And this one: Dumnorix. That's a person, not a tribe. Ever heard of him?'

'Can't say I have' shrugged Fabius, 'but maybe Priscus has. We'd best get straight back to camp.'

'That's several days ride. We need a night to recover first. I'm frozen.'

'Then I'll take the horses and you can run; warm yourself up. Come on.'

The pair moved back toward the narrow gulley that had afforded them a relatively simple access from the forest above. They would have to get back to camp as soon as possible. It may look like the depths of winter here but, despite the ever present snow, it was already Aprilis and officially spring. Soon, the army would be mobilizing for the coming season. The question now was: what would their objective be? Britannia again or the flattening of yet more Gaulish resistance?

Chapter One

<u>MAIUS</u>

Fronto flicked an idle finger at a garland of sweet smelling flowers that stretched from one peg to another on the wall of the spacious tablinum and wrinkled his nose at the scent that threatened to make him sneeze violently.

'I don't see why it couldn't be at our own property? It *should* be at the groom's property.'

Balbus sighed and patted him on the shoulder in a supportive - even sympathetic - manner.

'Tradition has it at my house, Marcus. Anyway, women are funny about holding celebrations in places where blood has been shed regularly. Lucilia would no more allow you to use your townhouse than a public arena, and Corvinia's on her side. When the pair of them set their mind on something only a lunatic would argue.'

Fronto nodded sullenly. He *was* that lunatic. The arguments over the past week had almost caused the calling off of the whole thing. Lucilia had proved to be more stubborn than Fronto could possibly imagine and he had decided it presaged a worrying future for him.

'But we could have had it at Puteoli. It's perfect.'

'And too far for some of the guests to travel. The gathering this evening will be well attended, Marcus. Half the luminaries of Rome that are coming would not have done so if they'd had to travel all the way down the coast to your villa.'

'The perfect reason to have it there.'

Balbus took a deep breath. 'Listen, Marcus.' he said with quiet strength, a steely edge in his voice making Fronto turn and frown, 'I know you're not a young man and that this is a very personal thing for you. I know that you think it should be as private and low key as possible and that you should be hidden away from public eyes. But Lucilia is a young woman - little more than a girl still, despite her strength of will. Young girls have few dreams and fears in life and one is the fear that they'll be married off to a sour old senator as a breeding machine. Lucilia has always known I would not do that, but she has, against all odds, actually achieved a match with someone she genuinely cares about and she wants to celebrate that; to shout it to the very halls of the gods. If you turn this ceremony sour I personally will plague you for the rest of your life. Do you understand me?'

Fronto, his brow furrowed, nodded resignedly.

'Sorry, Quintus. You know I want this, but you know how much I hate pomp. I feel like a general returning to Rome for a glittering public triumph. It makes my skin itch; and that's just the ceremony. I can't think as far ahead as the evening's festivities. Best part of a hundred sycophants, megalomaniacs and hedonists drinking all our wine and eating all our food while they pass judgement on us.'

'I know. But it's one day. You're not doing it for yourself - you're doing it for her. Now man up, rivet a smile on that sour cat's-arse of a face and straighten yourself. You look like a hunchbacked vagrant.'

'It's the knee. Something's still not right with it. Whenever I stand still for an hour I start to sag to one side.'

'I know. But that's because in six months you've carried out the exercises you were given - what? - three times? Wine and chariot races are no substitute for a health regime.'

'Oh piss off Quintus. You sound like Faleria now.'

He looked around at the garland strewn, drape-infested room.

'And you could have removed all the family death masks. Is that really appropriate?'

'Our ancestors have as much right to see this as I do. Pull that fake smile up a notch - the witnesses are here.'

Fronto's smile passed from the forced to the genuine as the ten witnesses for the ceremony appeared in the doorway, escorted by Balbus' body slave. The rest of the household were all busy attending the women, leaving them with one decrepit gardener and the reedy Greek that Balbus treated like a family member.

Galba, the former legate of the Twelfth Legion, had been a natural choice, having shared years of friendship and comradeship in the army and having returned to the city to take up the role of a praetor. He wore the toga strangely naturally, given his military bearing and stocky form, and he headed the group as the very image of the Roman nobleman.

Behind him, Rufus carried his toga yet more naturally. The taciturn, quiet man had been a last moment addition to the list when Fronto learned of his arrival in the city. Rufus had resigned his commission in the Ninth in order to return to Rome and work through his father's estate, following the old man's passing in the

14

winter. Despite the unhappy reason for his return, his presence was welcomed by Fronto. He added a certain gravitas to any occasion.

The same could not be said of the third figure. Galronus still shied away from the toga, despite having been officially granted citizenship just after Saturnalia and accounting himself the equal of any knight of Rome. His Gallic finery sat at peculiar odds to the rest, but somehow lightened the proceedings and helped Fronto relax just that tiny, necessary bit.

Faleria followed Galronus a little too closely, which brought the corners of Fronto's mouth up a tiny bit further. The Remi chief had made his intentions clear to Faleria at a family gathering with distant cousins and uncles at the villa in Puteoli during the Parentalia festival. Fronto had almost burst out laughing at the number of very serious relations who almost expired in shock at the audacity of the 'barbarian' as they saw him. Only Fronto, Faleria and their mother had managed to maintain their calm manner. The older lady had surprised Fronto by smiling and congratulating both the young Belgic warrior and her daughter, but the biggest surprise had been the complaint from Faleria that he had taken far too long in drumming up the courage to speak to her about it. Their betrothal was due to be announced at the wedding feast this very evening - a victory of Fronto's in the attempt to shift some of the focus from himself during the agonising parade of Rome's chinless, worthless upper class.

Behind Faleria came three of Balbus' relatives that Fronto had only met once during the arrangements, all of whom held position and property in the city.

After them, filling the final three places of the ten-person witness party, came three Roman luminaries that Faleria had secured: the orator Cicero, the poet Catullus and finally, surprisingly, Publius Crassus the younger, Monetalis and Augur of Rome and former commander of Caesar's Seventh Legion. While Cicero and Catullus' presence could easily be sought and bought by anyone with the right name and offers, Fronto had snorted when Faleria had suggested Crassus. Despite a certain grudging respect for the young martinet of an officer who had done as much damage to Rome's cause in Gaul as he had to the Gauls themselves, he was not at all sure why the young man had agreed to attend. Crassus was on a star-strewn path to glory in the Roman administration. Next year he would join his father in their attempt to obliterate Parthia and after that: probably a consulship, knowing the family's luck and connections. Crassus had never shown any real affinity with Fronto, but he did have a history of social activity with the Falerii. Fronto resolved to spend as little time in the man's presence as possible today.

Faces were missing - faces that made him sad. His mother, for one: retired now almost permanently to the villa in Puteoli, her strength in a gentle if saddening decline. The letter from Priscus apologising for not being able to be present was still on his desk. He had read it several times, finding it hard to believe that one of his oldest friends would not be here. But Priscus was still an officer and had duties. He was seemingly involved in something that simply would not afford him the time to take leave. He had intimated big things, but it was his absence that Fronto had fixated upon. He would have liked Carbo here too. Even in the just two years the man had served as his second, he had come to trust and rely upon that jolly pink faced centurion. But Caesar had denied all leave for anyone below staff rank - even Crispus, one of his dearest friends in the army was trapped with his legion in Gaul. Varus had accepted the invitation but had been struck down with a malady in the harsh Gaulish winter that had prevented him travelling.

Still, no use dwelling on the depressing absences. This was a 'happy occasion' as his sister had been drilling into his skull for the past two weeks of nightmarish organisation. Fronto had perfected his old trick of making himself so difficult and irritating that they sent him away and had managed to be ejected from the house by midmorning every day to spend his time with Galronus at the races or in the taverns of the city.

He couldn't help but wonder whether that was a situation that would change in the next few hours. Lucilia was a strong-willed woman.

'Marcus, you look well. Almost blissfully, in fact.' Rufus smiled warmly as he crossed the room.

'You think so? I think he looks uncomfortable and slightly sick' replied Galba with a grin that caused Rufus to elbow him sharply in the ribs.

'Glad you could come' Fronto replied weakly. He was starting to tremble slightly and had no idea how to stop it. He was also aware of the clamminess of his palms and hoped he would not have to shake hands with anyone. Perhaps he was ill? If he was properly ill, he might be able to delay proceedings?

16

Quickly, he ran a mental check over his body. Trembling. Sweaty palms. Churning stomach. Dry mouth. Headache. Sadly, nothing concrete for illness. They were all associated with nerves and there was nothing he could do about that. He had faced so many dangers in his time, from screaming, violent barbarians to murderous villains to collapsing buildings. But nothing brought the shaky fear to the surface like this.

'Time I moved away' Balbus said quietly. 'Be strong.' With a last gesture, he held up the small object he had been gripping the past hour. Fronto peered at the ring before reaching out and grasping it.

'A plain iron one would have done.'

'Not for my daughter. Behave and don't whimper.'

Fronto was about to deliver a cutting reply, but his old friend - future father! - had already stepped away into position near the witnesses. Time was almost up. With a shiver, Fronto shifted his weight to the other foot and faffed with the toga, trying to align it better and distribute the weight more evenly. How could a damn article of clothing weigh more than his armour?

But that was his lot in life now: No more cuirass and helm. Just a toga.

He squeezed his eyes shut to prevent the depression sinking in again. Any time he started contemplating the future he ended up in a grey miserable fog that lasted until he was safely drunk.

Aware that he probably looked deranged, standing with one leg slightly bent, shuffling and shaking and with his eyes squeezed shut, he straightened and opened them.

And remembered why he was doing this.

Lucilia was simply stunning. Fronto had seen dozens of weddings and dozens of brides in his time, and it was virtually impossible to tell one bride from the next until they changed out of the traditional garments, but somehow Lucilia managed to look individual, different and beautiful.

Her hair was bound up in the traditional six-locked cone shape, draped with the flame-coloured veil that shimmered and floated before her face, giving her features a gauzy, other-worldly appearance. Her white tunic, girdled with the double knot was somehow divine in its austerity. The saffron-shaded palla over her shoulders was quietly magnificent, cut in silk from beyond Parthia by an expert seamstress. Her golden sandals clicked lightly on the marble.

17

Fronto realised that his symptoms had almost entirely vanished, replaced by a speedily-thumping heart. He hoped he didn't look too vacant and reminded himself not to drool.

Corvinia and Balbina and the various women of the family came on in her wake, almost overshadowed by her stunning beauty. Fronto hardly noticed them as they moved from the open garden into the tablinum and greeted the witnesses with a simple nod. Fronto realised that he had started walking automatically, before his brain had even sent the message to his feet, keeping pace with the bride as she passed through the spacious room and into the atrium, where the altar had been placed next to the impluvium pool. From somewhere off to the left, an old man in the white robe of a haruspex shuffled into view, leading a thoroughly washed and deodorised pig, who snorted in a disgruntled manner. The old man almost fell over the pig which, Fronto knew, would be taken for a bad omen by many, but managed to right himself just in time. Old Bucco was Balbus' uncle and had the distinction of having been Pontifex Maximus for a brief stint following the Social War. How the doddery old lunatic managed to stay upright on his ageing bow legs was a matter of question for Fronto, but the man was undeniably the most qualified for the task.

Bucco raised his hands for a respectful silence and paused dramatically, the pig calmly standing by his leg, close to the altar and a smoking, glowing brazier.

'May the gods look upon this union... phlaaaaw... and bless it. We seek their... phlaaaaw... benediction and the omens in the... phlaaaaw... entrails of this noble beast.'

Fronto closed his eyes for a moment as he came to stand still beside Lucilia and in front of the spectacle. Balbus had warned him that Bucco had acquired an odd speech defect following the illness that had struck his left arm useless and made half his face slip, but Fronto had been unprepared for the strange exhaling, drooling drawl that punctuated his sentences. He tried not to laugh as the 'noble beast' left them the first gift of the day on the decorative marble floor.

Three of the house's slaves stepped forward and gently tipped the pig onto its side, holding it steady while Bucco brandished the knife, peering intently at it with one eye, while the other roved over the wall to one side.

18

Fronto raised his gaze to the doorway beyond and ran through a list of the upcoming charioteers at the circus in the next month and how much he was prepared to back each for, trying not to listen to the grotesque noises rising from the sacrifice before him. In fact, he became so involved in his mental list that he only realised the act was complete when Bucco rose into view, crimson to the elbows, holding something wobbly and purple that he dropped into the brazier beside the altar with a hiss and a smell that set Fronto's stomach rumbling.

'The organs are good' the old man intoned in a reedy voice. 'The liver... phlaaaaw... is particularly good. The gods bless this union. Let us now devote the heart to Venus and make the libation.'

Fronto dutifully stepped forward and took the bronze jug offered by a slave, tipping some of the best quality wine in the city onto the altar's depression where it sat amid the purple stains of previous gifts. Handing back the jug he stepped away.

Quietly he stood, watching the altar as the wretched carcass was hauled away from near his feet by two slaves, leaving a long trail of red. He found he was humming one of the Tenth's favourite marching songs under his breath and forced himself to stop.

'Ring' hissed Lucilia next to him. With a start, he realised that Bucco was watching him intently. Flushing, he produced the gold band and slid it onto the waiting finger, noting the look of triumph and... ownership?... that crossed his new bride's face.

In almost a dreamlike daze he repeated by rote the vows Balbus and he had drafted with the aid of Faleria three nights ago, and only half listened as Lucilia spoke her own. He dutifully smiled whenever it appeared to be appropriate, though he had hardly heard a thing in truth. In fact, the following quarter of an hour passed in a blur of nodding and smiling and speech impediments as his subconscious threw him questions to keep his mind busy.

What was he going to do?

Now *that* was a question that had been plaguing him ever since he had turned his back on Caesar the previous autumn. Soldiering was all he had ever known, and certainly all he was good at. Faleria and Lucilia would expect him to take a post in the Roman administration. He could very easily fast-track to the senate, given his age and experience. He might even be made a governor. But that would involve politics every day of his life, for as long as he lived. The very thought sent a shiver along his spine.

19

Balbus had managed a sensible enough suggestion, offering the possibility of simple retirement to the country to manage his estate. Other men his age did it, after all, and with the family name he had it would be a respectable choice.

But soooo boring.

Balbus might be happy cross-breeding vines or snipping roses, but the idea failed to appeal to Fronto. He might as well drop dead now.

He had come up with the possibility of setting up a ludus and obtaining a stable of gladiators. A lanista could make a lot of money and the life would be a little more exciting than trimming flowers or arguing with senators. Lucilia had made her thoughts on the possibility of a future as a lanista's wife quite plain.

So not that, then.

The only other possibility that had been raised by Galronus was to return to Caesar, helmet in hand, and request reassignment. Fronto didn't believe for a moment that Caesar would have him back even if he felt inclined to ask. He did *not* feel inclined to ask. The Remi chief had then suggested the possibility of Crassus' Parthian army, but the idea of spending a few years out in the expanses of deadly sand beyond Syria was hardly a draw. During winter he had been regaled with tales of that region by Furius and Fabius and everything they said had put him further off the idea.

So what was a man to do?

'Feliciter!' barked the old auspex before sagging and making a strange keening sound, drool dripping to his toes.

Fronto blinked, suddenly aware that the witnesses were cheering him.

It was over. He was a married man.

Lucilia was facing him, her face displaying a curious look which reminded him of that expression Faleria always had while buying slaves. Ah well. From a commander in Gaul to one in Rome. At least there would be fringe benefits from this campaign. Now all he had to do was survive the party and he and Lucilia could retire in peace.

* * * * *

'Have you given any more thought to the life of a country gentleman?'

20

Fronto felt that nagging itch that settled on him at formal occasions and took a sip of his extremely watered wine.

'Quintus, I'm no farmer.'

'Shame. See, I have a gift for you; for you and Lucilia actually.'

Fronto's eyes rose to the gathering in the large triclinium. Music wafted across the room along with the scented smoke from the braziers that kept the room lit and warmed. The guests had been doing a good job of keeping out of his way so far, possibly because of the look on his face that Balbus had told him was inappropriate for a newly-married man.

'A gift? It's me who gives the gifts to Lucilia.'

'I know. But still. You see I've been hoping you would decide to take up the life of a retired gentleman, and I thought that, to that effect... well the long and the short of it is: there's a villa waiting for you on the hill behind Massilia, adjoining my own estate.'

Fronto blinked. 'What?'

'I got the land very cheap as I know some of the city's council and they're eager to take Roman noble settlers. Gives the city a bit of security and legitimacy in Rome's eyes you see. I've had the same people constructing it as built my own villa, though that was a long time ago. It won't be finished until late summer at the earliest... possibly even next year, if the weather turns bad in summer, but it's yours. You need somewhere to go that's away from the rat race of the city and, let's face it, Faleria needs the villa at Puteoli. Her or your mother anyway.'

Fronto stared. 'It's... generous.'

'It's sensible. Have you given any thought to your future, then?'

'Almost nothing but. I love Lucilia, Quintus, and I'm happy as can be with the marriage, but there's this cloud hanging over me at the moment that I just can't shift. I'm no farmer or politician. As long as I've served with Caesar's guard or the Ninth or Tenth I've been absolutely certain of my place in the world. Now it feels like I've been set adrift on a raft and there's no sight of land. D'you understand?'

'Of course I do. I was lost for my first half year after I left the legion. I knew little else. You'll find a path, but you need to be patient. You need to be patient with the others too. Everyone has your best interest at heart and I know my daughters can be a little fearsome, but they love you - Lucilia especially. Take your time and relax. Treat this summer like an extended period of leave - that way you won't feel quite so lost. And remember that I'm always here to help.'

'That is actually surprisingly comforting, Quintus. Thank you.'

'Stop worrying about the future for the moment and concentrate on tonight. Your sister deserves your support and approval. There are a number of people who want to talk to you, probably to offer you opportunities, and Galba and Rufus are waiting for you to have time to reminisce. Even Crassus is waiting for a chance to talk. First thing's first, though. Catullus has asked me to introduce you properly.'

'Really? Can't imagine what the warbling fellow would want with me.'

'Be good. Catullus is in great demand and that 'warbling' was a composition in honour of you and my daughter. He gave of his time and skills as a gift to you and that deserves recognition.'

'I suppose. Come on, then.'

Balbus smiled and strode across the room to where a thin, well-dressed man sat quietly on a comfortable couch while three heavily white-leaded harpies gushed at him. He looked distinctly uncomfortable at the attention of the three women and that fact warmed Fronto toward him a little. As they approached, the poet turned to look up at him and Fronto was momentarily taken aback.

Catullus was a handsome man in his late twenties or early thirties with a clear - if pale - complexion and short, neat blond hair. He was clean shaven and unadorned apart from a single ring of gold. His toga was plain and old fashioned and he sat at ease, but his eyes almost stopped Fronto in his tracks. They were a glittering emerald colour and girls likely swooned over them, but they carried a hopeless hollowness in them that Fronto recognised all too well. It was a look he had seen in his bronze shaving mirror for years after the deaths of Vergilius and Carvalia. He understood what caused it and what it would do to a man. He also knew how dangerous it was.

'Ladies, may I introduce you to two veteran commanders of Caesar's legions' Balbus said expansively at the three women, who looked less than pleased about the possibility of being dragged away from the famous, handsome poet, but who recognised the barely concealed order from the house's master. As Balbus steered the women away from Catullus, the poet lifted a plain-sandaled foot and pushed another chair toward Fronto.

'Many congratulations, master Falerius.'

'No one calls me that. I'm Fronto to most; Marcus to friends.'

'I am as yet unaware as to my position in that hierarchy. It is good to meet you... Fronto. You have something of a reputation as a direct man - a man of action rather than words.'

'That sounds surprisingly double-edged for what I presume is a complement.'

Catullus laughed and once more Fronto noted the hollowness to the sound. It was mechanical and devoid of true feeling. 'I apologise. I am known for my somewhat cutting and edgy compositions, as your former commander will be well aware.'

'I think Caesar pays little attention to such lampoonery when he's got men like Cicero around bad-mouthing him. Apologies if I puncture your ego, Catullus, but you're only a small fish in that particular pool.'

Catullus snapped out the mechanical laugh again.

'Good. Straight talking as I was told. I have a question for you.'

'Go on.'

'I am informed,' the poet said, stretching, 'that you are one of very few men indeed who have had dealings with Publius Clodius Pulcher and come out on top; that he in fact is a little afeared of you.'

'Slimy, shit-ridden filthy catamite damn well *should* be frightened of me. If we ever cross paths again, he's going to be a shadow of his former self. In fact, I'd say there's probably only one man that hates him more than me, but that's another story.'

Catullus simply nodded at this sudden display of bile and invective.

'Good. Not that you hate him, particularly, but rather that you bested him. You see, I need information on something, and I am fast running out of avenues to search. Clodius is the only real source that I have not yet tapped and he has been the most likely possibility throughout, given his proximity to the subject. It seems that the events of the past few years have made him a very careful and defensive person, though. He never shows his face in public without a small army surrounding him. He even has a shield bearer beside him in public in case of disgruntled archers.'

'Again, much of that is my fault, but not all. I know of someone who's been waiting over a year for the opportunity to put a blade between those shoulders. Clodius would probably have been picked off months ago by any one of his enemies if he wasn't cocooned in the centre of an army and shielded. What's the son of a whore done to you then?'

'Not so much a 'what's he done', Fronto. More of a 'what might he know'. You see his sister and I were something of an item.'

Fronto felt his stomach turn over. Perhaps a handful of people in the whole republic knew what had become of the meddlesome Clodia: her untimely, if well-deserved death at the hands of the renegade officer Paetus. Official reports simply had her down as a disappearance. A brief and inexpensive memorial had been staged by her brother, during which he had hardly even paid attention, keeping himself busy with his murderous debt ledgers.

Catullus? This callow young poet had been romantically involved with the poisonous siren? There must be some steel in the man then, else she would have likely eaten him alive.

'Clodia?' He managed to say, hopefully without any unusual inflection. 'She disappeared over a year ago. I'm afraid I see very little hope in pursuing her now.'

'Regardless,' the poet responded quietly, 'I must do so. To not know… well let me try and put it poetically. She was the rosy fingers of dawn that began my days and the gentle shroud of night that closed them. She was the lamp that lit my way and the blanket that warmed me. Without her I am a shell, Fronto. A mere shell. I have to know.'

Fronto shook his head slowly. 'Don't get involved with her brother. The man is poison incarnate. Everything he touches withers. If you draw his attention he'll turn on you, and a year from now someone will be knocking on my door looking for the poet that vanished in mysterious circumstances. You understand that?'

Catullus simply nodded his understanding.

'When I ran out of worldly contacts to pursue, I started to seek the advice of oracles and soothsayers.'

'Always a laugh.'

'You may not put much stock in such matters, Fronto, but some things are a little hard to discredit. I heard the same thing from three different sources: that I *would* find her, but then I would die. Frankly that end is the most appealing for me now. Better to be reunited in death than alive and apart.'

'I note that doesn't say whether you'll find her alive or dead. Would you be happy to find she lives and then drop dead? I think not. Soothsayers cannot be trusted. I went to the oracle at Cumae once. Not exactly a satisfactory experience in any way.'

'I was told something else, Fronto. I was told that Rome was coming to an end. I was told prophecy, Fronto, and I suspect that if I depart this life with my Clodia found, I will be the lucky one.'

'Prophecy is all crap' Fronto replied flatly, though one eyelid jumped a little at the lie.

'I will be the first of four to die, they said. And those four will snap the threads that hold the republic together. The first by Socrates root, they said, so I think I can safely assume I will not pass peacefully in my sleep. The second, they said, would be by the Vulcan's fury, the third by the arrival of the sun, and the fourth by the Parthian shot. I'm no expert in these things, but I can't say it sounds good.'

'Don't put so much stock in this mumbo jumbo. And steer clear of Clodius. Nothing good will come of it.'

'I suspect otherwise. Are you saying you will not help me gain access to Clodius?'

Fronto shrugged. 'I'm saying I *cannot* help you gain access to him. There's no way but to walk up to his army and ask to speak to him, and I would heartily advise against that. Broken fingers and ribs are not pleasant. You're a celebrated man. For you to show up bobbing in the Tiber would be a shame.'

Catullus fixed Fronto with his sharp, emerald gaze and finally nodded and sat back. 'Then thank you for your time, Fronto. I hope the composition was up to expectations.'

'Lovely. Thanks.'

Turning from the poet, Fronto strode across the room and out into the peristyle garden. It was still early in the year and the evening air had a bite to it, though the rain had stopped blessedly a few days ago. It could be worse, though. Priscus' letter had told of an abominable winter in northern Gaul. Taking a deep breath, he strolled around the sides of the garden beneath the portico, breathing in the jasmine and marjoram.

'You look troubled, my love.'

Pausing, Fronto turned to see Lucilia standing in the doorway.

'I just spoke to your poet friend. He's a strange one.'

'Perhaps. You've had this pall hanging over you all day. I've not mentioned it, though many a bride might take offence at such an atmosphere on her wedding day.'

'Sorry, Lucilia. It's just the...'

'Future. Yes, I know. I'm well acquainted with how your mind works, Marcus.' She strode forward and hooked her arm through his, urging him to walk on. 'Put all of that aside. We can work it out in due course. For now, we have a summer coming that the auspices tell us will be a good one, and we have the city to play in, your villa in Puteoli to adjourn to and, of course, the new house in Massilia to visit. Think of it as a year-long leave break from the army.'

Fronto laughed.

'Sometimes I see so much of your father in you. Lucilia.'

'Hopefully not the baldness.'

Fronto sighed. 'I have this horrible feeling that we're heading for a fall again.'

'You and I?'

'The republic in general. Like the Social War. Troops in the streets; despots and proscriptions; blood and fire. I keep getting a whiff of it for just a moment and then the wind changes.'

'All the more reason to enjoy the time we have now. Anyway, I was coming to tell you something.'

'Go on.'

'You remember Julia? Atia's niece?'

Fronto's spirits sank a little again. Caesar's daughter - his only direct issue and the young wife of Pompey. The glue that bound the two politicians together.

'Yes' he replied apprehensively. 'She's an old friend of Faleria's.'

'I know. She's pregnant, you know?'

'I am aware.'

'Well she's determined to go to a performance in that monstrous new theatre her husband has built before she's too bulky to move, and she's asked if Faleria, Galronus, you and I want to join them. It's being organised now for a show in two or three weeks and I said we'd love to go. I hope you've nothing planned instead?'

Fronto's spirits sank ever further, rustling around in the soles of his boots. He had never yet sat through a theatre performance sober. Indeed, he had been forcibly ejected from the theatre in Tarraco twice in his time for drunken and lewd behaviour - when he was younger. Drama was anathema to Fronto. He sagged.

'Can we sit down? My knee's killing me.'

26

'I've told you to go back to that Greek physician and actually listen to him this time. I need you... active, if you get my meaning. Anyway, before you find a pathetic excuse, you needn't panic. It seems that Julia shares the bloodlust that runs in her family. It's not to be a play, but a contest of arms.'

'Gladiators?' Fronto brightened as he sank to a bench and rubbed his knee.

'Yes. All sponsored by Pompey. We'll have the prime seats with the games' editor. You'll be able to escape the humdrum world of the greatest city on the planet for an afternoon and imagine you're standing on a Gaulish hill, up to the knees in body parts.'

Fronto grinned.

'Well when you put it like that, it'd be rude not to accept an invitation from so illustrious a figure.'

'Indeed.' Lucilia reached up and placed her hands on his cheeks, gently but forcefully turning his head until he could see into her deep, hypnotic eyes. She leaned forward and kissed him.

'Let's get back to the party. I know you've managed to get your sister and her man to steal some of our thunder, but the guests might actually want to speak to us.'

Fronto nodded, his spirit lightening at the thought of an afternoon at the games.

'And then we can see if you can get me in the same situation as Julia.'

Fronto blinked and stopped, but Lucilia was already walking back to the festivities, laughing.

* * * * *

Gnaeus Pompeius Magnus, vanquisher of the Cilician pirates, twice consul of the republic of Rome, triumphant victor of the Sertorius and Spartacus campaigns, triumvir and son in law of Caesar, ran his fingers along the edge of the petals and smiled, leaning in to take a deep breath.

'Your aunt is a devious and dangerous woman, Julia, but she does send the most pleasant gifts when of a mind.'

The heavily pregnant Julia Caesaris, her face an aquiline mirror of her father, though as pretty as she was striking, smiled warmly.

'Be kind, Gnaeus. Atia has been nothing but accommodating and this ridiculous pissing contest between you and father needs to be kept well and truly away from family life. The medicus said that I need to remain as calm and content as possible, and that means no complaining about my family.'

Pompey turned, his jowled, jolly face breaking into a broad grin.

'Julia, my love, you are the tonic that calms my blood.'

Turning and leaving his young wife in the bright atrium, the great Pompey strolled into the vestibule and toward the door, examining the fresh decoration on the walls. When he had laid down the plans for the great new theatre complex that he had bequeathed to the city, he had had the foresight to add a luxurious new townhouse beside it to replace his old, plain and small home, but now he was having second thoughts about his new residence. To have common plebs running shops in the front may well be a common, profitable and space-saving practice in busy cities, but he should have stipulated that the entire block was to be self-contained as his property alone. Even though the house was so new that it still smelled of paint and plaster, he could almost hear the chattering and busyness of the future tenants of the two shops that flanked his front door. Maybe he should forego the rent they would net him and simply seal them up, knocking through a door inside?

The great general stopped, his finger tapping his lip, his head tilted to one side.

He *could* hear people and activity in the left hand of the two shops; it had not just been his imagination.

His jaw set in an angry fashion and he turned, striding back into the atrium where a surprised Julia raised an eyebrow at his expression.

'Something amiss, husband?'

'Someone's playing silly buggers in the empty shops out front.' Raising his voice so that it could be heard through the peristyle and in the slave and servant quarters out to the back of the complex, he bellowed 'Artorius?' - the name of the chief of his household security.

Within moments the stocky Sabine with a broken nose and scarred face appeared through the open doorway, three of his men at his heels. Artorius knew his master's moods and what his various tones of voice indicated, and that sharp command has suggested the need for muscled men.

'Domine?'

'Come with me.'

As the five men strode from the atrium toward the front door, Julia smiled a weary smile. 'Do be careful, Gnaeus. You're not as young as you seem to think.'

Pompey ignored the well-intended jibe and paused at the freshly-painted, bronze studded door, allowing Artorius to grasp the handle with its ornate lion head and swing the wooden leaf inwards. Inwardly acknowledging his wife's gentle reminder, he forced himself not to storm angrily out front before his men and waited until Artorius and two guards walked out, following them, with the last man taking up the rear place.

The street outside was as quiet as this region ever got during the daytime, with a few street sellers, the requisite number of beggars and whores, and the general populace going about their business. At this particular moment, however, their business seemed to be 'watching the front of the house of Pompey'. The general growled in irritation at the crowd of spectators that had paused and were observing his house.

Giving them but a moment's notice, he turned to see what had drawn their attention and his ire rose all the more.

While the house of Pompey was complete and freshly decorated, the two unoccupied stores that formed the frontage were still in the final stages of construction, their walls part plastered, the fronts still partly-bricked and partially still mere skeletal wooden structures.

The right-hand shop as he looked back toward his door was already near destroyed.

Three figures raged and fought around the small space, smashing wooden clubs into fresh plaster, waving knives, and shaking the timber frontage so that the tiles on the roof rattled. Two more combatants lay on the floor, plainly unconscious - possibly deceased.

Even as Pompey stared at the debacle, his face burning with anger, the larger, central figure managed to bring the odds closer, gripping one of his opponents by the shoulders and running him physically across the room, smashing his crown into the wall, behind which - in the general's house - stood the shelf that held the flowers Atia had sent. He could picture the ornate glass vase falling and smashing on the floor of his atrium.

Time after time his loved ones had warned Pompey about his temper. He may have the physical appearance of a jolly, good-natured fellow, but the fires of his anger were never truly extinguished, smouldering and bubbling even at his most peaceful, waiting to rage into a flaming inferno.

An image of Julia wagging a finger at him in admonishment flashed into his mind and he bit down on the rising tide of rage with great difficulty.

The big man in the shop let go of his most recent victim and Pompey noticed with distaste the cracked plaster and the smear of blood and lumps of something where the loser, his head smashed and broken, had left brain matter on the wall.

'Hold!' bellowed Artorius, his men fanning out around him to create a crescent that sealed in the shop. The big warrior either failed to hear over the rush of blood in his ears or blatantly ignored the newly-arrived hirelings.

Instead, the huge fighter turned to face his last surviving opponent. The smaller man had drawn a knife and was warily edging round him, possibly in an effort to flee the scene.

As the big combatant spun round and faced the street, Pompey looked him up and down. He was clearly no Roman. Well over six feet tall - probably over seven - and with a torso like Hercules, the man had straggly long straw blond hair that had been plaited until the fracas had dishevelled him, and a beard that almost obscured the lower half of his face. His bulging arms were marked out with strange designs and he wore only a ragged grey tunic, ripped open at the front, trousers after the Celtic style and fur-lined boots. He looked as though he would be far more at home wielding an axe in a snowy forest.

Even as Pompey watched, a small part of him was impressed as the barbarian giant gripped one of the upright posts that formed the frame for the wall and, grunting, tore it free from its position, turning back wielding the eight-foot post as though it were little more than a javelin.

Unable to escape the shop, the remaining opponent stepped forward and lunged with his knife, hoping to get inside the sweeping range of the huge club.

He was too late, as the big barbarian already had enough momentum on a swing that caught the knifeman a glancing blow - not heavy, but enough to knock him sideways and disrupt his attack. As he righted himself for another attack, he failed to notice the beam on its return journey and the barbarian caught him a hefty blow in the side that must have snapped the arm and broken several ribs.

The man bellowed his pain as he collapsed, but the barbarian was not finished yet. Stepping close to his last victim, he raised the beam vertically and then dropped it, end first, onto the convulsing man's face, smashing his head like an overripe melon and killing him instantly.

The big man heaved in several deep breaths and then turned to leave and registered Pompey and his men for the first time. With a strangely predatory smile, showing bloody, rotten teeth, the huge man barked something in a guttural language.

Pompey frowned and gestured to Artorius.

'Subdue him.'

The four men stepped forward toward the big thug and his beam, cautiously but without fear. These were no ordinary thugs, but warriors - former legionaries and gladiators chosen for their loyalty and their skills and strength. They were the best muscle Artorius could purchase for his dominus.

The first man feinted, causing the barbarian to pull back his beam threatening a wide swing. Even as he did so, the man at the far side slipped past the giant and into the shop, getting behind him.

The other two in the centre moved in for the attack, and the huge man swung the club. Both men ducked, allowing the beam to pass above them and strike the unfinished frontage, shaking loose dust, plaster and even a tile. The big man was a little shaken by the sudden impact that reverberated up his arms.

The first attacker, who had feinted to begin the fight, took advantage of the giant's momentary discomfort and ducked inside, delivering several sharp and professional boxer-like jabs to the man's stomach. Pompey's eyes widened as the big barbarian simply let go of his club and smashed his fists down onto the boxer's shoulders. Impressive beyond belief: those rabbit punches would have almost any man doubled over and winded.

Instead, the giant had smashed down his hands with such force that he plainly crippled the boxer, tearing the cord that ran from neck to shoulder on both sides and smashing one shoulder to a pulp of bone fragments. The guard collapsed to the floor, screaming and writhing.

Immediately, the two who had ducked were up again, knives out, sweeping them in arcs, keeping the big man at bay while the one who had snuck around behind him suddenly jumped on the giant's back, his arms locking around the neck, entangled fingers pressing up into the throat apple.

There was a silent, motionless pause and Pompey nodded, watching as the big barbarian began to sink forward with the pressure on his throat, but then the fight swung his way again. The giant had not been collapsing forward after all, but moving deliberately in a planned move to dislodge his strangler. As he lowered, he suddenly dropped forward to his hands, the guard on his back flung over his head and against the half-built frontage like a rag doll.

As the unconscious guard collapsed by the bricks and the barbarian sprang surprisingly lithely back to his feet, the remaining two men moved in, slashing with their knives.

The giant raised his fists ready to deal with them but the point of a long sword appeared just beneath his chin, the tip pressing into his neck and drawing a trickle of blood.

'Care to back down?' Artorius asked softly as he appeared around the big man's side, his hand gripping the sword's hilt in a professional manner. Pompey was impressed. He had never even seen Artorius leave his side, let alone get behind the big man.

The barbarian seemed for a moment ready to fight on, but Artorius pushed the blade and brought forth a small rivulet of crimson.

'I am very well trained with this, my friend. If you understand Latin, understand that you need to lower those fists and put the hands behind your back. I will not hesitate to push this blade right through your neck if you do not comply on the count of three. One!'

The big man's hands jerked indecisively.

'Two!'

The fists dropped, the hands disappearing behind him.

'Pelates? Goron? Bind his hands behind him.'

'What with, sir?'

'Use one of your belts.' Artorius glanced sideways at the hulking colossus who glowered at his captors. 'On second thoughts, use *both* your belts. Then go find some rope just to make sure.'

Pompey stepped forward, making sure to keep himself just out of the giant's reach.

'You speak Latin, then.'

'I speak Roman words.'

'That's some very impressive brawling, barbarian. Had you chosen somewhere else for your fight, I might have cheered you on or placed a wager; but this is my house that you are busy demolishing, and that peeves me.'

'Piss off, small Roman.'

Pompey fought the rise of his anger once more. Artorius was busy gesturing at the big man's neck near where the sword point had drawn blood.

'What?'

'Domine… there is a mark on his neck. 'LT''

'So?'

'It's the mark of the slave trader Lucius Tiburtinus. He's had so much trouble with theft and runaways he started branding his property even before sale. This is a slave!'

Pompey smiled unpleasantly. 'Then he will likely die a very unpleasant death for this show. Have him taken to the Tullianum and incarcerated until we can identify whose property he is. If the trader is in the city at the moment, it shouldn't be too difficult, and then the careless master can pay me for my walls.'

The big barbarian glowered at Pompey as Artorius and his two men manhandled him away from the scene and out into the street, heading for the forum and the infamous prison of the Tullianum.

Pompey sighed. It had started as such a positive day, too. He frowned at the guard who had been concussed in his fall and was busy rising to his feet slowly and shakily. He prodded the wounded man and pointed at the writhing shape of his companion with the broken shoulders.

Chapter Two

Brutus rubbed his chin reflectively as his eyes strayed back and forth across the sizeable fleet assembled before him. The ships, wider, flatter, and considerably heavier than the traditional Roman trireme, bobbed about in the harbour in response to the slight chop of the waves washing into the wide entrance from the channel. It was a breath-taking sight. Compared to the small fleet of the previous year it was as a legion to a century of men. The chill wind blustered at him and he folded his arms around his chest and hugged himself warmer.

'It's what the general wanted, and I know it's practical and sensible, but four of our most experienced trierarchs and marine commanders have requested transfers to the legions rather than deal with Celtic design ships, and the rest of them mutter prayers to half a dozen Roman gods before they set foot on the boarding plank. They don't think I've seen them, but they're not that subtle.'

Priscus, standing next to him on the dock at Gesoriacum, spoke through gritted teeth. 'I've denied all transfers. These overblown fishermen will get on whatever ship their commanders tell them to and they'll sail them straight onto the Styx if we demand it. I'm not about to be dictated to by a load of bearded, salt-stained arseholes who think they're indispensable because they know how fast a trireme can turn. We've risked enough rough seas with our own ships. The Gauls have been sailing these waters since Romulus hit his brother with a brick, so they know a thing or two about it. Time to learn from them.'

'I know.' Brutus sighed. 'I just wish sailors were a little less superstitious. It's been a rough month or two.'

'You think *you've* got problems' Priscus replied sourly.

Brutus turned a sympathetic smile on the camp Prefect. 'He's finally got round to sending for you then?'

'Not yet, but any moment now. All the senior officers have been called in bar you and me. Apart from everything else, I keep hearing rumours of transfers the general has decided on without even consulting me. I'm going to be picking up the pieces from it all for a month. I swear this job is the most pissy, irritating, mind-numbing career the military mind has ever devised. I've half a mind to resign the bloody role if the general's going to transfer people without my input.'

'If you resigned we'd be deep in the manure in a month. Since Cita retired there's no one else with the knowledge of camp administration and logistics. Crispus is a good administrator - he trained in the government back in Rome, but even he doesn't know the ins and outs of the army like you. You're it. I bet you're about to become official chief quartermaster too.'

'The general can go piss up a wet seaman's rope if he thinks I'm doing that too. I'm overdue my honesta missio. I could be running a nice little tavern back in Capua now, handling strong drink and soft pink women instead of standing in a wet wind watching ships bounce about in the current while my commander undermines me.'

'Hello' Brutus said with a resigned smile as his eyes settled on something past Priscus' shoulder. The camp Prefect turned to see two centurions striding across the muddy dock toward him. The two came to a halt before the senior officers and saluted smartly, three piercing eyes fixed on Priscus.

'Furius; Fabius. Trouble?'

'Not as such, Prefect - at least not for certain. The general's just told his secretary to fix him some food and then send for you. Thought you might appreciate the 'heads-up' sir.'

Priscus sighed and nodded.

'Thank you, lads. What are you up to at the moment, other than loitering outside the general's tent and eavesdropping?'

Fabius had the decency to look uncomfortable at the accusatory jibe.

'Marine training again, sir. Don't want to be caught unawares. And we've managed to procure a couple of the natives' chariots to practice manoeuvres against, so we've split into groups.'

Priscus nodded and gesturing a farewell to Brutus, turned and started striding back toward the fort on the hill, the two centurions falling in on either side.

'Good. Can you work with the other commanders to make sure each legion is familiar with them? There's a warehouse-load of shit poised to fall on us this summer and I want to be prepared for anything.'

Furius pursed his lips. 'Respectfully, Prefect, do you think the general will cancel his plans?'

'I don't see he has much choice. Can't go jollying off to piss-ridden islands on the edge of the world when Gaul's poised on a knife edge. You'd have to be an idiot and the general might be many things, but he's hardly an idiot.'

The three men stomped up the hill in silence toward the brooding fort. The light grey sky sat like a steel sheet over the town, depressing the spirits of everyone beneath it. Still, at least the snow had finally gone, leaving the entire north of Gaul a slushy, muddy quagmire. It was hard to imagine that Britannia would be any better, but at least the results of the centurions' investigations made that trip unlikely now. And of course, that would give Brutus more time to sort out his unruly sailors.

The town of Gesoriacum brooded beneath the hulk of the powerful Roman fortifications. Caesar's response to the rising of the locals the previous autumn had been typically severe. The T-shaped timber constructions that had seen a hundred crucifixions and hangings over the harsh winter still stood like scarecrows to warn the Morini against any further insurrection. Here and there a ragged, dry skeleton still clung to one, all meat and gristle long gone through scavengers. There had been no further noise from the local tribes, but Priscus had wintered here; could see what Caesar couldn't during his sojourn in Illyricum. The Morini might look cowed, but the signs were there for anyone who cared to look. Resentment was deep and had grown with every fresh corpse. That messages were being passed in secret between the tribes was plain, even before Priscus had sent out his men to start tracking them down and proving his fears.

A gesture meant to seal the lid on the fire pot of Gaul's rebel spirit had merely fanned the flames. The most worrying thing, to Priscus' mind, was the actual lack of minor revolts. Every season since Rome had followed the Helvetii into Gaul, some insignificant turd of a chieftain had roused his people to fight off the oppressor. And after the Morini, it had all stopped. No sign of trouble anywhere. Even the merchants had reported a Gaul at peace. Priscus was buying none of it from those traders - the lack of trouble did not spell acquiescence from the tribes. It spelled a change in the whole thing: a move from minor widespread rebellions to a deep, organised, hidden current of antipathy. Gaul was building to an explosion that would make Vulcan's detonating peaks look tame.

And Caesar was busying himself with swampy shit holes across the water.

36

Well Furius and Fabius' discoveries would have to change all that. Caesar couldn't ignore it any longer.

By the time they reached the headquarters building of the fort, Priscus was in a deeply irritable mood - a mood that was in no way alleviated by the brooding presence of the two dour centurions that had spent the late winter and early spring confirming the trouble heading their way.

The cavalrymen of Aulus Ingenuus, Caesar's personal Praetorian guard, stood impassive by the door to the timber building. Neither soldier blinked or made a move to stop the camp Prefect - the most senior soldier of the regulars in Gesoriacum - but both narrowed their eyes at the accompanying centurions, Priscus was expected; companions were not.

'You two head off to the mess. I'll meet you there once I'm done.'

Furius and Fabius saluted and turned on their heel, marching off toward the large hall that had been constructed to allow a warm, sheltered place for the soldiers to eat in the terrible winter of northern Gaul. Priscus straightened himself, wondered whether he should have changed, and decided against it. If Caesar disapproved of his scruffy appearance he could stick his thumb up his arse. It suddenly struck Priscus how he appeared to be slowly turning into Fronto, and his lip curled into a sour smile.

With a drawn breath of cold, damp air, Priscus stepped inside, his hobnailed boots tracking thick, brown mud into the dry interior, overlaying the dried dirty footprints of previous visitors. The building reeked of burning braziers and incense - the former a necessity against the cold; the latter a recent affectation of the general, picked up in Illyricum. At least it stopped the place smelling of dung like the rest of this fart hole of a country.

In the main room, the signs of almost constant activity lay all about: tables strewn with maps and tablets and lists, half a dozen chairs with bum-prints in the cushions, cups for water or fruit juice standing half drunk. Only two occupants remained in the room, though. Phillipus, Caesar's secretary, was busy gathering up documents and then scurried toward the door. As Priscus stood aside for the Illyrian scribe to pass, his eyes fell upon the figure of the general in his campaign chair.

Gaius Julius Caesar looked older than Priscus remembered. His hair seemed to have receded noticeably over the winter and new lines marked his face - worry lines one might say. He sat in thoughtful pose, his eyes straying across one of the maps. Priscus had deliberately avoided crossing the general's path in the two days since he had returned to the army for fear of being handed the shitty assignments as was oft the fate of the general's first meetings.

Priscus paused in the door for too long before announcing himself and the general suddenly looked up in surprise at the man loitering in the doorway.

'Priscus? Come in.'

No preamble. No surprise at the prefect's mysterious arrival just before the order sending for him had gone out. No shock for Priscus, either. The prefect saluted wearily and strode across the room to stand before the general, his vine stick behind his back, clenched in both hands.

'Sit' the general said quietly, indicating one of the cushioned seats with a casual gesture while his eyes continued to busy themselves with the map. Priscus dutifully did as he was bade and sat quietly, awaiting the general's attentions. Finally, after two dozen heartbeats - just the right amount of time to make a nervous man betray himself - Caesar smiled up at him. The man was like a lizard sometimes, he was so cold and calculating.

'Priscus, I am grateful to you for your superlative efforts this past winter to gather intelligence on tribal activity. I am surprised, given your abundant duties, that you managed to find time, but I am suitably pleased. You must commend your agents for me also.'

Priscus bowed his head slightly.

'Thank you, general. I am just pleased we've managed to grasp a thread of this evil blanket. Now we can pull at it and start to unravel Gaul.'

'Indeed.' There was something about the general's expression that unsettled Priscus and he narrowed his eyes.

'We *are* going to deal with them, yes, general?'

'Of course. That is the very reason that I have returned more than a month early. Your news is timely. Now I can take a force east and tread on the throats of the rebellious Treveri before we cross the channel.'

Priscus let out an exhausted sigh and squeezed his eyes shut.

'Surely, general, with such trouble brewing we should abandon the frivolous Britannia campaign and concentrate on consolidating Gaul? Iron out all the creases in one go?'

Caesar's eyes hardened for a moment and Priscus saw the muscles in his jaw ripple.

'I'm afraid I cannot afford to do that, Prefect.'

'But general...'

'No. The inconclusive result of last year's crossing has fuelled debate in the senate about my fitness to remain in the post of proconsul of Gaul and, while that gaggle of balding old women in togas do not unduly concern me, they are starting to sway the people; *my* people; my plebs. I must cow Britannia and chastise them for their interference in our affairs. I will not be bested by an island of barbarians. Besides, if the tribes of Britannia decide to throw in their lot with Gallic rebels we could face a much worse threat than we currently do.'

Priscus nodded slowly, aware that this was the sort of frank discussion that the general rarely held. In the old days it would have been Fronto that played the role of listener to such truths. No longer.

'Then we must divide our forces to breaking point to contain Gaul while we deal with their cousins across the ocean, general. It is dangerous.'

'One gesture will serve to keep the troublesome Gauls subdued long enough. I will handle the Treveri myself and defuse the situation for the time being, either by diplomacy or by extermination. Even if we cannot *keep* them down that way, it will buy me long enough to deal with Britannia. I shall take four legions east. Four will remain here.'

Priscus nodded, trying not to betray his true feelings on the subject. Britannia was foolhardy - a publicity stunt to repair the political damage from the failed landings the previous year. But the general had decided, and Priscus knew well enough when to leave matters alone.

'General, I have to broach the subject of transfers and the officers.'

'Of course. Go ahead.'

Was there a strange twinkle in the general's eye there? Priscus frowned. 'With the deepest respect, general, I've kept things running smoother than they had any right to for the past two years and I feel I should have had a hand in the transfer decisions I've been hearing about. It's part of my role here after all.'

There was a pregnant pause and a tendril of sweet smelling smoke wafted across between them for a moment, half obscuring the general's face. When it cleared, Priscus was surprised to see the old goat smiling.

'Sir?'

'I have given a great deal of thought to the transfers. It has been difficult to work through, especially without your help, but I feel I have made the best of what I have.'

Priscus' eyes narrowed further, a leaden suspicion weighing him down.

'General?'

'You have served excellently as camp Prefect, Priscus, and I can see no one who will adequately take your place.'

'Take my place?'

'When you take up command of the Tenth.'

Priscus blinked and suddenly realised he was on his feet, his finger wagging. Damn it! He would have to make a conscious effort to stop himself turning into Fronto.

'Respectfully, sir, I cannot accept.'

'You can. And you will.'

'You said yourself that no one will be able to do my job. Legates can be drawn from the nobs in Rome at the blink of an eye. You can have a dozen here in weeks. A camp Prefect has to grow through the ranks and learn the trade.'

'A dozen callow youths with no military abilities can be here in weeks. But you and I know the value of having seasoned commanders. Yes, the centurionate run the army. Everyone knows this - even the great commanders like Pompey or Crassus who like to say otherwise. The centurions control every battle and I am hardly unaware of the fact, but until said battle is joined, it is the skill of the senior commanders that makes the overall strategy successful. And even beyond that we also both know how much better a legion works with a good commander when stacked up against the bad or the ineffectual ones. Some legates are *so* bad they're more use staying out of the way, but a good experienced legate can be a boon, and my stock of good officers is running woefully low.'

'General, I'm not a patrician or even a gentleman.'

'Really?' Caesar raised an eyebrow. 'Gnaeus *Vinicius* Priscus? A man with three names is hardly from peasant stock? I'm aware of the Vinicii down in Campania. You may not play in the politics of the city, but one of your ancestors served as a commander under Scipio Africanus if I'm not mistaken.' He waved a hand dismissively, causing air currents to eddy the sweet smoke. 'Enough dissembling and argument. I need my best men in the most important positions and that means you taking over your old legion. No one knows them better than you.'

One man does.

'True, I suppose, general, but I'm no commander. Can you really not give it to anyone else? And bear in mind I have weakened bones and a gammy leg.'

'I told you, Priscus. I'm short on talented officers. Fronto's gone, Cita retired, Rufus returned to Rome to deal with his family troubles, Galba moving up the political ladder and leaving the military behind. I've lost four good officers in half a year, plus a number of the better tribunes and lesser commanders. And with Crassus and Balbus gone not long before them, things are becoming stretched. New officers will be arriving in due course, but they will be green and untried. With the Treveri brewing a revolt and Britannia standing defiant I need the cream of the Roman military by my side. As for your physical issues, even weakened you're twice as strong as Cicero or Plancus, and your leg is only actually bad enough to inconvenience you when it's cold and wet.'

'It's always cold and wet here, Caesar.'

'And I've even seen you run on it these past few months. No, you may not be what you were three years ago, but you've recovered far beyond the expectations of any of the medics. So that's it: you take command of the Tenth. You don't need to worry about any of the transfers. I've decided on them myself and informed those concerned, and I will promote a replacement for you in due course when I have the opportunity.'

'My centurions will piss themselves, general.'

'I think not. I've met them. Those remarkably few who don't hold you in high esteem are frightened enough of you they wouldn't even whimper at your appointment. I do have two sets of transfers I've decided to leave to you, though, as they both concern you. That excellent standard bearer of yours - Petrosidius - who took the initiative on the beach last year? I'm moving him to the Eighth to take on their eagle, as their aquilifer passed on during the winter and an eagle deserves a good man. So you'll have to promote appropriately among the Tenth.'

Priscus nodded unhappily. The thought of losing Petrosidius to the Eighth was irksome. Not only were veteran signifers hard to come by, but the grumpy old sod was one of Priscus' oldest friends too.

'And the other thing is your two spies - the centurions whose names escape me.'

'Furius and Fabius, general.'

'Yes. I need to move them from the Seventh. I have two other veteran centurions who have requested to be transferred out of Plancus' Fourteenth. It seems they are at serious loggerheads with their commander and they're about due their honesta missio. If I don't grant them their transfer they might leave the service and I'm not about to let veteran centurions go willingly at the moment. I'd like to bolster Cicero's command with quality men that I know will be utterly loyal.'

'Does it have to be Furius and Fabius, general? They're the top two centurions in the legion. Moving them could have knock-on effects.'

'I'm afraid it'll have to be. The two officers in question from the Fourteenth are Vorenus and Pullo. They're the top officers of Plancus' legion, so they'll be taking your men's positions. I know you'll find the pair some appropriate position with your last act as camp Prefect.'

Priscus' jaw firmed. 'With respect, sir, there's precious few places a senior centurion can move to that aren't a demotion. They'll not be happy.'

'Then you'd best make sure they are.'

'Do I have free rein, sir?'

'Indeed.'

Priscus nodded once and straightened. 'Then I'd like to assign them the rank of tribune and attach them to the Tenth under me.'

Caesar's eyes narrowed. 'They're both low rankers, right up from the roots. Good men, I'm sure, but not officer class.'

'Neither am I. You said you wanted good men in command? They're good men.'

Caesar opened his mouth to reply but paused, a faint smile touching his lips. Finally, he folded his arms. 'Very well. See it done, Legate.'

Priscus stood and saluted. 'Thank you, general.'

'Don't thank me yet. We have a lot of work ahead of us, Gnaeus, and only half the tools to handle it that we've had previous years. Go to your command. I'll have the relevant documents of commission

42

drawn up and delivered and since you're still nominally in command of the quartermasters you might as well go draw your own equipment. Don't go mad though. No golden breastplates or the like.'

Priscus shook his head slightly at the unexpected turn of events and, saluting once more, turned and strode out of the door. Over the years he had watched Fronto bend under the weight of his command until finally, last autumn, he had broken. Now Priscus would begin to test the strength of his own mettle under the same conditions.

Fronto!

How he missed the old bastard.

With a sigh, he exited the building into the cold, grey world of northern Gaul and made for the mess hall where Fabius and Furius would be waiting for him. They would not be expecting the tidings he was bringing, and he couldn't help a smile crossing his face as he imagined theirs at the news of their meteoric rise.

* * * * *

For the second time in two days, Priscus stood on the dock of the harbour watching the ships bob and bounce, the pale and drawn Brutus at his side.

'We'll be back within the month, and Sabinus and Labienus are able commanders while we're gone. I don't think you'll run into too much trouble.'

Brutus nodded with a resigned sigh. 'Dividing the army nearly did for me last autumn. I don't like this at all.'

Priscus shrugged. 'Itio is supposed to be little more than a fishing village with good sea access so you should have no problems. Anyway, Sabinus will meet you with two legions. Just make sure the fleet gets there in one piece. After a whole damn winter putting it together it'd be a shame if it turned up at Itio as floating kindling. You've got a month at most to get the fleet ready and all the supplies prepared. As soon as we get back from Treveri lands, the general's going to want to cross to Shitannia.'

'Don't get yourself killed out east, Priscus. It'd be a shame to get that shiny new helmet stoved in.'

'Don't drown. We'll be back in a month.'

Brutus gave him a half-smile and waved him away. 'Go on. They're waiting.'

Priscus nodded and turned to see Fabius and Furius standing at the far end of the dock, looking distinctly unimpressed. Despite

43

being dressed in the thin-striped tribunes' tunics and the armour and helm of a senior officer, both men somehow contrived to look baser and rougher than any ordinary soldier. Not scruffy or unkempt in any way - both men had too much attention to professionalism for that - but it was hard to see them as anything other than centurions in the wrong uniform - like a sweaty, blood-soaked bull wearing a sheepskin and shouting 'Baaaa'. He almost laughed. Fronto had said the same thing of him the day he had first donned the camp prefect's uniform.

'Morning.'

'Sir' the two men snapped off a salute.

'Is the legion ready?'

Furius nodded. 'We were the first to assemble outside the gate in full kit. That Carbo has them working like a machine.'

'He's a good man. After me he was the best centurion in the legion. What of the others?'

'The Seventh is lined up and ready. The Ninth are falling in now, and the Thirteenth are readying the supplies. Caesar's foregone a full wagon train for speed and settled for pack horses. Half the cavalry have given up their precious mounts to carry sacks of grain and timber. You've never heard so much grumbling.'

'Screw the cavalry. They only ever moan and chunter and most of them don't even speak Latin anyway. We'll be relying on resupply from the various store outposts that Cita organised before he left: Nemetocenna, Bavaco and Castrum Segnum are roughly on line for Treveri lands. Move fast and deal with them quickly is the general's plan. He doesn't want to be distracted from his Britannia campaign for too long.'

The silence that greeted that last comment spoke volumes about the two new tribunes' thoughts on the subject.

'Come on. Let's get to it.'

The three men strode across the harbour and through the gate in the town's ramparts. The four legions and their horseback supply train were assembling on the wide swathe of muddy grass to the east of the town. Three legions stood in perfect order while the last escorted the supply beasts and their handlers into position. It looked woefully light and under-equipped for a campaigning force. So long as Cita's planning and organisation held, the trip should be easy enough though. Two days between each supply base and the final one on the edge of the Arduenna forest that was home to the Treveri. In a week's time they should be deep in the heart of the midden.

Caesar and his officers sat ahorse at the front of the legions, ready and waiting to move out. In their absence, Sabinus and Brutus would move the fleet and supplies to Itio and Labienus would keep control in Morini lands with the remaining two legions. It was a remarkably simple setup, given the circumstances, and Caesar might well be right about one big gesture being enough to keep the natives in line for now, but Priscus would have been happier with two or three new legions raised first.

With a sigh, the Tenth's new legate and his tribunes started down the hill to take their command.

* * * * *

'What was that?'

Priscus turned in the saddle to look at Furius, whose voice had cut through the general hubbub of a marching army and drawn his attention.

'What?'

Furius pointed into the forest on their left and Priscus once again cursed the damned Gauls, the Belgae and every other race that revered woodland spirits. The journey from Gesoriacum had been mind-numbingly dull and each day, at the end of the march, the officers had sighed their relief and congratulated each other on a peaceful journey and the easy respect with which the locals had treated the passing army.

Priscus had *not* felt relaxed or congratulatory. He had spent time in the streets of both Capua and Rome and he knew that easy reverence for what it was. In the cities, men looked at you like that and you immediately checked your purse was still there and scanned the nearest alleys for their mate with the knife. This was the quiet subservience of a people with something to hide.

No amount of warnings had made the other officers pay any attention.

And now, having passed the final supply station and moved along the edge of the great sacred forest of the Treveri, Priscus could practically feel the revolution in the air, crackling like a spark of lightning.

And people constantly seeing things in the forest didn't help. Caesar had a few mounted scouts with the column, but they remained in the open, unable to penetrate deep into the trees and so steering well clear.

'It's just another deer, likely as not.'

'I don't think so, sir' Furius replied. 'Not unless the deer have started wearing armour. Sure I saw metal that time.'

Priscus frowned and focused on the treeline. After just a moment, he too saw a flash of metal within the colonnade of wide boles and the gloom of shadows their intertwined branches created.

'Get ahead and tell Caesar.'

'Should we not raise the general alarm?' Fabius asked quietly.

'There can't be enough there to be a threat to a four legion column in the open, not when they're only on one side of us. But whatever they're up to, they've not revealed themselves and so we can hardly account them friendly.'

Furius kicked his mount's flanks and rode off toward the head of the column and the commanders that rode together there. As the mounted figure disappeared into the dusty haze along the side of the elongated column, Priscus peered into the trees, wishing the sky was a little brighter. This dull, leaden-grey half-light played tricks on the eyes with forested terrain. Now that he knew what he was looking for, though, he could see them dotted here and there among the trees. Almost certainly they had archers with them, and the column was within bow range even for a bad marksman, so what were they waiting for?

His intense concentration was suddenly shattered by the braying of what might charitably be called a musical instrument. The unpleasant, droning cacophony was joined only a moment later by other similar noises being played just enough off-key as to send a shudder along his spine. He had heard the sound of the Gauls' carnyx horns before and, while it was true that the noise put the wind up many of the men, it in equal parts annoyed and amused Priscus. It sounded like a menagerie of distressed animals being physically abused.

His amusement remained suppressed this time, however. Too much of a coincidence to have a Celtic nobleman - for that was surely what the horn heralded - approaching the column at the same time as the forest to the side filled with apparent attackers. He had been sure there could not be enough men there to pose a threat to the legions. The woods would hamper the attack too much to be any real danger. And yet it had all the hallmarks of an ambush.

'Carbo!'

The pink faced centurion, senior in the Tenth, stepped out from the column and strode across to the new legate's horse.

'Sir?'

'Pass the word down the line. I want every pilum in the Tenth unshouldered and in hand ready to use.'

'Yes sir.' Carbo was peering into the woods. 'Treveri, sir?'

'Probably. It's their hallowed forest. Pass the word.'

As Carbo stepped back into line, Priscus turned to Fabius. 'Stay here and keep an eye on the woods. I'm going to see what the fuss is about.'

Fabius nodded and pulled in closer to the column as Priscus kicked his own horse and rode ahead in the wake of Furius. The Tenth formed the first legion in the column, with only the small cavalry contingent between them and the officers of the vanguard. As soon as Priscus moved ahead enough to see past the dust cloud kicked up by the horses, he spotted the source of the impossibly atonal noise. A small group of Gauls, perhaps a score in total - three of them on horseback - were issuing from some unseen trail in the forest on a course to intercept the column.

Steady, Fabius. This could turn ugly any moment.

As the small party approached, Caesar gave the order to halt the line, an order that was relayed in a heartbeat by the officers of the various units. As the legions and their cavalry escort came to an ordered stop, Priscus reined in alongside the officers. Furius was sitting close to the general and nodded to his legate.

'Ah Priscus,' Caesar said, turning to him. 'You've spotted an ambush I hear?'

'Perhaps, general. There are a number of men in the forest.'

'Then perhaps this noble comes to offer us an ultimatum? More fool him if he thinks to threaten or bargain.'

The less experienced of the officers in the van laughed dutifully, but Priscus simply squinted ahead, trying to make out the details of the approaching party. It was clearly a nobleman and his escort; his personal bodyguard. Priscus frowned. Why would the man put himself in such direct danger if he had a hidden army just waiting to pounce?

47

He continued to puzzle over the problem as the men approached and slowed. The leader was short and stocky, barrel chested and with the arms of a legionary blacksmith. His hair was a copper colour and braided, and his molten-bronze moustaches drooped past his chin, giving him a fatalistic, unhappy look. The ornamentation of his armour and helm and the high quality sword at his side spoke volumes about his rank. Here was a prince among the Gauls. For some reason he looked strangely familiar to Priscus. Caesar was wearing an expression of passing recognition too.

The Gaul must know that Caesar came to conquer; must know that Caesar was not a man to forgive or grant undue mercy. So why endanger himself when he could just send his men out?

Unless they were not his men…

'Shields!' Priscus bellowed to the column in general as he kicked his horse forward, covering the gap between the two groups of men in four bounds.

Even as Caesar opened his mouth to demand of Priscus what in the name of Venus he thought he was doing, the first arrow struck the nobleman's horse in the shoulder. Before the next could strike, Priscus launched himself from the saddle, slamming into the alarmed nobleman, knocking him from the horse's back so that the pair hit the ground in a tangle and rolled as arrows whispered through the air where the stocky nobleman had been moments before.

Uproar suddenly bloomed along the column. The continual clatter or men turning and forming shieldwalls was dotted with the bellowed orders of centurions and optios, the panicked shouts of green commanders, guttural cries of the nobleman's escort and the screams of both his and Priscus' horse as half a dozen more arrows thudded into them.

Instantly, Aulus Ingenuus was next to Caesar with the skilled manoeuvring of a veteran cavalryman, followed swiftly by half a dozen of his Praetorians, their shields creating a wall that protected the general. The last thing Priscus heard before his head hit the ground hard and shook his senses was the order for the release of pilum - the Tenth were prepared in advance and quick to launch a counter offensive.

Trying to think through his ringing ears and whirling senses, Priscus forced himself up to his knees and unfastened his helmet with considerable trouble. Removing it he noted with great interest the deep groove where his head had struck the rock. Helmetless, he would likely have died. Turning the helm to look inside he could see a smear of blood on the ridge that corresponded.

Blinking and trying to get hold of his brain through the roaring in his ears and the sickening, stomach-churning dizziness, he suddenly found himself being hauled upwards. As his eyes swam into focus, he realised that it was the Gaulish noble with the copper hair who was pulling him upright.

'Thank you' the man said in a thick accent as half a dozen sling stones whizzed through the air above them.

'Afnghhhh' was all he could manage in reply. Strange how a bump on the head made the tongue huge and numb and almost entirely useless. Blinking his rolling eyes again, he felt another hand come round to hold him steady and recognised in his swimming vision the chiselled, bristly face of tribune Furius.

There was no other explanation, now with the head-wounds into the bargain: he *was* turning into Fronto!

* * * * *

By the time Priscus' vision had properly refocused and the nausea had abated enough to allow him reasonable movement, the 'ambush' was over. The Tenth had taken the initiative, given their readiness and their position close to the van, and had peppered the forest's edge with deadly pila. In a display of incredible forward thinking and adaptability from their new primus pilus, the Seventh had appeared at a run from further down the column, pausing only long enough to ready their own missiles before sending a second wave into the forest into the seething, screaming aftermath of the first.

Priscus tried to bellow out an order, but his voice still seemed to echo quietly from somewhere deep in his chest, unheard by all but himself. He cleared his throat, wincing at the taste of bile, and looked around.

The legions were ready, swords drawn and shields up, awaiting the command to attack, following up on their devastating missile cloud. Priscus opened his mouth to shout the command, but paused, tilting his head. Turning, he looked at the stocky Gaul and at Furius.

'Did I hear music or is my head still playing funny buggers?'

The Gallic noble nodded. 'It is call for talking.'

Priscus frowned at the man. 'I know you from somewhere.' But before the man could answer, a small party of natives emerged from the forest's edge: another group of around a score, mostly noblemen in rich, heavy wool cloaks, with a small warrior escort.'

'Shooting before they talk? What are they: Parthians?'

The men of the Praetorian guard, along with their drawn, eight-fingered commander, manoeuvred their steeds into a protective circle around the senior officers, all-but blocking the view of Priscus and his two companions, now afoot.

'What is the meaning of this?' demanded Caesar of the new arrival and then, down to the man Priscus stood beside: 'out front!'

As the stocky Gaul moved forward, the Praetorian horsemen stepping their mounts aside to allow passage, Furius and Priscus followed at his shoulder.

The newly-arrived party fanned out, leaving one man at the centre, standing proud and tall in high quality bronze helmet and a clearly-Roman mail shirt. Despite the profusion of nobles in the group, he was quite clearly the leader.

'Man enemy.'

'That much is obvious' Caesar replied sharply. 'But not necessarily *my* enemy. Identify yourself.'

A man wearing a russet-coloured cloak stepped up beside him.

'This' he replied in good Latin with a faint Belgic accent 'is Indutiomarus, chieftain of the Treveri.'

Caesar shook his head and pointed at the dismounted Gaul with the two Roman officers at his shoulders nearby. '*This* man is Cingetorix, leader of the Treveri. He has commanded his tribal cavalry for me on several occasions over these past years, so I am familiar with his face.'

The tall noble and the man in the russet cloak exchanged a look and a few brief words in their own language and then the cloaked man addressed the general once again.

'Cingetorix is no longer of the Treveri. He is a crazed dog to be put down.'

Caesar glanced down at the Gaul close by and raised his brow questioningly.

'Indutiomarus is a usurping liar, Caesar. You know my loyalty.'

The general straightened again. 'I trust you understood those words, 'chieftain' of the Treveri? What say you to that?'

Again, the two men glanced at one another. 'Your former ally conspired against you with the Germanic peoples across the river, Roman. He is no friend of yours.'

'Indeed? And *you* are my friend?'

'Russet cloak' took a step forward. 'We have no love of Rome, it is true, but give us Cingetorix and we will give our oath to stop his German friends crossing the Rhenus.'

The man beside Priscus stepped out into the open, turning to Caesar. 'This man lies, general. He already has allies from across the Rhenus along with a growing force of his people in the forest. If I cannot return to Tielo and raise my own, loyal, men then by summer time, this usurper will have brought enough thugs from across the Rhenus to flatten all of Gaul, not just the Romans within it.'

Caesar sat back in his saddle.

'You put me in a difficult position. I have pressing business in the west, and I cannot tarry here long.' He turned to look down at Priscus. 'Take both these parties into custody and then have the Seventh and Ninth sweep the closest half mile of forest and round up anyone they find.'

'Caesar,' Cingetorix snapped, waving his hands, 'if you do this, you will give the friends of this son-of-a-German-whore time to build an army in the sacred forest; an army that will depose me and defy you.'

'I cannot set you free on your word alone, Cingetorix, regardless of your history of service. I will see that your enemy here is the first to be put to the hot irons to seek the truth of the matter, though, so you may yet walk free a friend of Rome.'

Priscus, looking back and forth between the two would-be rulers of the Treveri, suddenly focused on the group recently arrived from the forest.

'You!' he bellowed, pointing at the group. Caesar looked around and down in surprise at the interruption.

The entire crowd fell silent at the sharpness of Priscus' tone and the new legate stalked out half a dozen paces toward Indutiomarus, Furius bristling at his shoulder like a shadow with violent intent.

'You!' Priscus repeated. 'The cloaked man behind the spokesman. Show yourself.'

The rest of the crowd now peered at the group, focusing on the figure lurking among the Treveri nobles, wearing a long, grey cowled cloak.

51

'Come on!' he demanded.

A tense silence fell over the scene - a silence broken suddenly as the man in the cloak turned on his heel and made a break for the treeline. The world exploded into activity as though the man had been a trigger. Indutiomarus and his group of nobles burst apart like a kicked seeding dandelion, each man hurtling individually for the trees in the wake of the cloaked runner. At the same time, the Roman officers all began bellowing orders, with Caesar shouting over the top of them to take the nobles alive.

Priscus turned and gestured to Aulus Ingenuus, sitting in his saddle, impassively taking it all in, his primary duty the safety of the general.

'Ingenuus! Get your men to chase down that cloaked man and bring him back alive!'

The young prefect looked across at Caesar with an unspoken question. The general took a quick look at Priscus' face and then nodded. In response, Ingenuus gestured to two of his troopers and the three horsemen kicked their mounts into action, hurtling off at an impressive pace toward the woods and the running man.

Priscus watched the chase, ignoring what was happening with the rest. The Tenth and the Seventh were moving to the woods to round up anyone they could find and to prevent the escape of the party of nobles. But the cloaked man had distance on them all, having broken first. It was touch and go whether he would reach the woods before Ingenuus and his troopers but, if he did, he was as good as free. These men knew the forest of Arduenna as well as their own skin, and no horseman could penetrate it with any ease.

'Who is he?' Furius asked from close by. Priscus turned to him and saw Caesar leaning forward in his saddle behind the tribune, echoing the question with his own expression.

'I'm not one hundred percent sure, but I saw his face briefly and the fact that he ran tends to support my suspicion.'

Ignoring the irritation of the general at his non-answer, he turned back to watch the pursuit.

The man would only just make it. As he neared the first boles, he ripped away the cloak to give him a little more freedom among the trees and brambles but, with his back to them and the increasing distance, the view was no clearer. Ingenuus and his men were flogging the life out of their beasts to catch him, but they would not quite make it. Priscus smacked his fist against his hip in irritation.

The fleeing man sensed his freedom in his grasp and dived toward the woods, desperate to reach its shadowy safety.

Hauling back their arms, both of Ingenuus' men hurled their spears in a last effort to catch the man or to wound him at the very least. The first spear thudded into a tree bole less than two feet from the runner's head. The other, a magnificent or incredibly lucky shot, missed the man's thigh by a mere hand-breadth, but jammed into the leafy ground and stuck out at an angle, just high enough to catch the runner's ankle as he attempted to leap the obstacle.

Priscus closed his eyes in relief as the fleeing man suddenly sprawled head first into the mud and leaf-mould at the forest's edge. By the time the man had recovered enough to pull himself partly up, he found that he was at the business end of three cavalry swords, the ever-professional Prefect Ingenuus and his companions gesturing back toward the vanguard of the army.

The Tenth's new legate watched the approaching man intently, wondering whether he would try and make another break for it. He would be stupid to try, with Ingenuus and his friends' swords at his neck, but sometimes desperation led a man into the trap of stupidity.

Slowly, as he approached, the figure became more identifiable but it was only when he came close and raised his head defiantly that Priscus heaved a sigh of relief and felt the satisfaction of a task completed. Furius was still radiating confusion, but Priscus heard Caesar's breathing tighten.

'Dumnorix' the general hissed, his voice laced with venom.

Priscus nodded. Furius leaned closer. 'Dumnorix as in the one we saw on that message?'

Still nodding, Priscus turned from the sight of the weary prisoner and clapped his hand on Furius' shoulder. 'The very same. Soon as you mentioned that name, I knew we were on to something. I've been hoping we'd get our hands on him, but I didn't imagine it would be this quick and easy. Fortuna smiles on us, Furius.'

'But who *is* he, sir? Some kind of Belgic chieftain?'

'Oh no, Furius. No Belgian this one. He's Aedui, from down at Bibracte.'

'But the Aedui are long allies of Caesar.'

'Not *this* prick. When we last saw him he was a lot fatter and haughtier, but I know that face. Dumnorix was a ringleader of a plot four years ago, when we first set foot in Gaul; a plot which led to the death of a lot of good cavalrymen and the murder of a popular tribune, and almost the death of Fronto too. He was let off a bit too leniently, though, due to our need to stay in with the Aedui at the time - stripped of his titles and money and exiled. Soon as I saw his name on that scrap of message, I knew the knob-end was up to his old tricks, and what he's been doing since he was kicked out of Bibracte. And now we've got him without the need to keep the Aedui happy. This time I think the general might like to have him broken?'

He looked up at Caesar, who was still unleashing the full force of the infamous Julian malice at the scrawny, dejected figure before them, eyes burning and lip twitching. 'Bind him tight and strap him to a horse, none too comfortably either.' He turned to Cingetorix, who was still standing beside Priscus. 'My apologies for entertaining doubt, chief of the Treveri. Do you require our aid to secure your lands once more?'

The intended humiliation of the question was not lost on the chieftain, who tried to stand straight and proud, despite having been saved from an ignominious death by the timely arrival of Caesar's legions.

'Respectfully Caesar, now that your men are rounding up the majority of Indutiomarus' friends and warriors, I should have no trouble breaking his influence in the oppida of the Treveri. Should your legions remain to aid me, though, I fear it might send others running to his cause instead.'

Caesar nodded and looked up at the legionaries of the Seventh and Tenth herding captives from the forest.

'Very well. We look to have around a couple of hundred prisoners now. I trust you will have no difficulty with my removing them from Treveri lands and putting them under close guard among my veterans?' He glanced down at Dumnorix and then across at the tall figure of Indutiomarus who was being propelled toward them, his arms folded behind his back, struggling against the four legionaries who held him. 'And the interrogation of a few, of course.'

Cingetorix looked ready to argue for a moment, but lowered his head and closed his mouth, nodding silently.

'Go and quell the rebellious spirit among your people, Cingetorix. I have urgent business this summer, and I would hate to have to interrupt it in order to return here and remind you of your oaths. Do I make myself clear?'

Again the chieftain nodded, his head remaining bowed.

Priscus smiled at Furius. 'I couldn't have planned it any better. Two of the biggest ringleaders in chains at one accidental stroke. See? I'm wasted as a legate. We might just be able to avert this inferno before it builds ready to blow, Furius.'

The tribune nodded. 'Let's get Britannia out of the way first, sir, eh?'

Priscus grinned. 'Time to kick a few British arses, eh? Shame Fronto's missing this. Wonder what he's up to? He'll be married by now. Bet he's pacing like a caged lion.'

Chapter Three

IUNIUS

'There won't be any bookmakers.'

Fronto smiled at Lucilia. 'There are always bookmakers. Sometimes you need to know where to find them is all.'

The look in his young bride's eye seemed to be trying to convey some sort of warning, but Fronto shrugged off the worry. For the first time since last autumn he was in for a bloody good fight. He might not actually be *involved* in it - probably a good thing given how his knee was holding up and how he seemed to get out of breath even climbing a flight of stairs these days - but he would get to admire the skill at arms of professional fighting men. And perhaps make some money if he still knew form to any extent. And there might even be wine involved, since Pompey had pride of place and they were joining him.

The only minor irritation was that Galba was here somewhere in the throng but would not be in a position to share his encyclopaedic knowledge of the games. It was said that the stocky noble who had fought alongside Fronto for years now had such an intimate knowledge of the world of the lanista and his property that he had never yet lost a bet on a fight. He would certainly be a handy man to have close by, given the meagre amount of cash Fronto had managed to sneak out of the house. Lucilia had been adamant that Pompey was supplying everything they need so money was unnecessary. Not, Fronto simmered, when you knew where to look for a bookmaker.

Lucilia was suddenly waving, though she stopped herself short of shouting at the noble lady - such would have been inexcusable behaviour for a Roman matron of patrician blood. Even the expansive waving was perhaps over the top. But then, most noble-blooded visitors to the monstrosity that stood before them would be borne by litter and accompanied by guards. Not so the Falerii. Fronto had suggested transport, but Lucilia had chided him and suggested a walk, given the lovely weather, and that was *another* thing that had set him glowering: after the walk all the way from the Aventine, his knee was already playing him up and he knew he would be sitting with a painful throb throughout the games.

Perhaps wine would alleviate that.

His gaze fell upon the subject of Lucilia's gesticulating and he noted with sourness that the lady Julia, daughter of Caesar, had just alighted from a ridiculously comfortable-looking litter. Pompey Magnus, her husband, stood at the front of the portable couch, speaking to a heavy-set man with the look of a professional fighter as half a dozen hired guards kept a space open between the pair and the bustling crowd all about. The gulf between the two noble families - Pompeius and Falerius - was brought home to Fronto when his view was suddenly obscured as a man reeking of fish bumped into him, almost knocking him over. He spun to berate the man, but already had no idea where he was in the press.

'Should have had a pissing litter and guards.'

'Did you say something, Marcus?'

'Doesn't Julia look radiant, dear' Fronto said, smearing a horribly fake smile across his face - the one that made him look faintly constipated.

'She does. She's waving us over. Come on.'

As they moved forward, Fronto's gaze rose from the beauty of Julia and her bulging, pregnant stomach, past the litter and the private army of Pompey's to the enormous structure that the former general had commissioned several years ago and which had only just had the finishing touches added to it.

It was, he had to admit, a breath-taking piece of work. You could fit the entire timber and tile theatre of Tarraco inside this massive marble one five times over, let alone the huge portico and temple group that formed a part of the whole complex. It was easily the tallest building in the entire region of Rome.

It was almost impossible to get one's head around the sums of money that Pompey must have forked out to pay for this thing. It was a display of wealth and pomp beyond anything Fronto had previously imagined. The general had been granted three triumphs in his time - a magnificent achievement - and yet the people of the city would forget those ostentatious displays in short order as the political climate changed and swung about. But this enormous grand design would stamp the name of Pompey the Great on the city forevermore. It was a legacy, if nothing else. It was also the first theatre of any permanence that had graced the great city.

'Where are Galronus and Faleria? They were supposed to be meeting us.'

'Faleria said they'd join us inside' Lucilia replied calmly, still smiling at Julia. 'She and Galronus have a few things to attend to first.'

Grumbling, Fronto followed her through the crowd, grateful when it began to ease off as Pompey's mercenaries spread out and held the crowd back to facilitate their approach. Julia smiled at them warmly, holding out both arms in welcome.

'My dear Lucilia. Faleria has spoken of you numerous times. I am so pleased you could join us.'

As Lucilia bowed her head slightly in acknowledgement, Julia shifted her gaze to the sullen male. 'Marcus. You look well.'

Fronto gave her a weary smile. 'Kind; if not entirely true. Good to see you, Julia. How's knob-nos...' he shrivelled slightly into himself and coughed to cover his words. 'Sorry. How's life?'

'Life, Marcus, is superb and, despite the difficulties of having to heave this lump around on a daily basis,' she paused to pat the rounded bump, 'everything gets better day upon day. My beloved cannot wait to be a father again.'

Fronto's eyes slipped sideways to the well-padded figure of the general standing a few paces away. Pompey had become a little out of shape in recent years of political luxury. But then Fronto was hardly the frontline fighter he had been a few years ago. Something about the way the man stood, however, suggested that he considered himself anything but 'past it'. He would still present a powerful opposition in a fracas, the grumpy ex-soldier suspected.

'Fronto.' A curt, simple greeting. It could easily have been seen and heard as offhand, even insolent. Fronto knew this man, though. The greeting was simple enough in terms of words. The man's eyes, however, drank in every nuance of Fronto's bearing and attitude, filing away important details, identifying strengths and weaknesses. His expression moved from one of haughty distance to one of expectant companion. Fronto could feel himself being weighed up and tested. His greeting and first words to this man who had so opposed his own general at times would be paramount to the forming of any future relationship, good or bad. Fronto paused for only a heartbeat before allowing a friendly smile to reach his lips.

'It's hot as a camel's scrotum in this crowd. Let's get inside and find some cheap wine.'

He tried to ignore the horrified look his wife suddenly shot at him and the bemused expression on Julia and kept his twinkling, smiling eyes on Pompey.

The ageing general's eyelid flickered once and for a moment it looked as though he might explode. He did. In uproarious laughter.

Throwing his head back and letting out a bear howl of humour, Pompey Magnus reached out and threw an arm around Fronto's shoulder.

'Given our history, Fronto, I really did expect you to approach me with sour distaste, or at the very least unhappy respect. I am heartened to find you the same Fronto of whom tales are told in the military. Come. Let us cool down this 'camel's scrotum' and find some wine. Not cheap stuff though. I have three jars of the best stock waiting for us inside. I suspect your friend the Gaul will appreciate a jar?'

Fronto grinned. 'Galronus? I have no doubt. Come on then. Show us this theatre of yours then.'

Pompey, still chuckling, turned and strode toward the nearest entrance, two of his hirelings leading the way, clearing the crowd aside. Fronto reached out with his arm for Lucilia to lean on, but she had already stepped away from him and was deep in conversation with Julia. Shrugging, aware that the ladies' safety was assured by the ring of Pompeian guards, he strode off after the general, trying not to limp.

The arcade of columned arches that formed the ground floor arc of the theatre's outer wall presented dozens of points of entry, but the organisers of the games had placed railings across most of them, limiting access to only one point on the northern arc and one on the southern. As they made their way up to the southern access, the guards now physically pushing the general public aside to allow for their passage, Fronto realised how many people were going to be disappointed today. Certainly this monstrous theatre could hold a great number of spectators, but nothing like the number jostling toward the entrances to buy a small inscribed bone ticket.

As the guards cleared their way, Pompey simply waved to the factor at the table by the gate, who brushed aside his box of tokens and marked off the honoured editor and his guests on a wax tablet.

If anything, the heat was even less bearable in the confines of the tunnels, and once they made their way through the arched opening and out into the sunlight, Fronto breathed a deep sigh of relief. The theatre was all the more spectacular in its internal dimensions and, as they descended the half dozen steps to the front seating ring with an unrivalled view of the proceedings, Fronto drew a deep breath at the vast swathe of people already seated.

Not near the front at the centre of the arc, though. A space some twelve seats wide and four rows deep had been kept clear and, as they arrived and Pompey gestured to the seating, Fronto noted with interest the general's name inscribed into each of the seats.

'Reserved in perpetuity?' he enquired, lowering himself with his favoured knee first and brushing the chiselled name with his fingertips. Pompey, sitting next to him, shrugged. 'If I plan to attend, these seats will be kept for me - one of the benefits of having built the thing. If I have no interest in the entertainment on offer, those seats can be sold to the better classes and I will redeem the money.'

'Smart.' Fronto watched with some surprise as Lucilia walked on, almost entirely ignoring him, barring a brief flick of the eyes, and seated herself several spaces along, next to Julia, where they continued their apparently riveting conversation. He noted with interest they had left two seats vacant between the men and women. For Galronus and Faleria, presumably.

'Keeping the women out of earshot eh? Most sensible. I love Lucilia dearly, but sometimes she goes on like Aeschylus monologue.'

Pompey smiled happily. 'I like to give Julia her space and time with her friends. She is in a delicate way these days and needs to be indulged. Besides, we can make more of the sport, the wine and possibly even a wager when the ladies are not overseeing our actions, eh?'

Fronto grinned. 'I'll drink to that.'

Almost as if in response, a cup of wine was proffered from the side. The older man's guards had taken the perimeter seats, creating a wall of muscle between the ever growing crowd and the party of nobles. Within, other than the four of them, two servants attended with trays of food and jars of wine, the girl serving the ladies while the boy served the men.

'Thank you.' Fronto looked into the cup, somewhat disappointed at the minimal level of the wine inside as the jug of water was proffered to top it up. Fronto nodded and then jerked his hand across to signal a cut off, barely making the mix equal. The boy looked surprised but said nothing as he went on to pour a four to one mixture for Pompey.

'You're a fan of the games, I understand?' he asked, by way of casual conversation.

'I have had the privilege of seeing true contests of skill as far afield as Asia, Africa and Hispania. Each game I attend presents new fascinations. Every nation produces a different kind of fighter and they all have their interest for me. There are gladiators lined up for today from three different ludi, all chosen and paid for by my own eye and hand. I particularly like the look of the two Numidians and the Cretan from the school of Cornelius Vatia in Capua. Most surprisingly, one of the Numidians has been trained as a murmillo and not the usual retiarius or the natural horseman that most lanistas seem to think necessary for the desert-dwellers.'

'I shall keep an eye on them, then. I trust you're not expecting death matches?'

Pompey raised an eyebrow. 'Largely, no... it plays havoc with the purse-strings. But it will be necessary to offer the crowd the occasional death. You of all people should have no qualms about death in the arena, Fronto?'

'Not especially. When it's deserved. A fool or a coward deserves what he gets. A good man should always be nurtured, though. That's one thing commanding a legion for far too many years has taught me.'

An uncomfortable silence descended on the pair at the unfortunate reminder of Fronto's previous patronage. The former legate glanced to the side and was surprised to see just a flicker of something on Pompey's face that passed in half a heartbeat and was replaced by a serene calm.

Just for that tiny flickering moment, something had twisted the man's face and it surprised Fronto so much he had not known what to make of it. Rage. Pure, unadulterated rage, carefully controlled and concealed, but there nonetheless. Rage presumably brought on by the thought of Caesar. It occurred to Fronto that, were it not for the beautiful, pregnant young woman who sat a few seats further along and who created a bridge between two of the most powerful men in the republic, there was every possibility that Caesar and Pompey would have drawn blood from one another by now. Well... Julia and the shared knowledge that Crassus loomed in the east as a threat to them both.

According to Fronto's tutors when he was a young man, a tripod was the most stable base for any structure. Picturing Caesar, Pompey and Crassus together holding up the state in their quivering, blood-stained hands, he was inclined to doubt the truth of that statement.

Suddenly the pleasant host Pompey was back, reaching out to Fronto and tapping his cup.

'You're empty. Demetrios? Attend!'

'Yes, Domine.'

As the Greek boy filled the cup, Fronto moved the vessel along with the jar as the boy tried to take it away, doubling the intended quantity of wine in it. He grinned.

'Your health.' With an exaggerated flourish, he tipped the tiniest drop of water into the cup and lifted it to take a pull of the heady, rich liquid within.

'I note' Pompey said with casual interest, 'that you arrived on foot today? And unescorted too. Brave, given the crowds and the ugliness of the streets in these times.'

Fronto shrugged.

'Lucilia fancied the walk. To be honest, we don't keep that many guards or slaves in the house. More down in Puteoli, of course, 'cause it's a working estate, but not here.'

'You don't have a full complement of slaves?' Pompey asked with genuine and earnest concern. 'How does your house function? I could honestly give you half a dozen of ours. I seem to buy them monthly and I have trouble even remembering how many I have, let alone their names and functions. I could give you a dozen and not even notice they'd gone.'

Fronto shrugged. 'It was my father's doing, really. He used to keep plenty of slaves, but then there was the uprising down in Capua and all the trouble - well of course you remember it better than most.' Pompey nodded quietly. He had been one of the generals involved in ending the rebellion of Spartacus a couple of decades earlier. 'Well', Fronto went on, 'father came to the conclusion that unless a slave had proven his value, he couldn't be trusted. And those that he considered valuable, he tended to give their freedom anyway. By the time I came back from my first tour with Caesar, a few years after the slave war, there were only half a dozen slaves left in the villa and father had replaced them with paid servants, or kept on those he'd freed.'

'There is no danger of such a thing ever happening again, Fronto. I assure you. The keeping of slaves is only right and proper for a Roman.'

'Oh I have a few and I'm not against it. But I agree with my pater in that a trusted man with pay in his pocket is worth ten bound men. And besides, you say it'll never happen again, but that uprising you put down was hardly the first time it's happened. To be honest, I'm happy with the way we have it.'

'Things may have to change now that you're a married Roman gentleman, though, Fronto. You're no soldier now. The senate next, I presume?'

'Can't see myself lasting long in that august body without swatting someone. I'm still sort of finding my feet as a civilian and contemplating what to do about the future.'

Pompey smiled and Fronto was worryingly put in mind of a crocodile.

'Then we must have a long and frank conversation about your future, my friend. But another time. Look, the gates are opening.'

As Fronto peered into the orchestra and then up onto the stage, he saw the ornate bronze doors in the façade opening. The D-shaped orchestra had been ringed with raised boards and had sharpened stakes pointing inwards to protect the audience from the dangers in the arena, though the view was magnificent over the boards that sat at knee height for Fronto and his companions. Horns were blaring a fanfare as men of all shapes and sizes trooped out of the bronze doors and onto the stage where they stood and posed for the admiration of the crowd. From there they would be sent down into the orchestra for the individual bouts.

Pompey raised his voice to be heard by Fronto over the fanfare and the general hubbub of the excited crowd.

'Time for the man who paid for this to say a few words. But when this is over, you must come to the house for a chat.'

Fronto nodded, his mind turning over this strange progression of events. In fact, he was so deeply involved in his own thoughts that he almost jumped as a hand touched his shoulder and he turned, his heart thumping, to see that Faleria and Galronus had arrived.

* * * * *

The thraex gladiator leapt back out of the reach of the raking tines of the retiarius' trident. The idiotic Syrian net-man had overreached as he tried to lunge with the long pole-arm and, as he stumbled forward into a charge that met only with thin air, the thraex jammed his sword between the tines, twisting the trident and forcing it downwards. The now hopelessly-off-balance retiarius, already relieved of his net earlier in the bout, found himself falling forward with the shaft in his hands and let go reluctantly, aware that unarmed he was as good as lost, but knowing that holding on to the shaft he would end up prone, which was worse.

His life-saving decision turned out to be immaterial. The crowd were going wild and the swordsman, knowing that his success rested as much on the mob's whims as on his own skill, took advantage of the surge of blood lust and, his sword still entangled with the discarded trident, turned his small, square shield on its edge and swung it at the still approaching, half-falling man, catching him in the neck just beneath the chin.

The crowd's wild cries reached an ear-splitting crescendo as the disarmed net-and-trident fighter was swept from his feet with the force of the blow and collapsed on his back on the sand and temporary boards that covered the elegant, expensive marble floor.

Fronto nodded in approval.

'I think you owe me five.'

Pompey leaned across to be heard above the roar.

'I'd say the thraex overstepped the mark there. That looked an awful lot like an intentional killing blow without awaiting approval.'

Fronto shrugged. 'I'd say that whatever the intention, that *was* a killing blow. I know the retiarius just looks winded but I'll tell you for nothing that blow crushed his windpipe and his throat apple. The man's a goner in less than a dozen heartbeats.'

Pompey raised his brows in surprise. 'I defer to the expert opinion of a man who's probably dealt such a blow. What to do with the victor then?'

'Congratulate him. It'd be a waste to discipline him for that, and the crowd are behind him.'

Pompey nodded. 'Expedient. I agree.'

Standing, the editor raised and lowered his arms several times in a motion for silence. At the third gesture, the horns blared and quietened the crowd.

'Victory to the Thracian. A noble end for the vanquished. See how he dies even now!'

The crowd surged their appreciation while the prone form of the retiarius shuddered several times. As the thraex inclined his head to the editor and then spun and issued theatrical bows to the rest of the crowd, two attendants rushed into the orchestra from the small wooden shed that protected them in the corner, a third man behind them in a long black cloak and with a huge fake beard, hefting a giant-sized mallet over his shoulder. The victorious gladiator was lifted from the arena onto the stage, where he went to stand with his fellow survivors, blood and sweat spattering the floor beneath them all. In the arena, the figure of Dis Pater, lord of the underworld, raised his hammer over the head of the fallen retiarius. He paused. He was supposed to make sure the fallen were not faking their death, but he was no executioner and he could still see the choking man's legs kicking spasmodically. He looked across at Pompey, who nodded.

Fronto watched with distaste as the enormous hammer smashed open the dying man's skull, smearing his life's essence across the sandy boards. It was no way to go, but at least it was fast. Faster than choking to death with a crushed throat.

'You have an interesting sense of morality Marcus Falerius Fronto' Pompey noted, watching his companion's sour look with interest. 'Unconventional, to say the least. I think I would appreciate your opinion on a personal matter. Perhaps, instead of visiting me tomorrow, your dear wife could spare you for an hour when the day's events have ended?'

Fronto shrugged. 'I expect she'll be happy to stay in the company of your wife and my sister. The three of them are as tight as the vestal sisterhood now.' He glanced across to the three women who were talking in conspiratorial tones and occasionally issuing a burst of laughter. As far as he was aware not one of the women had even looked at the arena in an hour of bouts. Such a waste of good entertainment. Galronus had managed somehow, after an initial exchange of pleasantries, to slip away to find Galba, leaving Fronto with the statesman.

'Ah,' Pompey said with a self-satisfied smile, gesturing at the temporary arena on the theatre floor. 'This should be a good one. I do like to watch a dark-skin in action. They seem so much more lithe and energetic than the rest of us.'

Fronto turned his attention to the stage once more to see two more gladiators being lowered down to the orchestra on the wooden platform suspended by ropes.

On the right, an unusual sight: a scisor gladiator. His pale skin spoke of a Gallic or Germanic origin, though little of it could be seen. His torso was encased in a mail shirt, his head in an egg-shaped bronze helm, undecorated apart from two circular eye-holes. His arms were covered with padded leather sheathes and his legs protected by bronze greaves. But the speciality of the scisor lay in his weapons. A short, straight blade in his right hand was paired with a fearsome engine on his left. His forearm was encased in a steel tube, at the end of which, instead of a hand, was a wide, fan-like semi-circular blade, glinting evilly in the sun.

On the left, paying him no attention, stood a dark-skinned Numidian equipped as a murmillo. Along with a heavy, ridged and decorated crested helm that bore a grilled face-guard, his only defences were a ridged leather protector on the arm that bore his short sword, and a rectangular shield on the other. His chest was bare, as were his legs. It appeared a hopeless match.

Pompey and Fronto looked at one another and both spoke at once.

'Five on the murmillo.'

'The Numidian for six.'

They paused and shrugged. 'You care not to wager for the scisor?' Fronto hazarded.

'I like a Numidian in a fight, as I said. And you?'

'Your Numidian's going to win. The scisor's an unknown, but the murmillo hardly seems bothered by his presence. That kind of confidence wins fights.'

Pompey nodded slowly. 'I agree. It looks an unexciting match.'

Standing, he motioned to the stage. A trumpet rang out and the wooden platform jerked to a stop halfway down.

'Let the murmillo face a *pair*' he announced. Give them someone fresh... the crupellarius.'

The crowd bayed their approval of this bloodthirsty largesse, as a man almost entirely encased in iron was urged forward until he stepped over the edge and dropped to the platform with a heavy, weighty crash, causing it to sway a little. The man was so heavily armoured that not a morsel of flesh showed on his person.

'A more even match?' Pompey asked slyly.

66

'Perhaps a little too far the other way now.'

'Then you will take my bet?'

Fronto blinked. 'Six? On the one Numidian against two of the heaviest men there, including a bloody crupellarius? Yes I'll take your bet. Confidence only goes so far. Might as well set him against a lion and an elephant.'

The two spectators smiled and turned back to the arena just as the platform hit the sand, sending up a small cloud of dust. The three fighters stepped from it, two of them bending their knees and stretching their arms in preparation for the coming trial, the crupellarius unable to do so due to the sheer weight of inflexible iron that covered him.

Pompey stood and waited for the crowd to gradually subside, the three gladiators separating and walking to equidistant places in the arena as the wooden platform was raised to the stage once more. Finally, everything was quiet.

'A special bout in honour of my beautiful wife and the child she bears. I will donate a bag of gold coins to the winners. Begin!'

The crowd surged to a roar once more and then fell to an expectant, hushed quiet as the three men took their first steps toward one another. The scisor and the crupellarius looked at one another and then nodded, sharing some unheard plan. As the latter stomped inexorably forward like a living statue, his iron cuirass and laminated arm guards clanking and screeching, his chain breeches, apron of protective strops and iron greaves groaning, the scisor scraped his curved fan-blade down his sword edge, drawing a spray of sparks and sending out a noise that cut through the nerves like an audible wound.

The Numidian murmillo flexed his arms and walked half a dozen steps forward, stopping and standing in a relaxed fashion, as though waiting to be served in a bar. Fronto frowned, starting to suspect that Pompey knew something he didn't. One man could not be that good.

As the Numidian's opponents approached, they began to spread out, forcing the murmillo to turn his head back and forth to keep an eye on them both.

'See how they flank him' Fronto pointed.

'Note how slowly the iron giant moves' Pompey countered. 'He will have an age to deal with the scisor first before having to turn his attention to the other.'

'Perhaps,' Fronto conceded, 'but they're both heavier armed and armoured than him. He'll have to be a champion to get out of this intact.'

Pompey shrugged. 'Intact is immaterial, so long as he lives.'

'I doubt he feels that way.'

Fronto forewent any further conversation as he turned his attention to the action in front of him. Sure enough, as Pompey had pointed out, the weight was slowing the crupellarius, and he approached at around half the pace of his companion. The Numidian glanced once more at him to make sure he was as slow as expected, and then stepped across into the line of attack of the scisor, who once more scraped his weapons together to create the sparks and the ear-splitting shriek of tortured metal. How the Numidian could stand it, Fronto couldn't imagine. It was making *his* head ache this far away.

And then, finally, judged just right to put the crowd at their most tense and expectant, the two gladiators were within fighting range. The scisor began to swing his sword and his razor-fan in figure-eight motions, creating a whirling web of death. Fronto grinned.

'He's better than I expected. Not just a showman. He knows killing too. Your man's bollocksed.'

'My man's agile' Pompey noted quietly.

As Fronto watched, the dark-skinned murmillo ducked and weaved, thrusting his sword to try and create an opening, but always, while failing, nipping back, swaying and dodging out of the way of the swinging web of sharp steel. Still, he was gradually being forced backward toward the edge of the arena by the pressure. Soon he would run out of space to dodge.

The crupellarius was approaching now, slowly, but with infinite menace, a clanking statue of deadly, impervious iron.

Fronto shook his head. The Numidian was good, but he was nearly penned in. Soon, he would be minced meat.

Even as he watched, Fronto felt a thrill that began in his purse as the Numidian lunged with his blade and had it caught by the spinning web which sent it hurtling out across the sand to land half way across the arena. The unarmed murmillo leapt back out of the way, throwing up his shield, which was steadily, methodically shredded into strips by the spinning blades. He was almost at the wall now.

At a last, desperate moment, the Numidian lifted his tiny remnant of shield - now little more than a boss with a hand-grip - and tossed it away.

Fronto realised that he was gripping the edge of the seat and forced himself to relax. He was not a ten year old at his first match. Prat!

As he focused, his jaw twitching with the excitement, everything changed in the blink of an eye. The desperate Numidian, devoid of weapon or shield, had shrunk back, his arms coming up to cover his face. The scisor, sensing victory, had moved in to deliver a crippling blow - enough to end the match without an instant, unworthy kill.

But his victim was no longer there.

The Numidian had continued back from his shrinking in apparent fear and had fallen flat to the floor, prone but apparently intentionally so. Fronto wondered what the hell the man was planning.

The scisor's spinning web of horror passed over the prone form as the attacker staggered forward, unable to halt his momentum quick enough. In half a heartbeat, he was standing over the prone Numidian, one leg on either side, the spinning blades starting to swing down toward the target. As the sharp steel approached the prone man, the Numidian reached up with his free hands, pulling aside the man's loincloth, and grabbed the testicles, wrenching them from his body with a single, muscular move.

The screech of the brutally castrated gladiator echoed across the great theatre, stilling the crowd into a shocked silence. Even the impervious crupellarius faltered in his step at the horrifying cry of pain. The stricken fighter, still standing, cut himself twice as his sword stopped spinning and fell away to the earth, forgotten, the other hanging deadly but useless in its razor-ended metal case. A huge splash of blood washed across the dark-skinned gladiator beneath him and, even as the unfortunate man's free hand came down to try and find his missing manhood, the Numidian was already out from beneath him, coming up behind.

Leaving the ruined scisor screaming and probing between his own legs with an armoured hand, the Numidian almost casually strode across to the fallen sword and picked it up before sauntering jauntily across the arena and collecting his own discarded blade.

The crowd exploded in applause and cries of excitement as the blood-slicked Numidian murmillo, now armed with a sword in each hand, strode back toward the iron monstrosity, ignoring the howling eunuch he had created, who seemed unable to move, groping his own ruined parts.

The crupellarius turned to face the approaching Numidian, whose small square shield was raised, despite the fact that it was largely pointless, given his full-body coating of iron. His long, narrow sword came up, the dangling apron of metal strops that protected his groin jingling against the chain breeches as a reminder that his opponent would be unlikely to pull the same manoeuvre here.

The Numidian strolled toward him calmly.

Observing from the stands, unable to ignore the excited air of anticipation emanating from Pompey, Fronto began to feel the money he had envisaged tipping into his purse evaporate before his very eyes. The murmillo *couldn't* be that good. But clearly he was.

The crupellarius stomped two steps forward and then braced to meet the approaching dark-skinned gladiator who paused, just out of sword reach, and let go of both his own blades, reversing his grip as he caught the falling hilts, now holding them face downwards as though for an overhand stabbing motion.

Taking one more step to bring the fight to a conclusion, the crupellarius thrust his shield forward to take any stabbing, raking blows from the two swords, drawing back his own blade to strike as soon as the opening came, sure in the knowledge that he was all-but impervious to blades and could withstand even a couple of direct strikes if necessary, waiting for his best moment.

In the most unexpected, unlikely move, the Numidian dropped to his knees, right beneath the crupellarius' shield edge. Fronto frowned, wondering what use being that close would be, particularly now that he was on his knees, a position in combat which almost universally led to defeat. Yet somehow he knew that the man would win. The crupellarius had every advantage but Fortuna and Mars sat on the Numidian's shoulders, watching over him. Despite the damage being done to his purse, Fronto found himself rooting for the kneeling warrior.

It was beautiful. A stroke of genius. Fronto watched with impressed admiration as the Numidian murmillo completed his intended manoeuvre. From his kneeling position, both swords reversed and held downwards, he jammed the blades behind the knee-top edge of the iron giant's greaves, one each side, driving down the blades inside the man's armour in the tiniest gap possible, so that both swords brought sparks from the greaves' edges as the blades scythed down the man's shins inside, the points driving through the bones of the crupellarius' feet, almost severing them, all inside the man's impervious plating.

The iron man screamed at the dual crippling blows and wavered for a moment before toppling backward to the earth, the weight ripping the hilt of both jammed swords from the Numidian's grip as he fell.

Again with the casualness of a man at a quiet dinner, the dark-skinned murmillo rose to his feet, unstrapping his helmet and pulling it away in one hand to allow his sweating, shiny face the blessed breath of air. Fronto was surprised. The man was clearly older then he himself. It was exceedingly rare for gladiators to last that long. After half a dozen years they were either dead or freed and rich - invariably the former.

Fronto stared as Pompey rose and began to applaud, the entire arena joining in, raising an uproar of approval. The man's two victims stood and lay where they had been crippled, bleeding and screaming. Neither would die if they were tended quickly, but whether they would ever fight again was a different matter.

'Who *is* he?' Fronto asked Pompey, certain that he had somehow been duped and this astonishing fighter was one of the world's greatest champions sneaked in among the group - a freed hero who fancied another bout for the money and the fun.

Pompey shrugged. 'His name is Masgava, if I remember correctly. Impressive, isn't he?'

Fronto shook his head. 'What is he? Some kind of ringer? A freedman? A provincial champion?'

'No. He's a genuine ordinary slave gladiator - not even that expensive. Apparently he has a habit of being disobedient and forward, so he keeps getting sold on. More trouble than he's worth, so to speak. A good warrior though.'

Fronto stared at the grinning Numidian. That, he most certainly was!

* * * * *

'I still cannot get over it. That was, without a doubt, the best fight I've seen in any arena.'

71

Pompey nodded. 'I told you, always watch the dark-skins. They're simply always better.'

'Where are we going?' Fronto asked as he strode alongside the former general, his knee sending him urgent messages to sit down at the earliest opportunity. They had strolled eastwards from the theatre following the final bout of the day. The three ladies had waved them off, returning to Pompey's house close by with a well-muscled escort, while Pompey elected to walk, leading Fronto and Galronus away with only half a dozen men around them. The ladies would await their return.

Now, some distance from the theatre, they were passing close to the Temple of Juno that towered over the Capitoline.

'To the carcer, my dear Fronto. To the carcer.'

Fronto frowned and looked across to Galronus expecting to share a surprised and unspoken question, but the Gaul's own frown spoke only of complete incomprehension.

'Carcer?' The big man repeated, rolling the unfamiliar word around his tongue.

'It's...' Fronto said, trying to explain as best he could. 'It's where convicted criminals and prisoners are held before they're killed.'

'A prison?'

'Not as such. No one stays there very long. In fact most of its visitors come out on their back within days.'

Galronus nodded sagely. 'Among the Remi, such punishments are carried out when judgement is made. It is the way.'

Pompey gave a half-smile. 'Among the Romans we like to wait for a big occasion to celebrate to get the best value from our corpses. Stranglings always go down well on a festival day. There's nothing like a seafood fricassee and a cup of rich mulsum accompanied by a state execution, eh? The kids love it.'

Fronto glanced up at the undecorated brick façade just ahead that fronted the most fearful, infamous place in the centre of the city. A single door of heavy oak stood in the wall, no sign to announce what lay behind it. Fronto had visited the carcer only once, as a boy, when his grandfather had taken him to show him what happened to the enemies of the state, expecting Fronto to seek a career in the city. At the time, he had shivered at the awful place; at the four men who had waited there for the time of their execution.

A shiver ran up Fronto's spine at the sight of the building.

'Why in the name of Jove's balls are we going to the carcer?'

Pompey pursed his lips. 'As I told you earlier, I seek your opinion on a personal matter.'

Fronto frowned as they approached the door. The three visitors stood in the street as one of their accompanying guard knocked on the door and spoke to the single-minded public servant who maintained the security of the carcer's main doorway. As Pompey's hireling stood aside and motioned to the open door, the general strode inside without pause. Fronto took a deep breath and swallowed a last lungful of good air before entering. Galronus followed up with an air of inquisitive interest.

The half dozen Pompeian men waited outside the building, and Fronto found himself in the front chamber of the complex, where three guards sat sharpening swords. They were three of the very few people allowed to bear a weapon within the city's sacred bounds, given the nature of the chambers they watched over. Galronus looked around with interest and nodded a greeting at the guards, who pointedly ignored the odd foreigner, despite his Romanised dress sense.

'Let us through' Pompey demanded of the three men. 'We need no escort and shall only be a quarter of an hour at most.'

The guards looked for a moment as though they might argue, but one quickly crossed the room and unlocked the heavy door to the next room. 'We cannot let you enter unescorted, general.'

Pompey fixed him with a look. 'Think hard to whom you speak.'

The man actually held Pompey's eye for a moment, and then bowed and stepped back. The general waited for him to swing the door open and stepped through, Fronto and Galronus following on. Beyond the door a large trapezoidal chamber, some twenty feet across, sat in subdued gloom. Fronto was immediately chilled to the bone and deeper still - a chill that had nothing to do with cold. In fact, it was curiously warm and damp - sweaty even - inside. The room, constructed of heavy stone blocks, was faintly greened with age and mould, strange shadows flittering around the rough-hewn stones in a dim glow cast by the three oil lamps that lit the chamber. In the floor's centre, a circular opening gaped like the maw of Hades itself. Ahead, a passageway led off into the rock beneath the Capitoline hill.

'This' Pompey said to them, gesturing around the room like a tour guide, 'is the carcer. Down the hole you can see there is the Tullianum, where the stranglings are carried out if the prisoner is not worthy of a good public death.' Fronto tried not to look, but Galronus was peering around with interest and, as they approached the hole, peered down it. Fronto shied away, repulsed more by the smell of urine and (possibly imagined) dead sweat than by its actual physical presence.

'Down here' the general continued, now apparently speaking mainly to Galronus and gesturing to the tunnel ahead 'is where we keep the prisoners awaiting their turn. These chambers were quarried out in time immemorial and the stone from them supports some of the great buildings in the forum. The Tullianum we passed back there was an antique cistern, dating from before the draining of the marsh and the construction of the aqueducts.'

Galronus was nodding like a student filing away knowledge as they strode across and into the passageway, Pompey pausing at the entrance and collecting one of the three oil lamps from the main chamber. The passageway was more a series of doorways that connected three chambers at one end, creating a sort of gallery. Fronto remembered it well, despite all the years that had passed. Each chamber was barred off half way in with iron railings to create three separate cells connected by the gallery, each of which would hold one or two prisoners, though as often as not they would remain empty. Few people stayed here long.

Fronto blinked in surprise as they entered the first chamber and the flickering orange glow of the oil lamp picked out the half dozen dirty, shit-smeared, naked figures lurking beyond the bars.

'What's going on, Pompey?'

'Fronto?'

'Why so many? Are the other rooms being repaired or something?'

'Hardly' Pompey replied quietly. 'Each is as full. It's been a busy time for traitors to the republic and for unforgivable criminals.'

Fronto stopped in his tracks. 'This is inhuman. They should either be done away with or freed, not just left here.'

Pompey shrugged. 'They're awaiting their time, Fronto. It's the way of things.'

'Oh come on! Look at *him*! He must have been here *months*. He's almost starving to death and that beard has too many weeks' growth for a man awaiting his execution.'

Again: the shrug. 'I don't make the rules, Fronto. I've put a few of them here, for sure, but I don't control their progress beyond arrival. That's down to the legal system.'

Galronus cleared his throat. 'Marcus is correct. This is not honourable.'

'I say again, this is not my decision. But we are becoming side-tracked from my purpose. The next room, Marcus.'

Unhappily, Fronto and Galronus shuffled into the second chamber behind Pompey. Again, half a dozen dirty, naked creatures backed away from the intrusive light. As Pompey stepped toward the bars, closer than Fronto would have advised, one figure moved out of the shadows and stepped toward them. He was enormous and clearly a northerner by his appearance. Fronto came to a halt where he knew he was still very much out of reach.

'You!' the big man spat the word at Pompey with thick Celtic overtones, his straw blond beard hiding much of his fierce expression.

'Yes, me. I have done some research on you, my big ox-like German.'

The barbarian's eyes narrowed.

'Yes. Of the Suevi I believe' Pompey went on. 'Your name is Berengarus. The records of the slave traders are duplicated into the city records of the tabularium above us. It seems your former owner - Lucius Tiburtinus - disappeared last week after a big sale. You were not crossed off his list, so you should still be unsold in his pen. You are not, and he is missing, presumed dead. The evidence, I would say, does not look good for you.'

'Piss off, Roman fat man.'

Galronus folded his arms. His face had taken on a hard look. Fronto knew there was little love lost between the Germanic Suevi and Galronus' own Remi tribe. The two had fought each other uncounted times over the centuries. Pompey turned to Fronto.

'So tell me, with your unusual morality and sensibilities, Fronto, what I am to do with this thing' he gestured at Berengarus. 'He almost certainly murdered his owner, definitely killed a number of plebs before my very eyes, and seems to be entirely unrepentant.'

Fronto frowned. 'What?'

'You have fought these people. You own slaves. It has been in my mind to simply have him killed, but Artorius, my chief enforcer, thinks I might be able to make use of him myself. My friend Policus thinks he should be given to a lanista to train for the arena. And my wife thinks I should wash my hands of the whole affair and let the state take over his case.'

Fronto shrugged. 'He'd certainly make a tough fighter, but maybe not a gladiator. To be honest, I've found the Germanic peoples to be too wild and crazed to be controlled. Not sure I'd trust him in my employ if I were you. Galronus?'

'Kill him now. He is an abomination.'

Fronto looked closer at the huge barbarian and realised with a start that the man was staring at him with some sort of vicious hunger or deeply-ingrained malice. Not the look he had directed at Pompey, but something different. Nastier. It felt as though the man seemed to know him enough to hate him without reserve. Fronto shuddered involuntarily.

'I think I'm done here.'

'Not yet, Fronto the killer of Gauls' hissed a reedy voice from the shadows. The sound was so unpleasant that even Galronus and Pompey took a step back, joining Fronto well out of reach.

Some sort of wraith appeared in the dim circle of lamplight, stalking forward toward the bars, where he came to stand next to the huge barbarian, whose malice-filled gaze was still locked on Fronto. What in the name of all the gods was going on in this place? The new, terrifying figure gripped the bars, his parchment thin skin barely concealing blue veins that throbbed rhythmically. His rheumy, pale - sightless? - eyes were locked on Fronto and a grey tongue flickered around the thin, desiccated lips as a wisp of his wild grey hair flopped down over one eye. Fronto shuddered again. It was like looking at the long-dead still standing unnaturally and speaking to you. Silently he uttered a prayer to Fortuna to get him out of this unpleasant place immediately.

'The killer of Gauls and Germans. Lapdog of the bald eagle of Rome. How is your master, Fronto?'

'Do I know you?' Fronto managed, his voice cracking slightly with nerves.

Pompey cut in to answer. 'I doubt it. This is Tulchulchur, the Monster of Vipsul. Don't let his apparent age and infirmity trick you, Fronto. It is said that he has killed more people than old age.'

Tulchulchur grinned, revealing only ten teeth, though including all four canines which were curiously and worryingly prominent. 'At your service, General Pirate-Killer. But I can hardly claim the record... there are men in these chambers who would seek the title themselves.'

Fronto shook his head. 'I've seen enough. Do what you want with the barbarian, but I wouldn't trust him as far as I could kick a ballista ball up a chimney. Come on. Let's get out of here.'

Pompey gave him an indulgent smile and turned to follow as Fronto strode for the exit, Galronus at his heel. As they left there came a series of kissing noises, hisses, growls and shrieking laughs from the cells, and cutting through them all, a deep, Germanic voice. 'I work for you, Pompey general! I work for you!'

Fronto paused for breath only when they had left the building entire, stooping to rub his sore knee. Galronus looked distinctly unimpressed.

'Thanks for that, Pompey.' Fronto snapped angrily. 'Was there a point to that unpleasantness?'

Pompey shrugged. 'I was simply interested to see what you made of Berengarus. What else transpired in there was entirely unintentional. My apologies for subjecting you to it. I assumed you would not be perturbed by such a place - you who have stood knee deep in the entrails of Gaul.'

Fronto fixed him with a hard glance. 'An open battlefield and an enemy with a sword is one thing. That place and the poor bastards wasting away in it is different. They should all be executed or freed.' His mind furnished him with an image of the ancient spectre of the rheumy-eyed killer. 'I'd plump for executed, to be honest. It's going to take a week and a lot of wine to shift the smell of decay and faeces from my nostrils.'

Pompey put a friendly hand on his shoulder. 'Truly, Fronto, you have my apologies. I had not intended such a show of unpleasantness. I needed to check on the German before I made my decision and I thought that perhaps your opinion might swing me.'

'And has it?'

'Perhaps. Come. Let me make it up to you. A visit to the baths to wash away the stink and then you can rape my wine cellar to numb the memory.'

Fronto nodded and followed on, though his mind would not stop throwing back snippets of the visit to the carcer: images of the cold-eyed barbarian and the thin, pale wraith next to him; the phrase 'killer of Gauls' and the creeping feeling that he must know this Berengarus from somewhere. Certainly Berengarus seemed to know him.

Not for the first time this year, Fronto wished he was standing on a field in Gaul with a shield and a sword, watching hairy lunatics running at him and screaming. War was so much more simple than this private life crap.

Chapter Four

'Soon as we stop, I want you two to take charge of that load of shitbags back there and get them in the stockade, all apart from Dumnorix - put him in solitary somehow with a double guard - and then get some rest before you meet me at my tent at sunset.' Priscus took a weary breath. 'I'll have to go and listen to the general rant about Aeolus once we've got the legion encamped.'

Furius and Fabius gave a tired smile. The general's mood had been steadily declining as the army approached the coast and the newly established temporary camp at Itio. The calm harbour that Caesar had selected for embarkation had been freshly and grandly renamed Portus Itius, despite the local's tendency to ignore their settlement's enforced Latinisation. The winds had shifted round to the northerly a few days ago and had since refused to change, bringing a fresh cold gust that pushed any wind-powered vessel straight back into port and declared flatly 'no sailing the channel until I've moved again'. This further delay had deeply irritated Caesar, and the general had become waspish and difficult to such an extent that officers now flipped coins to decide who would face him over even the simplest query. Furius and Fabius heaved a sigh of relief that their tasks were simple military ones.

As the column approached the timber walls of the Portus Itius fort, half a day's march north of Gesoriacum, the fresh smell of cut pine emanated from the stockade and the two or three buildings that had been constructed within. The general and his small party of senior commanders led the van as usual, the forward scouts having arrived an hour or so ago. Behind them came the cavalry contingent and then the Tenth, followed by the other legions. However, between the rear ranks of the Tenth and the front of the Seventh, space had been made for the two hundred and nineteen prisoners they had taken in the forest of Arduenna, all roped at both wrist and neck, their ankles unfettered to allow for swift transport. The two dozen Treveri nobles - and one Aeduan - among them expressed outrage at being roped among the common warriors - a sign to Priscus that Gallic culture was considerably more 'civilised' and therefore uneven and debased than he had previously realised. Only an advanced culture

79

could boast such smug, snobbish inequality. They might as well be Roman already, Priscus had smiled to himself.

It had, in fact, already become necessary to separate Dumnorix from the other nobles in the roped party, placing him toward the rear and among the more subdued lower warriors. He had by pure chance been overheard by a passing legionary trying to exhort the Treveri nobles to throw in their lot with him in an attempt to overcome their jailors and flee. How he had expected to escape a four legion column with cavalry contingent and mounted scouts was unfathomable, but Priscus had kicked the Aeduan noble until he coughed blood and then moved him away from potential conspirators. After months of investigating and unravelling the threads of an apparent Gallic plot to rise up against Rome, he was not about to take any chances with a man who appeared to be at the centre of it all.

The column came to a halt outside the east gate of the fort that had been constructed by Sabinus' force and which had only the facilities to accommodate those two legions and the command party. Caesar issued a number of commands to his couriers, who turned their mounts and rode down the line with instructions for the individual commanders. The mounted clerk reined in before Priscus and saluted - a salute that was returned somewhat wearily and half-heartedly.

'With the general's complements, Legate, your men are to encamp off the south wall of the fort as best you can. He realises that you may have to remove some of the treeline to accommodate the legion, but space around the fort is at a premium and as soon as the wind changes the legion will be embarking anyway, so he hopes your discomfort is short-lived.'

Priscus rolled his eyes. 'Thank the general for his concern and inform him that we will do so and I will attend him presently.'

As the clerk rode off once more, Priscus gestured to the two recently-raised tribunes. 'As I said, take command of the prison detail and get them slammed up. You might even want to give that Aedui bastard a bit of a going over. If we can deliver a nugget or two of useful information to the general it might stop him being such a miserable and vindictive sod.'

Furius and Fabius saluted and rode away along the line of the legion toward the roped slaves. As they left, Priscus turned to the primus pilus, whose shiny pink head was brighter than usual after the sweaty day's march.

'Carbo? I presume you overheard the general's instructions? Get the legion settled in, set the watch and passwords, make sure the standards and eagle are secured at the legion command tent, check on ration distribution and then meet me in the headquarters for a briefing at the sixth watch. And bring whatever booze you can track down among Sabinus' supplies.'

Carbo saluted and began to issue the orders to his centurions, directing the setting up of camp in the narrow strip of clear land between the timber stockade and the dense forest close by. There would have to be more than just a little deforestation to give the legion any security. To have the treeline right at the edge of the camp would be to grant any potential interloper the opportunity to get so close they could climb into bed with the men before they were even seen.

Furius and Fabius reined in ahead of the four roped lines of captives, who were guarded by men of both the Tenth and Seventh legions who'd had a hand in their capture. An optio from the Seventh was busy walking up and down the lines, smacking shins and shoulders with his stick, moving the prisoners into straighter lines.

'Optio? We'll take charge of the prisoners from here. You can return to your unit.'

The optio frowned for a moment and then saluted with a slight shrug.

'All yours, sir and good riddance to the shit-stinking heap of 'em.'

'Wait a moment' barked a deep voice. Furius looked up to see a familiar face approaching. The Seventh's new primus pilus was striding along the column, vine staff jammed under his arm, an air of haughty irritation about him.

'What can I do for you, *Centurion*?' Furius smiled, adding a stress to the title. The primus pilus frowned at the tribunes sitting astride their mounts by the prisoners.

'I know you... sir.'

'Yes. We met in the snowy woods hunting Gauls a few months ago. Pullo, yes?'

A sour look passed across the officer's face. 'Yes, sir. Field promotion, sir?' Furius smiled indulgently, feeling the warmth of successful one-upmanship flowing through his veins. 'Sadly, I had to vacate my previous position so that you could fill it.'

81

Pullo reined in his anger with visible and somewhat understandable difficulty. 'Legate Cicero has ordered that I take the captives and put them to work on the trench and rampart for the Seventh's camp.'

Furius turned to Fabius and pursed his lips. 'It's a good idea, really. Shame to let the Gallic bastards sit in comfort while good legionaries dig and sweat.' He turned back to Pullo. 'I'll compromise with you, Centurion. The nobles are all going straight to the stockade, but there's almost two hundred others. Split them half and half. Take one lot with you to build your camp and the other can go and serve the Tenth in the same role. Good enough?'

Pullo mulled it over for only a moment - just long enough to almost count as an act of defiance to a superior officer, and then nodded. 'Very well, sir. I will inform the legate of your request.'

'Decision.'

'Sir?'

'It was not a request. It was a decision. If your legate has a problem with it, he can argue the toss with ours.'

Again, Pullo paused and pondered. Furius and Fabius could almost see him weighing up the likelihood of Cicero even considering entering an argument with the veteran of the Tenth and coming down on the side of 'not even on a quiet day in Hades'.

As the primus pilus turned and left with no further salute, Fabius pulled his mount alongside. 'You're going to have trouble with him and his mate. I reckon he sees you as a rank-jumper. He's going to want to one-up you at the first chance he gets.'

Furius shrugged. 'Let him try. Him and his pet... Vorenus was it? We're not new to that game.'

'You could always just drop him in the shit for back-talking a superior?'

'Not likely. It's only a stroke of luck that separates us rank-wise - he's just another 'better than you senior centurion'. If he wants a pissing contest, I'll beat him on his own level. The chain of command's one thing, but a little competition between units is healthy and you and I both know that the Seventh is still far from its best despite all our work, while the Tenth has gone from strength to strength. I can piss higher than him on my worst day and then wash the floor with his face. Come on.'

Turning, he rode back to the rear of the Tenth, where an optio of his own legion was changing the men on prisoner duty.

'Optio? Separate out all the leaders and nobles, have them roped together and led to the stockade in the camp. Then work with the officers of the Seventh to divide the rest and put them to work on the defences; but before you get to that, detach Dumnorix from the lines. We're taking him with us.'

The optio saluted and the two tribunes sat and watched patiently as the Aeduan nobleman was wrenched clear of the lines, his hands still roped together, a legionary from the Tenth holding the end of the cord.

'Where do you want him taking, sir?'

Furius made a dismissive gesture and reached down to grasp the rope. 'You go about your work, soldier. I'll take this shitbag.'

As the legionary obediently let go, Furius tied the rope tightly to his saddle horn leaving just enough play for the captive to stand five or six feet from the horse.

'Walk!'

The Aeduan glared sullenly at him. Furius smiled. 'I'd *advise* you to walk. The alternative is uncomfortable.'

Still, Dumnorix poured his immobile malice and scorn at the two tribunes. Furius pursed his lips and flicked the reins, urging his horse into a walk. As Fabius fell in beside him, Dumnorix suddenly found himself wrenched from his feet, one of his shoulders dislocating with the sudden jerk, and dragged along the floor, his knees bouncing painfully from the rocks, roots and packed earth. By the time Furius had counted to ten, the Aeduan was on his feet and stumbling alongside, groaning at the pain in his shoulder.

On the brief ride up to the fort gate, the tribunes amused themselves by occasionally increasing the pace and then relaxing it, forcing Dumnorix to run for short periods, during which he invariably fell, further wrenching his damaged shoulder and bouncing along the floor before he could find his feet again. At the gate, the legionaries from the Eighth on guard duty did not request a password, given that officers, scouts and cavalry from the entire column were pouring through in a constant stream, but they did watch with interest as the captive Gaul bounced from the gatepost on the way, grunting and cursing in his own language.

'Which way to the latrines?' Fabius said quietly.

The legionary, a curious look on his face, gestured to the right side of the gate. 'Nearest one's away to the south, sir, but you really don't want to go in there. The better, clearer one's up there.'

Furius nodded. 'Thank you, soldier, but the shitty one will do nicely.'

Angling his horse south along the intervallum road that followed the inside of the rampart to the south, and with Fabius at his side, he rode on to the latrine - a small affair separated from the camp by a dozen leather tent sections tied together in a fruitless attempt to contain the horrendous odours.

The drifting aroma of ammonia and faeces easily escaped the surrounds and the two tribunes found their eyes watering as they approached. The gate guard had been right. This latrine was ready to be closed down and backfilled. Perfect.

Dismounting, Furius whistled, attracting the attention of a legionary standing near his tent and emptying the half-eaten contents of his mess tin into a slop pile. The man turned and, recognising the uniforms of senior officers, saluted.

'Take our horses to the cavalry compound, hand them over to the equisio, tell him they belong to the Tenth's tribunes, and then you can go about your business.'

The legionary saluted and grabbed the reins of the horses, waiting until Furius had untied the rope and dragged the panting Gaul to one side before leading them off at a respectful walk toward the centre of the camp. Dumnorix stood, hunched despite his bad shoulder, and glared defiantly at the two tribunes.

Furius dropped the rope. 'Get in the latrines.'

Dumnorix stood motionless and Fabius took a step forward, wrenching the pained man around to face the doorway, raised his leg and gave the Gaul a hefty shove with the hobnailed sole of his boot, sending him staggering forward into the stinking leather room, where he collapsed onto his knees in the reeking muck of the churned ground.

'Juno, someone in the Eighth must have shit himself to death in here' Fabius exclaimed as the pair stepped through the gap between leather walls and hauled the prisoner to his feet, pushing him further inside, past the dogleg entrance that provided minimal privacy for the occupants.

The temporary latrine was some ten feet by fifteen, the three sides without an entrance occupied by deep turf-cut trenches that were now almost entirely filled with the unthinkable. Only one had even the slightest room left. The tent sections that formed the walls were streaked with stains and marks and the ground had long since lost any sign of its original grass, now displaying only rutted and churned mud and other less pleasant substances.

Fabius pushed Dumnorix until he fell on his knees again.

'He's still way too defiant' he said matter-of-factly.

Furius nodded. 'Let's give him something to think about, then.'

Reaching out, he grasped the knot that bound the man's hands together so tightly it had rubbed his wrists red raw and stained the rope with dried blood. As Dumnorix still stared silently at him, he raised an eyebrow and then, suddenly, jerked the knot upwards and over the Gaul's head. The Aeduan noble screamed in agony as his dislocated arm was almost wrenched clear of his body with the motion. At the end of the move, his bound hands were together behind his neck, still held by Furius, who began to tug them slowly down his back, putting painful pressure on his good shoulder and sending waves of blazing agony through the bad one.

Fabius leaned close to the man's face as Furius relaxed the pressure a little.

'You're going to tell us everything we want to know, you Gallic turd. I just want to make sure you understand that. We've practiced interrogating giant African thugs, Parthian zealots, drugged Greeks and even veteran Roman soldiers. You hardly present a challenge. And even if you exhausted all our techniques, there are men around more expert than us. So do yourself a favour and start singing out now, so that we can all avoid the worst of this.'

Dumnorix hesitated for only a moment and then spat in his face.

Furius jerked down hard, causing a howl of pain from the Gaul. Tears flooded the prisoner's eyes.

'Care to reconsider?' Fabius asked, wiping the spit from his eye with his scarf. Dumnorix hawked to spit again but Fabius stood and moved out of his way with a shrug. 'Shit face?'

'Shit face.'

Hauling the Gaul painfully around, Furius pushed the man forward, flat onto his face, having positioned him carefully so that his head fell into the fullest of the latrine trenches, his face deep in the foulness. As the Gaul struggled to breathe in the muck, Furius kneeled on his back and almost casually snapped his little finger at the top knuckle.

Dumnorix howled in pain and made an unpleasant wet gargling sound.

'Nasty' Fabius commented. 'Didn't want to open your mouth at this moment, eh?'

After a pause of three counts, Furius broke the next finger, slightly slower so that the dreadful anticipation could build along with the physical pressure. Another count of three and he stood, the two tribunes hauling the spluttering, coughing man from the trench. A fresh waft of foul air circulated in the partly-contained yet roofless room and both officers winced, closing their eyes.

'Ready to chat yet?' Fabius asked, his voice hoarse with the conditions of the barely-breathable air.

Dumnorix coughed up a foul black liquid and then heaved and retched his guts out for a long moment. Furius and Fabius, aware of the very real possibility of their charge drowning or suffocating if they were not careful, relaxed the pressure on his arms and let him haul in a dozen ragged breaths before the grip was tightened again, pulling his arms up.

'So...' Dumnorix tried, collapsing immediately into another coughing and gagging fit. After a moment more, he straightened and took another breath. 'So that you can just kill me anyway?'

Furius grinned evilly. 'If you think death is what you need to be afraid of, have *you* got a surprise coming!'

Fabius nodded. 'We're pretty good at this, but by the standards of some people we're still novices. There are men on the general's staff who could keep you alive for a year. 'Course you'll be half burned by then and missing most of your extremities. Your face will be lacking all its recognisable features and your remaining stumps will be all smashed and jellified. If he's got a man anywhere near as good as Pompey used to have, he can even peel off a lot of your skin and keep you going to watch it happen. You'll be *begging* for death in an hour. All we're up to here is a gentle threat. Feel like talking yet?'

Dumnorix pulled himself upright again and spat in Fabius' face once more.

'I guess we can spare an hour before we have to go meet Priscus, eh Furius?'

The more senior of the two tribunes jerked on the rope, causing a hiss of pain from their victim. 'Oh he'll be chattering away long before Priscus needs us. You got your Parthian knife on you?'

* * * * *

86

Gnaeus Vinicius Priscus, legate of the Tenth Legion, reached under his tunic and gave his undercarriage a good scratch. He sighed with relief. He'd had an unbearable itch for the best part of an hour, but one could hardly stick one's hand down one's breeches and have a good rummage while standing in a tent full of senior officers and one of the most powerful men in the republic. Fronto had once confided that he had a trick for dealing with that very problem, but had never actually enlightened him as to what it was. Priscus had experimented a couple of times, raising some odd looks, but had never managed to work it out.

Somewhere out across the camp horns sounded the sixth watch and almost simultaneously there was a rapping on the wooden strut of Priscus' tent door.

'Come in.'

Furius and Fabius filed into the tent and stood near the door as the portal smacked shut behind them. Priscus sat heavily on his cot and began to unlace his boots. The tent was fairly sparsely furnished. Unlike other legates, Priscus had been a centurion for so long that he had never racked up the cartload of home comforts most senior officers preferred to drag round on campaign with them. The small battered table that had been with him since Hispania held a tray of bread and fruit and jugs of water and wine that a thoughtful legionary had supplied when they'd erected the tent. He was damned if he would have a body slave or tent servant peeling him grapes like some officers he could think of.

Something drifted past Priscus and his nose wrinkled.

'What, in the name of sacred Minerva, is that smell?'

Furius and Fabius looked at one another and then back at their commander.

'Sort of a combination. We had a bit of a latrine situation, so we've both washed down as best we could and loaded up with alum and rose scent to try and cover the remnant.'

'It's not working. You two smell like a pig shat in a bowl of perfume.'

'That'll be the boots. They're going to need some work.'

'Then could you kindly leave your latrine-soaked boots OUTSIDE MY BLOODY TENT!'

Trying not to laugh at the expression on the legate's face, the two tribunes bent and unlaced their boots, slipping them off and tossing them back out of the door to one side.

'Sweet mother of Dis, that was some smell! So tell me why you felt the need to go swimming in dung.'

Furius nodded professionally as Fabius grinned.

'We had a little chat with Dumnorix of the Aedui.'

'I hope he's intact still?'

'More or less. He pretty much confirmed what we've thought from the start. He was surprisingly talkative once he'd had a turd or two down his throat.'

'Nice. Anything useful?'

'Depends on your definition of useful - one or two things piqued our interest, certainly. There's a grand scheme underway, just as you originally suspected. A number of tribes are already signed on to this great cause, and the word has been passed to some tribes beyond the Rhine, across in Britannia and even down across the mountains in Hispania. Dumnorix claimed it was all the doing of a bunch of druids, which is quite feasible, of course, and he claimed not to know any of them but under extreme duress, he named one: his brother, Divitiacus, who rules among the Aedui.'

'So I guess we can stop thinking of the Aedui as our great ally in Gaul, then.' Priscus sighed, allowing his mind's eye to drift back over four years of stomping across this Godsforsaken land to a beautiful summer at Bibracte and the hospitality of the welcoming Divitiacus. That nice little tavern with the shady oak tree in the corner. The memory wrenched at him suddenly with the shades of absent friends: four men sharing a drink and a laugh - Priscus, of course, with Longinus, Balbus and Fronto. The slain, the wounded and the retired - all gone.

'It would seem so' Furius said quietly, drawing his attention back to the matter at hand and the infidelity of the Aedui. 'The druids are passing word and drawing together a huge web by the sound of it, rousing, bribing or even blackmailing chieftains and nobles into joining them. There was reference to a particular man they call Esus, who seems to be important, but I get the impression that this one is tight among the druids and even Dumnorix doesn't know much about him.'

'Do we have any idea of what they're planning? Any chance of finding out more about this Esus? How likely are we to get more from Dumnorix?'

'Very definitely we have an idea of their plans, but only in the broadest terms. The son of an Aeduan whore is real proud of his secret rebellion, but it seems he's become just a cog in the grand scheme now and his knowledge is limited to specific local groups and a general overview. It seems the druids are planning to build up the resentment across all the Celtic people and prepare until they reach a point where their whole world is ready and set against us. Then they can all rise up as a nation in one army.'

Priscus pursed his lips. 'It's bold. And more elaborate than I thought the Gauls capable of, but then those druids are a devious bunch. And what of this Esus and Dumnorix?'

'I suspect that this Esus character is little more than a rumour or a minor deity to the general insurrectionists, his details kept among the druids. But he has to be someone important from the way Dumnorix spoke of him. I don't think you'll find out anything about him until you manage to peel open a druid and look inside his mind. Dumnorix I reckon still has stuff to spill, but probably nothing vital - just low level stuff - general blustering and threats. I get the feeling he likes to think of himself as some great liberator and hero to his people. Basically a midget playing the giant. If we get the chance I'd like to lay my hands on that Divitiacus man, though. Or this mysterious Esus. Or even a druid who can help point the way. Whatever the case, I think we're beyond being able to deny that Gaul is building up ready to explode.'

Priscus nodded. 'I think I'll have to go back and face old eagle-nose again. There's no sign of us having a good wind for sailing in the near future and with this information I might just have enough leverage to turn him away from Britannia again.'

* * * * *

Caesar sat in his campaign chair, hunched over his map table, pinching the bridge of his prominent nose. Dark circles ringed his eyes, which surprised Priscus. As long as he had known the general, the man had never taken more than four or five hours' sleep each night, and yet greeted each day sprightly and energetic. Sleep must be evading him altogether to cause such apparent weariness.

'General.'

Caesar looked up and Priscus noted that it took a moment for the man to focus on him - another solid sign of sleep deprivation. For a moment he wondered whether this was a good idea. Shaking it off, he saluted.

'Ah, Priscus. Something important I presume, then? Come… sit.'

The general gestured, open handed, at the seat opposite and Priscus strode across and dropped into it with a groan.

'News from the captives, general.'

'Some grand scheme to throw off the yoke of the conquering Roman, yes?'

Priscus narrowed his eyes.

'Legate, I am far from uninformed, especially in my own camp. Fill me in with the details I don't know.'

Priscus scratched idly at his chin. 'Dumnorix and his brother, the Aeduan chief Divitiacus, seem to be involved, as well as - from what we can gather - the entire sect of the druids and some half-mythical character called Esus. It appears that the general theory is to rouse all the Celtic peoples from Gaul, Britannia, Germania and even Hispania against us in one 'glorious' freedom fighting army. Whether or not such a thing is truly feasible remains to be seen, but if it is, it could spell the end of our time in Gaul.'

Caesar shook his head. 'There is little more there than I had already anticipated. Sooner or later every tribe finds its Hannibal; it's just a matter of being prepared to remove that leader before he actually causes any damage. The Gauls had their first such man in Brennus centuries ago, and he took them to the very slopes of the Capitol. I won't let that happen again, but then we are more organised and prepared than that Rome of ancient days, while the Celts are, if anything, even more fractious.'

'I wouldn't be too sure about that, general.'

'We can keep them from centralising their resistance by playing off one party against another, much as we did with the Belgae. The most salient point you provide is the name of what might very well be their new Hannibal. This Esus needs to be identified and dealt with at the earliest opportunity and in the meantime we can continue to sew discord between the tribes. I see no greater threat than those we have already put down as long as we can stop a new head growing on the hydra and keep it busy.'

'With respect, Caesar, I think this is a great deal different. Before, we've had chieftains and nobles raising their men against us and it was always possible that a particularly charismatic one would draw a group of tribes together. These bastard baby-eating druids, on the other hand, could raise every man, woman and child from the border of Italia to the frozen wastes of Thule against us. I don't think we can keep setting them against one another for long. We need to concentrate on this and deal with it once and for all.'

Caesar gave a weary smile. 'You sound more like Fronto with every passing week. For the very last time, I am not abandoning the Britannia campaign in order to face a nebulous threat from a hidden group of unknown size and strength. Legions will remain here and you can set men to work rooting out the trouble while my own agents deal with influencing the tribes. We need only keep them off-balance for the one campaigning season while I put Britannia in their place. We may even find something useful for your investigations there in any case, since their tribes have also been implicated. Then, once the season is over, we can concentrate on your Gallic insurrection and pulling it to pieces. All things in good time, Priscus.'

'I just hope leaving it for a season isn't giving them the time that they need, Caesar.'

'Then we had best set our agents to work. I have it on good authority that the winds will change favourably within the next month. That gives us plenty of time to arrange matters in the meantime, yes? The gods appear to have brought us a compromise in their infinite wisdom.'

''Good authority'?' frowned Priscus.

'It is a rare occasion when two augurs agree, and when they also agree with experts on the subject - in this case the local fishermen - I am inclined to pay attention. The wind will change within the month and we can cross.'

'And while we're in Britannia, those chieftains and nobles who have cause to dislike us will continue the trend of rebellion.'

'We shall take all our noble Gallic hostages with us to Gaul and take whatever precautions we can with the rest. We lessen the dangers if we keep a tight rein on those we know to be untrustworthy.'

'You seem awfully confident with all of this, Caesar?'

The general sighed and leaned back. 'Never do anything without the weight of your confidence behind it, Priscus. That is the way men fail. It doesn't matter whether you're in the right or in the wrong, so long as you're the one still standing at the end to tell the tale.'

Priscus nodded slowly. 'I will talk to the few we trust: the Remi cavalry for instance. They will be able to supply me with men who can investigate the matter further, since my own officers will be in Britannia I presume.'

'Indeed.' Caesar took a long, slow breath and tapped his lip thoughtfully. 'At your best estimate and given your experience with logistics, Priscus, how long would it take to get a man to the far end of Gaul and back?'

Priscus frowned. 'Are we talking courier changeover, general, or river barge or what? A fit and keen soldier, or a fat one legged comic actor?'

'Using whatever resources you could glean from our supply system, and ordinary men.'

The legate's frown deepened a little. 'With a few horse changes I could get a small group of riders to Narbo and back in between three and four weeks, without allowing for bandits, weather problems and such, and only if we use the open country and main native roads. Weather could seriously alter the estimate, though. Why?'

Caesar gave a crooked smile. 'We don't want the leaders of Gaul to become organised while we're away, so let's take them with us. Not just our current hostages but the rest too.'

Priscus blinked. 'Sir?'

'While you're arranging to send out your native spies, have a group of half a dozen cavalry, mixed native and regular, visit each of the tribes that officially swore us fealty and 'invite' their leader to join us at Portus Itius. With the exception of certain groups that you feel we can trust, such as the Remi, of course.'

Priscus bit his lip. 'It's a dangerous gamble, general. It will keep them off-balance for sure, but it might very well anger them enough to give extra impetus to the rising.'

'As I said before, Priscus, I only wish to buy us the time to deal with Britannia. Then, we will bring our heel down on Gaul once and for all. Let's get to work and waste no more time. We have but a month.'

Priscus' face spoke eloquently of his own opinion on the matter, but he rose slowly from the chair and saluted anyway. A month. Just a single month in which to push the tribes of Gaul to breaking point. It was like having young Crassus back with the army.

* * * * *

Aulus Crispus, legate of the Eleventh Legion and former archivist of Roman records, rubbed his earlobe and gestured wearily at the cavalry officer in front of him. The regular Roman cavalry made up less than five percent of all Caesar's mounted contingent, and nominally outranked even the auxiliary noble commanders.

'I do not give a squashed fig what Varus' spurious orders were, I cannot believe that such an educated and sensible man intended to choke the parade ground with native horsemen milling around in chaos at that very time of the day when the legions are expected to carry out their parades. I have the Eleventh sweating in their armour over there, waiting to line up and carry out manoeuvers, and there are two legions behind them awaiting their turn. We have already waited almost a quarter of an hour for this debacle to end, but there just seems to be a steady influx of wandering horses.'

The decurion, seriously outranked by this angry yet softly spoken young officer, had the grace to look sheepish.

'The commander told us to commandeer whatever space we needed, sir. We've got to walk every horse and then run them and check their levels of fitness before we decide who to take across the channel and who gets to stay here and be given further exercise and training. The auxiliaries have been stood down all winter and a lot of them are under strength or out of condition.'

The man caught Crispus' expression and coughed. 'With respect, sir, a horse is a big thing and nearly all the land hereabouts is covered with trees. The parade ground can only be the space he expected us to take, sir.'

'You are churning the damned thing up with your hooves, you moron!' Crispus snapped. 'Much more of this and it'll be totally unsuitable for even a German horde to jump around on. You'll simply have to find somewhere else to carry out your little tests. I will brook no further argument. Get this heaving mass of horseflesh off my parade ground by the time I count to a hundred or you will be carrying your teeth back to Varus to explain the problem. Do I make myself clear?'

The decurion went pale and Crispus was further aggravated to see the man's eyes slip past his shoulder and widen with even greater fear. He closed his own eyes and counted silently to five, trying to calm his hammering pulse. *All* he needed now was to be reminded that he was not the angry, fire-in-the-blood officer that some of the legions had. He had worked hard these past few years to throw off the veneer of the studious administrator and achieve some semblance of the military commander that his mentor Fronto had always been. When he opened his eyes again, they fell upon the two tribunes from the Tenth and he sighed. At least these two answered to Priscus and he felt they might be on his side.

'Is there a hold up, legate? The Tenth is due on the ground shortly.'

'Nothing I cannot handle, thank you, Tribune. Decurion Death-Wish here is just shifting his troopers now,' he turned an angry face on the cavalry officer. '*Aren't* you?' he hissed.

With a hasty salute, the decurion turned and waved at the musicians. Calls were suddenly blasted from two cornu, followed by the eerie, chilling wail of the Gallic dragon banners being waved and catching the air. Troops of horse began to assemble into groups in preparation to leave the ground.

As the decurion strode off to remount his horse and lead the column away, Crispus stepped onto the edge of the huge turf square flattened deliberately to serve as a full legion parade ground. Standing disconsolately as the horses milled, he peered down at the churned grass and the deep ruts and hoof prints.

'Idiots.'

His gaze rose to the horsemen in front of him and he frowned.

'Wait a moment. You're not one of the…'

The young legate's words trailed off as the man on the heavy, Gallic roan mare in front of him suddenly lunged forward, thrusting a spear into his face.

Furius and Fabius, a mere half dozen paces away and busy sharing a private joke, suddenly looked around at the commotion in time to see the spray of blood as the iron spear tip emerged from the back of Crispus' head at the base of the skull, pulling through part of the internal matter of his head with it. The two tribunes, stunned by this sudden turn of events, looked back along the line of the spear and blinked in recognition.

Clutching the haft of the weapon was the bruised and battered figure of Dumnorix the Aeduan, somehow not only free from custody but on horseback among - a quick glance around confirmed the tribunes' fears - among the Aedui cavalry contingent!

Even as the world exploded into action, the Gaulish escapee releasing his weapon and gripping his reins, the limp form of Crispus dropping to the churned turf with the spear still transfixed in his

94

head, the Aedui cavalry turned and began to canter off the parade ground making for the only wide path through the surrounding forest.

The rest of the horsemen appeared stunned, milling around uselessly, the pale decurion staring in shock at the body of the twitching legate as the Aedui fled the scene.

Furius and Fabius exchanged a look.

'Get after them and bring them back!' Furius bellowed at the five hundred or so horsemen gathered on the turf, his tone and resonance easily enough to cut through the general murmur of shock. Simultaneously, Fabius had run over to the decurion who was sitting with his musicians and signallers and staring at the scene in shock. With no preamble, the tribune grabbed the decurion's steed's bridle and pulled down so that the horse almost knelt, the officer slammed forward in his saddle until his eyes were a hand-width from Fabius'.

'Dismount, soldier.' He turned to the musician a few feet away as the horse staggered back to its full stance. 'And you!'

Obediently, still in shock, the two men did as they were bade. By the time Furius had bellowed at half a dozen groups of riders, sending them off after the Aedui, Fabius came up alongside him on horseback, leading the other mount. He gestured at the horse

'Come on.'

With a nod, the senior of the two tribunes clambered up into the saddle and the pair began to race their mounts off toward the wide roadway that had been cut through the forest in the direction of Gesoriacum, down which the Aedui had fled, the rest of the cavalry right behind them.

'How in Hades did he get out?' Furius growled as they pounded along, in the wake of the others.

'Can't have been too hard. Clearly the man's making friends in low places. The bloody guard on the prisoners could do with a bit more discipline, mind!'

Furius' face darkened. 'I imagine they're beyond all discipline now. Priscus is going to want an investigation into this.'

'Let's just catch the bastards first.'

Fortunately the two horses they had taken belonged to senior regular cavalrymen and consequently were among the better mounts to be found in camp and it was only a moment before the two tribunes began to pass the stragglers among the auxiliary pursuers. Another few heartbeats and they passed into a wide, shallow valley, a stream meandering along the centre, a shimmering pool off to the right.

Already some of the pursuit appeared to be breaking off here and Furius was about to vent his anger at the horsemen before he realised that groups of them here and there were actually Aedui horse, surrendering to their pursuers, the other cavalry reining in to take them into custody. With a nod of approval he rode on after the diminished group heading for the forest path on the far side of the open space.

'Dumnorix could be among them?' suggested Fabius almost breathlessly as they rode.

'Not likely. He'll not come back by choice. He knows what's ahead for him.'

'Then he might have veered off into the woods? Gone to ground or fled on foot leaving the rest as a distraction?'

Again, Furius shook his head. 'He's not that brave - you know that from how easily he caved in to interrogation. He can't be sure of the locals' loyalty and he feels safe with his Aedui around him. Fortunately it doesn't seem that they're as true to his cause as he expected. One small pursuit and they're just giving in. They probably outnumbered their own captors too.'

Again, the pair plunged on into the shade of the forest thoroughfare. Even here and now, small groups of horsemen were coming to a halt at the sides of the path, half a dozen Aedui giving themselves to their pursuers and turning their back on the would-be rebel.

'There!' Fabius shouted, and Furius peered ahead. Sure enough, they had caught up with the core of the fleeing cavalry. By now less than forty or so men surrounded the hunched figure of Dumnorix, and the pursuers were more than double that number. Even as they closed in on the lead, the two tribunes watched with suitable appreciation the way the loyal native cavalry managed to push an extra turn of speed from their mounts, peeling off to the sides of the track, ducking the overhanging branches and flanking the fleeing horsemen, effectively blocking the path ahead.

All of a sudden, the Aedui seemed to come to the conclusion that the game was up and that they had lost. Their mad flight into the woods had been a dismal failure, largely due to their having drawn too much attention to themselves with the murder of the legate before turning to flee.

Dumnorix found himself in trouble. He was in the midst of the group of warriors - it had been the safest position to take during the flight, surrounded by his countrymen and safe from outside blows. However, now that those same warriors were slowing their mounts to surrender, he found himself slowing and stopping, unable to break from the group.

His protection had become his prison.

Furius and Fabius slowed their mounts as the Aedui began to throw down their spears and swords and raised their hands to show their empty palms. Within the tightly packed crowd, the tribunes could hear a commanding, if desperate, voice bellowing orders in the Gallic tongue. Apparently Dumnorix was still hoping to exhort his men to flight. They would not be following his orders.

As the pursuing cavalry began to gesture small groups of Aedui away from the main force, binding their hands with their own reins, Furius and Fabius watched the protective screen in front of the fleeing noble shrink and then finally vanish, leaving him centred in a horseshoe of his former allies.

Defiantly, the Aeduan noble walked his horse a few steps back toward them, a sword in his hand.

'You intend to take me back and torture me again for more information, I expect.'

Fabius let his lip curl slightly.

'Not at all. We intend to let someone much more experienced and inventive do that.'

'I will not surrender simply, like these sons of she-dogs.'

A few of the Aedui turned angry glances on their former charge at the insult. Furius chuckled at the sight of the false bravado turning away any hope he might have of reclaiming an ally among the crowd.

'I imagine not.'

'I will tell nothing else. I am not privy to the most important facts and before I can tell you even the most harmless of titbits, I will die.'

Fabius looked across at his fellow tribune and raised his eyebrows questioningly. Furius nodded once, and Fabius turned to the remaining Aedui who sat, mostly unarmed, upon their horses in a horseshoe around the renegade.

'No punishment for any man who helps beat Dumnorix the traitor to his well-deserved death.'

Dumnorix's eyes widened as Fabius grinned at him.

'Now wait!' he barked, followed by another short statement in his own tongue as the arc of horsemen began to close up and form a circle around him. A moment later the first blow rang out, followed by a cry of pain. Clearly Dumnorix had decided to fight back - one of the unarmed assailants suddenly toppled from his saddle, a nasty sword wound in his chest. But even with most of the circle of horsemen unarmed, the former nobleman stood no chance. The remaining twenty two Aedui warriors went about their grisly business - a business unseen from the tribunes' position - with efficiency and even grim satisfaction. After a few moments, a gap opened up in the lines for just a heartbeat and Dumnorix's horse trotted out, frightened, coming to a halt some way down the road.

Again the circle closed up. There was no noise but for the regular clop and slap of horse's hooves coming down, eloquently describing in simple sound what was becoming of the body in the centre of the circle.

Fabius counted past two hundred before the circle of men broke up and the Aedui filed out, weaponless and with hands raised to meet their captor. The mess in the centre of the mass of dark, red-brown hoof prints could barely be described as human. Only the recognisable signs of the clothing Dumnorix had worn could have identified who it was. It briefly passed through his mind that perhaps some sort of switch had been pulled and that the prisoner had got away, but one look at the faces of the villain's fellow tribesmen - his killers - made it clear that they had done their distasteful duty as requested.

'Drape that thing across it's horse and let's take it back to Priscus.'

Furius straightened in his saddle. 'Warriors of the Aedui. You took an oath to Rome and to Caesar when you joined this army on behalf of your tribe. By attempting to aid the escape of this dangerous mad dog, you broke that oath. But in taking his blood, you have renewed it. Get back to your units and prepare for the passage to Britannia. Hail Caesar!'

The reply of 'Hail Caesar' was less heartfelt than one might expect from a parade ground of legionaries, but the fact that not a voice remained silent amid the crowd satisfied Furius.

Watching the Aedui slowly return in the direction of Portus Itius, the mess that had been Dumnorix stretched over a saddle, Furius and Fabius squared their shoulders.

'Remind me again why we came back after winter?'

Fabius smiled at his friend and the pair shook their reins and kicked their heels, heading back to Caesar's camp.

Chapter Five

QUINTILIS

Fronto rolled over onto his chest, his face buried in the soft, scented sheets, and groaned with comfort. Outside, the sounds of a full working day for the folk of the city were well and truly advanced. How long had he slept? Lucilia hadn't even bothered waking him.

Rolling over once more, he came to the edge of the bed and swung his legs out and down to the floor, wincing at the jarring in his knee as the foot hit the carpet - an import from Parthia of all places that Lucilia had desired enough to spend a centurion's yearly pay on. With another groan he pulled himself up to a seated position and stretched before knuckling the sleep from his eyes.

Gods it must be halfway to noon! He was getting lazy with this relaxed lifestyle. In the preceding years he would have been up, cleansed, broken his fast, addressed the troops and marched ten miles by now. He smiled a private smile as he realised how much he stretched the truth even speaking to himself. Over the past few years the pressures of the post had turned his always prodigious drinking from a carousing hobby to a necessary habit. Only now that he was out of the armour could he realise just how much he had declined in the past four years. When they'd first marched into Gaul he had been up before the birds in the morning and gone to his cot after the rest of the army. By last year he was dragging himself from his pit after Carbo had already done half the morning's work for him, his head clouded and fugged with last night's wine.

These past few months back in Rome he had tried to rein in his drinking a little - not *that* much, obviously - but the aches and pains in his battered body often required that little extra numbing, and so he had largely failed in the attempt. One thing he *had* noticed, though, was that imbibing on a fun evening with Galronus, Rufus and Galba at the races, or with Lucilia in the privacy of their own rooms, was not leaving him with the sour mood and stinking head that he remembered from preceding years in the wilds of Gaul. Somehow the good humour and circumstances that surrounded each cup made it lighter and healthier. Despite the plethora of aches and pains, the worryingly expanding waistline, the general decline in his fitness and the weakness of that damned knee, Fronto hadn't felt as relaxed and healthy in years.

Standing, he stretched again, listening with interest as a new click added itself to the morning symphony of cracks and creaks. The left shoulder one was new. Was that from that fall down by the Victoria Virgo temple last month after Rufus' get-together?

Stepping slowly over to the column of light that sliced through the room from the atrium doorway, Fronto found himself wondering whether it would be nice after all to move to Balbus' generous villa above Massilia. A country villa with wide open windows that would let in light and display views of open hills and vineyards instead of high, featureless walls that kept the city's stink and press safely hidden. Lucilia was keen enough that she was trying to persuade him to spend summers there away from the dung-filled super-heated stink of the city.

She might be right.

Where *was* Lucilia, anyway? What did she have planned this morning? Would they be able to stroll down to the Forum Holitorium once again? They might see that beggar with the twisted arms again. He was funny - a deformed beggar who had turned his misfortune into a street act and seemed to be making a small fortune. He *was* good though. Good enough that Fronto would happily go watch and pay again.

What had woken him?

Fronto suddenly had a memory of his first roused moments of the morning. The door. A knock at the door. Obviously nothing important, though, as they'd let him sleep on. Yawning and scratching himself, Fronto strode out into the atrium, feeling less self-conscious in his expensive silky subligaculum than he had when Lucilia had first presented him with them. They were ridiculously comfortable but had an unfortunate tendency to drop to the floor when he pulled his stomach in or reached up with both arms. He had almost frightened the bed linen girl to death when stretching one morning as she came up from bed level. He grinned at the memory and then instantly felt guilty - damn this married life for its added veneer of guilt.

'Lucilia?'

A muffled reply came from somewhere out in the garden and he strode through the atrium, along the short corridor and out into the open peristyle, beneath the walkway that surrounded it. Lucilia sat on the small marble bench with the animal head decorations near the central fountain, Faleria by her side with a small vellum scroll on her knee.

'Good morning, Marcus. Have you thought yet of putting on some clothes?' Faleria raised an eyebrow meaningfully. Fronto frowned at her, then looked down and hastily rearranged his underwear with a shy smile.

'You're late up' Lucilia commented.

'You left me to sleep. Who was at the door?'

'A courier bearing missives.'

Fronto's attention sharpened. 'From?'

'Yes, there's one for you.'

As Lucilia drew a small scroll case out and proffered it, Fronto reached out eagerly, only for her to swipe it out of reach and lean forward, puckering her lips.

'Lucilia!'

'Just a kiss, Marcus.'

With a sheepish look at his sister, which Faleria judiciously ignored, he leaned forward, gave Lucilia a quick peck on the lips and yanked the scroll case from her hand. She laughed and sat back.

Fronto straightened and looked at the case. It was a standard, military issue case that had clearly come from the armies in Gaul. He noted, with interest, that a similar one sat on the bench between the girls. Whatever Faleria was reading had also come from the army. From the look on her face it had not best impressed her.

Greedily, he tore at the seal bearing the insignia of the Tenth Legion. Carbo, then? Or Atenos - could Atenos write in Latin?'

Jerking open the case, he tipped out the small scroll page, crammed with miniature writing. Vellum was expensive and hard to come by out in Gaul, so correspondents were as economic with materials as possible. What surprised him was that the scruffy, spidery handwriting was actually that of Priscus.

'News from your beloved Legion?' Lucilia goaded.

'Mmph.' Fronto replied, running his eyes along and down the vellum, frowning, smiling, his eyes occasionally widening in surprise.

'Well, come on!' Lucilia prodded him. 'Don't forget some of these people are my friends also.'

Fronto looked up. 'Sounds like I got out just in time. Caesar's running out of senior men. He's made Priscus legate of the Tenth!'

'Good for Gnaeus. He deserves it.'

Fronto glared at her. For all the fact that he would support his oldest, closest friend in the legions to the end of the world and beyond and wanted nothing but the best for him, for some reason it rankled badly that Priscus had been given his former position. But then, would he have preferred a stranger commanding his beloved Tenth?

He silently chided himself. Legates served at their commander's whim. That he had commanded the Tenth long enough to consider them his was unusual in itself. No other general would have kept commanders in charge of a single unit for so long. But still it felt somehow like a betrayal. He realised he was muttering under his breath.

'What was that?'

'I said he's going to get more than he bargained for. Sounds like the officer corps is stretched to the limit. He won't be simply commanding the Tenth. I'll bet he ends up serving as camp prefect or Quartermaster as well, or even running two or three legions. The general's even had to promote centurions into the tribunate. I bet the old bastard's regretting driving me away now.'

He became aware that Lucilia was peering at him with a penetrating gaze as though she was picking apart his inner thoughts - thoughts that he now realised were horribly suddenly filled with jealousy that he was not involved in it all.

'Priscus suspects some big revolution among the Gauls is coming. Sounds like he's right too, from what he says. But the general's still going ahead with his second jaunt to that piss-wet island. Furius and Fabius are now serving as tribunes in the Tenth, apparently!'

'Another deserved set of promotions.'

'But an unheard of one. Centurions to tribunes? Come on... we'll be having slaves in the senate next.'

'Have you any idea how pompous you sound?' Faleria snapped at him and Fronto recoiled suddenly.

'Sis?'

'Sorry, Marcus. I realise that was a little sharp. Ignore me - I'm being waspish.'

Fronto narrowed his eyes.

'What's up, sis?'

Faleria, her eyes dark and troubled, held out the scroll that she had been reading. Fronto took it and began to read. The note was short and succinct, written out by the praetor's clerks as attested by the mark at the end. Dictated directly by Caesar. Fronto re-read it just in case.

By the order of Caius Julius Caesar, Proconsul of Gaul and Illyricum, all officers and nobles of the native auxilia are called back to service as per the requirements of their oaths of fealty to the state.

You are required to attend the army under the command of Titus Atius Labienus in Gesoriacum as presently as travel allows and no later than the Kalends of Septembris. Further orders will be issued upon arrival.

In the name of the senate and the people of Rome.

Fronto shook his head.

'He doesn't have the right to call Galronus back at his whim like that. I was there when the oaths were administered. The units are under oath to serve with a commanding noble from the tribe, but which one is never stipulated. I know for a fact that Galronus left his Remi under the command of his cousin, who is also a noble of the same line - a prince in his own right. Don't let this get to you. It's Caesar doing his best to fill his diminished command with tried and tested men.'

Faleria shook her head. 'It's more than that, Marcus. If there's some big rebellion looming, it's Caesar pulling in all the officers he trusts to help him deal with it, and all the ones he *doesn't* for...'

She fell silent, and Fronto nodded slowly. It made sense. Fronto knew that Galronus was hardly about to rise up in opposition to Caesar, and it appeared that the Remi were one of the more supportive and accepting of the allied tribes. But Caesar would be taking few chances now.

'I'll write to Priscus - tell him that Galronus isn't coming back for the time being and ask him to explain why to the general.'

'Thank you, Marcus. I just don't know what to do with this. Galronus will be back from the market any time now. Do I show him it? If I do, he might just go anyway - you know how seriously he

104

takes these things. But if I don't, he might be offended later that I hid it from him.'

Fronto reached down and collected the scroll case from the bench, allowing the vellum to curl into a roll once more and dropping it into the cylinder. 'Not your problem. *I* got the message and it was *me* who didn't tell him.'

'Marcus…'

'No. Forget about it. My problem now and I'll sort it. Now what delights do you two ladies have lined up for us today?'

Faleria arched an eyebrow, some of her sharp humour returning as she said 'You mean you're having a day away from the races and the fights?'

'Can I help it if all these Pompeian luminaries keep inviting us to them?'

'You don't have to say yes to everything they invite you to. We only get to see you two days a week.'

Fronto sighed. '*Anyway…* I have nothing on today, so what would you like to do?'

'Lucilia would like to take a walk down in the woodlands beside the Via Appia, Marcus. I thought we could take her and show her the Egeria spring and the pools. Maybe even pick some of those gorgeous mushrooms for the evening meal?'

Something inside Fronto deflated. A walk - bad for the knee, combined with a sacred nymphaeum - bad luck in Fronto's experience, followed by picking mushrooms - a dirty and irritating task resulting in the collection of one of the few foods that he would be happy never to eat again. A perfect day, then.

'Come on, then' he said, wearily.

'Hadn't you better put on some clothes first?'

Fronto glowered at his sister as Lucilia let out a light, tinkling laugh. Turning on his heel, he strode back through the house to the room where, he now realised, Lucilia had already had his day's clothing laid out. He eyed the toga on the chair with distaste. The heavy, itchy thing was little more than an encumbrance of the wealthy used to display their superiority. Carefully ignoring it, he changed his underwear for a very similar new silk subligaculum in Tyrian purple (what was he? A king?) and pulled on the dark green tunic and breeches. Pulling the chair out of the way, he reached round behind the folded toga and opened the cupboard, withdrawing a well-worn grey cloak. So what if he was mistaken for a pleb?

Suitably attired - at least as far as he was concerned - he stepped back out into the atrium and wondered whether he should visit the house baths first? With a smile, he reached up and snagged a hand in his tangled hair. No. If he went out messy it would be an excuse for them to visit the baths down near the Porta Capena on the way out, which would lessen the time spent trudging through woodlands pulling up fungi.

As he turned toward the garden once again, the entrance hall behind him echoed to a knocking at the door. Turning, he strode toward the door, but the figure of Posco, the longest serving member of the household staff, scuttled from the other side of the atrium and rushed ahead of him, unlatching the door. As he opened the portal, Fronto heard a familiar voice entreating entry and smiled.

'Let the gentleman in, Posco.'

'Of course, Domine' the little man replied in a slightly offended tone, as though it were unthinkable that he might do anything else.

Balbus strode in, lithe and sweat-free despite the heavy toga. Fronto smiled as he spotted the litter in the street and the four burly slaves rubbing their sore hands and shoulders.

'Marcus' Balbus said in greeting, and Fronto's brow creased instantly at the serious intonation in his friend's voice.

'Something wrong?'

'Depends on your perspective, I guess. You've not heard the news then?'

'Just got up. What news?'

'Catullus.'

'The poet? The loverboy one? What about him?'

Balbus began to stroll on toward the atrium and Fronto swung around and fell in alongside him.

'He was found on the floor of his townhouse this morning. He'd apparently had some sort of fit. There are a hundred different stories going around already, but all of them agree that he was found in a pool of his own vomit, all twisted and tensed. Some say he shat himself and others that he's bled from the ears. Any which way, the city's in uproar. The superstitious are saying it's a sign from the gods and spouting the usual rubbish. The mindless are saying it's the plague from Parthia finally hit Rome and that we're all going to die. The sensible are saying that he probably ate and drank himself to death like most rich layabouts.'

'And the correct will be seeing poison' Fronto replied quietly.

'Poison?'

'Hemlock to be precise. 'Socrates' Root'. He told me of it himself in a conversation at our wedding feast. He'd had it predicted by augurs.'

'Coincidence?'

'Not when he was getting involved with that snake Clodius.'

Balbus stopped in his tracks.

'Clodius? Why would he poison a celebrated poet? Hardly his style. Politicians and wealthy plebs, yes. Poets?'

'Catullus was in love with Clodia - or at least infatuated enough to obsess about finding out what happened to her. I suspect he pushed that stinking rectum of a rat bastard Clodius too far asking questions about his sister, the poor sod. I suppose I'll have to try and remember the rest of his prophecy now.'

Again, Balbus frowned. 'Prophecy?'

'I'll tell you later, when I've had a think on it. I sort of dismissed it offhand at the time, but perhaps a little prematurely in hindsight. In the meantime, we're planning a little walk into the woods to pick mushrooms. Care to join us?'

The older man's face creased into a smile. 'Sounds pleasant. Why not?'

In the privacy of his head, Fronto ran through the reasons.

* * * * *

Three days had passed since the death of the handsome young poet and still the streets abounded with wailing lovelorn girls - and often boys too - as well as doomsayers and lunatics claiming divine disfavour or the spectre of plague creeping through the twisting thoroughfares of the city. Their numbers lessened with each day though, at least.

The details were becoming distilled.

The cause of Catullus' death was now being attributed to eating the wrong mushrooms - a fact that struck Fronto as particularly unfunny, given how he had passed his time the day of the body's discovery. But the symptoms as they had been recorded and released were also conversant with a man who had taken - or been fed - hemlock. The coincidence was all too much for Fronto, who could hardly blame an innocent mushroom, given his prior warning.

And for three days he had also been wracking his brains trying to recall the prophecy the poet had repeated to him. Four people were going to die and it would be cataclysmic for Rome or some such rubbish. There was something about Vulcan, he was sure, and something to do with the Parthians, but beyond that he was drawing a blank. He doubted he would even have remembered the hemlock part had Catullus not just passed that way.

He had confided what he did remember to Balbus, who had urged him to visit a soothsayer and try and have the prophecy revealed once more. Fronto couldn't think of a more effective way to waste both an hour and a purseful of money and had refused flatly. The day he put his trust in a dishevelled dribbling idiot who claimed to know the shape of things to come because he had got a wart on just the right part of his buttock or because he had been hit on the head with a dead duck was the day he might as well sign away the last of his sanity and stand for the senate. If the prophecy was really true, it would play out and then he would remember it in due course. And, of course, if it was true there would be nothing he could do about it anyway.

Turning his thoughts from such irritating and nebulous matters, he peered at the door in front of them. Lucilia nudged him.

'Stop looking so gormless and distant. And straighten your toga.'

Grumbling, Fronto did as he was told like a good soldier and fixed as genuine a smile as he could muster on Pompey's closed door just as there was a click and an olive-skinned man opened it and bowed, ushering them inside. Fronto gave a last longing look at the litter that had brought them here from the Aventine and then followed his wife inside.

Everything about Pompey's new palatial town house echoed the personality of the general or of his beautiful wife. It was tastefully wealthy and with an edge of the austere, as one would expect of Caesar's daughter. No gilt glamour and opulence; almost martial in its severe simplicity. The décor was picked out in pale pastel colours and marble white, with subdued and quiet landscapes and cityscapes painted on the wider surfaces, and yet the upper walls, almost hidden from initial sight, were crimson.

That, to Fronto, summed up what he was rapidly coming to see as Pompey's personality. While the Caesarian blood tended toward Spartan and austere wealth, the Pompeian blood was the boiling red of violent rage, covered or masqued with a thin public veneer of calm white. A dozen times or more now Pompey had socialised with him, always skirting the subject of Fronto's future - something that had occurred during that visit to the carcer had put the general off the subject apparently. Every time, he felt he knew the general that little bit better. Pompey was as much the soldier as Caesar - that much was plain and clear. But their paths and purposes could not be further removed from one another.

Caesar, as Fronto was well aware these days, had taken to military command like a duck to water. But his love of the campaign, of war and of battle - his sheer ability and comfort in the role - were all born from the need to advance in political and personal circles. Caesar became the perfect soldier in order to climb the ladder to - what? Godhood? A martial man by necessity.

Pompey was very much the opposite, Fronto suspected. He had not taken military service in order to build his stature in Rome or advance his cause - after all, he was of a better family than Caesar to begin with. He had little real *need* to do more than achieve one victory. But Pompey was a soldier for the love of war - for the love of the fray; for the desire of blood? Far from using military service to gain position, he had repeatedly used his political weight to secure himself military campaigns. Much of what he did in Rome seemed to be an attempt to get back into the field once again. Fronto recognised the trait in much the same way as he had long recognised it in himself.

But even then there was a difference between Pompey and himself, despite their love of the martial life. Fronto loved the simplicity and the camaraderie; he appreciated the sense of order and discipline that came from the life as well as the freedoms it granted. Pompey, he was sure, fought because his blood demanded it. His temper showed sometimes when he was tested and Fronto had, in fleeting moments, seen something in the man's eyes that bore more resemblance to the crazed battle-lust of the Celtic warrior than to anything Roman.

Whether all this was a good thing or bad, he was still trying to weigh up. In the last year he had come to believe that Pompey was the pleasant, popular - even liberal - character that was Caesar's antithesis. He had thought Caesar to be a cruel shadow of Rome's celebrated pirate-killer. Now, he was beginning to reform his opinion. Could it be that for all Caesar's treatment of people like tools and his cold calculating attitude, he was still actually the more human and reasonable of the two. Fronto found himself wondering what opinions he would have been forming of the third member of this powerful triumvirate had he decided to make for Syria and serve under Crassus?

'Lucilia! Marcus!' the lady Julia beamed, waddling uncomfortably from a doorway off the atrium, one hand beneath her swollen belly, lending extra support. Fronto notched up his 'I am greeting someone who is pleasant and yet I hardly know' smile, but it was largely unneeded as Lucilia and Julia were already rushing into close conversation. It had been this way the last few times they had visited.

As often as Fronto met with Pompey out in the city, the couple met with Julia at her house. Pompey's young wife was now in the advanced state of pregnancy and her movements were necessarily restricted. She had stopped leaving the house at all weeks ago and welcomed every visitor as a chance to relieve the boredom and ennui of the same surrounding walls every day. Faleria and Galronus were alternating visits in order to give her all the more social time.

The girls had started wandering off toward the first of the house's two spacious gardens, totally ignoring Fronto as usual, and he pottered along behind, half-listening to their conversation as he studied the walls and images of Pompey's house.

Closer inspection of the décor revealed something else telling about the house's owner: Every scene seemed to have some relevance, now that he paid attention to the individual - very well executed - wall paintings.

The atrium displayed scenes of a lush valley and its surrounding countryside. It was only when one really peered at the detail, though, that one could make out the tiny figures of the Roman legionaries and their foes. Pompey's victory over the gladiators of Spartacus' army in the north: a small victory, but one that the general had blown up enough to claim responsibility for ending the whole damn war. The whole atrium told the story of the battle, but only if you knew what you were looking at. At first glance, they were peaceful country scenes. He wondered whether Julia had not noticed or whether she rather indulged her older husband's militaristic whims.

'The midwife says it is a boy' Julia was announcing to Lucilia. 'She's absolutely certain of it, she says. Gnaeus is blissfully happy, of course. He already has his two strapping sons, but what man doesn't want another, eh? Besides...' her voice fell to a loud whisper,

110

'he confided in me that he never truly loved Aemilia or Mucia, and a son made between us would have all of his favour.'

Fronto grunted. He remembered the marriage celebrations to Mucia Tertia, back in the day. As *he* remembered it, *that* was supposedly a true match of love after the death of his previous wife.

Lucilia shot him a warning glance, but Julia either had not heard or had ignored his grunt.

'Personally,' the waddling mother-to-be added, 'I think it to be a girl. There is nothing but difficulty and discomfort. Only girls are this difficult, or so my mother told me!'

The two ladies laughed and Fronto turned his gaze to the décor once more, rolling his eyes at the ridiculous conversations of women. The corridor that led through into the first garden was painted with delightful views of the city in all its glory. Suspiciously, he leaned close and examined it. What he saw made him grin.

At first open glance, it was most definitely a series of views of Rome. When one examined the images close up, though, one could see that they depicted the route of a victorious general's triumph. Every time Pompey stepped from his atrium into the garden he relived the triumph over and over again. Were three real ones not enough for him?

The light was suddenly blotted out and he looked up ahead, frowning, to the garden doorway. Julia and Lucilia were gone, wandering out among the flowers, talking of children and menfolk. But the light was now blocked by a hulking figure.

'You?' Fronto whispered, straightening and looking up into the eyes of the enormous barbarian that he had last seen behind the bars of the carcer on the slopes of the Capitol.

The figure remained silent, but the very fact that he all-but blocked the exit from the corridor spoke of violent intent. Fronto closed his eyes for a moment and tried not to panic. He bore no weapon of course. He was a nobleman in the city of Rome, in a toga that Lucilia had insisted he wear, visiting a friend with his wife. The thing in front of him bore no blade but with arms like that, who needed a sword? Fronto had the horrible suspicion that if he turned around, he would see a second figure blocking the other exit behind him, but to look around would announce his fears and that would do no one any good.

Would the barbarian really try anything? In the house of Pompey?

Unless, of course, it was by Pompey's will…

'Marcus. Falerius. Fronto. Legatus.' Four separate words. Spoken as if they were unfamiliar and at the same time horribly distasteful.

'Listen…' Fronto's voice came out slightly cracked with nerves and he cursed himself for it. 'I don't know what I've done to you, but I am here in peace to visit with Pompey's wife. You serve Pompey now, I presume? I remember you understand Latin, if not courtesy.'

The bulky barbarian shifted slightly.

'You are worst of Roman.'

Finally! Something other than platitudes and vague threats. Something annoying enough to snap him out of the nerves and warm his blood.

'Oh don't be so bloody dramatic. If you know many Romans, then you'll know there's a damn sight worse than me!'

'Not to kin of men who die in river.'

Fronto shook his head irritably. 'What river? Make sense!'

'Great river. You call Rhenus.'

Fronto paused. 'The Rhenus?' Something clicked. 'You were there last year? When we fought on the banks? You're of the Suevi?'

'I hear you fight and build bridges. But Berengarus remember much before. Long memory, I. Three years in Rome, in chain. And still I know you.'

'Three years? So, Ariovistus then? You fought us back then? You've been a slave since our first year in Gaul?'

The giant's glowering silence was confirmation enough.

'Look… Berengarus, was it? You can blame who you like, but remember that you were invading Gaul yourselves. Battle's battle. I hold no grudge against the Suevi who fought us.'

The huge man stepped forth and leaned forward, almost nose-to-hairline with Fronto. 'That because Suevi not kill Roman children; Roman woman.'

'I seem to remember the Suevi rather differently' Fronto snapped. 'I think they'd snap a baby in half if they were in the right mood.'

'Wife murdered by Roman horse.'

'Condolences' Fronto snapped angrily.

'Son drown in river in escape.'

The irritated Roman took a step back and folded his arms indignantly, and with some difficulty, given the toga. 'Alright, so you had it bad. Tough. War is no walk in the woods for anyone, you idiot. You think the young men I led last year who were pinned with arrows near the river deserved to die? You don't want women and children to suffer? Well here's an idea, you giant genius: don't bring the poor bastards to the battle! Then they won't get killed. I've precious little bloody sympathy for any of your kind. I've met your women before. Four years ago one of them took a bite out of my pissing heel! Blame who you like, but my conscience is clear.'

He realised with some surprise that he had become so angry he was jabbing his finger into Berengarus' chest and withdrew it, slowly, so as not to appear timid. The German was actually shaking.

'Get out of my way you shambling heap of pointless horse dung.'

Without looking the barbarian in the eyes, he ducked to the side and pushed past him, out into the corridor beyond. Striding off, he emerged into the light and stood in the doorway actually shaking slightly himself, half with nerves and half with anger. How *dare* that big thing accuse him of being a murderer of women and children?

He momentarily glanced around and realised with a start that Berengarus had turned and followed him.

'Never turn back on Berengarus again' the Barbarian growled. 'You do: I kill. Simple.'

'Oh just piss off and leave me alone' Fronto snapped, deliberately and provocatively turning his back on the brute and stomping out across the flags into the garden, where Lucilia and Julia reclined on a bench in the sunshine while a slave served them chilled fruit juice.

'Marcus! There you are.' Lucilia announced as she spotted him approaching. 'Where did you get to?'

'Just reliving old campaigns with one of Pompey's guards.'

'Someone you served with?' Lucilia smiled.

'After a fashion.' He turned to the slave with the jug. 'Do you have anything stronger?'

'At this time of the morning?' his young wife disapproved.

'Old campaigns sometimes need dulling a little.'

Julia nodded calmly. 'My dear husband says much the same sometimes.' She peered around the garden and then smiled and waved. 'Berengarus? Be a darling and fetch an amphora of wine and a jug of water.'

113

Fronto felt his pulse speed up just a little at the lightness in Julia's voice as she turned a conspiratorial smile on Lucilia.

'He's big and hairy, but he's such a kitten really.'

The sound of Fronto's grinding teeth echoed dully across the patio.

* * * * *

Fronto rolled the leg of his faded military issue breeches down over the padding around the knee, where they rucked up a little and failed to reach the full length to just below the joint. There were still some officers and men in the legions who preferred to go all natural and airy under their tunic the way everyone had back in Hispania, but with the weather further north, every year saw more men adopt the Gallic tradition. Soon, they'd probably be wearing the full length wool things and damn the consequences. It was better than your legs turning blue in winter.

Stretching the leg, he winced once again. The Greek medicus had told him to wrap it as tightly as he could to get the greatest level of support, while still allowing reasonable movement.

It felt peculiar and looked worse, but he had to admit that, as he put pressure on the floor with his foot, the knee pained him less than usual. The medicus - he had finally relented yesterday and visited the quack practitioner - had carefully checked him over and announced that, despite the pain, there was actually nothing wrong with the joint. It was simply a bad 'sprain' or something that should have healed long ago, but instead of strengthening it, Fronto had been favouring the other leg and allowing it to weaken yet further.

It had actually surprised Fronto when the man had measured his legs and showed him the comparison. His good leg was considerably bigger and more muscular. His weak one had seemed spindly and stringy by comparison. Half a year of neglect and his leg was pathetic. It was that more than anything that had made him decide he had hit the bottom of the trough and it was time to start climbing up again.

He was not a young man, and he knew it, but he had always had a level of fitness well below his age. He had used to outrun the young raw recruits. Now he wheezed when he climbed out of the bath.

No more.

He looked the length of the running track. It seemed impossibly far. The sounds of laughter and splashing from the Piscina Publica - a wide open swimming reservoir - saturated the area. Here, alongside the public pool where the children frolicked, a private running track and small palaestra stood for the exercise of the Roman physique.

Fronto tried to ignore the perfect specimens of manhood that used the park, all rippling muscles and firm abdomens, oiled and tanned in the early summer sun. He tried to ignore the fleshy folds he knew were safely hidden inside his faded military tunic and peered at the hairy, less-than-muscular leg.

All this would change.

Nearby a man grunted as he lifted a bar of weights that looked to Fronto impossibly heavy. Behind him, a man vaulted over a low wall again and again, sometimes spinning or somersaulting in the air. Fronto called him some unkind things and stood, wincing.

Fixing his gaze on the far end of the track, which looked like it might be halfway to Syria, he took a deep breath. One glance and then he dropped to a crouch, his mind replacing that featureless brick wall at the far end painted with rude graffiti, with an image of a nice bowl of pork loin and buttered flatbread. Mmmmm.

He ran.

The first hundred paces were fine. In fact, he began to wonder what all the fuss had been about and why he had been putting all this off for so long.

And then, suddenly, the pain leaked through his euphoria and into his brain. The only reason he didn't collapse in a rolling ball of tangled limbs was the sheer confusion as to the pain's source. Clearly, the sharp, shooting agony was the knee, but it appeared to be fighting for prominence with the feeling that apparently someone had extricated his lungs and was grilling them while they were still in use. The burning was so intense he panicked and stumbled to a halt.

His hands dropped to his knees and he felt at the wad of bandaging.

It was intact. And apparently his lungs were still on the inside, despite the pain.

Still, it was the first time he had done more than amble across a tavern room in half a year. Not bad.

Turning, his face fell. The starting line from which he had set off was nightmarishly close. Turning back he frowned irritably. The end wall was still so far away he couldn't pick out individual bricks or bits of graffiti. He had made it barely a third of the way along the track! It had felt like a thousand paces, but in the old days he could have spat this far.

With a clenched jaw, he realised that this was one of those make-or-break moments, like the ones he had faced in so many battles. Either he would succumb to the pain and discomfort and the laziness, accept that he was getting too old, give up and go home - or... he would take the failure as a challenge and learn from it. Use it in a manly fashion to challenge himself and push through the limits, seeking to run a little further each time until he was sprinting the track with no trouble.

The guilt repeatedly smashed him in the face as he stooped to collect his belongings by the starting line and left the complex.

Perhaps there was a third option: a sensible and timely withdrawal to marshal his forces and bring forward the reserves.

He would come back tomorrow.

In the evening.

When all the Hercules wannabes would not be there to watch him flounder and fail.

With a sense of having neatly sidestepped failure with a spurious plan for future attempts, he strode toward the slope of the Aventine and home. At the corner of the street that led up toward the house of the Falerii, where a popular bakery stood, a wall was given over to the display of public notices. While the majority of these were private and sometimes cryptic, interspersed with the crude and rude comments scribbled or illustrated by the few commoners who could write, this was one of four cardinal points in the city where inscribed copies of the 'acta diurna' - the official public daily notices - were posted for those few who could read. Every hour or two a helpful priest from the small Temple of Picumnus across the road would pop out and read aloud the acta diurna for the rest.

Fronto approached with interest, noting the two servants of the state hanging the latest news on the wall and then pushing their cart off back into the city. The higher strata of society present milled around before the wall, running through the notices, and Fronto joined them. It was always worth catching up on the news before Faleria or Lucilia chided him for not paying attention. Besides, there might be the latest tidings from Gaul or Syria on there.

His eyes scanned the tablets, picking out small points of interest. There was very little of note and certainly nothing of martial interest.

116

He was about to turn and leave when he paused, a nagging feeling clawing at his consciousness that he had totally bypassed something he should have paid more attention to. Once again, this time taking more care, he scanned the tablets and finally, on the third one, there it was.

Deaths.

Should it worry him that notification of deaths were the only things that seemed to be of import to him? No one else seemed to have noticed the important piece of news. Or was it maybe that no one recognised its importance?

How many people in the city even knew who Aurelia Cotta was?

Apparently no one in this crowd, as he could not sense even a single intake of breath.

Fronto had met the lady Aurelia maybe half a dozen times in his life and always in the presence of her only son: Gaius Julius Caesar. While Fronto had never known Caesar's father, who had died some thirty years ago, the elderly Aurelia had been a force of nature who had always impressed him. There was no other way to describe her. It was quite clearly from her that Caesar and his two sisters had inherited their shrewdness, intelligence and self-control. The lady Aurelia had held the family together with her strength and fortitude despite having been made almost destitute during the proscriptions of Sulla. She was one of the cornerstones at the very least of the entire Julian family. She was also, though he would be loath to admit it, one of the few human beings that Caesar would willingly and readily bend his knee to. A woman, in fact, who Caesar would flip the world on its back to please. It was just possible that, apart from his own daughter, the lady Aurelia was the only person that Caesar would ever truly love.

Fronto pictured the general, sitting as he was accustomed, in his folding campaign chair, poring over a table full of maps. Unbidden, an image of Caesar receiving this news leapt into his mind's eye, and the resulting picture was almost unbearable. Heart-breaking.

Suddenly, Fronto felt a wave of guilt. For the first time since he had turned his back on the general last autumn, he realised that no matter how many capable officers Caesar might have, there were some things that, Fronto having spent so long with the man, only he was qualified to deal with.

Grief was one of them.

117

For the first time in years it was distinctly possible that Caesar might need his shoulder to lean on; his and only his. And for the first time in years he was not there to provide it.

Ideas of a mad horse-relay ride to northern Gaul popped into his mind. If he left quickly enough, it was just possible that he might beat news of the death to the army.

No. Stupid!

It was no longer his place to be that person. And he had responsibilities here that he couldn't simply drop.

A moment later, his face set grim and his failed exercises entirely forgotten, Fronto was striding up the hill, wincing with every other step but otherwise ignoring it and making for home. By the time he reached the door, his mind had run through everything he could remember of his conversations with Catullus on the night of the wedding feast, but he was no closer to piecing together his forgotten foretelling. While Fronto was no great believer in prophecy - actively, rather than passively, disbelieving it - it was more than tempting to see the death of Aurelia Cotta as part of the same prediction.

He tried the door but found it locked tight. Of course. Hammering on the wood, he waited until Posco opened it and then strode inside. Faleria stood in the atrium as one of her endless young women arranged her best midnight blue stola and hung the gold necklace around her neck, adding a gold hair net, while another produced her best sandals.

'Going somewhere nice?'

'Not exactly' Faleria shot back at him, rather harshly. 'The house of Pompey.'

Fronto stepped forward and raised his hand. 'Now might not exactly be the time.'

'Now is *precisely* the time. I take it you refer to Aurelia Cotta?'

'Yes. Young Julia's going to have a lot on her mind right now.'

'Why do you think I'm going, Marcus? Do use your brain once in a while.'

'It's a family thing. Maybe you should leave her alone.'

'Her father is a thousand miles away, Marcus, surrounded by barbarians. She hardly speaks to her aunts, and her husband might not be sympathetic enough an ear. At times like this, she needs a friend.'

Fronto nodded slowly. 'Then be careful. Want some company?'

'From you? No. I don't think that would help at all. You stay here and keep your wife busy - she wanted to come with me and I don't want to crowd poor Julia.'

Fronto nodded and strode past her toward the peristyle garden, where he could hear voices. As he passed from the shadow of the house's interior out into the sunlit courtyard, he could see Lucilia sitting on that white marble bench, chatting away to Galronus, who stood nearby looking distinctly uncomfortable, as though he had been left guarding the lady and didn't know from what.

'Psst!' he hissed at the Remi officer, trying not to attract the attention of the Lucilia. After a moment, Galronus turned and saw Fronto. With a nod of recognition, and pausing politely only until Lucilia finished her diatribe and returned to her reading, he strode across the garden, his feet crunching on the gravel paths, and came to a halt in front of the house's master.

As usual these days, the Gallic nobleman was attired in the Roman style, but had opted against the toga - a tendency the two men shared. His long hair was well brushed and braided, but his chiselled, clean shaven jaw tore away most of the signs of barbarism from his person. Only the hair and the gold torc at his neck would really give him away. Otherwise he might as well be Roman.

'You've heard?' he asked.

'Just. I saw the acta diurna on the corner of Ostia and Lampmakers. A courier will be riding his horse to death to get the news to Caesar already.'

Galronus nodded. 'How will the general take it?'

'Badly, I suspect, though no one will notice. He'll contain it and force it down inside until he's alone in the winter, when he'll have the time and space to grieve. At least by then he'll have a grandson to take the edge off it.'

'A bad way to go.'

Fronto frowned. 'I've not heard? I assumed it was peaceful. She must have been heading for her seventh decade.'

Galronus' face took on a dark edge. 'A fire in the subura. It took the whole household: slaves, servants, and of course the lady herself. Only two or three people made it out alive.'

Vulcan's fury.

Suddenly, Fronto realised he had gone rather cold despite the summer heat pouring down from the golden orb above. Vulcan's fury. Socrates' root had taken Catullus and now Vulcan's fury had

119

consumed Caesar's mother. Two more to break the republic? And Gaul apparently poised to rise up. It was like standing at the gate to Hades and peering inside.

'Galronus, I think I need a drink.'

The Remi officer nodded quietly and gestured to the door that led into the triclinium, where an amphora already stood open in the room's centre, a tray of cups and glasses on the low table nearby.

As Fronto entered and sank onto one of the cushioned couches, Galronus doing the honours with the drinks, the former legate once again pictured Caesar receiving the news - he would grieve, but it would hardly break him. What had Catullus' prophecy meant? The republic was *strong*.

But then Fronto had a sudden and different picture of Caesar, raging in a private hell over the death of his mother; he pictured Pompey, keeping his boiling fiery blood contained beneath a sheen of calm and pictured himself watching that sheen gradually buckle and fail. Pictured Crassus - he'd only met him the once, but his reputation was one of greed and heartlessness, and his eldest son was hardly a positive advertisement for his blood?

Three men - all volatile in their own ways. Suddenly the republic didn't look half as secure as he had previously thought.

Chapter Six

Priscus rubbed his chin as he watched the ships bouncing and jostling in the harbour. It seemed like only a moment since he had been here last, contemplating the crossing and listening to Brutus complaining, while in reality it had been a number of weeks ago now - a whole trip to Treveri territory and almost a month longer of dealing with scouts and waiting for the wind to change.

'It's still a bloody stupid idea.'

Titus Labienus, one of Caesar's most senior lieutenants and an increasingly outspoken opponent of the general's more aggressive policies, sighed and patted him on the shoulder. 'I argued with him 'til I was blue in the face, and 'til his was purple. We're crossing today and nothing any of us can say will stop that.'

'Frankly, I'm surprised he listened to you at all. Cicero was only in there for a count of about twenty before he was thrown out on his ear for gainsaying the general. Your words must carry more weight than his.'

Labienus shook his head wearily. 'Not really. I'm walking very close to the edge with the general these days. I can see in his eyes the question of whether he can trust me, and I suspect he has already answered that with a negative, but there are so few of us left on his staff with any talent or even much command experience. Caesar tells me that he's got a few clients and friends of friends who are looking to gain field experience and they should be with us before winter sets in, but they'll mostly be eager young puppies without an ounce of skill. Frankly I'm dreading it, given the likelihood that they'll be my responsibility over winter. There's even the possibility that Crassus' younger son will be coming, so that's a joy in itself. I can't imagine that particular sour apple has fallen far from the tree.'

Priscus shrugged. 'I saw that a few have already arrived: three new officers were in the mess hall last night. Two chinless babies, but with them a tall, thin one who seemed to have a clue what he was talking about. Maybe it's not as bad as you think?'

'Trebonius, that is, and I suspect he's the shining diamond among the dull stones. Besides, Caesar's already said he's taking him across to Britannia, so it's no use to me. I'll be left with the two pale and reedy children with the flapping lips and no chin.'

121

Priscus pinched the bridge of his nose. 'At least you get to stay and play nursemaid to the Gauls while we get to cross to 'swampland' and get tenderised by a bunch of naked savages plastered with white mud. You've got my list of names and locations for while I'm away, yes?'

Labienus nodded sagely. Priscus' somewhat expansive and ever growing network of spies had been documented on seven tablets in the sort of detail only a former camp Prefect or chief quartermaster would ever consider. In his head, Labienus corrected himself. *Not* 'spies'. 'Scouts'. Priscus had flown off the handle when Labienus had referred to the man's 'web of spies', snapping and raging about how only dishonourable and twisted politicians used spies. Even 'agents' was a touchy term to the Tenth's legate. As far as he was concerned the men he had sent out to the various tribes to try and unearth any details of this mysterious figure at the heart of Gallic rebellion were simply scouts and nothing more. It was a military use of a military resource.

'Don't act on any information that you get unless it's of critical urgency. I've spent a long time setting all this up and there's a lot at stake. Everything should be handled slowly and carefully.'

Labienus patted him reassuringly on the shoulder again.

'I'm not about to do anything precipitous. I'm a great believer that we could still settle all these troubles diplomatically.'

'I used to think that was possible too, until last year. That Morini rising at Gesoriacum just goes to show, though, that even when you think everything is calm and quiet it's just building up for another kick in the teeth. I'm rapidly coming to the conclusion that the only way to stop these constant risings is to bring the whole bloody lot to battle, stand on their neck and break them once and for all. Like Carthage, or the Greeks at Corinthus.'

Labienus turned, a suspicious frown creasing his forehead.

'Wait a moment... you're not trying to stop this rebellion at all, are you?'

'Pardon?'

'You're keeping tabs on it all and aware of what's happening, and you're investigating it, but you're not actually trying to stop any of it are you?'

'I have no idea what you're talking about.' Priscus shifted uneasily.

'Gods above and below! You're actually fostering it!'

'Shhhhh!' hissed Priscus. 'That kind of talk could get a lot of people into a lot of trouble.'

Labienus, eyes wide, was shaking his head. 'I underestimated you. You're even playing the general, aren't you? Do you really think you can *direct* an enemy rebellion?'

Priscus glanced round to make sure no one was listening and then glared at his fellow officer. 'I'm not 'fostering' or 'directing' *anything*, and I'm not 'playing' anyone, but it struck me recently that these druids and their mysterious leader are doing us a bloody favour. We could spend another ten years stomping around Gaul putting out little fires and still never see an end to it. But if they truly are trying to band the whole nation together into one great army and face us, then we could finish it in one blow; break them like Hannibal's mob. We can't deal effectively with these little risings, but no army the world across can stand against eight legions in the open field.'

'Juno, man, are *you* playing a dangerous game! What happens if we let them fan their fires of rebellion and then discover all too late that they're better than we expected. They can field more men than us. And a man fighting for freedom will always fight harder than a man fighting for coin. You're madder than Fronto!'

'Quite possibly; I served with him a long time. Feel free to spend the weeks we're across the sea in trying to quench those flames with words and promises. Good luck to you - until a few weeks ago I was intent on trying to stop the Gauls rising until I had this epiphany and I'll be the first to buy you a drink if we come back to find Gaul peaceful and content. But I think that's an unachievable dream. And when your diplomacy fails I want their collective neck in one place to stand on.'

Priscus narrowed his eyes.

'This was all off the record, I presume.'

'Don't worry. I'm not about to go around blurting this out. Who'd believe me? And if they did they'd likely think it insane. I hope for a better path, but I'm no fool, Priscus. I can see the sense in a single strike policy to fall back on. Just don't tell Cicero. You do that and word of it will be whispered round the senate in a month.'

Priscus nodded as his eyes strayed once more across the vessels in the harbour. There were so many of them, and of such an unfamiliar shape and size. His gaze came to rest on two ships that sat somewhat apart from the rest - as far as that was possible in the rather packed harbour - with a strong legionary guard patrolling both the vessels and the dock at which it stood.

'What happens if those sink?' he mused. 'Would it solve a problem do you think? Or make your diplomatic option non-viable?'

Labienus peered at the two ships - impromptu floating stockades that played host to a surprising number of nobles from almost two dozen of the larger tribes of Gaul, Aquitania and Belgica. In addition to those captured in the forest of Arduenna, more had been escorted into the camp over the past week by Priscus' and Caesar's assigned units, nobles from as far afield as Vesontio, Burdigala and the tip of Armorica.

'I think it would make things more difficult for all of us' Labienus said quietly. 'Other men would rise to take their places and we would have to familiarise ourselves with a whole new generation of leaders. Besides, if we happened to be responsible for the deaths of over a hundred Gallic chieftains, I suspect we would be handing them all the more reason to...'

He paused and narrowed his eyes at Priscus' carefully blank expression.

'Tell me you wouldn't sink a ship full of prisoners just to push the Gauls together against us.'

The Tenth's legate sighed and allowed his shoulders to slump a little.

'Sadly, no. That would be murder pure and simple and a soldier kills on the battlefield - not like that. But I'd be lying if I said it hadn't crossed my mind. Although the general and I have not discussed the matter, I have the deep suspicion that he is of much the same opinion as me in terms of Gallic rebellion, so you never know - those two ships may not weather the storm regardless of my lack of interference. I think Caesar's taken the murder of that poor young bugger Crispus badly. He may well want to punish the whole of Gaul for it. I'm dreading writing to Fronto with *that* bit of news - the old bastard treated Crispus like a son.'

Labienus sighed. 'Try and keep the general from doing anything dangerous or inflammatory.'

'And you look after our ports. Don't want a repeat of last year's debacle. We want to get back here in a month or two and find a friendly port waiting for us, not a bunch of natives with pitchforks. Make good use of the Eighth.'

124

'Priscus, I have been commanding legions for more years than I care to think. Please don't treat me like an idiot.'

'It's just… well the Fourteenth are still so largely untried and the Twelfth are half raw recruits after Octodurus.'

'Yes. I know. The Eighth are my veterans. And I have a couple of thousand horse too. Just go organise your own legion. Caesar wants everyone ready with the tide.'

Priscus peered once, suspiciously, at the ships and then turned, clasped hands with Labienus and then strode off toward the camp of the Tenth.

* * * * *

'I swear I just felt a spot of rain' Carbo frowned, plucking the helm and lining cap from his head to reveal his shiny pink scalp and rubbing away the sweat.

'Fronto said this land just seeps rain' Priscus grumbled. 'There's not a damn cloud in the sky but I can feel it too. There's probably so much of the bloody stuff it's raining back upwards to refill the sky.'

'But it's a blue summer's day. How can it rain?' Carbo stared at his hand as he felt a tiny droplet ping off it and then scoured the cloud-free sky with suspicious eyes.

Around them the Tenth slogged up the beach in neat formations, shields to the fore, prepared for the inevitable resistance of the Britons. It was new territory to Priscus, of course, who had stayed in Gesoriacum last year while Fronto led the Tenth across the sea, but it felt little different to northern Gaul, and so it held a slightly irritating familiarity for him. Apparently, this gentle sloping beach was where the army had landed the previous year and Caesar had aimed for it from the start, knowing it to be a good place to beach. Priscus had been suitably impressed by the huge white cliffs that had slid past on their left this morning, but other than that, little of Britannia recommended itself to him.

One thing nagged at him, though: the absence of locals. The officers and men had been full of the stories of last year's landing, when half the population of the island had apparently arrived atop those cliffs and shadowed them round to their landing place in order to launch into the invader and drive them back into the sea. Despite keeping his eyes peeled, Priscus had seen a grand total of four figures in all the miles of coast they had followed, and each of those

125

had been a shepherd or a child who had paid the massive fleet below no attention whatsoever, totally unconcerned. Surely these lunatics could not be so blind to the Roman threat that they thought they had sent Caesar packing for good last year? Or worse still, that they could easily do again what they had done last year?

This army was a different proposition to that of the previous year. Treble the size, for a start, and with cavalry support.

And yet the five legions were unimpeded as they moved from their ships up onto the beach and assembled by cohort and century, the cavalry contingent forming up to the northern edge as the ships constantly arrived, unloaded and then backed away in rotation.

No sign of a welcome party.

'Make sure the entire legion's properly turned out and ready, and then have three centuries of the best veterans picked out - men who remember this beach and its surroundings well. Have them pass their pack to the rest and be ready for action. I'll be back shortly, after I've seen the general.'

Caesar stood as an island of collected authority in a constant stream of men, animals and equipment, the flood of disembarking soldiers flowing past, yet allowing a respectful six paces of calm around the general and his officers. Cicero had also left his legion under the capable command of his primus pilus, Pullo, while he addressed the commander, as had Trebonius - the newly assigned legate of the Ninth. Trebonius had already impressed Priscus with the ease with which he had assumed command, as though born to it. Tall and almost skeletally thin, the man had sharp cheekbones, pale grey eyes and almost white-blond hair in a severe cut. The overall impression was on the disconcerting side of striking, but he had an easy humour that seemed at odds with his appearance, and a good way with his officers and men.

Cotta, one of the longer-serving though less 'hands-on' of Caesar's staff, and currently filling in as legate of the Eleventh following the demise of Crispus, stood beside the group, running down a list on a tablet in his hand. Priscus strode through the tide of men, still displaying the slight limp from the almost lame leg that had earned him the nickname 'lefty' - the men thought he didn't know. The steady flow of legionaries parted respectfully for the veteran officer and Priscus came to a halt before the general, saluting crisply.

'Ah, Gnaeus. The Tenth appear to be in good shape.'

126

'Yes sir. With respect, general, the lack of a welcoming party is making me twitch.'

Caesar nodded as he scratched his chin. 'The same thought had occurred to all of us, Priscus, be sure of that. And because these Britons can be treacherous, I want the entire army disembarked and ready for anything before we run the risk of triggering any unpleasantness. The full force should be formed up within the half hour.'

Priscus became aware that his hand was clenching and unclenching rhythmically in the way it did when he was waiting impatiently to get moving. With conscious control he flattened his hand by his side and held it there.

'The Tenth will be in position in moments, Caesar, but I beg leave to take a small detachment and check out the surroundings. I'd rather know what was going on before we're all stood in nice lines on this beach presenting a nice shiny target.'

Caesar began to shake his head, but Trebonius cut in with his quiet, calm voice.

'The legate speaks sense, general. It will be a while before we can muster cavalry patrols - many of the horses are still nervous after the crossing and adjusting to land, but a few centuries of veterans could sweep a quarter of a mile of the surrounding forest in no time.'

Caesar stood, looking back and forth between the two men, weighing his options, and then nodded. 'Very well, but just a few hundred paces and stay within signalling distance of the beach. I don't want units being lost and butchered deep in the woods without us even knowing about it. Priscus, you can search out the left. Trebonius, your Ninth can cover the right. Cicero: send a few centuries out forward to the edge of the beach. Let's check the lie of the land.'

Priscus saluted the general and his fellow legates - Trebonius returned it with a smile, while Cicero looked less than impressed and Cotta barely looked up from his list - and then tramped back across the beach to the Tenth. Carbo had three centuries of veterans from the First cohort standing out front, armed and ready, their bulky equipment in the care of their fellows.

'We're to check out our surroundings.' He gestured at the three centurions standing before their men. 'Spread out in loose formation but every contubernium needs to stay in sight of the next and stop once you're far enough into the woods that you can't see the beach anymore - we go no further than that. Satrius: you have the left, from the shore to that big sycamore. Caecina: you cover from there to that little stream bed. Liberalis: from there to that earth bank. All got that?'

The men nodded and Priscus turned to Carbo.

'Get the rest of the men as ready for action as you can without looking like it. Caesar seems to be of the opinion we have the time to organise and fortify before dealing with the locals. I'm less sure.'

He squinted across the beach to a series of bumps in the ground ahead.

'That would be last year's defences, I take it?'

Carbo nodded. 'They were fairly well deconstructed when we left, but the rudimentary ditch and mound are still there. It'll cut camp-setting times in half.'

'Good. It was designed for two legions, and I can't imagine Caesar wanting to leave more than that here - probably Roscius' Thirteenth. The rest of us will be moving inland in due course, depending on what we find. Come on. Let's move out.'

With a last nod to Carbo, Priscus crossed to the wiry, walnut-skinned form of centurion Liberalis. 'Let's go.'

'Sir, you should stay with the legion.'

'And you should mind your tongue, Liberalis. Move out.'

Moments later the three centuries were reforming as loose lines, moving toward the forest's edge. Priscus trod the gentle slope up toward the forest with the casual interest of a man entering a new land. The signs of last year's landing were here for anyone to see if they knew what they were looking for. Quite apart from the earthworks over to his right that marked last summer's camp, there were numerous other tiny signs: the lack of obstacles near the top of the landing area, for a start. Even in the barest beach there would be rocks here and there jutting from the ground, and saplings and scrub bushes. Not here. The stones had been removed, probably to be reshaped for catapults and ballistae. The scrub was new grown this spring, very low-lying, confirming that it had all been stripped clear last year to give an excellent field of view from the camp. Everything was clear as far as the treeline.

Then, as the men approached the woods, there were the signs of deforestation on a legionary scale. The stumps left were not the work of local woodsmen, but the systematic removal of timber to construct palisades. Each stump displayed the tell-tale marks of Roman picks and mattocks. Even the roadway that stretched ahead through the forest had been widened and showed the ruts formed by traffic, long since grassed over.

With quiet commands and simple gestures, the centurions and their optios split the centuries into contubernia - tent parties of eight men - and moved in among the boles of the trees, stepping high above the undergrowth and moving carefully and as quietly as eighty armoured men in a forest could hope to.

Nothing.

Pace after pace they moved into the forest and Priscus was quite aware that there was no chance of hiding more than a small group of men in such a place - not enough to threaten five legions, anyway. Maybe in one of the clearings or back a mile or two, but not close enough to represent a present threat.

As if sensing his acceptance of the emptiness, the centurion gave the signals to halt and turn back, having come far enough from the beach.

Priscus amused himself on the return journey trying to count the different sounds made by a century of men trying to be quiet: the jingle of belt fittings and baldric attachments; the chink of mail shirts; the metallic scrapes of helms, shield rims and sword chapes rubbing other metal objects; the steady tramp of boots and heavy breaths of men working their muscles hard; the occasional indrawn breath as a bramble hooked bare skin, though no open cries - the men were well enough trained to avoid such dangerous behaviour. Other, smaller noises, too, and all above the general hum of nature: the rustle of leaves and the occasional patter of the impossible rain dancing off them. The crack and scrabble of low wildlife scurrying out of the way. The buzz of insects and the chittering of birds. The plaintive, quiet call of an owl...

Priscus stopped dead and a legionary almost knocked him over, coming up short in surprise.

The legate swept a hand in an arc, palm flat down, and the century of men stopped instantly. The Tenth were, and would always be, trained to perfection by its veteran centurions.

Three quarters of the sounds in the woodland died instantly with the cessation of movement, eighty highly experienced soldiers suddenly clenching anything that might scrape, clang or jingle. The noises of nature went on, but the single owl hoot was not repeated. Surely...?

A distant 'twoo' called out from the deep woodland.

Priscus remembered his uncle teaching him about birds - mostly about trying to bring them down with an arrow so that they could be slow-boiled - but the man's almost encyclopaedic knowledge of avian life stretched beyond simple hunting and culinary techniques. Even now, decades after the old man had died, Priscus could still identify a bird's species from its call more often than not. He also knew that the traditional 'twit-twoo' of an owl was actually *two* owls calling and answering.

He couldn't identify the specific species from the sound, which might mean that it was a native breed, but it more likely meant that the native scout who was using the owl call to alert his fellows in the wood was not very good at mimicking it. Certainly not too bright, anyway. An owl just before noon? Not unheard of, but highly suspect.

Priscus' face turned slowly upwards and an evil smile reached his lips.

'If you understand Latin, then understand this: you have the count of ten to get down here and drop that blade or I will have you split open, stuffed and then put back up there as a warning to others!'

Glancing around the men with him, he frowned for a moment and then gestured as his eyes fell on a stocky legionary with an unsightly bulbous nose-wart.

'Pontius? You're from some piss-stained native town in Narbonensis if I remember rightly? You speak the language?'

'I speak the tongue of the Saluvii, sir. My granddad taught me.'

'It's all the bloody same. Just sound threatening and repeat what I said.'

As Pontius cleared his throat and began to work through the unfamiliar sounds, Priscus emphasised what he hoped were the right words with gutting and stuffing and hanging motions. Whether the man fully understood Pontius or not, he seemed to get the idea, as a heavy hunting blade dropped from the branches above, sticking into the loam with a thud. A moment later, the figure that had been holding it dropped and then rose to its feet proudly, stripped bare to the waist above the same sort of patterned wool trousers worn by the Gauls. His hair looked as though he'd had a fright, standing proud and spiky, hardened with pale mud.

Priscus rolled his eyes. The lad couldn't have been older than eight or nine summers, not a wisp of fluff on his chin. A scout? A spy? Did they set their *children* out as pickets?

'Pontius, tell this little shit to walk ahead of us back to camp and if I hear an owl hoot out of him, the sole of my boot will be the last thing he ever sees.'

Falling alongside the legate, Pontius did his best to repeat the threat, using his fingers to make walking motions just in case. Without waiting for further instructions the boy strode back toward the beach.

'Good. He seems to understand you. Ask him who he was calling to.'

Pontius repeated the question and, when greeted with silence, did so again, louder and more threatening. Again, no response.

'I don't think he understands me, sir. The Saluvii dialect's probably totally different to *his* tongue.'

'He understands just fine. Let me help.'

Reaching out, Priscus gave the boy a hard slap round the back of the head, making sure the two heavy shiny rings on his fingers connected with scalp. Without being bidden, Pontius repeated his question a third time.

Recovering with a scowl, the boy rattled off something in his unpleasant, barbaric tongue. Pontius concentrated hard, his head cocked to one side as he tried to unravel the unfamiliar words.

'It's hard to tell, sir. Remember, I'm not a native speaker. It's just me granddad was...'

'Just tell me.'

'It sounds like there was a whole load of warriors watching when the fleet first showed up, but then they went away.'

'And?'

'I don't know, sir. You need someone who speaks a closer dialect. Maybe one of the Belgae in the cavalry?'

Priscus nodded. 'With the help of Blattius Secundus.'

Pontius shivered at the mention of the Tenth's most infamous 'immune'. Secundus was a man skilled in the use of the knife, and not for any savoury purpose. He had started skinning coneys as a boy, but his talents for cutting, combined with his love of causing damage and pain had brought him to the attention of his commanders, who often turned to him when time-sensitive interrogation in the field was required.

'Listen, boy. I don't like hurting little children, but if *you* don't know where your warriors are, then whoever you were hooting to certainly does. By the time we get to the general I want a location, or a very unpleasant man with a razor sharp knife will find it out for us.' He turned to Pontius. 'Translate it.'

As the centuries stomped down toward the assembling Roman army on the beach, something Pontius said had struck home, as the boy began to rattle out a torrent of words like a stream in flood.

* * * * *

It was late in the day when the legions marched out from the beach - too late for the liking of several of the officers, who complained bitterly about leading their legions into unknown territory in the dark. The sun was little more than a pale purple glow among the trees ahead, and wild night time winds tore at the leaves and branches around them as four legions and several hundred cavalry headed inland along the wide rutted path through the forest.

The native boy had been rather talkative even before Secundus had started playing idly with his skinning knife, and had been positively eager to help then. In the end, not a single jab had needed to be inflicted. Though Secundus had returned to his unit quietly, Priscus had the distinct feeling the man had been disappointed at the ease with which the scout had caved.

The local force the boy had estimated at some two thousand warriors, plus perhaps twenty chariots and a hundred horsemen. Even allowing for a fair margin of error in one so young, it was not a force to frighten the legions based here. Enough to cause serious damage if they were allowed the freedom to entrap and ambush the Romans, though awed by the sheer scale of the Roman force, the natives had decided against an attack and had withdrawn to some local fortification ten miles or so from the beach. The directions the boy had given had sounded vague to Priscus, but Furius and Fabius, who had fought in the area the previous year, apparently recognised some of the landmarks the boy referred to.

And so at sunset the bulk of the Roman force had marched west, leaving a caretaker garrison to guard the ships. Quintus Atius Varus had clearly been disappointed to be left commanding the beachhead, though he had not said as such. Caesar had assigned Roscius' Thirteenth and much of the cavalry to the beach head. The expanse

132

of woodland in the region - attested from visits the previous year - rendered the use of cavalry less effective, and so Varus' talents would be of little use. And so he and Roscius were charged with refortifying the camp and protecting the ships that bobbed about in the water, riding at anchor.

The journey since then, deep into the forest, had been both irritating and nerve-wracking.

Night fighting! Priscus' face took on an extra level of sourness. Next to him Carbo gave a legionary a crack round the back of the helmet with his vine cane, causing the bronze bowl to ring like a bell and half-deafen the soldier.

'Pick your feet up, Plotius. You fall over and you'll bring a dozen men down with you.' Turning, he frowned at Priscus, his rosy face - usually given to a humorous good nature - full of concern. 'You alright, sir? You've looked pained ever since we left.'

A legionary in the column whispered something to his companion and Carbo delivered another ringing blow to the helmet of the transgressor without even looking around. More than a decade of experience as a centurion gave a man a sixth sense and an unerring accuracy with his vine staff.

Priscus nodded. 'I'm fine. Not happy, though. Night campaigning's barbaric. Stupid. No one can see the standards move. People mistake calls and whistles and cornu blasts from other centuries' signallers. Soldiers get lost. Tree roots become snares and traps. It's unremittingly horrible. And the locals know this ground as well as they know their own pimply arses. We outnumber them about ten to one, but they're tucked up in a fort, so that changes the odds, and the dark and unfamiliarity halves it again. I reckon we'll effectively be at about a two to one advantage.'

'It's still an advantage.'

'But not a good one. We should have waited 'til morning.'

Carbo shrugged. 'The general was probably right about that, though, sir. With their scouts compromised, they'd probably be gone by morning and retreated to some other, unknown place. Gods, they might even have gone already. If they have, this is just a nice walk in the woods.'

'Nice?'

'Figuratively speaking, sir.'

Priscus tried not to voice his opinion any further. The legion would already be grumbling and it was unseemly for them to hear a

133

senior officer moaning too. He had chided Fronto enough about it over the years and now here he was doing exactly the same. Was it something that legionary command did to you, or was it too much exposure to the scion of the Falerii?

He glanced around in the dark. They must have come seven or eight miles now. The sun had set two hours ago, leaving a chilly, oppressive darkness surrounding them. Not above, of course: the sky was still as clear as it had been through the day, the crescent moon and myriad stars twinkling merrily away, while the strong winds had not let up yet and caused a constant rustle of leaves and eerie howling. But even with the track wide enough for eight men to march abreast, the silvery light glinting off their armour, the gloom among the trees to either side was worrying - given what it might harbour.

Though they had followed a series of wide roads and tracks, Priscus would easily admit that he was turned around and lost and would totally fail to find the beach again if left to his own devices. They had taken side paths and turned at junctions more than a dozen times, and every meeting of paths in this endless woodland looked identical.

'Did you hear that?' Priscus said suddenly. Carbo frowned. 'Heard all sorts, sir.'

'The owl.'

'Heard owls hooting all evening in these woods, sir. About the only thing you *can* hear over the damn wind. Nothing unusual there, though.'

'There is with *that* owl. The call's faintly reminiscent of a snowy owl such as you get all over the north, even down to Cisalpine Gaul, but much more like the spotted owl that's common to the south of the Mare Nostrum. Either we have an owl that's well and truly lost, or we have another native scout who doesn't know the difference between species!'

Carbo nodded and gestured to his optio, who jogged forward. 'Sir?'

'Get ahead to the officers of the Seventh and tell them we might be about to have company.'

The junior saluted and ran off to the Seventh, who were leading the column. Behind them came the Tenth, then the Ninth and the Eleventh, with Caesar's staff and then the cavalry tagging along at the rear, the latter ineffective as scouts in dark woodland.

As Priscus scanned the pitch black boughs of the forest for the hidden scout - something he was unlikely to spot with the branches waving about in the wind like this - the column marched on. From ahead came the sounds of the Seventh splashing down into deep water, crossing a narrow but fast flowing river. Another hoot drew his attention, this time from ahead, across the river. His eyes tried to pick out details in the darkness. Ahead, the land rose to a wide prominence - a hill that stood out from the surrounding woodland like the bald-spot on an old man's crown. As they emerged at the river's edge, however, he could see a stretch of open ground from the river to the summit.

It was a hill fort. Not like the walled and gated oppida they had faced in Gaul - such places were clearly the Gauls' version of a Roman civitas. The defensive ring around this hill consisted only of high ridges and dips designed to wear down attackers while the defenders poured missiles down upon them. There could well be a small palisade at the top, of course, but it was a far cry from the heavy defences of say Bibracte or Aduatuca. More of a fortified gathering place then than a permanent defended settlement - a place to retreat in times of danger, which is just what the Britons had done.

'Carbo! Look ahead. That must be where they're hiding.'

'Then why all this hooting? They must know we're here by now.'

Priscus nodded. The same question had occurred to him. 'Well it confirms that they've not fled, anyway.'

The last men of the Seventh dropped into the chilling waters of the river just ahead, holding their shields over their helmets with their weapons atop it to prevent rust damage. Pausing only long enough to allow the stragglers of Cicero's Seventh to clamber up the far bank and rearm, separating the two legions by a healthy thirty paces, Carbo gave the order to cross and the men of the Tenth drew their blades and placed them and their pila onto their shields, hoisting them over their heads and stepping down gingerly into the freezing flow. Priscus, at the head of the legion and bearing no shield, simply raised his sword high and plopped down into the water, clenching his teeth as the biting cold flowed around his crotch and thighs.

The following journey, struggling across, almost armpit deep at the centre, was among the least comfortable moments Priscus had endured in recent years and it was with audible relief - accompanied by chattering teeth - that he clambered up the north bank of the river and lowered his sheathed sword to hang on its baldric once more.

This side of the river, he noted as he stamped his feet to bring some life back into them, the edges of the forest lay some three hundred paces away to either side, leaving a wide swathe that opened up like a broad avenue leading all the way up the ever-increasing slope toward the hilltop fort. Ahead, the gap was opening up between the Seventh and the Tenth as the latter slowed to negotiate the river and reform on the north bank.

Three owl hoots came in quick succession from the edges of the woods to left and right. Priscus' head snapped round, the cold instantly forgotten.

'Carbo...'

'I heard, sir.' Turning, Carbo eyed the men crossing the river. There were two full centuries on the north bank now, but the bulk of the legion were still on the south side.

'We're in trouble, sir.'

'I know.' Even as Priscus swept his eyes to the woodland on either side, figures began to issue from it. Eerie in the silver light, the figures of the Britons moved like ghosts, mostly naked to the waist and painted with patterns and images, their arms covered with swirls of dark paint and lines and dots that made the pale flesh almost vanish among the dappled moonlight. They were hard to concentrate on, difficult to precisely locate while they stayed close to the trees, especially with the branches and leaves waving in the winds and covering much of the movement. One thing that was instantly obvious to Priscus was that every last one of them was armed with a bow, drawn ready to release or a sling whup-whupping around their hand.

'To arms!' Carbo bellowed. 'Look to the woods!'

All around, centurions began to bellow orders to their men. The two centuries that had already formed up on the north bank formed hasty testudos with their shields to protect from the missiles that were already being loosed. The century busy crossing the river was already doomed, arrows and sling stones smashing into men unable to bring their shields to bear. The choppy waters were a scene of carnage instantly.

Priscus looked this way and that from his position of dubious shelter between the two testudos. It was chaos. The question was: what to do about it?

136

The eerie figures that had emerged - several hundred of them - were standing at the edge of the woodland where they could easily retreat and melt away into the forest. The small force of legionaries would never catch them. On the other hand, the following legions had faltered in their crossing, the rest of the Tenth forming a shieldwall on the south bank to protect from arrows, so Priscus' diminished force could hardly wait for the rest of the legion to cross. The Seventh were already moving away at speed up the hill. For a moment, Priscus wondered what in the name of Janus' anus Cicero thought he was doing, but the reasons came clear soon enough. Ahead left and right a second force was pouring from the forest edge: horsemen and chariots. Cicero had his own troubles.

Again, Priscus regarded the shieldwall that marked the lack of advance by the rest of the legions. As long as the crossing point was under the attack of those sling and bow men, no centurion was going to have his men wade across nipple-deep and largely unprotected. Nine of every ten men would fall before crossing, as was evidenced by the number of bodies from the third century already disappearing beneath the surface of the water, concussed, wounded, or dead and dragged to the river bed by the weight of their mail shirts.

Two centuries. It would have to be enough.

'Carbo! Satrius! We need to break that missile attack. Carbo: go left. Satrius: right. Don't stop until you've secured the bank.'

The two centurions gave the orders and the testudos separated, peeling off left and right, heading toward the missile shots at the forest edge. Even as the Romans moved toward their targets, half the Britons turned their shots from the shieldwall on the far bank to the mobile tortoises that bore down on them.

Priscus, shieldless, ducked inside the shielded formation as the century's optio opened up the rear and made room. This would be bloody work; and fruitless. Given the number of archers and slingers they faced, they would lose anything up to a dozen men to stray shots on the way - at least one man from each tent party - and when they finally got to the treeline, the Britons would melt away out of reach and disappear into their familiar forest. But at least the rest of the legions would be clear to cross.

Biting down on the inside of his cheek - a habit he had recently recognised in himself when faced with an unpleasant but unavoidable task - Priscus marched with his men into the storm of arrows and stones, trying to ignore the crack of missiles on wood and leather that came so thick it sounded like rain and the periodic cries of pain as a shot found a hole in the defensive formation.

It was a noble sacrifice. What more could be asked of a soldier of Rome?

* * * * *

Titus Pullo looked left and right at the vehicles and horses pouring out of the forest's edge. They presented a very real threat to the Seventh and it was abundantly clear that the legion was on its own with no hope of support from the rest of the army. The Tenth were split and in trouble at the river and the rest trapped off to the south somewhere. Cicero, somewhere in the press of men nearby, was bellowing orders to reform and stand fast.

Pullo had no such intention.

Turning to Vorenus, the second most senior centurion in the Seventh, he pointed at the hill fort that loomed ahead, above them.

'Get the men up there. The cavalry and chariots won't pass that first ridge, 'cause of the slope. We'll be safer there.'

As Vorenus nodded and exhorted the men to a fresh turn of speed, running up the slope with little attention to formation, Pullo singled out the legate, easily recognised due to his position on horseback amid the infantry and accompanied by standard bearers and musicians.

'Sir! We have to get high enough up the slope to get away from the chariots!'

Cicero guided his horse forward, fury and desperation fighting for control of his face.

'We can't let ourselves get trapped between the fort's defenders and the cavalry, Centurion!'

'Sir, the numbers we had are wrong. There's enough chariots and cavalry there to turn us into minced meat. They'll just ride over the top of the men and break our formation.'

Cicero glared at him, aware of the fact that his legion was surging fast up the slope already, fleeing the vehicles.

'We cannot get trapped between...'

Pullo pointed at the hill. 'I'm not going to get us trapped, sir. I'm going to take the bloody hill!'

Cicero stared at his senior centurion as though the man were mad. Pullo's jaw twitched defiantly. 'Do you think...?'

'Legate Priscus can handle things here, sir. They just have to clear out those archers and then the army can cross. The chariots and cavalry will be little use to the Britons at the water's edge - no room to manoeuvre. We need to get up the slope and safely out of their way too.'

Cicero dithered for a moment and by the time he nodded his acceptance of the choice Pullo was already gone up the slope, catching up with the foremost men of the Seventh. Briefly the legate cursed the loss of Furius and Fabius and the arrival of their replacements from the Thirteenth, but he could hardly kid himself that Furius would have made any other decision. No officer had more knowledge, skill, or authority in the thick of battle than a veteran centurion, and only a stupid legate would ignore their advice. Putting his heels to his horse, he urged the beast up the slope.

* * * * *

Priscus reached the first tree trunk with a great deal of relief, though that was tempered a little as he looked back and saw the bodies littering their wake. More than a dozen men, in fact. More like a score of them. Satrius immediately began to give the orders to his men, and three contubernia lined up as best they could in the woodland, their shields presenting a wall against the odd stray shot coming from the deep forest where the straggling archers took an opportunistic pot shot.

There was the distinct possibility the enemy might reform, and so a good number of men had to create a shieldwall to protect the rest. Even as Priscus looked across the open ground, noting the fact that Carbo's century appeared to be mirroring the activity at the far tree line, he realised they were not 'out of the woods yet' so to speak. Some half a mile up the slope already the Seventh appeared - perhaps out of some mad lust for glory - to be launching a full scale attack on the hilltop fort. Behind them, the Briton cavalry and chariots had come very close to catching the rear of the legion, but had been prevented from pursuing them by the gradient of the last quarter-mile of slope.

Clever. He belatedly realised that Cicero had examined the poorly-defended camp and the mass of vehicles and horse, and had shrewdly decided that the former was the safer option. He was taking

139

the camp not because he wanted to, but because he had to. The alternative was likely destruction.

Of course, that had freed the Britons' vehicles and horsemen to turn to their other threat.

Even as Priscus watched, the mass of cavalry and chariots was already beginning to thunder down the slope toward the rest of the army.

Decision time: To re-cross the river, re-join the rest of the army and leave the Seventh to it? Harsh on Cicero's men, but so long as they achieved the fort, they could probably hold it until the army found another crossing point elsewhere. Or to stay where they were and try to hold off the mass of cavalry and chariots while the rest of the army crossed? Extremely hazardous, of course.

He found his gaze wandering along the bank opposite and smiled at what he saw.

His newly-raised tribunes, Furius and Fabius, were attacking the problem with the sharpness and decisiveness of veteran centurions, not the dithering foolishness of most of their rank. The two men had split the rest of the Tenth Legion and were moving them both ways along the bank, sending their men across the river within the protection of the forest to either side, where they ran the risk of meeting fleeing archers who could cause damage, but where they could safely assemble on the north side among the trees without having to withstand cavalry charges or chariot attacks. It was a playoff of potential dangers against definite ones, and Priscus approved wholeheartedly.

'Alright, gentlemen. The rest of the Tenth will be joining us presently. Break up that rear-facing shieldwall and get back here to the treeline. As soon as those horses and chariots get here, I want every pilum we have thrown in among them to keep them milling about. They can't cross the river and they can't enter the woods, so we should be able to hold them off. As soon as you've thrown your pilum, start hurling rocks and logs at them. If you find a discarded bow or sling, pick it up and use it. Whatever we can to keep them disorganised.'

'Why disorganised, sir? What can they do to us here?'

Priscus eyed the young legionary - he had not seen him before. A new recruit, then.

'Because as soon as they organise, they'll dismount and come at us on foot. Then the odds'll be about ten to one in their favour, so we have to keep 'em busy until the rest of our boys join us. Come on.'

* * * * *

Pullo rushed up the steepening incline. Vorenus, just ahead, was yelling commands that formed each century into a testudo. It slowed the advance considerably, but the defenders had kept a few archers and slingers at the hill top and they, added to the bulk of the warriors hurling random stones down, were creating a veritable hail of missiles.

There was at least four hundred paces to go yet to the crest, and the gradient was gruelling. The men were beginning to flag and lose heart, knowing they were cut off from the rest of the army. Somewhere back there Caesar would be fuming at the hold up.

With a manic grin, Pullo stepped out into the open, ignoring the falling missiles, despite the fact that three of the smaller ones bounced from his mail shirt.

'Five amphorae of wine and a week excused duties for the first century over the top!'

He laughed at the sudden surge of enthusiasm as the half dozen centuries that led the assault suddenly pushed hard up the slope, the rest - still forming testudos below - rushing to catch up in the desire to collect such a valuable prize.

Caught up in the surge of spirit, Pullo fell in behind his century, already one of the leading units. The ground was eaten up pace by pace at a surprising speed, the only thing to mar the splendour of such a glorious assault being the legionaries caught by lucky shots. Every five heartbeats or so there would be a shriek and another body would fall out of formation and tumble back down the slope, his helmet a flattened, concave mess of blood and hair where a heavy stone had smashed his skull or an arrow jutting from beneath the chin of a surprised legionary face.

Death went hand in hand with victory in the legions. Attachments were formed between friends, but no legionary ever called a man friend without the underlying knowledge that the next morning they might be withdrawing his funeral costs from the kitty and divvying up his gear.

Pullo was no green recruit. He silently wished well to every man who fell as he ran, but his eyes and his mind remained locked on that bank ahead. The earthen rampart had been hastily bolstered by the addition of intertwined branches and felled tree trunks. A poor defence even against their own kind of disorganised mob. Against a legion of trained soldiers?

The primus pilus grinned as he selected a spiky haired head jutting up from the defences as his first target...

Afterwards, Pullo would forget which century was first over the defences. It was Vorenus who distributed the wine; he who had watched that first man over the wall.

Pullo, however, had only the vaguest memories of the battle. As he neared the top of the slope, a sling stone hit him a glancing blow in the forehead that skimmed past his temple drawing blood and tearing out his hair until it lodged painfully inside his helmet, just above the cheek piece. The capsarius would later tell him just how lucky he was to be alive.

All *he* could remember was the sudden stunning blow and then the resulting loss of temper.

He had taken out his anger on the defenders, not even pausing long enough to loosen his helmet and dislodge the stone. As he had clambered across a sycamore trunk, sharpened branch ends sticking out, he had gone to work with his gladius, plunging it again and again into the panicked Britons defending the bank.

It might have been the unexpectedness of the attack that broke the enemy. It might have been the sheer voracity of the Roman force. It might have been the crazed bloodthirstiness of their senior centurion as he ripped and tore, stabbed and sliced his way into the fort's central space. Whatever the reason, before even the last of the Seventh Legion were over the bank, the defenders had broken and run for it. Whooping, cheering Romans went to chase on down the far slopes of the fort as the defenders fled for the woodlands, only stopping as their centurions bellowed threats. Even then, the jeering invaders picked up the defenders' own rocks and hurled them down on the survivors, smashing and dismembering the fleeing Britons as they ran.

For Pullo the attack ended as the adrenaline surge passed and he sank to his knees in the grass, sprayed with blood and gore, his sword crimson right to the pommel, his dented helmet still trapping the slingshot against his bruised skull.

* * * * *

The sun rose on a scene of blustery tranquillity that sat at odds with the night's activity. The trill of waxwings and the buzz of bees accompanied the muted shrieks of the wounded as the capsarii worked on them and the buzz of flies around the pile of Briton corpses at the far end of the hilltop.

Tribune Furius, tired but hale, strode across the grass, his face a mask of grave concern, the Belgic scout who had arrived at the camp a few moments ago scurrying along at his heel. He paused as he passed a capsarius working on an officer.

'Nice work last night' he commented.

Pullo looked up, his vision slightly hampered by the linen wrap being wound round his head by the young man.

'I won't let it go to my head' he grimaced as the capsarius pulled the wrap tight.

On Furius strode again, his gaze fixed on the small knot of senior officers standing outside the front doorway of one of the sparse collection of huts which made up the farm that occupied this end of the fort. Caesar was deep in conversation with Priscus and Cicero. Of the other commanders there was no sign - the Ninth and Eleventh had been sent out to try and track down the survivors who had fled the attack and both legions had been gone since before first light. The Tenth and Seventh, having carried out the bulk of the attack, had been granted the morning to rest and recover as they secured the hilltop. Once the two pursuing legions returned, the general would decide whether to move on or to return to the beach and consolidate before planning the next move.

Caesar was the first of the three to look up as Furius cleared his throat noisily. 'Yes, Tribune?'

Furius gestured to the scout to step forth in front of the general. The Gaul looked extremely nervous. It was not unknown for messengers to suffer at the hands of Caesar for delivering bad news.

'With respect, general,' the man stuttered uneasily, 'I bear greetings from Quintus Atius Varus, commander of the...'

'I know who he is!' snapped Caesar impatiently.

'Err... the commander regrets to inform the general that terrible winds in the channel last night caused collisions. Err...'

143

Caesar pinched the bridge of his nose and held up his hand to silence the man. The scout paused, looking nervous. 'What is the damage?'

'Sir, the ships were riding at anchor out...'

'*What* is the *damage*?' the general repeated, his voice taking on a dangerous edge. Furius could quite imagine what was going through the general's mind. Almost exactly the same thing had happened the previous year and had wrecked the fleet, almost endangering their chances of returning to Gaul. The scout swallowed.

'Commander Varus has confirmed forty two ships lost and only five remain undamaged.'

Caesar trembled, just once, and even Furius found that he had taken an involuntary step back. 'This is *unacceptable*. Why were the ships not beached?'

The scout was now visibly shaking and Priscus and Cicero had subtly taken a step back to allow the general a little room. As the silence in lack of a reply became oppressive, Priscus sighed.

'With all respect, general, the only man with any real experience in this sort of thing is Brutus, and he's back in Gaul commanding the Eighth. No one in authority had given the order.'

Silently, Furius allocated blame to the general himself, who had moved off into a hasty night time march and assault without securing the beach head first. Beaching the fleet had clearly been the general's order to give, but who would dare challenge Caesar. He wondered how Varus would fare as a result. There was little doubt that culpability would end with the senior man left in charge.

'Send out the scouts and recall the legions' Caesar barked at no one in particular. 'We return to the coast to assess the damage and rebuild the fleet!'

As men scurried around to carry out the instructions, Priscus found himself watching the general trembling and wondered if this was how Fronto generally felt?

Britannia was clearly cursed. And this was only the opening fight of a campaign!

Chapter Seven

SEXTILIS

It was an impromptu gathering in that there were no musicians or poetry recitals or other trivial patrician ephemera, no two weeks of ladies planning what to wear or having the house moved around to make it 'just right'. Fronto glanced around the room and noted with a strategist's eye just how carefully Lucilia and Faleria had planned the seating. The pair of them next to one another and directly opposite Fronto, where they could watch his every move, make subtle motions and mouth words to him easily. Where they could best control him. Balbus and Galronus next to them on either side, where Faleria could rein her husband-to-be in at any time and Lucilia could guide her father's moods as she was often able. And next to Fronto? Galba and Rufus - two people who he respected and liked, but who owed him nothing and were unlikely to take his side automatically. It was as well planned as any battlefield he had ever seen.

He had not had a declaration of war - no blooded javelin jammed in the floor as he slept - but it had the feel of the girls preparing to take him on in battle.

The only thing that reassured him just a little was the fact that none of the other male guests looked particularly comfortable or sure of themselves either. Clearly none of them had been enlightened any more than Fronto.

Posco stood by the door as the household staff brought in the drinks - Fronto noted a distinct lack of wine; just fruit juice - and platters of cold meats and simple delicacies. Once they had delivered their wares they shuffled back out quickly, Posco bowing once and then, pulling the door closed behind him, leaving the nobles in the triclinium with no attendants. The two less regular visitors raised their eyebrows in surprise at the lack of slaves present.

'Our apologies to you gentlemen for asking you to join us' Faleria addressed Rufus and Galba directly. 'Lucilia and I may need a little advice and support, and our dear Marcus' comrades from the legions seemed the best place to turn.'

Fronto felt a cold stone in his belly. This was about him, just as he had suspected.

'Marcus?'

Uh-oh. What now? 'Yes?' he replied suspiciously.

Faleria cleared her throat preparing to go in for the attack. 'You have spent half a year now moping around Rome, splurging the family's savings on chariot racing, gladiator fights, cheap wine and the like. You wake late and are rarely abed before the moon's apex. Your wife is patient, but not endlessly so, and I have little of that particular virtue left. Mother would have thrown you out of the house in the old days. It is time that you turned your mind to the future.'

'I've had my mind on little else anyway.'

'That seems unlikely. What plans do you have?'

Fronto sighed and leaned back. 'I am torn, dear sister. I miss my command.' He held up a calming hand as Faleria narrowed her eyes and started to interrupt. 'The Tenth has been my life for nearing a decade, and the Ninth before them. Half my good friends are either still serving out in Gaul or lying under a marker somewhere in a sodden valley. When it's silent and my mind wanders, it wanders back there. But I drew too thick a line beneath my name in Caesar's ledger last autumn. I was right in what I said and possibly in what I did, though, and I'm not sure that I would wish to serve under him again, even if he would have me. But that's the crux of the matter - I fear the general would not accept my service again. And so Gaul is out.'

Balbus and the others nodded seriously. They all had experience with the general, who was not known for his forgiving and kind nature. Even Faleria, who was on good terms with the general's daughter, harboured a glint of steel in her eye - it was a man known to serve Caesar who had taken her and Lucilia captive last year, after all. Whether true culpability lay with Caesar as well, or just with Clodius, the connection drove a wedge between the families.

Fronto sighed and continued.

'I suspect that Crassus would welcome me in Syria. It's said that he's building an army to rival that of Caesar in order to head east and squash the Parthians once and for all. He'll want experienced officers and although his son and I don't generally see eye to eye, young Crassus knows my worth. I could probably do well under Crassus in the east as he values useful commodities. The only problem is...'

'...is that I will not let him go' Lucilia said flatly. 'The Parthian deserts are a death sentence for all but the Parthians themselves.

146

Stories abound of Roman subjects found dead along the Euphrates from Parthian incursions. The republic has not dealt well with Persia and I see no reason for Crassus to achieve where so many others have failed. Even if he does take Parthia, there is a high likelihood that half his army will die from the conditions out there. No, I will not have my new husband ripped from my arms and parched to death in an eastern desert. Better he fawn to Caesar and serve in conquered Gaul.'

Fronto gestured at his young wife. 'There, as you can see, is the issue with Crassus.'

He sat up straight again. 'Pompey is on the verge of making me an offer, I believe, though he keeps dancing around the subject. He's sitting in Rome playing with politics, but I sense he's twitching to take to the field once more - he's just waiting for the time to be right. The problem is: with Caesar conquering Gaul and Britannia and Crassus moving against Parthia, Pompey's in danger of losing his military credibility. He needs a new victory to stay safely ahead of his peers. Once he's decided what to do, I suspect he'll have an offer for me.'

'You'd take up a command with Pompey?' Galba frowned. 'You say there's no going back to Caesar now, but you'll *really* have crossed the line with him if you do that.'

Fronto sank back uneasily. 'I'm not sure. The offer would be tempting and might be the only military option open to me, but' he lowered his voice somewhat unnecessarily given the company, 'the problem is that I'm not sure I trust Pompey any more than I trust Caesar. Possibly even less.'

'But you are set on a military command?' Rufus asked quietly.

'I'm not built for anything else really. I can't even conceive of how a man can sit in the senate without losing his temper and beating them all to a pulp. Or falling asleep. Or one and then the other. And I'm no gentleman farmer. No offence, Balbus, but I've no idea what end of a vine goes in the ground and which serves the wine. I'd die of boredom. So any offer of military command is my only real choice, I suspect. Of course, I could just wait and see who's made consul next year and get in with them, maybe get myself a more independent command?'

Galronus nodded and glanced briefly at Faleria. 'I have no urge to rush back to Caesar's command. Either Gaul is settled and now all-but Roman, in which case there is no need for us, or - and I suspect

147

this to be the case - my countrymen will rise in ever greater numbers, in which case I would sooner or later be forced to choose between my old family or my new.'

'Not a happy position' Fronto agreed, trying not to think about Galronus' recall orders that sat safe in Fronto's desk, unseen by their intended recipient. 'But perhaps we could still serve on staff somewhere. There's always revolts and incursions in Africa and Numidia, or the old northern Greek states. Sooner or later an army will be sent out there. And there have been stirrings in Noricum, Illyricum and on the borders of Aegyptus with the strange people south of them. Something will come up, and we might get a command with a less political, more objective commander.'

Balbus cleared his throat unhappily. He looked painfully embarrassed as he turned to Fronto. 'I don't wish to sound unkind, Marcus, but you're not really suited to the military life anymore, no matter what you might wish.'

Fronto stared in surprise at his friend, who recoiled a little sheepishly.

'Explain.' He said flatly.

'Well, without dancing too wide around the subject, you're a bit of a mess.'

A dangerous flash of anger passed across Fronto's gaze, but Faleria was nodding. 'Quite right. Out of shape. You've put on a lot of weight Marcus, and I hear you wheezing when you come in, having climbed the Aventine.'

'I...'

'And your knee is weak as anything' Lucilia added. 'You can't walk more than a mile or two without needing to sit and rest it.'

'Now listen...'

'I have to admit that I'm having to walk slowly so you can keep up' Galronus added unhappily.

'Anyone else? Am I ugly too? Or too old?'

'Marcus, we're not trying to be mean but you are badly out of shape. You're not the man who went to Gaul five years ago.'

'It's just a bit of extra padding and a weak knee. It can all be put right.'

'Then do it.'

'What?' he turned to stare at Faleria, whose defiant gaze bored into him.

'You say you can put it right? Do it. Get yourself fit and healthy again. Then you might be able to obtain one of these military commands you so desire. And at least in the meantime it'll give you something to do other than drink, gamble and sleep.'

Galronus was nodding seriously.

'And you!' Faleria snapped, turning on him and causing the Remi nobleman to blink in surprise. 'If you seriously intend to take me to wife, you need to curb your own circus-going habits. Marcus may be fatter than you...'

'Hey!'

'... and drink more, but you're in danger of becoming one of those slaves to the races and I have no intention of living my life as a 'circus-widow'.'

'Not fat!' yelled Fronto angrily.

'Oh be quiet, Marcus.'

'I think perhaps we ought to be going' Rufus said hurriedly, rising from his seat, his eyes meeting an equally uncomfortable Galba. 'Time is running away with itself.'

'Sit down' said Faleria forcefully, a deliberate hard smile on her face. 'You haven't touched the food yet.'

* * * * *

The guard at the gate eyed Fronto up and down suspiciously.

'What you want?'

'To speak to the owner of the establishment.'

'Who you?'

'My name is Marcus Falerius Fronto. Now please either fetch, or escort me to, the lanista.'

The guard ran his tongue around misshapen yellow teeth and finally shrugged, unlocking the gate and swinging it open. Fronto stepped inside, his gaze following the sounds of furious combat off to the left, where the gladiators of the school could be seen behind the training area's surround - a solid wall to waist height, with a barrier of iron bars driven in above, creating a barrier some fifteen feet high, with spikes facing inward at the top. Twenty or more men hammered at the palus or moved through a series of planned strikes and parries on the far side. To one end a huge, shaven headed creature was lifting a roof beam with one of his counterparts hanging

149

from each end, the strain showing on his face but not stopping him lifting it past his head.

Despite his reservations and his denial of how bad he had let his fitness level become, Fronto suddenly felt tremendously old, weak, fat and lazy watching the men beyond the bars. Turning his attention back to the guard, who'd now locked the gate once more, he strode across the paved courtyard to the house attached. The sweaty, filthy guard passed him off at the door to a house slave - probably a eunuch - in a green tunic, who made motions to follow, unable to address Fronto due to his lack of a tongue.

Fronto followed through the overly-opulent house that reeked of overcompensation for a low birth, and entered the tablinum, where he was bade to sit and offered wine. He smiled his acceptance, but changed his mind at the last moment and waved the jug away.

For a while he sat alone in the office, his gaze taking in the gaudy decoration and wondering if this was what most people thought the older patrician families did with their houses. So much gold and crimson it was actually quite painful to look at - as though the legendary King Midas had exploded in the centre.

Finally, as he was beginning to become restless, Lucius Tubero, owner of the house and the fourth-most successful lanista in Rome, entered with a warm smile and a low, sweeping bow. Of course, there *were* only four lanistas in Rome.

'Master Falerius, it is an honour to extend to you the welcome of the house of Tubero. Will you take food or wine?'

'Thank you, no' Fronto said with a friendly smile. 'To be honest, I'm in a bit of a hurry.' He shifted the bulky weight of his toga slightly. He still hated wearing them, but as a badge of rank they helped people take you seriously. They also, as Faleria had pointed out none-too-kindly, hid a bulging waistline rather well.

'I was not warned of your visit, sir' the lanista went on, sycophantically bowing again. 'Had I been, you would have been welcomed fittingly.'

'This is fine, thank you, Tubero. I'm not in the market for pomp and splendour. I'm in the market for a gladiator.'

Tubero's face fell, though only for a heartbeat before being replaced by a hopeful smile. 'Just the one, Domine? Difficult to hold even the simplest match with one.'

'I'm not staging a match or any sort of game, private or public' Fronto said in a business-like manner.

'Oh?' the face fell a little again.

'I'm looking to purchase a single man for myself.'

'Oh...' the man leered.

'Not like that!' snapped Fronto angrily. 'I want a personal trainer... for my nephew' he added weakly.

'Ah. Well my gladiators are the best in Rome, Domine, so you have come to the right place, but they are not cheap, I will warn you.'

Fronto nodded. 'I had a feeling.'

'Could I ask how you came to choose the house of Tubero for your needs?' the man asked hopefully. Fronto smiled. Almost anyone reputable would have gone elsewhere, but Fronto had his reasons.

'Of course. I am informed that a week or so ago you came by a fresh purchase from the house of Oculatius? A Numidian.'

'Him!' the lanista almost spat, and then his mouth curved into a smile and his face took on a desperate hope. 'Oh him? You mean the murmillo?'

'Masgava. I am led to believe that he is troublesome. Even the harsh rule of Oculatius could not control him. It's said that he sold him on to recoup some money, as the alternative was just to dispose of him.'

Tubero's fake smile became wider and easier. 'I fear you hear falsehoods, sir. The one they call Masgava is spirited, certainly, but no trouble. He will be the pride of my stable when he is broken.'

Fronto smiled in return. 'He has now been in the stable of all four of Rome's lanistas, and I suspect half a dozen others before he reached the city. If he's not broken now, you're unlikely to manage it.'

Tubero's smile slipped and a lot of his hope vanished down the lopsided lip. 'What's your bottom line, Domine?'

'Three hundred denarii. No more.'

The lanista shook his head, the usual business patter taking over. 'Respectfully, three hundred is *ridiculous*, Domine. Even a green, untried youth would go for more than that. Masgava is a veteran of the games - a champion. He could command ten times that.'

'He could if he were less trouble. I don't know how much you got him for at your bargain price, but I know that Oculatius only paid two hundred for him, so you can't have spent more than two hundred and fifty. Probably less. You've had him for a week and I'll wager that already he's causing issues.'

'He is calm and happy with his lot, Domine. I couldn't possibly sell him for less than five hundred.'

'Let's go have a look at him' Fronto suggested, standing. Tubero, his face starting to take on a distinctly unhappy taint, rose and followed him back out to the courtyard. The ugly gateman glanced once at Fronto and then turned back to the street outside. The three other guards who patrolled the courtyard and the divide between training area and private domicile moved slightly more to attention as their employer arrived. Fronto instantly wrote them off as unworthy when compared to a real soldier. The house of Tubero was not wealthy enough even to hire ex-legionaries as guards - these were thugs, beggars and criminals with cudgels.

Beyond the wall the training was still going strong, and Fronto strode across to the bars easily. One of the guards motioned him to step back and he did so, just enough so that no arm thrust through the gaps could grab the folds of his toga.

Masgava stood at the far side of the yard, immobile, watching the rest with a blank expression. Fronto spotted the doctor - the chief trainer - moving about the yard, encouraging, shouting and complaining.

'Call him over.'

Tubero, his smile now entirely vanished, shouted the doctor, who gave a gladiator a thump with the thick end of his coiled whip and then stomped across the yard to the barred wall.

'Yes, Domine?'

Fronto gestured to him. 'The Numidian at the back?'

'Yes, Domine?'

'Is he ready for a match yet?'

'If he feels like it, Domine.'

'Sorry?'

'He's trouble, that one.'

Fronto turned a beatific smile on Tubero. 'Three hundred. No more. And to sweeten the deal, I shall pass word around those I meet at Pompey's next reception that the house of Tubero is worthy should they be seeking to host a match.'

The smile came back, slightly shaky, but there nonetheless.

152

'Three hundred, Domine? Very well, though I will be breaking my own back with the financial burden. Shall I have him roped and delivered to your villa?'

Fronto grinned. 'Actually, no. Have him gather what gear he has and just release him out of the side gate.'

The lanista stared at him, but Fronto produced a weighty purse of coins from beneath the voluminous folds of his toga and dangled it in front of the man, who watched it swinging hypnotically.

'He's a wild beast, Domine. He might kill you before he runs for it!'

Fronto shrugged. 'I'll risk it. See to it. I shall be in the street outside, waiting.'

The lanista stared at Fronto and then at the purse that dropped into his hand. The noble visitor with the insane purchasing habits was already marching for the gate, where the ugly little guard was unlocking it.

He would wait until he was inside once more to gloat. That old bastard Oculatius had been so damn glad to see the back of the Numidian he had almost given him to Tubero and even then, he had been thinking he'd been overcharged.

Three hundred denarii! Now he could buy a *real* gladiator for the stable.

* * * * *

The heavy wooden door bound with iron strips opened slowly to reveal the hulking shape of the Numidian almost filling it. Fronto smiled warmly at the colossus, who eyed him suspiciously.

'Masgava, I believe.'

As the big man ducked to step through the gate, the guards closing it and locking it behind him, Fronto felt the first thrill of something unusual and new running through him. He was used to the military life, but this was different. The man two feet from him in the quiet alley was a trained, expert and inventive killer with a track record of disobedience. It was almost as good as standing on a battlefield.

'You want to kill me?'

The Numidian frowned and glanced to both sides, as though expecting to see the usual archers waiting to pin him to the door if he moved wrong - a standard gladiator's lot. No archers were evident, and he looked back at Fronto with increased suspicion.

'You want to own me?'

Fronto laughed and the Numidian cocked his head to one side. 'They said your name is Falerius. I do not know of a ludus of Falerius?'

'That, my dear Masgava, is because I am not a lanista.' Reaching out with a grin, he grasped the big man's extraordinarily muscular upper arm and turned him to walk down the street. Or so he planned. In fact, the big man proved as immobile as a stone wall, and Fronto simply felt the muscles move beneath the skin.

'Come' he urged, calmly and not unkindly. Masgava frowned again but turned, hoisting his sack of personal goods onto his back.

'Where are you taking me?'

'To our family's house on the Aventine. I have need of you, Masgava.'

'I do not like to fight unworthy opponents and I am not a whore to be used' the man replied flatly.

'No wonder you're trouble for the lanistae. I'm surprised they've let you live at all. *No* gladiator sets his own rules.'

'When I do fight, I make them a great deal of money.'

Fronto shrugged. 'Anyway, as I said: I'm not a lanista. And I am not in the market for a man to fight in a match, whether it be for blood or to the death. And I'm certainly not looking for a man-whore.'

'Then why do you need a gladiator, Domine? Are you building an army?'

'Not really. I need a personal trainer in arms and fitness - largely the latter' he added sheepishly.

'For your son?'

'Actually, for myself.'

'You are too old to train well.'

'Gods, but you're outspoken for a slave. We'll have to do something about that!'

'I do not respond well to beatings.'

'That's not what I meant. Tubero's man will be delivering your documents later today when they're drawn up. As soon as he does, I'm signing them over to you.'

'What?'

'You'll be a free man, Masgava. Happy with that?'

'Why?'

'Because I need a trainer, not a slave. I need a man who feels he can talk to me on the level and who's not afraid of pushing me. And frankly because a man works better and is less likely to kill you in your bed when he's free.'

Masgava frowned. 'You want me to train you properly?'

'Yes.'

'Then you need to do as I say.'

Fronto grinned. 'Obedience is well taught in the legions. Go on.'

The big dark-skinned man paused and looked around. They were in one of the narrower streets on the lower slopes of the Aventine, looking back down toward the Tiber and the docks where barges were loading and unloading. There was no one else in the street, and no faces in evidence at the windows. The sun was high and hot and the population of this area, generally the more wealthy, were either in their houses cooling off, or at the baths.

'Take off the toga.'

Fronto paused for a moment, about to argue. It was not a thing to ask of a nobleman even from a freedman, let alone a slave, but then he hated wearing the damn thing anyway. With some difficulty he struggled out of the hot, heavy, itchy garment and Masgava grasped it and draped it over his taut, muscled shoulder.

Feeling curiously like a boy who had angered his tutor, Fronto stood in the silent, empty, hot and dusty street in just his tunic and sandals, surprisingly exposed under the appraising gaze of the huge Numidian. Was this how slaves felt on the block? He mentally chided himself for the unworthy comparison. While his future was uncertain and there were things about his life he might change, he could never hope to feel how this dark-skinned killer had done on the sale podium.

Masgava walked slowly round him in a circle and then stopped again in front, his chin resting in a huge palm.

'Problem?' Fronto asked quietly, wondering if the big man was about to check his teeth.

'You were trained in arms, clearly, and trained well. The muscle on your sword arm still outweighs that of your left, so you rarely used a shield, but you clearly used a weapon a great deal. Your stomach sags but still shows the marks of having been taut less than a year since, and you have a number of battle scars. You were a centurion in the legions?'

155

'A little higher than that. A legatus and a tribune before that.'

'Then you were an unusual officer; trained and fought like a soldier. You have let yourself decline since your retirement?'

'Something like that. I injured my knee and it led to me taking it a bit too easy this past half year.'

Masgava nodded thoughtfully.

'Two months and you could be fit. Three and you'll be as fit as you've ever been. Give me six months and you'd make a champion in the arena. Ex-soldiers make good gladiators, when they're obedient and enthusiastic.'

Fronto laughed. 'The former I can claim. Enthusiasm, however, depends on what I'm asked to do. I've tried binding my knee and running on it, but I can't make half a length of a stadium. I can't see my general fitness rising too high until I can sort that problem out.'

Masgava crouched and peered at his leg, causing Fronto to feel stupidly self-conscious. He hoped to the gods he wasn't blushing. When the big Numidian jabbed a finger with the consistency of a pilum haft into the wobbly bit below his kneecap, he shrieked and almost collapsed to the floor, his leg turning to jelly. Despite the sack over his shoulder and the toga draped on top of that, the big Numidian still managed to catch Fronto with the probing hand and stop him falling. Slowly he rose, Fronto's eyes leaking with the pain.

'You tore the cable in your knee some time ago. The actual injury has healed, albeit badly. I suspect you failed to rest and exercise it, and went on as normal?'

'Sort of. I was in Germania and Britannia. Can't really relax and spend a month doing knee bends in that situation.'

Masgava nodded understandingly. 'Your main problem is not your injury. It comes from lack of care and rest and the jarring you kept giving it when it should have been healing. The medicus in any ludus will tell you all about it. It happens a lot among successful gladiators.'

'Why successful ones?'

'The rest are not around long enough to suffer it.'

Fronto smiled weakly. 'So what do I do?'

'There is a lining on the bone that wears and even sometimes becomes detached. With a little support and the right exercise it will heal to some extent. Never expect it to heal *fully* though. You will have an aching knee for the rest of your life, but with the will of Fortuna, a few healthy offerings to Aesculapius, and the right regime of strengthening, you could reach a passable state and minimise the ache. The upshot is: you should certainly be able to act more or less normally, but get used to preparing for trouble in cold damp times.'

Fronto wiped the pain-tear from his cheek and rolled his shoulders. 'You'll happily train me then?'

Masgava gave a noncommittal shrug. 'What else will I do? I am a slave at your beck and call, and you say you will make me free, but free also means poor. I cannot afford to return to my homeland, and starving in the streets does not appeal. I have seen how Rome treats its poor. They envy the slaves a roof and a meal.'

'I'll take that as a yes, if a reluctant one. If you are to be a paid, free member of the household you will need more than a gladiator's loincloth and a strong will. Once I've shown you the house and you've settled into the room, I'll give you a month's wage up-front and you can have the rest of today to head into the markets and purchase a good cloak and boots and some reasonable clothes. I don't know what you have in that sack, but I'll wager it's not a clean tunic. Can you read? Can you write?'

Masgava shook his head. 'Not the first priority for a fighter.'

'Then I shall have Posco start showing you. It may not be the first priority, but I like any servant of the house to know their letters if they can. Saves no end of trouble later.'

'You wish me to go into the city, then? On my own? Do you not fear I will flee? Or commit deeds worse than simple flight?' he added darkly.

Fronto grabbed the heavy toga from the big Numidian and draped it around himself in a rough approximation of the correct manner, turning and gesturing up the slope of the Aventine. 'Are you likely to kill us in our sleep? Tubero seemed to suspect it.'

'Tubero was an idiot. A runaway slave - even a gladiator - risks torment, but one who killed his master? The way he would be sent to walk among their ancestors does not bear thinking about. He would *dream* of a quick death. I have been troublesome to the lanistae, but never enough to bring such punishment upon myself.'

The big man fell in alongside and the pair strode up the slope, emerging into a wider street where half a dozen citizens went about their business, ignoring the other half dozen residents who sat at the edge of the road with suppurating sores and twisted or missing limbs, arms outstretched for a coin. Beggar and citizen alike peered curiously at the strange mismatched pair: one huge and dark and almost naked, the other pale by comparison and stocky, wrapped badly in a huge white toga.

'I saw you fight in the theatre, you know? Against the crupellarius. Impressive. I had sword tutors as a young man and I trained alongside the soldiers of my legion in the Ninth. My friend Velius taught me every trick he knew. But what you did was frankly astonishing.' Fronto pursed his lips. 'Twice in recent years I have found myself the target of enthusiastic killers and if I'd met them in the level of fitness and ability I currently maintain, I'd be dead in moments. It's important that I become fit once again, but I want more than that. I want that skill that allows you to take on a crupellarius without blinking.'

'I will make you a killer of men if that is what you wish.'

'Do that. And pull no punches. In return I will make sure you want for nothing and leave my service with the funds to go home a wealthy man. Or even start your own ludus if that's what you'd wish.'

He locked his eyes on the end of his street ahead and missed the glint of satisfaction in the Numidian's eyes.

* * * * *

Faleria raised an eyebrow in that manner which suggests dangerous things might be about to happen.

'And you thought to do this without even asking the rest of us our opinion?'

Fronto grinned. 'You told me to get fit. That's what I'm doing.'

'By bringing a conscience-free killer into the house and giving him free rein to gut us in our beds?'

'You're usually a good judge of character Faleria. Are you blind?'

The lady of the house stepped forward past Fronto and looked the Numidian up and down... mostly up. For a while she rested her gaze on his eyes, which were a piercing and unblinking green, and her brow furrowed.

'He's an honest man. How unexpected. And somewhat forthright, if I'm any judge.' Then, addressing the gladiator directly: 'Why should I give you room in my house?'

Masgava's eyes locked on hers. 'Because, domina, if you do not, the master here will be little more than a soft cheese with feet by the end of the year.'

Fronto turned an indignant face to the big Numidian behind him, shocked at the sheer insubordination of which the man appeared capable. What he saw was the wide grin crease Faleria's face.

'I like him, Marcus. He's going to work you hard.'

* * * * *

Fronto peered down the running track, trying to ignore the stares from the athletes oiling themselves. Next to him Masgava crouched, tying the single support bandage tight around the knee and knotting it below. The chilly morning air blew around parts of him that were rarely open to its caress, adding to his self-consciousness. He looked down at his slightly overweight form and sighed. Years of serving in the military had left him with a reasonable weathered tan on his arms and legs and face, but his torso and pelvis were almost translucent they were so pale, darkened only slightly by the hair. And even that was starting to go grey.

He was horribly aware of how underdressed he was. Gods, he was underdressed for a brothel! There was actually more material covering his bad knee than the rest of his body.

'Tell me again why I'm almost naked?' he asked the Numidian bitterly. The big man seemed to have taken his new role very seriously and roused Fronto from sleep blearily almost an hour before sunup. In fact, by the time Aurora had tickled the horizon with her rosy fingers they had already swum at the baths and done some knee bends, arriving at the track just as it became light enough to see the far end. Fronto glanced once more longingly at the pile of his clothes that lay on the bench.

'You are baring flesh because this is not about modesty, but about strength and endurance. Because you need to be committed and not go at this with only half a care. Because I want the added incentive to keep running - if you fall over naked on this grit the result will sting you for days. Because a bit of air and sun on the skin is good and healthy for you. Because you'll sweat out the fat. And, of course, because I told you to.'

Fronto took a deep breath. He had quite literally asked for this, but that didn't make it any easier. He'd had this idea of a long-term training program that would slowly build up over the year or more to put him back in condition. Not so Masgava. The Numidian had been insistent from square one that barring unmissable engagements every day would involve at the least eight hours of training. Moreover, he had imposed a limit on dining and drinking. Fronto had been shown the chart, devised by the Numidian and written up by Posco, early this morning and had resolved to purchase and hide at least five amphorae of wine and half a roast hog each month. There *were* limits, after all.

'In the first run I will allow you one rest break for the sake of your knee. Savour it. The second and third will have no such respite. For every unscheduled break you take, I will add one run to the day's total, even if it takes us until sunset to complete them.'

'Juno! You should serve with the legions' interrogators.'

'And you should try training as a gladiator. There is no such thing as pain. It is a fantasy of the weak mind. Do not allow yourself that weakness and you will train yourself to ignore all pain. Be the master of your own body. If you do not, your body will master you and you will be little more than a bloated sack of organs.'

'Nice. Did your own tribe sell you into slavery by any chance?'

'Take three slow, deep breaths to steady the beat of your heart. This run is not about speed - that will come in a week or so. This run is about endurance. It is about finishing the track without falling and collapsing. Three breaths and then go from a standing start, picking up speed as you feel you can. Anything above a walk is acceptable for the first run.'

Fronto stood miserably and dutifully took three deep, slow breaths, the third of which fetched with it a wracking cough brought on partially by the foul tainted gusts from the tanneries in the street beyond the stadium. Recovering, he took another three and squinted at the track stretching out beneath his feet toward the brick wall at the far end. As before, it seemed half a world away.

It came as more than a mild surprise when Masgava gave him a ringing slap across the bare buttock next to his extremely skimpy loincloth, and he was already twenty paces down the track before he could think of anything other than running, his red, heated fleshy backside steadily cooling in the breeze even as the muscles strained.

He was running.

It was a moment of elation to realise that it wasn't as bad as he had been expecting. His knee felt sore, and his muscles were already complaining, but he was applying a trick of Velius'. The grizzled centurion from the Tenth - may he reside happy in Elysium - had taught his men to *count* the steps, *feel* the steps and *live* the steps.

160

That way all else became background. And he was entirely correct: as Fronto jogged at the comfortable, mile-eating pace taught the legions, he was able to suppress and push down the pain in his knee and his muscles with the force of his will. His mind had no time to dwell on them - his mind was locked on not only counting each footfall, but naming each one for a city where he had lived, served or fought or a person he had lived or fought with. Perhaps it should be alarming that there were enough of them to cover a full stadium run, and impressive that he could remember enough.

Whatever the case, it was helping. Of course, it was also helping that he was keeping a steady pace and not sprinting as he had tried last time he was here.

And then, with little warning, it became too much. The footfall that was 'Ampurias', or 'one hundred and sixty seven' saw the temporary end of his endurance. For some reason on that step his foot came down seemingly harder than the others, jarring his bad knee enough that the shock of white pain broke through his counting and attacked his senses.

He managed, despite the agony, to slow and come to a steady halt rather than stumbling and rolling naked in the painful grit. He coughed and spat on the track, wheezing in deep breaths, and glanced over his shoulder to see Masgava nodding his approval and holding up his index finger - not as a gladiator's plea for life, but to remind Fronto that he was to have only one stop.

It irked him. It actually irritated him that he was subject to the harsh rules of Masgava, and by his own design, too.

He looked up angrily at the track ahead and blinked.

He was no more than ten paces from the wall - just two paces from the end of the track itself. His running pace must have been longer than he had expected. With a grin, he turned back to the Numidian, his heart warming with the realisation that the raised finger had not been a reminder of stops, but a count of completed runs. Or was it the fiery breaths and rising bile that warmed the heart? Either way he couldn't wipe the grin from his face.

If he could finish the run first time, he could finish anything.

'It's not...' he paused for breath, 'It's not just a fitness thing... though!' he bellowed at the dark-skinned figure at the far end of the track. 'I want you... to teach me the rest too!'

Masgava pointed at him.

161

'Two more runs without a break and I'll slide in a little weapons practice tonight.'

Fronto's grin widened.

* * * * *

Faleria and Lucilia smiled warmly at their hostess as Julia moved her considerable bulk slightly on the couch to achieve a more comfortable position. It was becoming more of a chore by the week. While the young wife of Pompey was blissful at the thought of being a mother and doing her best with the pregnancy, it was quite clear that her frame was not naturally given to such labour, and the midwives fussed around her continuously. Faleria had introduced the poor girl to an infusion the elder lady Faleria swore by, based heavily on raspberries but, if the draught was working at all, it was having an inadequate effect.

'So your husband is training under a gladiator? My husband will laugh himself sick when he learns of it - rest assured he shall not hear it from me - though I suspect my father will think it a stroke of genius.'

'He is finding it harder work that he expected, I fear' Lucilia smiled. 'Every time he speaks of it, the poor dear puts on this manly look that so clearly barely covers his weariness and pains. As he walks in through the door, you should see his legs shaking. But every day he is looking more like his old self. By the time winter sets in, he'll be at his peak again.'

Julia threw her head back laughing, and then wished she hadn't, pulling herself forward once more, wincing and cradling her belly.

'Perhaps after Marcus is finished with this gladiator he will lend the man to Gnaeus. He's putting on a little too much weight for my liking. I saw him the other day standing in his office, staring at his cuirass from the days in Pontus. I don't know whether it was a wistful look - probably was - but it was also quite clear that it would barely go round him these days. All his extra stomach would squeeze out of the sides.'

The mistress of the house gave a pleasant, loving chuckle and her guests joined in.

'Marcus is missing the military life also' Faleria put in. 'Why do we always find ourselves with men whose love of battle surpasses their love of the home?'

'The alternative is hard to find in Rome.'

Almost as if on cue, the door swung open to a cacophony of voices and bodies. Artorius, the head of Pompey's household guard, hurried in, shouting for water and towels. Behind him Berengarus, huge and hulking, dragged an unconscious togate man in each hand, both spattered with blood and displaying battered heads. Three other men in white togas were in the group, followed by half a dozen guards.

What drew the sharp, terrified gaze of the three women though, was Pompey. Surrounded by his guards and retinue of sycophants, it took them a moment to notice that he was being helped inside, and a moment longer to focus on the crimson stains and marks all over the chest and belly of his toga.

Faleria was on her feet immediately, adding her voice to the call for water and towels, a surgeon or medicus and a priest. Lucilia, her own focus more on Julia, rushed across to the couch just in time to catch Pompey's young wife as she fainted dead away at the sight of her husband, slumping from the recliner. Had Lucilia's reaching hands not been there, the mother-to-be's head would have connected hard with the floor.

'What in the name of sacred Vesta happened?' Faleria demanded of the guards. Artorius took one look at her, frowning at this guest who seemed immediately to have taken it upon herself to assume the role of matron of the house, and his gaze slid past her to Julia, lying at an awkward angle, cradled in the arms of the other houseguest.

'What the...?'

His face a mask of panic, Pompey suddenly pulled his arms free of the men supporting him and leapt forward from the group.

'Julia?'

Faleria stared at the former general, covered in blood splashes and yet now apparently vital and urgent as he almost ran across the room to take his wife from Lucilia's arms and lift her gently back to the seat.

'What happened?' Lucilia asked, shocked.

As Pompey continued to concentrate on his unconscious wife, Artorius crossed the room to her. 'Fear not, my lady. The blood is not the master's. There was a disagreement at the Aedile elections that got out of hand. There was some trouble, though Berengarus helped sort it out.' He gestured at the big thug, who still held a battered, unconscious man in each hand.

Faleria turned a sharp look on the general. 'My lord Pompey, your wife is heavily pregnant and delicate. The last thing she needs at a time like this is a shock!'

Pompey - conqueror of the pirates of Cilicia, vanquisher of Spartacus, victor over Mithridates and the most powerful man in Rome, recoiled at the tone of her voice and found his mouth was opening and closing with no sound emerging.

Faleria turned back to Artorius.

'Fetch the midwives and slaves. Have the lady Julia taken to her bed and made comfortable. Do not attempt to bring her round until then, unless she surfaces on her own.'

Artorius dithered, glancing across at Pompey, seeking permission, but the general was entirely focused on the woman in his arms. When Faleria spoke again, the steel in her voice could have cut Artorius in half.

'Fetch. The. Midwife.'

As the head guard ran off, the rest of the entourage dispersing so as not to become part of this uncomfortable scene and the hired thugs scurrying about their business, Faleria turned back to Pompey and Lucilia.

The general looked up at Faleria, his face ashen.

'I fear the midwives may be too late.'

Her heart in her throat, Faleria's gaze slid past Pompey to the woman in his arms and to the spreading stain of red on the pale blue stola at her pelvis.

'Merciful Venus!'

Chapter Eight

Priscus sat in his tent, trying to ignore the sounds that filtered through the thick leather from the camp outside. The Tenth was packing up to head inland, along with most of Caesar's army. Everything was busy - chaos of the most organised kind. Ships were pulled up on the gravel while men patched, repaired and tended them as though they were wounded legionaries - men from the mixed cohorts that would be staying at the beachhead. Other ships had remained intact or were already repaired and had been beached further along the gravel slope. The ones beyond any hope had been torn apart and now formed three enormous heaps of timber waiting to be reused for construction, ship repair, or campfires. A small squadron had been sent back across the sea to Labienus to request the construction of further vessels to supplement the damaged fleet, and the senior officer over in Gaul had confirmed that he had begun the task, sending the squadron back to Caesar immediately.

Ten days had passed since the routing of the Britons at their rampart-encircled hill, and the beach fortifications were now complete, the fleet well on its way to repair, the legions in high spirits; as high as one might expect, anyway.

The parts played by the Seventh and Tenth legions in the fracas had been lauded by the general and his somewhat sparse staff, as well as the other legates who had been delayed by the crossing and had arrived only to find it all over bar the abortive chase.

A curious state had arisen, however, between the two leading centurions of the Seventh, who had been almost entirely responsible for the success of the attack, and the two new tribunes of the Tenth, who had been responsible for the army managing to cross the river and come to their aid. While Pullo and Vorenus, Furius and Fabius had all been cheered for their actions and had clasped forearms in respect for their parts in the fight, there was an undefinable tension between the two pairs that Priscus had noted on more than one occasion.

It was understandable to some extent, of course. Two senior centurions moved to a new legion without any noticeable promotion only to take the place of two men of equal rank who had now been made tribunes. It would mar the relationship between many officers.

But Priscus had truly thought these four men too professional to let such matters get to them. Unless, of course, the tension went all the way back to that reported encounter in the woodland during the winter when they'd argued over the Gaulish courier. Could it really run that deep?

It would certainly need an eye keeping on the situation. The fact that the four men were so rigidly polite and militaristic around each other reeked of worsening relations. Most centurions and their ilk were quite free with one another and relatively relaxed among their kind. If things did not improve, there could be trouble between the two legions as a whole, and that would do nobody any good.

Priscus huffed and shook his head angrily. He was letting his mind wander on purpose, trying to fill his thoughts with anything other than the task at hand. Nibbling his lower lip, he returned the stylus to the ink pot, dipped the split nub in it, rattled it against the glass bottle neck to remove the excess, and then lowered the pen to the small sheet of vellum.

Marcus Falerius Fronto, from Gnaeus Vinicius Priscus, legatus, Legio X.

The header had sat unchanged for a quarter of a useless hour so far.

My apologies, my friend, for the long delay in writing. Things have been very busy here and I have only

The legate sighed and reached for his sharp knife and rag, blotting the fresh ink and scraping the words from the vellum amid the numerous other marks of deleted writings. He was either going to have to commit to a sentence or find a fresh sheet of the expensive material. Perhaps he should have used a wax tablet.

I have tried ten times ten ways now to tell you of the passing of our friend Aulus Crispus and I give up. The latest in the long line of good men lost to this army, Crispus died fast but dishonourably at the hands of a treacherous Gaul.

Perhaps he should pull the blow a little and not talk about the manner of the man's death? But lying and omissions would never help when the truth came out. Priscus paused and closed his eyes, picturing Fronto as he read the words. His stomach twisted at the sight. The former commander had lost so many good friends over the past four years and each time he had taken his grief, honed it to a keen edge, and then inflicted it on the men responsible. Yet in this case, even had Dumnorix lived, Fronto was half a world away and impotent to do anything about it. Perhaps it would be kinder not to write the letter at all? Certainly it was way past due now. But when the day came that Fronto found out from someone else, Priscus' name would be unspeakable.

He was sent to Elysium with rich gold on his eyes and a good attendance by his pyre. The remains are already on their way to Rome for interment, should you wish to pay your respects to him and his family. I suffer a heavy heart to be the bearer of the news. There are hardly any of the senior staff now who marched with us against the Helvetii.

Still, we have taken captives in Britannia and have won a first small victory. The captives have given us information as to where we will find a ringleader named Cassivellaunus who has drawn together all of the aggressive local tribes, and the legions are preparing to march out and deal with him. Hopefully in a few weeks we can wrap up this entire expedition and get back to Gaul, where I will set about exacting revenge for Crispus. Would that you were here to help - I sorely need it and, while he would never say as much, so does Caesar. Of his senior men, the only ones now who can claim even remotely the same experience and ability as you are Sabinus and Labienus, and the latter is still hovering on the edge of Caesar's trust at the best of times.

Again, Priscus paused and re-inked the pen thoughtfully, staring at the vellum. He cursed himself for a bad letter writer. The news of Crispus, while being the most acceptable attempt so far, was still brief, sharp and poor. The rest read like a status report and then a stream of whining and complaining. This was why so many officers left their clerks to compose such letters and simply put their mark at the end.

I trust that all is well with you and your kin. Pass on my regards to those we hold dear and I pray that I will see you all when the season is over. With my newfound rank I see no reason to winter here with the men when I can return to Rome.

Another pause as Priscus wondered what else to say. There was only a little vellum left. With a shake of his head, he gave up and signed it, rolling it into a scroll and dropping it into a standard military tube-case. With clenched teeth, he dripped wax on the join to seal the case and then pressed his signet - the heron and olive branch of the Vinicii - into it.

'Courier?'

The young soldier who had been hovering just outside the door of the tent for the past half hour at his request pushed aside the flap and came to attention inside, saluting.

'Sir?'

'Take this, visit the chief clerk at Caesar's praetorium and check if there are any other messages awaiting the trip to Rome. If there are, take those too and head down to the ships, find the one set aside for courier duty and accompany the messages until they reach Gesoriacum and the supply chain. Then check for incoming messages and bring any you find back here. When you return, wait at this camp. The army may not have returned from our march, but there will be a resident garrison. You got all that?'

The messenger nodded. 'Yes, sir. Anything else, legate?'

Priscus shook his head, motioning the lad to leave, and stood, reaching for his embossed helm with the ridiculous horsehair plume, and grabbing his sword and baldric before turning to leave the tent. This bloody Cassivellaunus had damn well better either capitulate quickly or run until he reached the edge of the Styx. Priscus was in no mood to mess around.

* * * * *

Tribune Fabius cleared his throat. 'It's no good, sir. There's nothing usable here.'

Priscus sagged, pinching the bridge of his nose irritably. 'Nothing?'

'Not a thing, sir. All the animals that couldn't be taken away have been charred beyond edibility. The crops have been harvested early or burned where that's not possible. All the veg have gone. I swear the bastards have even picked all the fruit and berries from the trees!'

Priscus closed his eyes. Caesar was going to rant again. A week now the army had been on the move inland, crossing rivers and traversing forests, always heading west, forever stretching their communication and supply lines, and every mile west had been a chore.

The first two days had been perfectly acceptable, the army moving in good spirits, eating well from the supplies they had brought, and with no sign of the Britons. Day three had changed all that. The natives had appeared among the trees of the seemingly endless forest the army crossed. While the legions had hurriedly responded by drawing close and preparing for action, it appeared that the Britons were content to keep pace and watch the invaders from a distance - a habit that quickly began to unsettle the Romans.

By that first night, it became evident that their apparent non-involvement was an untruth. The army settled in to make camp, a heavy guard out against local incursions, and waited for the standard small rear-guard of men from the Ninth and Eleventh to arrive with the supply wagons.

They never came.

The first scout party sent out to find them also disappeared without trace.

When four cohorts of the Seventh were sent to discern what had happened, they discovered the supply train ransacked and the entire rear-guard still in position, minus their heads.

On the fourth day the army had stayed put while a strong force returned to the beachhead to collect more supplies, and then on the fifth they marched on, only to encounter a grisly tableau in a forest clearing involving an altar to a misshapen native deity surrounded by in excess of two hundred severed Roman heads. While a number of the rankers began to question the wisdom of continuing on into this barbaric land, the grim spectacle simply hardened Caesar's resolve, and the army marched on, crossing a second large waterway that morning that the locals called the 'Medu Wey'.

That night, the new rear-guard and replacement supply wagons failed to arrive and Caesar snapped one of Priscus' wax tablets in half in his anger.

It quickly became painfully clear that, unless the legions were to leave a continual line of men all the way back to the beach, they were unlikely to maintain a working supply train with these nightmarish hidden ambushes. Caesar decided on the sixth day that the force would have to become fully self-sufficient, cutting the standard daily rations and living from foraging and the commandeering of local resources.

It was an easily workable plan. It had seen Roman forces through hostile lands over several centuries.

It was also a complete failure in Britannia.

This Cassivellaunus, who - the questioned captives had confirmed - had managed to bring half a dozen tribes together in the single cause of resisting the Roman advance, was quite clearly dangerously insane, and possibly brilliant.

After the assault on the hill fort, the man had realised that this Roman force was unstoppable in the field, even with his novel tactics. And so he had combined with all the other tribes in a unified network of resistance, refusing to meet the Romans in battle, but continually severing the lines of supply and communication and effectively blinding the army. It was no longer viable to send out scouts and patrols in numbers of less than a thousand and comprised of both infantry and cavalry. The smaller groups had been all too easily picked off and then left, dismembered, in the path of the army.

And now that Caesar had decided the army could live off the land for the length of one short campaign, Cassivellaunus seemed determined, willing even to kill his own people if it stopped the Roman advance. Every farm they reached had been burned, slighted and raped of anything useful. Every orchard was picked, every field harvested. Even the woods seemed suspiciously empty of deer and game birds. Could the Britons really be overhunting their own forests to excess just to stop the Romans eating?

And it was working. The army was hungry and starting to slip into despondency. Gone were the high spirits gained from the hill fort's conquest. Now, every man trudged slowly and miserably, trying to ignore the grumble in his stomach and living off only the dry rations he carried in his kit.

Then, last night, a shock arrow storm had swept down from a hill nearby, killing dozens of men and wounding many more. The whole thing was over before even a buccina call could go out, and by the time soldiers had reached the ridge, the archers were long gone. Since then, no man had left his shield out of reach.

170

And now here were the Tenth, standing in a deserted farm, looking at a field of inedible stubble and smelling the charred remains of the too-old, too-young, and lame animals that formed a carbonised smoking pile near the main hut.

Another failed foraging mission. Four hours of hunting the surrounding lands with almost two thousand men and what had they to show for it: a stray cow that had somehow escaped the mass cull, two unfortunate ducks and a hare. Oh, and a basket of mixed nuts, berries and fruit. When divided between four legions'-worth of men, it wasn't going to supplement the dry rations a great deal.

'What are your orders, legate?' Fabius asked quietly.

'What else? We return to camp. I face Caesar and everyone else makes a piss-poor stew out of the half dozen scrawny animals we found. I hope someone likes to eat arse meat, as that constitutes about ten percent of what we've recovered. Brains, bums and balls.'

'Sounds like the Seventh… apart from the brains' smiled Carbo from where he stood nearby, who then snapped to attention and straightened his face as the two officers turned to glare at him.

'When I find this poor excuse for a lame donkey's pizzle Cassivellaunus, I'm going to make a stew out of him.' Priscus growled.

His hand fell to the water-skin at his side - of which the contents only comprised three parts in four of water - and he unstoppered it, lifting it to his lips and cursing the fact that every day saw him turning more and more into Fronto. *That* thought, in turn, brought him back to the letter he had dispatched, which would now be somewhere in northern Gaul, winging its way to Rome where it would make Fronto thoroughly angry.

'What's that?'

Priscus looked in the direction of Carbo's gesture. Flashes of bronze glinted in the sunlight among the trees at the far end of the farmer's field. There, a century of the Tenth were busy trying to hack the remaining few stalks of some crop from the ground.

'Ambush. Surely not enough to challenge four damn cohorts?'

And yet as the legate watched, arrows, sling stones and spears began to arc from the tree line and into the century of working legionaries. Fortunate were they that recent experiences had taught them to be ready at all times and to never underestimate the enemy. In a heartbeat every man had risen from his work, sword already in hand and shield unslung from his back. Nobody even bothered putting the leather cover on their shields these days.

Eight men lay dead or writhing from the onslaught, but seventy had survived, largely through their preparedness.

And then Priscus witnessed the latest in a long line of disasters engineered by the bastard Cassivellaunus.

The century - under Centurion Allidius if he wasn't mistaken - quickly formed up into a testudo exactly as Priscus would have ordered, had he been close enough, but then marched at double time to the treeline. That, Priscus would *not* have done. With the trouble and trickery of the Britons this past week, it paid to retreat in good order and re-form with the rest of the army.

Allidius, however, seemed dead-set on taking the fight to the natives who had pinioned a contubernium of his men. The sour-faced Sicilian had always pushed his men a little too far. Five years ago, Priscus remembered having been forced to rein the man in during the Helvetii battle as he had been about to break formation and push forward. And now the man had done it for the last time.

Priscus turned to the cornicen by his side, opening his mouth to demand the recall be blown, but his gaze had not left the century of men out by the woods and he realised all too quickly what little difference the call would make.

The men of Allidius' century charged on the men hidden among the boles of trees, bellowing their love of Rome and their hatred of the Britons, only to run directly into the covered trench that had been prepared lovingly for them and carefully lined with sharpened branches. Not a man of the unit escaped the trap, the second and third lines stumbling into the deep, wide pit on the heels of the first and plunging to their agonising death.

Even across two fields by the farmhouse, Priscus could hear the pained screaming. Already the natives had left the woodland and were plunging long spears down into the pit, killing the few active and dangerous survivors, but not bothering with those who would quickly die of their wounds.

'Sir?' the cornicen prompted.

'What?' snapped Priscus.

'Sound the rally? The charge?'

'No point. Poor bastards are already dead. Dead *and* stupid' he added bitterly. 'By the time we muster and cross two fields those native arseholes will be half a mile away in the woods and lost to us.

Just sound the muster and when the cohorts are in position we'll go and collect the bodies and head back to the army.'

As Priscus stormed angrily away toward his horse and the cornicen blew the call, Furius strode across to his friend. 'If we don't find and skewer this Cassivellaunus soon there'll be no one left to cross back to Gaul in our rebuilt fleet.'

Fabius nodded. The list of the dead was lengthening, despite the low numbers falling to each individual incident. And with each fresh trouble and resultant burials, the army lost more heart.

Britannia truly was a cursed land.

* * * * *

'Priscus? Cicero? What do you see?'

The general sat atop his white steed on the rise above the river, hand across his brow, shading his eyes from the glare, calm and collected as though the entire campaign and journey had gone entirely according to his design.

Sitting on their own horses to one side of him, Priscus and Cicero shared a resigned, weary look. Neither of them was rolling around with enthusiasm at this point. They glanced across the wide Tamesis river at the north bank.

'Enemy horse and chariot wheeling around at the back' Cicero shrugged. 'Most of the warriors on foot in the centre, close to the bank.'

'Unseen, but almost certainly archers, slingers and spearmen hidden in the three or four small copses we can see over there' Priscus added.

'Your assessment?'

Cicero took a deep breath. Clearly, Caesar would not be happy to hear anything negative at this point in the push. 'It will be an extremely hard fight. The men will have to slog across the river very slowly. This may officially be a ford, but it's still deep enough to drown a short man. All the way across they'll be in danger of enemy missiles with just their heads poking out. The other bank's as good as a fort's ramparts - a natural defence. Those infantry will cut to pieces anyone who reaches the far bank. Even if enough men make it in force to actually do any damage, there's not enough space for them to form up. In the vernacular, as Front... as the centurions would say: 'we're buggered seven ways from market day'.'

173

Caesar's gaze hardened as he turned it on Priscus, who was nodding seriously. 'They've set sharpened stakes along the far bank and - if you look carefully enough general - under the water too across the latter half of the ford. They're a death trap that'll need weeding out as we advance, which will risk ever higher casualties.'

Caesar frowned. 'You think it impossible?'

Cicero shrugged. 'Nothing is impossible, general, other than making a vestal smile. But it *is* impractical. Can we not keep heading upriver and find a better crossing?'

Priscus shook his head. 'Nearest crossing upriver is many days round, according to our information. And if they've got this place sewn up like a vestal's undergarments, I imagine they've some pretty unpleasant surprises for us there too. The way is here, but it's difficult.'

His mind roved back over the past four days since the Tenth had lost a century of men in a farm. The endless cycle of loss and ambush had far from declined as they closed on the Briton's home ground, but rather had increased in intensity with each day. The one time the legions did seem to achieve the upper hand, routing a small enemy ambush of horse and chariot, they had pursued them, only to find half of Britannia waiting on the far side of the hill. Few men of that force had returned to tell the tale and the enemy had vanished by the time a punitive force hurried out to deal with them.

Worse still, a small force of particularly determined Britons had made a suicidally dangerous attack last night as the army made camp, aiming for the gap between two legions where a group of officers stood discussing the defences. Their attack was so small, swift and carefully aimed that they managed to cut down two centurions and Durus - a tribune of the Ninth - before any kind of force formed to stop them. Of perhaps a score of insurgents, more than a dozen managed to continue on out of the half-built camp and escape into the woods unharmed.

And now this.

Unhappily, Priscus peered into the water and then lifted his eyes to the massed enemy at the far side. No matter what they did, they would lose an unhealthy number of men today. Even putting aside the difficulties of the terrain, this was the largest force they had yet seen - though almost certainly not the full force of men that Cassivellaunus could call on - and it attested to the continually growing sureness and confidence of the natives that they felt they could face the invaders en masse now. Conversely, the legions slumped unhappily, following a week and a half of watching Charon dog their footsteps and now staring yet more death in the face. The morale level of the army would be very influential in any Roman assault.

They *would* win - there was little doubt in Priscus' mind about that. Rome had the advantage of numbers still, and the legions were disciplined enough that no matter how bad things became, they would do their duty even as they grumbled about it. But the losses would be appalling and would put any further campaigning in doubt.

'Then we will frighten them into submission' Caesar announced boldly.

'I beg your pardon?' Cicero frowned. Priscus turned his own surprised look on the general, who straightened and gestured at the ford - some ten feet wide.

'The ford is a killing zone, as you say' the general stated. 'It is impeded with sharpened stakes, in much the same fashion as the whole of the far bank. It is deep and the legionaries will struggle across in constant danger from the enemy. At the far side they must deal with the enemy pushing back at them, and then they will have no room to form up. That is the essence of your observations, gentlemen?'

'It is, Caesar.'

'Then we must do the unexpected. The unthinkable. We will commit to a charge with cavalry support.'

'Caesar?' both men said at once.

'There is an interesting thing I have noted about fords. The water level is shallower there than the normal river bed, as you will note, but in addition upstream of any ford, the close stretch of river bed also becomes shallower over time. I know not whether this ford is a natural underwater causeway or a native construction of timber or stone, yet it matters not. Look upstream and you will see, if you look closely, that decades or even centuries of silting have built up the river bed against the ford to almost the same depth. That section is crossable almost as easily as the ford.'

'Almost, Caesar, but it's still a little too deep. Even on the ford, men will only have their head above water. They'll drown there.'

'The cavalry will not.'

175

Priscus blinked. The thought hadn't occurred to him. With perhaps ten feet extra width, devoid of sharpened stakes, the cavalry would have a reasonable crossing alongside the infantry.

'They would still have to negotiate the river bank stakes at the far side and the waiting Britons' Cicero countered, though his voice had taken on an almost eager note even as it voiced his concern.

'They will manage. They must.'

Priscus nodded. 'And if the cavalry can break the defenders at the bank, the legions will have time to remove the stakes and they'll have space to assemble. It *could* be done. We'll lose a lot of the cavalry, mind.'

'Gauls are in almost infinite supply' Caesar replied drily. 'And reducing their fighting numbers might be no bad thing if your fears are accurate.'

Priscus sat back on his horse and glanced across at the auxiliary cavalry, extremely glad that Galronus was not here to be privy to such comments. It occurred to him as Caesar began to send out orders through the various message riders that a large proportion of the Briton leader's force had gathered here to stop the Romans in one major strike.

Given the nature of the sly bastard who ruled this group, the chances of he or his trusted companions actually being present was small, which meant that this was likely a force formed mainly of his allies under their own leaders. And if that was the case and the army could put the shits up them deeply enough, Rome might today have the opportunity to drive a few of the tribes away from their alliance, weakening Cassivellaunus' overall strength.

'Who gets to walk into the lion's den across the ford, general?' Priscus asked, nodding at the river.

Cicero straightened in his saddle. 'I respectfully request that honour. My primus pilus and senior centurions have proved their valour recently.'

Caesar tapped his lip. 'That right could easily be claimed by the Tenth, Cicero. Or even the Ninth, who are also a veteran legion?'

Priscus could feel angry eyes boring into his back and turned slightly to see Furius and Fabius close by, both giving him a look that demanded he intervene. Again, the rivalry between they and the centurions in the Seventh was starting to spill over. Better not to pour any kind of fuel on that fire. Neither legion should take the honour. So perhaps the Ninth, or...

176

'Caesar, why not give the honour to the Eleventh? They recently lost their legatus to a Celt spear. They will be hungering for revenge and so far they've been in support.'

Slowly, the general nodded. It was a sound idea.

'Cornicen? Signal the Eleventh to form at the river's edge beside the cavalry.'

* * * * *

'Felix' - born Titus Mittius in a house of ill repute in Ravenna - looked down at the deep, fast waters of the Tamesis and fidgeted with the harness of medals that picked him out as a centurion. In fact, he was the primus pilus of the Eleventh and now, by his reckoning anyway - the third most senior, long serving centurion in the entire army. He had led the Eleventh since its formation at the outset of the war, but had served in senior centurion roles in the Ninth before that. His nickname - 'the lucky' - was something of a joke among his peers, given the regularity with which he injured himself in curious and often idiotic ways or came a cropper through random acts of misfortune, but never had it impinged on his ability to do the job, and do it better than most other men could.

Today, particularly, he did not feel lucky.

Reaching across, he wrenched the small shield from the signifer's arm and cast it to the grass.

'Sir?'

'You'll need every ounce of strength to keep that standard aloft in the water. Besides, if I don't need a shield, neither do you.'

The signifer nodded quietly, his eyes reflecting the same uneasiness Felix felt. It was an honour, of course. There would be awards and rewards for the first men across and the front position naturally went to the primus pilus. One thing that was missing from both his harness and his unit's standard was the mural crown for being first over the wall. Did that river bank count as a wall? It bloody well should!

Somewhere behind, the musicians blasted out the infantry advance, quickly followed by the call for double time. Double time? In neck-deep water? Who did the general think he was kidding?

'Right lads. Fast as you can.'

Without further delay or thought, Felix dropped into the current, feeling the chilly waters suck the energy from his flesh, along with every prickle of heat. Corpses had been warmer than this. Next to him, Montanus the signifer disappeared beneath the water in a brief splash, the standard dipping alarmingly and then righting itself as the heavy-set man straightened and his head appeared above the water, arms gripping the heavy decorated pole with rippling muscles. Even as Felix and Montanus took their first sludgy, sucking underwater step at 'double time' he heard the first line of legionaries dropping into the water behind, eight abreast, their swords unsheathed but held close to their chests beneath the torrent to prevent extra drag and resistance, their other hand holding their shield above their head, creating a strange testudo-style roof that moved gradually across the water. At least they had a little protection from enemy missiles.

Not so the two officers at the front.

Four steps further into the water and the primus pilus was half deafened by the sound of horses and riders entering the river just to their left, the spray of green-brown water splashing across the men and soaking their bull-emblem-painted shields.

And then all became a sensory battering of discomfort.

The sound of shouts and pained cries as men called out to one another, officers urged their men on, and Gallic and Belgic cavalry ploughed through the water noisily, yelling in their own tongue combining with the brief, flashing, strobe-like vision as the disturbed water's surface lapped at his face, interspersed with open sky and a view of the far bank with its defenders. The numbing cold of the torrent vied with the burning of his muscles to see which could cause him the most discomfort.

Somewhere in the first rank just behind him, a man stumbled, his ankle caught in weed, and his mate went to help him, moving aside his shield just long enough to haul the first man back up above the surface. The recovered legionary turned to thank his mate only to see his rescuer disappear beneath the water, a grey-fletched arrow shaft protruding from his open mouth, blood fountaining out around it.

The legionaries - and the officers leading them - found a renewed reserve of strength in their muscles for an extra turn of speed at this sudden reminder that they were well within range of enemy archers.

Felix pushed on, his feet finding the heavy sunken logs that formed the base of the ford, covered with sand and gravel and treacherous sharp rocks, weed growing up from the cracks here and there, threatening to bring him down the same way it had the man just behind him.

With a measured regularity, he called out encouragement and yelled profanities at his men every three steps - a practiced talent that required no attention; he had none to spare if he were to keep moving and retain his footing.

The location of the hidden stakes was lost to him in the chaos and the murk. From the bank, they had been just about revealed by the whitening of the water rushing over them, but with the foam kicked up by the cavalry who had already charged past on the left, the water was too turbulent to give any indications.

The first stake he came across almost did for him, angled toward him with its wicked point at sternum height. With a surprising hand from the lady Fortuna he hit it at a slight angle, turning as he was to shout at Montanus. Had he walked straight into it, he would now be a Roman-on-a-stick. Instead, the surprisingly sharp point tore a few links from his mail shirt and then he found himself snagged as his leather medal harness caught on it as he slid past.

'Stakes!' he bellowed in warning to his men.

Desperately, and yet trying to retain his outward composure, he unhooked the leather harness, cursing as he saw one of his prized silver phalera - the one with the double-faced Janus - disappearing through the murky water and down to the river bed, where it was lost to him for good.

A sling stone 'whupped' past his head, tearing off a piece of his earlobe and refocusing his attention on the task in hand, forcing him to forget the vanishing medal.

Now his arms, vine staff providing an extension, were sweeping out ahead beneath the water. Four paces on, his wrist found the next stake, its point drawing blood and leaving splinters.

Nine paces to the next stake. Beside him, Montanus disappeared with a shriek that was cut off almost instantly as his mouth filled with the dirty water, his face a mess where the sling shot had neatly struck directly between his helmet's cheek guards, pulping nose and eye and driving into the brain behind.

Before he could shout the order a legionary behind grabbed the falling standard, discarding his own shield, and raised it proudly. Should he survive the day, that man had gained promotion the old fashioned way.

Six paces to the next stake, which caused a bruise upon its discovery. Somewhere behind, the second century would be starting to remove the stakes as their companions waded on past them. Felix looked up and realised suddenly how close he was to the enemy. Perhaps eight paces away, the bank rose steep and evil, more jagged points jutting out toward them barely a foot apart, with others offset below. The climb would be difficult and all the more so with the enemy above. He could make out the infantry above, seething, awaiting their arrival.

No. Not seething like that. Seething almost in panic! He frowned and looked around as he closed on the bank.

The cavalry were gone from the waters now. Already hundred upon hundred of the Gallic buggers had stormed across and gained the far bank with relative ease. His roving eyes caught the sight of their arrival point and he winced.

Dozens of men and beasts lay dead and dying at the river's edge, impaled on the spikes and turning the torrent crimson with their sacrifice. But their rapidly-pulping remains had formed a living ramp for the rest and had protected them from the spikes. With no more than a passing thought for their fallen comrades, the surviving bulk of the cavalry had leapt up to the fresh grass, their spears jabbing, their big barbarian swords cleaving and slicing, smashing and crushing.

In fact, the western half of the north bank was already clearly in Roman hands, the savage, unstoppable and almost suicidally-reckless assault of the auxiliary riders having pushed the defenders back and back, partially with the weight of muscle and the strength of their iron, but mostly with the brutality of their charge and the unwavering ferocity of their desire to win the bank and kill the enemy.

So it seemed to be with the Belgae in Felix's experience. As often as not, they didn't care who they were fighting, so long as they *were* fighting.

The natives ahead and above Felix were pulling back from the bank, joining in the general, panicked, disordered retreat of the enemy. Gallic riders pushed along the bank to aid the clearance, and Felix suddenly felt his tension at the dangerous crossing and his urge to get 'stuck in' to the bastards give way to the most astounding frustration. For the first time in many months, the Eleventh had been granted the opportunity to win glory, and it had been snatched from their grip by a bunch of hairy Gauls on glorified donkeys!

180

Just as he remembered his silver Janus phalera disappearing into the murk of the river, so the mental image of the Mural Crown that would adorn either his harness or the century's standard retreated into a depth of sweaty barbarian horsemen.

'You alright, Centurion?' asked the legionary who'd taken on the standard, his attention suddenly drawn to the angry mutterings of his commander.

'No I'm bloody *not*! I'm buggered if this win goes to the Gauls. Treble time. Get the men up on that turf long enough to kill a few of the bastards and take some prisoners.'

The legionary grinned.

'Will do sir. Mopping up time.'

Felix glared at him as he reached for the stake driven into the bank and began to climb.

* * * * *

Sego of the Catuvellauni watched the first figures of the Roman infantry rise from the river like a swarm of midges at dusk. They were shockingly fast, given their equipment and what was being asked of them. They had crossed the river relentlessly, even with arrows and sling stones pelting them, felling one man in every ten. They had negotiated in short order the sharpened points that had taken the defenders half a day to position, the front rank climbing past them as the second fought off any warrior brave enough to get close to this killing force. The ranks that followed up would then remove the stakes, clearing the way for the great steel beast to follow.

Alongside their unexpected and astonishing cavalry charge that had essentially outflanked Sego's force at the outset, this unrelenting assault made it abundantly clear that the river was not going to be the barrier Sego had hoped.

The young warrior shook his head in amazement. Their trade-brothers from across the waves had told them the Romans were unstoppable. Cassivellaunus had laughed at that, pointing out that the Romans had been driven away the previous year with little difficulty. The greatest chieftain the tribe had ever had was a charismatic man. His words grabbed the brain and soul of the listener and made him want to follow. Without Cassivellaunus, his people would not have managed to band with the other tribes north of the great river and several south of it too.

But it now occurred to Sego, as he watched the steel monster tramp across the grass, shedding water like a wet dog, that Cassivellaunus had dreadfully miscalculated.

Here, the combined forces of three large tribes were intended to stop the Romans crossing the great river. The Catuvellauni - probably by their chieftain's design - formed only one tenth of the force, the bulk being made up of warriors from the Dobunni and the Trinovantes, who were like slave dogs now to Sego's tribe.

But no matter how much fear or respect they had for the Catuvellauni or the charismatic chieftain, nothing was going to hold the allied tribes in place against this beast of an enemy. It was clear to Sego that the Dobunni, who were mostly to the right of the field, were in chaos, many having already disappeared into the surrounding woodland after the crushing charge of the cavalry and run to find their cowardly women and runts. The Trinovantes would likely have done the same, even though they had not faced the horses, had they not been largely trapped between the Romans and Sego's own men.

It would be over in a hundred heartbeats. Sego took a deep breath and lifted off his precious bronze helmet - a prize that had been taken from a dead Roman the previous summer and had reached Sego via an enterprising trader of the Cantiaci. Rubbing his short, wild, blond hair and biting his lip, he tried to decide what to do. He was young for a war leader, but fearless and bright, and both he and Cassivellaunus knew it.

Many warriors would surrender their wits to the song of the blood at this point and lead their men to a hopeless, if valiant, death by the riverside.

Sego could not afford such heroic insanity. The Romans could not be held here and that was obvious. And when they marched on against the tribe's sacred settlement at Wheat Valley, even though the main force of the Catevellauni waited there and the ditches were deep, they would be fighting for their life against a powerful foe. To waste men here was a foolish notion. The chieftain would need every spare warrior at Wheat Valley if he was to hold off the Romans long enough.

It was, Cassivellaunus had said with certainty, all a matter of time. The Romans would not winter here, when the tribes' brothers across the sea were already starting to rise and throw off the

182

republic's yoke. All the Catuvellauni would need to do was keep the Romans at the hut's door until the snows and rains came and the temperature fell, and this chieftain-dog Caesar would take his men back across the sea. There he would be kept by other troubles until he was finally killed or thrown back to Rome an abject failure.

The tribes of this sacred island, beloved of the druids and of Belenus would hold against this would-be invader.

But Sego must end this madness first.

The Roman infantry smashed their way through the first gathering of Trinovanti warriors in the manner of a smith's hammer on a too-brittle sword. Sego was close to the front, as was fitting of the nephew of a great chieftain, and he would have to withstand the initial assault and hold it back long enough for the Catevellauni to abandon the fight. If he made to run without facing down a single man, his honour would be lost to him and the Trinovantes might just kill him themselves.

With gritted teeth, he locked his gaze on the man with the strange head-plumage that marked him as a leader, but the Roman chief was quickly lost in the press of men, and Sego found himself instead looking at a common warrior of Rome. The man, some decade older than Sego and far heavier equipped, threw up his shield and made to barge him, the bulging bronze boss meant for the young war leader's face.

But these Romans were also slow, weighed down with the water of the river that dragged their sodden clothes and armour toward the ground. Almost contemptuously, Sego battered the large shield aside with his own sword and stuck his spear in the Roman's gut, snarling his distain at the man's mail shirt as the decorative leaf-head of iron tore through the links and sank into warm guts.

Just to be sure, Sego took a step to his left, wrenching the spearhead a foot sideways inside the man's belly, before turning it through half a twist and yanking it back out. The Roman screamed and fell to his knees, his sword discarded as he clutched at his ruined gut.

It was a glorious feeling to destroy these men in battle, and Sego savoured the moment as long as he could, but it could not last and he could not repeat it. Already the man was down and a handful more were jostling to take his place. He had been seen to kill and the allies would fight for him.

Allowing two warriors of the Trinovantes to take his place, he stepped back. There, not far behind, were Sego's own men: three strong warriors selected by Cassivellaunus to serve the young war leader.

'Get the warriors away from here and back to Wheat Valley.'

The older of the three nodded his agreement and reached for the horn at his side. The younger, roughly Sego's age, pointed at the fray.

'What of the Trinovantes?'

'They will hold the Romans until we are gone and then flee back to their hovels.'

As the warrior nodded and watched the raging battle with the gaze of one who will miss all hope of glory, the third man, a distant cousin of his, gave a brief bow.

'I must leave, Sego.'

'What?'

'Cassivellaunus saw this. He is wise, and so I ride for the Cantiaci at Durovernon with a message from their overlord. I must go. The gaze of Belenus be on you, uncle's son.'

Sego fumed for a moment, angry that their chieftain might plan for an eventuality without even informing him, but nodded and gripped the man's shoulder. 'Luck surround you.'

The man jogged to the treeline, where his horse was held by the bearer, and leapt onto the mount with practiced ease, disappearing into the woodland, where he would follow hidden, secret trails to the crossing only five miles away. In a few days, the rider would be at Durovernon near the coast, speaking to the Cantiaci. About what, Sego would not cast a guess, and he could not afford the time to think upon it. Already his men were pulling away from the fight.

He would have to join them presently. The battle here was over almost before it had begun, but the next fight would be critical. Wheat Valley must hold until the Romans turned away for the autumn, or the Catuvellauni would be destroyed.

Chapter Nine

SEPTEMBRIS

Fronto alighted from the litter in a sombre manner. Next to him Lucilia dropped down lightly, aided by the large, imposing form of Masgava, dressed now in a plain tunic and boots, cut of good cloth at a well-regarded seamstress'. He had no weapon and yet Fronto felt safer in his company than had he a half dozen knife-wielding thugs by his side.

'Remember to be patient and easy' he reminded his wife. 'Julia tires very quickly and anything could cause her difficulties. At the first sign of weariness or trouble, we make our apologies and leave.'

'She might appreciate the support.'

'She will appreciate the freedom and relief that solitude affords more.'

For eight days now Fronto and his wife had alternated with Faleria and Galronus in visiting the stricken daughter of Caesar. Galronus always looked strained and faintly uncomfortable before and after the visits - Pompey and Julia were nothing to him - but he bore the burden for Faleria, who he loved.

Since that incident a week previously when Pompey had returned home, healthy but shaken and spattered with other men's blood, Julia's health had risen and fallen like the waves of the Mare Nostrum. She had borne all the pain and trouble stoically. Amazingly so, in fact, and if anyone ever needed proof of her familial connections with Caesar, then her hardiness, her bloody-minded refusal to succumb to despair and her sheer strength of will were that proof.

The midwives had clustered around Julia and worried and clucked and flustered. The three women had all agreed that the child had been unharmed, despite the torrents of blood, but that Julia had been weakened to a dangerous degree by the shock to her system.

A medicus had arrived on the scene in moments, demanding that she be bled to balance the humors in her body, but the midwives had little need to argue with him as the general himself, quickly disrobed of his grisly garment, had personally slapped and ejected the physician. She had bled enough, he said.

185

Fronto felt slightly uncomfortable himself now at these visits. His only ties to Julia were though the former commander who he had forsaken and his sister, who was never present at these times. Lucilia was a friend of the poor girl's, but a recent one, and Pompey was still at best a social acquaintance. Every visit brought with it the difficulty of being in the former general's presence as he watched his love struggle. And every visit brought him into the presence of Berengarus the north-man, who seemed to be ever at Pompey's side these days.

As usual Fronto quietly asked Masgava to stay with the litter. Bringing a dangerous professional killer into the general's house would hardly be the best, most sociable of decisions.

Lucilia rapped on the door and waited.

Behind her, Fronto moved from foot to foot, not through nerves, but more the urge to get this uncomfortable visit over and get back to his routine.

Routine.

That meant the exercise and training to an extent that would make most legionaries quail. Velius was the only man Fronto had ever known to run a trainee from dawn 'til dusk with no break for food, pausing only to keep the victim watered. It looked worryingly like Masgava was building up to the same. Yesterday, Fronto had jogged from the house down the slopes of the Aventine, past the carceres of the Circus, skirting the Forum Boarium and then back along the narrow way between the Circus and the Palatine before trudging wearily back up the south-eastern slope of the hill and home. Masgava had claimed it less than two miles in total though Fronto found it difficult to believe it had been any less than three.

One thing was certain: it was working.

For all his grumbling and shirking (wherever possible - which was sadly not as often as he would like under the watchful gaze of the master) his knee was strengthening all the time. Between the running that built it up and the exercises to carry out in the morning and evening, he no longer needed to sink to any available seat after walking a hundred paces.

His reverie was interrupted as the door opened just wide enough to show the man-mountain that was Berengarus behind it. Fronto frowned. The Germanic thug was not doorman material and never would be. Pompey had less hairy, belligerent slaves in his household for such duties.

'We are here for Julia.' Lucilia announced with a smile that would cheer most men. The barbarian, however, narrowed his eyes in a manner that Fronto really did not like.

'Lucilia...'

His wife waved him aside with a negligent hand and Berengarus made to close the door again until a voice from inside said something that was not quite audible through the gap. At the unheard order, the door swung open and the barbarian stepped aside.

Fronto knew something was dreadfully wrong the moment his foot crossed the threshold. He had never been a really devout man, his devotions to the gods mostly simple lip-service or the desperation of the near-terminally endangered, but he had a soft spot for Nemesis and Fortuna - vengeance and luck quite simply - who had become his patron Goddesses. A healthy and balanced, if confused and conflicting, belief in both fate and chance - a grudging recognition of the former and a high regard for the latter - had given him a strange sense of impending troubles that had manifested in various manners through the years. He refused to think of it as anything other than a natural ability.

His natural ability was playing him up something terrible this morning telling him fairly urgently to piss off and come back another day.

'Lucilia, this is a bad time. Let's go home.'

'Hush, Marcus.'

As Fronto, starting to feel distinctly uneasy, reached out to grasp his wife's shoulder, Pompey appeared in the atrium from the 'triumphal' corridor. His face was an ashen grey, his eyes puffy, pink and bloodshot. He was simply attired in a very military style red tunic, and that colour was shockingly echoed by the crimson that stained his hands and lower arms - blood that had dried on some time ago and which no attempt had been made to remove. He could easily have been ritually sacrificing a goat or some such, but Fronto's preternatural senses were telling him something else.

'Lucilia...'

'How fares Julia?' she asked the house's patron, though her voice shook as she saw his arms and realised that something was, as her husband's tone had suggested, quite wrong.

Pompey's eyes, 'til now downcast, came up to meet those of his guests.

Lucilia actually took a step back, bumping into her husband.

Though the puffiness and colour of the old general's face clearly told of hours of tears and the wrench of grief, it was not loss or despair they read in his cold eyes. It was rage, barely controlled beneath a seal of steel.

'Lucilia…' Fronto urged once more, as his wife trod on his toe stepping back.

'Master Pompey?' his wife asked, quietly, with a carefully measured combination of sympathy and guardedness.

'You have the temerity to come here? Today?'

Fronto was edging back toward the door, his hand on Lucilia's arm, encouraging her to follow him, but he paused for a moment, that same strange sense warning him. He glanced over his shoulder only to see that Berengarus had stepped between them and the door.

'Pompey' he said quietly. 'Julia is not well?' He knew the answer, of course, but the question bought him conversation time during which he could try and think his way out of their apparent predicament. In the old days, he would have faced up to the old general, meeting anger with like, prepared to fight tooth and nail to leave. Not so now, with a young wife sharing the same danger. Now, his first thought had to be her safety. And of everything here, two things were certain: Julia had died, and they were anything but safe.

'Her weakness finally overcame her in the middle of the night' the general said, his voice quiet and carrying an undertone of menace. 'She passed while birthing the boy.'

Lucilia jerked in Fronto's grasp, her urge to run to the pleasant, young mother almost overwhelming. Fronto tightened his grasp. None of the other doors in the room would lead anywhere useful. Only the exit to the garden, blocked by the general himself, and the door to the street, covered by the barbarian. Unless they could talk their way out, which seemed increasingly unlikely, he would have to put one or the other down. His mind reeled. He was in better shape than he had been for many months but nowhere near the peak of his ability, and he hardly fancied his chances against the aging general, let alone the colossus behind him.

Helpfully, Lucilia continued to string the discussion along, buying him time.

'A boy? The gods be praised for taking the oppressive darkness and drawing from it a small light.'

'A *snuffed* light' Pompey snarled. 'Dead before he could ever even see his father. As dead as my heart. *As dead as my joy.*' The muscles in his arms flexed a warning. 'As dead as my ties to your monster of a master' he added, his eyes slipping from Lucilia to her husband.

Fronto nodded fractionally. *An argument.* He had to draw Masgava's attention without supplying due warning to the pair in the room, else they might bring the rest of the general's motley force of thugs into the fray.

'Hold!' Fronto barked loudly. 'Firstly, Caesar is *not* my master. Secondly, your ire is ill-aimed. We have visited your wife and supported her in every way possible. My wife and sister have been with her and helped her every step of the way. That she did not have the robustness to bring your child into the world is a tragedy, but not our doing. What cause have you to launch your anger at us?'

It mattered not, in truth. Fronto had known from the first time he had socialised with the general, months ago now, that Pompey had the heart and spleen of a savage animal, carefully encased in a veneer of civilisation. The man could explode at any time and Julia's passing seemed to have been enough of a trigger. Fronto's voice had risen in a tone of defensive anger - faked, of course, as he was too busy keeping the situation in mind, with the corner of his eye flicking back to Berengarus to make sure the thug was not closing on him. The loud, sharp tone was designed in truth not to stand against Pompey, but to cut through the atmosphere and pierce the door, hopefully reaching Masgava where he waited near the litter. Would the gladiator know to do anything? Would he *choose* to?

Pompey took a couple of steps forward, his hand coming up pointing, accusingly with a blood-stained finger that quivered a little.

'I know you're Caesar's creature. You always were, like that runt Clodius, even when he claimed to be serving me, or Brutus, or Antonius or any of the whole shipload of whoremongers, catamites, villains and traitors. I should have known to what lengths you would go two years ago when you had the audacity to interrupt a meeting of your betters and threaten me on the beak-nosed despot's behalf. But I chose to believe that you had broken your ties to him and that perhaps you might be of use to me.'

The hand stopped wagging its index finger and made a sweeping motion instead.

'But no. You were, are, and forever will be Caesar's monkey, doing his dirty work and poisoning the world for the rest of us.'

Lucilia's mouth formed a shocked 'O'.

189

Fronto's voice became indignant - strangely so as he pushed it up a notch of volume again, willing Masgava to be close to the door and not testing the ripeness of fruit on the stalls at the far side of the street.

'Whether you think me Caesar's man or not, what has that got to do with this nightmare? Your wife failed to birth a child. It's horrible, but hardly a first. These things happen. Have you lost your wits? Your reason?'

The general stopped, his eyes bulging, the veins at his temple throbbing faster. Fronto realised Pompey was ready to explode and that every tiny push from him could cause the whole situation to become deadly dangerous.

'I found your poison' Pompey spat. 'The vial that has been ruining her. Did your sister plan this herself, or did you supply her with the toxin?'

Fronto's brow wrinkled. What was the old man blathering about?

His memory furnished him with an image of Faleria giving the heavily pregnant girl an elixir of Raspberry and calming herbs in the hope that the old traditional infusion would help ease her difficulties.

'Don't be an idiot.' His tone had dropped again, because now he really was angry. Too angry to push the volume of his voice. 'A herbal infusion to calm a pregnant woman! Nothing more.'

A low growl rose in Pompey's throat.

'I knew that eagle-faced lunatic would eventually turn on me, but I had not realised just how far he would go. To kill his *own daughter* just to deprive me of a love and an heir. Because this has his brand stamped all over it. You are a mindless lackey, Fronto, without the balls for this wickedness, but Caesar would drown Rome in a sea of blood if it suited his purposes.'

It struck Fronto just how easily that last statement might just as easily be applied to the general in front of him as the one in Gaul. Again, Fronto felt his own ire grow and forced himself to keep it in check. Lucilia had to be his first concern.

'You can believe what you like, Pompey, but neither I nor my wife or sister had any hand in Julia's death; and Caesar may be a touch manipulative and heartless, but he would no more subject his own daughter to the slightest pain than he would himself. He may play wild with the lives of his enemies, but his family and friends are inviolable!'

190

The ease with which he had instantly leapt to the defence of his former commander startled Fronto. The general was shaking now and the former legate of the Tenth felt the tension in the room rising to a critical level.

His time was up.

No help was coming.

Turning, he came face to chest with Berengarus and angled his eyes up to meet the big barbarian's glare.

'I would suggest you step aside, sunshine, and let the lady and I out before we cause you any trouble.' He smiled. 'She's a biter.'

The mountain of muscle and bone stayed put, but Fronto felt his heartbeat ease as the big man suddenly became a silhouette, the door opening behind him to admit the streaming sunlight. Of course, Berengarus was a guard, not a doorman. It had not occurred to him to lock the portal after letting in the visitors.

'Step aside or your dominus will be pulling splinters from your spine until the day the Styx runs dry.'

Fronto could just make out the ebony skinned legs of Masgava between the tree trunks of the barbarian's own. As Berengarus moved to the side - not in obedience, but rather to avoid having his back to this new potential enemy - Fronto grinned at the Numidian in his service who stood in the doorway, hefting a makeshift weapon formed of a narrow wooden plank sheared off at a diagonal halfway its length, leaving a nasty, jagged, splintered tip.

'I am truly sorry for Julia and for your loss, Pompey. I think you need to consider your accusations before you level them, but grief does stupid things to people so we'll go now and leave you to your mourning.'

As the general's eyelid flickered in irritation, Fronto turned to the Germanic thing by the door. 'And you and I are going to part ways now too. I pray it will be the last time we meet, but I don't like to be threatened. Bear that in mind in case it isn't.'

Turning his back on the tableau, he guided Lucilia gently but firmly by the arm, out into the street and toward the hired litter, where the four slaves waited to hoist it to their shoulders. As he passed, he nodded gratefully at Masgava, who returned the gesture, made some arcane gesture at the barbarian by the door and then casually tossed his makeshift weapon into the atrium before backing away and joining the Falerii.

The door stood open, the Germanic giant watching with angry eyes, as Lucilia mounted the litter and it lifted and moved off down the street, Fronto electing to walk alongside with his Numidian companion.

As they turned a corner and made for the Capitol, the bulk of Pompey's new theatre disappearing from view, Lucilia pulled aside the litter's curtain and leaned out, regarding her husband and his retainer.

'Are we safe? Should we run?'

'He's not stupid enough to send someone to stop us in the streets.'

'And later?'

Fronto and Masgava exchanged a look. The latter shrugged and Fronto rolled his shoulders. 'He'll probably begin to calm down and see it for what it is: terrible misfortune. If he doesn't, then he's going to have a bad time bottling it all up.'

'And the elixir of Faleria's?'

'He can have any physician or herbalist look at it and they'll all tell him it's harmless. He can suspect what he likes, but there's no evidence that we had anything to do with Julia's death. There can't be, given that we *didn't* have anything to do with it.'

Lucilia seemed a little happier at that and disappeared inside to be alone with her thoughts. At a gesture from Masgava, the two men slowed their pace, falling slightly behind, out of earshot of the litter.

'Do you really think the general will calm down and see sense?' the Numidian asked quietly.

'Why?'

'I saw his face from the doorway. It was not the face of reason.'

Fronto thought back on everything he had learned of the general and came quickly to the inescapable conclusion that Masgava's fears were far from unfounded.

'I think he will have trouble letting go of this. It will drive such a wedge between him and Caesar that their differences will be irreconcilable and he still thinks of Caesar and I as close. With Crassus out east and half Rome bought by Pompey, he has virtual autonomy in the city. I think he will try and revenge himself on Faleria and myself.'

'Will he send men?'

'Doubtful. His position is too public. Such an act, if it were uncovered, would ruin his popularity. He is the noble victor and the benefactor of Rome's people with only Caesar to rival him. He will try to ruin things for us, but it will all be by legal means.'

Masgava gave him a meaningful look. 'Respectfully, Domine, would you wager your wife and sister's lives on that?'

Fronto glanced at his companion, wondering how he would be coping with things had he not employed the outspoken, forthright Numidian. It was almost like having Priscus at his side again. He had missed martial companionship more even than he'd realised. But most important of all, the man had raised a vital point. He *was* sure of Pompey's need to stay clean, but not sure enough to bet Lucilia and Faleria on it.

'When we get back to the house, I'm going to go speak to the girls. I need to persuade them that now is a good time to go back to the villa in Puteoli and visit mother. If they are out of the city, I don't have to worry about them.'

'Will they be safe there?'

'Galronus will accompany them and there's some good men at the estate, and plenty of strong arms for hire at the port of Neapolis. A little coin and they could be as safe as a legion in a fortress.'

'And what of you, Domine?'

Fronto smiled. The big Numidian had been rebellious in his tone when first they met, using the word 'Domine' - in the manner of a weapon, coated with bile - to address Fronto. Since becoming a paid, trusted member of the household, he had been advised that he could be informal with Fronto when they were alone, and yet he had continued with the word, though now infusing it with a surprisingly amount of respect.

'Me' Fronto replied. 'I will continue to train and heal, with your help. I fear I have broken my bridges with this general now, too. First Caesar and then Pompey. I am becoming an island in a sea of dangerous fish, Masgava. I had best learn how to fight them off or how to swim damn fast!'

'Then perhaps it is time you began to hire a small guard of trustworthy men?'

Fronto shook his head. 'Gangs of thugs never improve the situation, they just exacerbate things. We've done nothing wrong and I intend to go on as though that's the case. We devote this afternoon to seeing the ladies packed and prepared to leave in the morning with Galronus and most of the staff. Then you and I get back to the routine.'

Masgava nodded and the pair picked up their step, falling in alongside the litter as it turned once more, heading for the Forum Boarium that lay between them and home.

* * * * *

The early afternoon sun beat down mercilessly, baking the life out of the gardens, wilting the flowers and draining the energy from the two men in the wide peristyle garden.

'We should train with the wooden swords' Masgava reproached, two of the heavy practice weapons in his hand, eyeing Fronto with a strange, unreadable expression.

Fronto smiled and drew the blade from the sheath, raising it so that it caught the bright sunlight and sent blinding flashes around the garden as he turned it. The perfect, Noric-steel blade with the straight fuller showed no sign of wear or neglect. The perfect orichalcum hilt with the figures of the Capitoline triad was polished to mirror brightness. The ivory handle was now wrapped with burgundy-coloured felt to negate the slightly mis-sized hand-grip. Fronto had continually toyed with the idea of having the hilt replaced. A new ivory grip that better matched his hand and a new hilt that displayed Fortuna and Nemesis perhaps?

Masgava pursed his lips.

'That's not a soldier's weapon.'

'No. But it's perfectly weighted and formed, nonetheless. Its former owner was a master swordsman. It's a special piece of equipment.'

'You will train with the wooden swords now, though.'

'I don't need to build up my arm muscle so much, Masgava, so I don't need the weight. And the added danger of a real cut might improve my reflexes.'

'We start with the wooden swords for a week and more. You think your arm muscles are strong? Bulky? I see what looks like a purse drawstring with a knot in it. There is much more muscle to be had and a lot more strength. If you need the extra edge, we will then move to real swords soon, but not your pretty toy.'

'One gladius is much the same as another, and I want to get used to this one. It's sort of special to me. It has a lot of evil history to make up for.'

194

'No' Masgava said, stepping forward and knocking aside the raised blade with the practice weapons. 'You will begin with wooden swords and then you will move on to whatever blade I place in your hands. It will like as not be a different blade each day. You will train with the Thracian sica and the Gallic broad-blade. You will train with the Dacian falcata and the Arcadian Xiphos and Kopis. You will train with every type of sword I can lay my hands on. And sometimes also with axes, tridents, forks, spears, javelins... the dagger, the cestus, the naked fist. Sometimes you will learn how to down a man with an elbow or a thumb. And when we have exhausted weapons and body parts, you will train with chairs and vases, amphorae and' his eyes roved around the garden. 'And anything that comes to hand.'

Without warning, the big Numidian spun, his foot connecting sharply with a small statue of a nymph that stood at the corner of the garden's pool, shearing it neatly at the base and sending it with staggering accuracy straight at Fronto's face. The pupil, startled, raised his perfect sword just in time to stop the marble nymph breaking his nose, though the lovely orichalcum hilt took a dent in the process. He glared angrily at the former gladiator.

'Was that strictly necessary? That's my mother's ornamental fountain!'

'Would you try and argue a murderer out of such a tactic?'

'Of course not' Fronto snapped.

'Then accept it and learn. Everything is a weapon. The dust that blinds when thrown; the position of the sun to discomfort an attacker; the loose rock that can be turned into a missile. Any object, in fact, can become a missile, a blade or a club. To be prepared for any fight is mostly a matter of mental attitude rather than skill. See everything around you not for what it is, but for what it could be.'

Fronto nodded, glancing guiltily at the broken nymph lying on the gravel. His mother would certainly make him pay for that.

'I shall need a lot of money' Masgava said in his flat, matter-of-fact voice.

'Oh yes?'

'I need to procure weapons and armour of various types, and not cast-offs that are brittle and damaged. If you wish to learn properly, it is not a thing to try and do cheaply.'

Fronto sagged.

195

'Look, Masgava, I'm not really sure just how necessary all of this is? I mainly wanted to get fit and to improve my skills after letting them slide for a year or more. I'm too old to start training as a gladiator.'

'Really?' the Numidian asked scathingly, walking slowly around him in a circle, eying him like a purchaser at the slave block.

'Well, when am I ever going to need to know how to kill someone with a marble nymph, no matter how pretty and full-breasted?'

Masgava stopped once more in front of him and folded his arms. 'You do not listen to your own tales, Domine.'

'What?'

'In two years alone, you have fought a gang of men through your own burning house, been set upon by gladiators in your bath, been taken on by assassins in your camp and hunted through these very rooms by murderous officers.'

Fronto blinked. Had it happened that often?

'And that is without considering the dangers you faced against the Celts. And if you go east to join Crassus, you will face the Parthians and their desert allies who know how to kill better than any Roman and who revel in the joy of blood. And if you sign up to serve in Africa in the expectation of rebellions, you will have to face *my* people. Do you relish *that* thought? How long would you last against five of me? Fifty of me? Five hundred of me?'

Fronto spread his free hand in a conciliatory gesture, noting with irritation how three of the fingers were slightly raised from the rest after being broken last year and not quite setting correctly. In cold, wet weather they ached as badly as his knee.

'Very well. I have a habit of getting eight shades of shit kicked out of me. You've made your point.'

'I do not think I have' Masgava replied and crouched. Fronto eyed him suspiciously, shifting his grip on the sword hilt.

The Numidian messed with the ties on his sandal, refastening it, and stood again.

'See that the nerves are making you twitchy. Instead of pouring all your concentration into being ready with the blade to counter whatever I am doing, pay better attention to what exactly that is, and then you will be more able to counter appropriately.'

'But you just retied your sandal strap.'

'Did I?'

In a blur, faster than Fronto could have imagined possible, the Numidian flicked his foot forward and up. The sandal-boot, the same style as worn by the military, came free, the tie having been loosened enough. The hobnailed sole flew with once again unerring accuracy for Fronto's face. Fast as he could, and proud of his speed, Fronto jerked his blade to the side and knocked the flying boot out of the way.

In the blink of an eye, as he looked down, a smug grin plastered across his face at so outwitting the manoeuvre, the big Numidian's bare foot kicked him in the bad knee, having continued upwards after flicking off the sandal.

The blow was clearly a 'pulled' one, deliberately light, so as to cause no real damage. Still the gentle strike was enough to crumple Fronto's leg, causing him to collapse, smug grin still forming, in a jellied heap on the floor.

'Still think I'm overdoing things?'

Fronto stared up at the Numidian, trying to ignore the throbbing in his knee which, he was fairly certain, would have been utterly shattered had Masgava wished it. He'd barely had the time to react to the flying shoe that would have bruised and disoriented him, but even that had been simple distraction while the foot came in to do the damage. The man was a marvel!

'Fine. Your point has been adequately made. And now that you've undone a few weeks' work on my knee, what do you propose we do for the afternoon.'

Masgava reached down and gripped his wrist, hauling him upright. Fronto hobbled around the gravel for a moment, testing the weight on his knee. The blow had been miraculously aimed, actually doing virtually no harm, just temporarily weakening the knee enough to collapse him. As he hobbled, he felt the strength returning.

'This afternoon we fight with wooden swords, as I said.'

Fronto shook his head in wonder at Masgava as the big man strode across the gravel to retrieve his discarded sandal. The man didn't even wince at the sharp stones that dug into his bare foot. He must have soles made of leather himself!

He was still shaking his head as the wooden sword hit him in the stomach, felling him again.

'Concentrate!'

* * * * *

197

Fronto rose blearily at the hammering sound. Blinking away the sleep, he shuffled across the bed, dropping his feet to the cold marble floor with a slapping sound. Pushing himself upright and stretching, he strode out of the room in just his subligaculum. It was too hot in Rome at the moment to sleep in a tunic.

Aware that he was all-but naked, he shrugged and strode through the atrium toward the front door. He could hear the birdsong and could judge from both that and the angle of the light in the atrium that it was barely dawn. Anyone who knocked on the door at this time of the morning deserved anything they got.

Fingers wrapping around the hilt of the cudgel he had taken to leaving on the altar near the entrance, Fronto hefted it and crossed to the door, unlocking it and swinging it open, weapon ready to strike.

Galba - former commander of the Twelfth Legion and now a praetor of Rome with standing in the courts - stood in the slanting morning light, his bristly, dark face grave. His brow furrowed at the sight of the house's owner.

'Good morning' Fronto greeted him, replacing the club on the altar top and stepping back to open the door.

'What's happened to Posco?' the heavy-set visitor asked, stepping inside and adjusting his toga.

'Sent him, Galronus and most of the slaves and servants south with the girls to Puteoli. Just me and one man left here, and Masgava doesn't strike me as a born doorman. Probably never even thought to come and see who you were. You're up early.'

'Thought I'd drop in before I get to work. A praetor cannot afford to be abed after sunrise.'

Fronto closed the door and grinned as Galba looked him up and down with a furrowed brow.

'Yes. You got me out of bed. I don't habitually accept visitors naked.'

'You've been exercising I see.'

Fronto pulled an exaggerated pose, flexing his arm muscles. 'Shows then?'

'Doesn't make you less of an idiot, but at least now you're a thin idiot.'

Springing back to a normal stance, the house's owner gestured his guest toward the tablinum. As they strolled Galba relaxed a little.

'You may have it right, parading round in your underwear, though. It's damnably hot today in a toga.'

'I can imagine. That's the price you pay for public service. It's just one of many reasons why I'll never take position in the city. Now what brings you here so early in the morning?'

Galba entered the office and sank into the proffered seat.

'A warning. Pompey appears to have it in for you. I don't know what you've done to piss him off, but ever since Julia's death, he's been like a bull behind a gate. I'm told he rarely sleeps, and then badly. He's worried all his people and his clients to the point of panic.'

'He's just looking for somewhere to lay the blame so he can feel better. He'd be fine if he were in Caesar's position - or Crassus'. Then he'd have a nation of Rome's enemies to take it all out on. But in Rome he has to be restrained; careful.'

'Not over-restrained' Galba said quietly.

'Go on?'

'He's been blackening your family's name throughout the senate and anywhere he has influence.'

'Should I really care?'

'Yes. You should. You personally might not care if your father's alcoholism was publically advertised, or even that you might be said to be following the same trail. You might not care that you're called dissolute and even an opponent of the senate because of your ties to Caesar.'

'I have no ties to Caesar.'

'Perhaps not in your eyes, but the great and good - and the bad, for that matter - of the republic see it another way. Your sister and your wife will hardly appreciate the way the Falerii are being systematically diminished. Good job they're in the south. If Faleria finds out about this you'll have to physically restrain her.'

Fronto shrugged, though the thought that Pompey was besmirching his father's name rankled more than a little.

'We'll live. It's a few weeks of bad-mouthing. Soon he'll change his tack and find something else to obsess over and forget all about us. And then things will begin to right themselves. A name blackened in Rome is only of import as long as the news is fresh. As soon as it stops being spoken of it will fade. Look at all the names blackened under Sulla. Most of them are now the top families of the republic'

Galba nodded, though his face was still dark.

'I tend to agree, though I think the problem is a little more serious than you seem to realise. And if that were the only trouble I would have waited and seen how things panned out before bothering you, but there's more.'

'What?'

'The old general is trying every trick he can to damage you. He's got a gaggle of lawyers poring over the tablets of law in the tabularium, trying to find anything he can use against you.'

'We've broken no laws, Galba.'

'Of course you have. Every day, every inhabitant of Rome breaks some law. There are so many of them - and some so obscured by the endless years since their institution - that people aren't even aware they're breaking them. Have you ever bowed or stopped to acknowledge a high official in the forum?'

'Of course not. You watch a consul make an appearance and the crowds rush to see him.'

'Then they're breaking ancient laws. Once upon a time a horseman was condemned for riding past a consul. See what I mean? It only takes a few rabid and inventive lawyers with enough precedents and you could find yourself spending the next six months in court answering one charge of inanity after another.'

'Is he that petty?'

'Again, I suspect you underestimate, Marcus. They may be petty, but if even half the obscure laws are invoked, convicted and go through, you could end up flat broke, homeless and with a ruined name. Be very aware, Marcus, that Pompey has resources you couldn't even dream of. Without Caesar's support or that of Crassus, you form a fairly solid and naked target to a man with a thousand bows and a million arrows.'

Fronto leaned back. 'So what do I do?'

'Nothing. Keep your nose clean and provoke no one. Don't drink. Don't gamble. Don't even go out if you can help it. Stay out of the light for a while.'

'And all that time Pompey gets free rein?'

'Hardly. I am a praetor, remember, with no small power. And there are men in the courts, the senate, and other positions of power who fear or distrust Pompey. Leave it in our hands and we will block every move he can make as well as any man could. Just lie low until he runs out of options. Sooner or later it will end and he'll have nothing else to throw at you. You're an easy target, but there are people out there who'll make a shield for you even if they don't like you or don't know you, just to oppose Pompey.'

'Should I go to Puteoli as well?' Fronto asked quietly and earnestly.

Galba shook his head. 'Not now. At this point it would seem like an admission of guilt; fleeing the scene of the crime as it were. In time, it might not be a bad idea, but not now. For now, just stay down and be quiet.'

The praetor shuffled uncomfortably in his seat in the silence. Fronto narrowed his eyes.

'What is it?'

'There is one other thing you could do?'

'Go on' Fronto asked suspiciously.

'Clodius.'

'Shit, no!'

'I know you have a history with the man and that he is in Caesar's purse up to the drawstring, but the man has power among the low and a personal dislike of Pompey these days. You may find that he hates his former master enough even to overcome his dislike of you.'

'No. Absolutely not.'

Galba shrugged. 'Just a suggestion. Bear it in mind.'

Fronto's mind wandered back over his involvement with Clodius over the years and centred unexpectedly on an image of a man crouched on a wall opposite his own front door. Paetus? The former prefect in Caesar's army who had been disgraced, betrayed and then given up as lost in battle was somewhere in the city. He had sworn vengeance on both Caesar and Clodius and - as far as Fronto knew - had no trouble with Pompey, but if anyone was an expert at staying out of the light while keeping apprised of everything that happened, it was he. Fronto wondered for a moment how he would go about contacting the man, if he were still about, of course. There'd been no sign of him in over a year, so it was more than possible Clodius had found him and dealt with him.

'Anyway,' Galba said, rising from his seat and drawing Fronto's attention back to the matter at hand, 'this was just a quick call to let you know what's happening. I will arrange to see you again, or send word with someone as soon as anything happens worth reporting. In the meantime, stay safe.'

Fronto nodded and expressed his thanks as he escorted the nobleman out through the atrium and into the street. As he closed the door, he pondered on just how things had collapsed so much so quickly. Turning, his heart jumped into his throat as he spotted the two figures in the doorway to the garden.

'Trouble?' Galronus asked quietly, Masgava standing next to him with his arms folded. The cavalry officer must have come to the rear door into the garden while Fronto and Galba had talked.

Fronto nodded. 'Seems like it. Pompey is conniving to kill me with bureaucracy. Galba thinks he could do it, too. It'll cost him a cartload of coin, but Pompey's got enough to buy a small city.'

He frowned.

'You should be in Puteoli now, relaxing in the sunshine and keeping the girls safe.'

'The girls have Posco and all your men and women at the villa, and Faleria's already hired a dozen new fairly muscular 'labourers' to ward off any would-be trouble. I thought I might be more use to you here.'

'Thank you. You might be right though at this point all I'm doing is training and staying out of sight.'

'One other thing occurred to me' the Remi chieftain said, relaxing and leaning against the wall.

'Go on?'

'You said this prophecy of the poet's...'

Fronto slapped his head. 'I'd forgotten about that. So much shit since Julia's death I haven't had much time to think. I wrote it down as best I could remember.'

He scurried back into his room and retrieved a much reused wax tablet from his desk and then returned to the atrium, running his finger down the words and crossings out.

'Socrates' root: Catullus and his hemlock. Second one was Vulcan's fury, and Aurelia burned in her house. Third one was... I've put something to do with Apollo.'

'Apollo?' Galronus frowned. 'Can't see how that fits. Could be unconnected.'

Fronto shook his head. 'I was prepared for coincidence after the first one. I don't like to believe in prophecies, since most of them are the written variant of horse shit. But after two deaths coming to pass the way I was told, I'm less inclined to put it down to accident. I don't like to favour the gods with too much influence in our affairs, but it's hard to deny them when they're tapping you on the head with their divine finger.'

'Apollo' Galronus mused. 'Archer? Arrows? Helios? God of the sun?'

Fronto sagged.

'The sun!'

'I don't understand.'

The near-naked former legate shook his head. 'No. Not the sun shining in the sky. The son. The son of Pompey. The son did for her.' Bloody prophecies are always tricky things. Remind me sometime to tell you about my visit to the Sibyl at Cumae.

'And what was the fourth, then?'

'The Parthian shot.'

Galronus raised an eyebrow meaningfully. 'Good job you're not planning on running out east to join Crassus' army, then?'

'Crassus' Fronto said in a whisper. 'Catullus, Aurelia and Julia. Pompey and Caesar's ties are pretty much severed. If something happens to Crassus too, we could be armpit deep in the shit.'

Masgava pursed his lips.

'All the more reason to finish training, then.'

Chapter Ten

Priscus rubbed his temples and winced. The last few days had offered precious little in the way of sleep or relaxation, the army marching back east and slightly northwards in response to information from captured Britons, bearing down upon the fortified settlement that this Cassivellaunus had made his centre of operations.

The column had been pushed to and beyond the limit by the demands of the General who wanted ever more speed from his army. Caesar had demanded of his officers that the Britons be brought to heel in plenty of time for the Roman forces to settle the matter and return to the boats to cross the channel before the dreadful weather in this part of the world made crossing unsafe or even impossible. In that matter Priscus could only agree. The very idea of being trapped here for the winter didn't even bear thinking about.

But alongside the natural weariness and stress caused by a forced campaign at speed, there was the constant interference and trouble caused by Cassivellaunus' tribe and their allies. Individually, to a force of this size, each incident of chariot strikes against outriding scouts or ambushes of foraging parties were little more than ghosts of gnats pestering a horse, but taken as a whole, the morale-destroying tactic was having a profound effect on the men of the legions.

The lack of any real food supply was also having consequences. Every day more soldiers were coming down with dietary disorders, having now spent some two weeks on nothing but stream water and the hard biscuit emergency rations they carried with them. It was starting to look to Priscus as though every farm, forest and fishpond for a hundred miles had been wiped clear of anything edible.

It was not uncommon now to see a legionary fall out of line trying to gather what looked like edible fruit or berries. Even the beatings such activity bought them from their officers did nothing to prevent repeat incidents. Valuable pila had been cast off into the woodlands and lost in vain attempts to pin what might have been a deer, but could just as easily be a figment of the mens' imaginations.

Trebonius had offered the suggestion that the army divert from their course and move on one of the other tribal settlements in order to attempt to secure a source of fresh grain, but Caesar's flinty gaze

204

was set upon Cassivellaunus and nothing short of a slap from one of the gods would have turned his head from that now.

And finally last night the scouts had come back unmolested - a rare occurrence in itself - and proclaimed that the settlement had been located.

Following the battle, such as it was, at the river Tamesis, the few captives had been examined by the officers and subdivided. Those men - the bulk - who were poor and stupid warriors of the various allied tribes were simply disarmed, beaten a little, and ejected into the woodlands to run home and tell of the clemency and power of Rome. After all, the column could hardly spare the men, let alone the food, to keep guard on a chain of prisoners. Those few who were apparently powerful men - a couple of nobles, a rich warrior and a man who looked suspiciously druidical to Caesar - had been kept in the column as potentially useful and important to keep separate from their people; those eight captives made little difference, But the three who belonged to the Catuvellauni tribe were given to the vanguard to help them navigate and move on the settlement. The poor bastards had been defiant at first, but half an hour with Blattius Secundus and his selection of hunting and skinning knives had made them remarkably compliant and talkative. The two who still had their eyes helped their friend to move as they aided the scouts in any way they could to track down and enslave their own people.

No one stood up to Secundus for long.

Now, as the sun sent glittering rays through the trees, Priscus had to admit that they would probably never have found this place without Secundus' unpleasant methods.

The captives referred to it as 'Wheat Valley' and Priscus could see how it had acquired that name.

A low rampart ran across the land before them and, while they could not see the far end of the enclosure, it must be a remarkably sizeable area. A pool and long, narrow waterway lay at the base of the rampart facing them and, apart from a few coppices like the one the small Roman party now occupied, the entire wide, open countryside around the settlement was covered with grain fields - all harvested, leaving nothing of use for the outsider, and probably stored in bulk somewhere behind those ramparts.

Behind Priscus, Cotta, currently commanding the Eleventh, snorted.

'Call that an oppidum?'

'What?' Priscus asked sharply, despite his weariness.

'Well, the oppida we've seen in Gaul were all on high bluffs, well defended with heavy towered walls and the like. This is a slight lump in the flat land surrounded by a small mound and a fence. My aunt could take that if she armed her gardeners.'

'She must have a sodding big and dangerous garden then. Look again.'

Caesar nodded slowly, standing off to one side. 'Ditches, you think, Priscus?'

'Hades yes, sir, ditches. Big ones too, I reckon. They're not relying on a natural slope - it's a plateau, but only a low one. Instead they've done exactly what Roman architects would do. Those mounds - which, by the way, are actually rather big - are the spoil from the ground in front of them. The only place the mound's low and there's no ditch is where all that stagnant water is. Anyone fancy wading into combat through a swamp?'

There was a silence interrupted only by the guffawing of a blackbird somewhere above them. Priscus peered between the branches and across the raped fields once again.

'The southwest approach is the only feasible one. The mound is suspiciously low there and without a water channel. I'm guessing that the ground was resistant to ditch digging. See how the hedge and stockade atop it is considerably stronger there? That's to counteract the failure of the topographic defences. To the south-east there's the water and to east and west those big mounds suggest deep ditches. Easier to take the stronger stockade than cross the deeper ditch.'

'What of the north' asked Trebonius, pointing into the distance which sat in the early morning haze. 'I can see no mound anywhere.'

Priscus turned and pointed off to the east. 'See the river?' The officers turned as one, almost comically, and peered through the foliage spotting the winding ribbon of silver that shimmered off to the east, curving round toward them until it passed out of sight.

'And there' he added, pointing west. Again all eyes followed his finger and saw the waving silver serpent straying across the landscape. 'Runs just past the north side of the settlement, I'd say.'

'It's tiny' Cotta snorted. 'A horse could jump it.'

'Look again' Priscus sighed. 'Widens out in a lot of places to ponds and lakes. That means there'll be fens and bogs and reeds and the like - a nightmare to cross, despite looking suspiciously narrow. And then there'll be the slope up from the river to the settlement, no doubt defended by a stout stockade that we can't see from this angle. I tell you now: the southwest is your favoured approach. It's the only place where legions can be deployed effectively. That should be enough of a reason on its own.'

Caesar nodded. 'You have the right of it. Remember, Cotta, that Priscus has years of the first hand assault experience that we all lack.' He tapped his chin reflectively. 'The north will be their bolt-hole.'

'General?' Even Priscus joined in the confused query.

'Where the tribe will run when faced by our attack. The south will be our focus and the east and west are unfeasible. The tribe will run north.'

'So you want a force there to stop them?'

The general smiled knowingly.

'Hardly. We cannot afford to smash or enslave them. We are far outside our own territory here and not in a position to claim the lands.'

'But you wanted…' began Trebonius.

'I wanted to show our strength enough to persuade the tribes of this accursed island to keep their claws out of Gaul. I will not tolerate interference with our progress there. This place is the focus of our opposition in Britannia. I want it to fall easily, quickly and efficiently. And there is no point in making a bold statement of our ability to crush the opposition if there is no one left to witness it and spread the word.'

A nod of understanding passed through the officers and Priscus smiled with relief. Even since Gesoriacum, the general had been adamant that Britannia must go ahead, but the legate had assumed - as had everyone else - that this campaign was either an extension of Gaul, trying to add yet more territory to the control of the republic, or a stunt to raise his standing with the mob in Rome.

Of course, *whatever* his motives, if he was successful, he would achieve the latter.

But the general was ever one for keeping his wagers and plans to the last moment; until the dice needed to be rolled. It made sense now why Caesar felt it wise to leave an unsettled Gaul for this: because he had to make sure that the vast hordes of barbarians from this land kept their noses out of affairs across the water. And to do that he had to prove to them that Rome could come in and stop them, chastise them and even destroy them if it felt so inclined.

207

The only hiccup was that Priscus was not entirely convinced that the attack on 'Wheat Fields' would be as simple as the general hoped. It should, but the column had no siege weapons with them - only light artillery - and the army was underfed, hungry and miserable. Morale was low enough to affect their ability to succeed here. Under normal circumstances, the legions would take this place in a matter of hours. Like this, could they even realistically camp down here for that long?

Of course, if they could lay their hands on the grain stores inside that settlement...

'Fulvius! Get those natives over here'.

As the optio and his contubernium of men coaxed the three captives across to the commanders, Caesar gave Priscus a quizzical look but remained silent. In a short time he had already come to respect the former centurion's opinions.

The natives - two broken and hopeless, one crippled and blind - sagged in their captors' grasp as they were forced to their knees before Priscus, who gestured for them to rise again. As the weakest of them, a young man in his twenties who was hardly warrior-material, turned his pale face to the legate, Priscus grasped his chin and turned him to face the settlement.

'Where will Cassivellaunus store all the grain they've harvested?'

The Morini scout who accompanied the small prisoner escort repeated the question in a dialect close enough for the captives. At first the man was defiantly silent but a quick cuff round the head from the optio loosened his tongue. His fellows glared angrily at him, but did nothing to prevent him answering the question. The scout nodded and then raised his gaze to Priscus.

'Town have four grain store near west side. Lots extra grain mean more store. Not time to build extra so keep in house near grain store.'

Priscus frowned and rubbed his forehead where a bead of sweat was starting to trickle down toward his nose.

'If we could seize a supply of that grain we could maintain a siege for a lot longer and the morale of the troops would increase a great deal. The lads love to eat and to pull one over on the locals.'

Caesar shook his head. 'I have no intention of tarrying for a long siege. I want this over with in short order. Besides, you know how dangerous and unlikely it would be to manage to bring any sizeable quantity of grain back out of there. But if we cannot raise our troops' morale and feed them well, we could perhaps even the odds the other way.'

'Sir?' Trebonius frowned.

'Destroy their grain. Lower their morale and make them equally hungry.'

Priscus nodded slowly, his eyes glinting with devious thought.

'It has some merit, Caesar, but there is a serious problem with the idea: when we do take the place, we still have no food. We need that grain when the town falls.'

'You have a better idea, Priscus? I recognise that look.'

'The scout says they will have too much grain to keep in the granaries and it'll fill the closer houses too. So we could destroy just the granaries and not the nearby houses. Specific targeting. We know they don't build in brick, so those granaries will be wood and will go up a treat with fire arrows. But we need to make sure we leave all the excess in the other buildings to feed the men. The archers will have to be careful.'

'Fire spreads, Priscus' Trebonius reminded him gently. 'Among wooden buildings on a dry day you'll be extraordinarily lucky if the other buildings don't catch.'

'That's why we attack slowly and sporadically. We attack at night and use Decius' Cretans - they're the only archers good enough to pull that off. We need the inhabitants to have time to realise what we're doing and rush across to limit the damage. If they've an ounce of sense, they'll realise that the granaries are done for straight away and pull the wreckage down, throwing water on the walls of the other buildings. We have to hope they're not stupid enough to miss that or we'll lose all the grain anyway.'

Trebonius smiled slowly. 'I see where you're going with this. There'll be such a focus on the grain stores that their attention will be distracted.'

'Absolutely. And that might give us just enough advantage to get a force across the southwest rampart easily.'

The two men turned to look at the others. Caesar nodded his approval as Roscius, so far quiet at the general's shoulder, shared a look with Cotta before the two men smiled and nodded in turn.

'Get it done.'

* * * * *

Auxiliary prefect Titus Decius Quadratus waved to his centurion. Calatorius - a veteran of the Sertorian war and a dour, disapproving old man - left the protection of the wide-boled tree and scurried through the undergrowth with a speed and dexterity that belied his years.

'Sir?'

'You've served with archers longer even than me. What's your opinion?'

Calatorius gave one quick glance toward their target and shrugged.

'So long as they're the right buildings the boys will have 'em to ash in half an hour.'

'But that's the very problem. Can we rely on those being the right buildings?'

The two men peered again. Decius' unit of four hundred Cretan archers had been split, half remaining with the force guarding the ships and beachhead, the other half with the army that had advanced west. Three slightly depleted centuries of lightly armed sagitarii had waited until dusk and skirted the wheat fields at a mile distant so as to remain undetected by the settlement, coming in from the west and toward the 'oppidum' using overgrown hedgerows and small copses and plantations of fruit trees for cover. They had reached their destination over an hour ago and the men were resting from their exertions, sipping from flasks and rubbing sore muscles. In order to cover their plain white linen tunics, they had donned their travelling cloaks of grey coarse wool, despite the balmy evening, and had moved like ghosts across the landscape, their lack of armour, helm or shield lending them surprising stealth, their only equipment a bow and quiver and a short sword at their belt.

And here they were, waiting for the moon to reach its apex, when the attack would begin.

It had surprised Decius how much the officers argued over tactics - he had never been privy to staff meetings before. Some of them had been insistent that a night attack was dangerous and stupid, regardless of the bright moonlight and clear sky. Others had argued that Rome was known for its dawn assaults and rigid adherence to certain norms of warfare and that a night assault would give them the edge of surprise.

It was true, of course, but there were so many dangers in the dark.

The Cretans had fallen foul of some of them. Men with ankles twisted in unseen hare-forms and badger setts, others caught by sharp protruding branches. And these were unencumbered lithe soldiers. The legionaries would hate it.

Decius narrowed his eyes. Their position gave them the only advantageous view of the settlement to be had from this side. In the coppice an ancient tumulus rose, already decayed and partially collapsed, but affording the only view that showed anything of the buildings beyond the ramparts.

The inverted 'v' shape of a thatched roof rose just enough to be visible beyond the defensive stockade of heavy timbers. It certainly could be a granary, as could the four or five more they could make out just beyond. They could equally be someone's home or an arms store. Gods, they could be a tavern or a whore house for all the Cretan unit could tell from this point of view.

'We can't rely on it' Decius sighed. 'If we launch an attack against the wrong target, we might not draw enough attention from the locals. We need to be sure. I'm going in to have a look.' He glanced up at the high moon in the clear black, star-studded sky. 'The main attack will begin in less than an hour, and we need to have the buildings ablaze before then. Get the men into position quietly and carefully. Have everything ready, and then watch for me. When I wave my arms, light the arrows and shoot.'

'Respectfully, sir, you can't do that. That's what scouts are for.'

'All the archers are needed here and I don't want to rely on someone else's senses anyway. I want to check this myself. Just be ready.'

Calatorius saluted and started gesturing to the other centurions and optios, moving their men into positions where they were still obscured by foliage but could see the ramparts well enough to shoot. He considered arguing with the prefect, but Decius was not a man to hide behind rank and the two of them had served together long enough for the centurion to spot a lost cause. Briefly he offered up a prayer to Mars and Fortuna that his commander be safe.

* * * * *

Decius dropped to a crouch in the undergrowth at the edge of the coppice, realising only at the last moment that it contained a patch of stinging nettles and cursing Fortuna, who clearly was not watching him tonight.

The ground from here sloped very gently downwards toward the oppidum, offering no real cover. A few saplings and shrubs dotted the grass, but even the wheat fields had not extended so close to the defences, and only turf lay before him until the ground dropped out of sight. That, presumably, was the deep ditch of which Priscus had warned. On the far side of it the rampart rose tall and imposing, topped by a fence of heavy timbers, reinforced with whole tree trunks and ancient hedges that tangled and intertwined.

'Fronto, you old goat. Wherever you are, this has all the marks of one of your stupid ideas.'

Back in the woodland he had already slipped off the mail shirt and his helmet that would shine in the moonlight and attract too much attention, but now he paused long enough to remove his shiny, bronze-plated belt and drop it to the ground, unfastening his sword and holding it still sheathed. Nothing that might catch shining moonlight and nothing to make too much noise.

Dressed only in tunic and breeches, boots and scarf and with his sheathed sword in hand, Decius took a deep breath and prayed to any god that might be listening that the defenders on that rampart were busy playing dice or something.

It was a hair-raising run, especially with his legs tingling painfully from the nettle stings, and he almost lost his footing once before he reached his first objective, dropping to the ground and sliding the last ten feet into the dubious cover of a large shrub with sweet smelling flowers.

Barely daring to breathe for fear of drawing attention, Decius slowly rose to a crouch and peered between the swaying fronds of the thicket of flowery shrub-life. It took him a long moment to see the first movement: a head appeared above the palisade and moved along it a few paces before vanishing from sight. Nothing else. No cries of alarm. No warning fires. Nothing.

Thank you lady Fortuna. If I get through the rest of the night, there'll be a small altar to you when I next get to winter somewhere civilised.

Another deep breath. Decius peered ahead. Roughly the same distance again until the ditch. Now, he was closer to the defences, but he was also further down, below them. Less visible, despite the increased proximity.

Clenching his jaw and squeezing his eyes shut for just a moment, Decius leapt out from the shrub and hurtled down the gentle slope toward the lip that hid a drop of unknown dimensions.

He kept his eyes locked on that edge as he ran, fearing even to look up for fear of seeing a spear being hefted ready to cast down at him.

And suddenly he was there. In fact, his momentum was such that he failed to pull himself up adequately and hit the edge at a run, pitching forward and having to throw himself onto his back to prevent tumbling down into the morass.

His breath coming in rapid gasps, he came to a halt gripping the roots of a tree that had recently been felled, probably to shore up the ramparts across the ditch. The slope was sharp - almost too steep to descend on foot - and it was something in the region of fifty feet deep, the lowest section showing signs of recent work that had cleared and deepened it. The far side was much the same, rising even higher to the palisade. It was quite an impressive piece of work, despite being largely invisible from a distance.

His heart thumping, Decius scrabbled down the slope as quietly as he could, taking care not to fall, using only one hand, the other gripping his sheathed sword. After what felt like an hour, he finally reached the bottom and scurried across to the far side, his feet sinking into the freshly-excavated earth at the bottom.

Another deep breath and he began to climb. His muscles strained and complained - he was not a young man these days - but he ignored the discomfort and scrabbled up the slope, gripping roots where they presented themselves or tufts of grass elsewhere to aid him. He made surprisingly good time and was starting to feel extremely pleased with himself when it all went wrong.

His hand reached out for a tuft of long wild grass and paused at a sudden sound of clinking metal above. Decius had been a military man for much of his adult life and a man could not wear the uniform for long without recognising the sound of a mail shirt being disturbed. The fact that it was so loud and clear indicated how worryingly close it and its owner were.

Holding his breath, the prefect pulled himself in to the slope, gripping the best handhold he could find and bringing his sheathed sword close to his body. Above, horribly close, there was a rustling sound and then a man whistled through his teeth.

Moments later the urine began to spatter Decius' head and shoulders. He closed his eyes and cursed Fortuna, mentally revoking his offer of an altar. Risking the stream of steaming liquid, he glanced up for a moment.

He was almost at the point where the ditch ended and the rampart began, where there was a very slight lip. The Briton stood on the grassy foot-wide ledge relieving himself, having clambered across his own barricade in order to urinate in peace.

Even as Decius looked past the man to make sure he was alone, the warrior's eyes widened as he saw the figure on the slope only feet below him. The man's mouth opened to yell a warning as he let go of his crotch mid-stream and reached for the spear he had jammed in the ground beside him.

Decius, all thought of subtlety gone, reached out with his free hand and grasped the warrior by the ankle, yanking him back so that he fell, his fingertips only just brushing the spear shaft before he hit the slope on his back, winding him. Not a sound left his lips, but he was already struggling, his hands coming round to grasp at the Roman beside him.

The prefect was faced with two choices and he recognised them as such instantly. He could either throw the man down the slope - easy enough given his position and the precarious unbalanced senses of the Briton, or he could kill him here. Both had their downsides. To throw him down the slope would likely kill him, or at least knock him flat unconscious. But he would likely scream as he fell and alert the whole settlement that something was up. Or he could kill the bugger here, but his sword was still sheathed to prevent the metal shining in the moonlight.

With a regretful sigh, Decius let go of the grass, using that hand to bat away the Briton's reaching grasp as he drew back his other hand and thrust.

He watched with irritation as the chape of the scabbard - beautiful bronze and fashioned into an image of Mars wielding a pilum - pushed against the Briton's tunic just below the mail shirt for only a moment, presenting resistance to the blunted weapon. Decius knew his own strength, though, and the Celt's eyes widened as the blunt decorative bronze work broke his skin and pushed on into his belly, followed by a scabbard of some of the best, most expensive Hispanic leather. The sword cover had cost Decius a small fortune.

As the man's hands jerked in his agony, Decius' free hand left them and clamped itself over the mouth just in time to stifle the cry. Gritting his teeth, the prefect pushed on with his other hand, feeling the sheathed blade slide through the man's innards, pausing for a moment as it encountered the spine and then sliding past it and exiting to push against the mail shirt and the ground below.

Decius kept his hand over the mouth and levered the sheathed blade left and right with some difficulty, watching, impassive, until the light left the man's eyes. As the Briton's hands fell back lifeless, Decius removed his own from the mouth which lay open in a silent scream, and fished in the small pouch that hung on a thong around his neck. Hurriedly he removed a small brass dupondius and pushed it into the dead man's mouth beneath the tongue. A habit he had picked up from his chief centurion, it supposedly kept the man's spirit from hounding him over the ignoble manner of his death.

With a deep breath, the prefect pushed himself up from the slope and pulled the scabbarded sword from the man's gut with an unpleasant sucking sound, noting the damage to the bronze work and the mess that would ruin the leather for good.

Another ten feet or so up this slope and he would be able to peer over the top of the rampart and confirm their targets. One wave of the arms and...

The warrior who appeared at the top of the slope saw Decius instantly - he must have been checking on his friend. Whatever the case, his spear appeared in his hand instantly, raised to cast down. His mouth opened to bellow a cry of warning and the prefect realised that there was no time now for stealth. Launching himself upward, he ducked out of the spear's direct path.

But the man never cast it anyway. As Decius leapt up, his dripping, gore-covered weapon brandished in his hand, an arrow, flaming with bright orange, whistled out of the darkness and thudded into the warrior's neck, the flames immediately catching his beard and hair and setting his face ablaze even before he toppled backward out of sight.

Before Decius could turn to wave, two dozen other burning arrows streaked across the sky and disappeared within the settlement, their grouping so perfect they could only have come from his unit of Cretan veterans. Bless that centurion. Fortuna may be a fickle - *and altarless* - bitch, but Decius would definitely pour a few libations to Centurion Calatorius when this was over.

* * * * *

Atenos, a huge blond centurion of Gaulish extraction with a deeply tanned face, turned to frown at his superior, the primus pilus of the Tenth Legion.

'Looks like it's started early.'

Carbo, his shiny pink face running with sweat that trickled down from beneath his hot, heavy helm, nodded. 'Wait for the count of a hundred and then give the signal to advance.'

As Atenos turned to peer at the oppidum ahead, Carbo addressed the musician next to him. The soldier looked at a loss without his curved horn, but there was no need for an audio signal, and so his role had been shifted to that of 'messenger'.

'Get back to command and inform them that we're advancing early, as the archers have begun.'

The musician ran off and Carbo turned back to Atenos to hear him counting. With irritation he realised the big centurion was talking in his native language. The primus pilus tapped him on the shoulder and gave him a pointed glare. Atenos frowned and then nodded his understanding, the count shifting from a Gallic tongue into Latin at thirty seven.

Leaving him to it and picking up the count at thirty eight, Carbo moved off to his own century and fell into position. There was an eerie silence broken only by the hooting of an owl and the distant cries of alarm within the settlement and then finally, almost simultaneously, Carbo and Atenos gave the hand signals to advance. The motions were picked up by the other officers and passed down the line, where they would be picked up by the Seventh to their left and the Ninth to their right.

The legions marched on Wheat Valley

* * * * *

Sego of the Catuvellauni danced impatiently from foot to foot.

'Why do we sit here, my chief, while they burn the granaries?'

216

Cassivellaunus, chieftain of the Catuvellauni and overlord of a loose alliance of Briton tribes, gestured at his youthful war leader with a placating hand.

'Calm, my young friend. Precipitous action is what ends lives unnecessarily. You seek to bring battle to those who would burn our grain?'

A nod - an impatient one.

'A brave thing - and noble too. But only a warrior can afford to be brave and noble alone. A leader must temper his bravery and nobility with planning and understanding.'

'But I do *not* understand, my chief. If we keep our grain we can hold Wheat Valley for months. The Roman dogs will starve and the crows will pick their bones in our fields. But we *must* protect the grain.'

'Sego, the grain attack is a diversion. And regardless, I had the bulk of it moved to the *Willow Trees* Oppidum three days ago. We have only enough here to see us through a few more days anyway.'

'But why? If...'

'Sego, you are blinded by your desire to fight these men. They are an enemy and an invader, yes, but there are many ways to scratch this itch. We cannot hold Wheat Fields against them. These people destroyed the greatest fortresses of the Belgae. We simply cannot beat them by strength of arms and we must therefore defeat them with guile.'

'I do not understand' grumbled Sego sullenly, batting the cheek piece of the captured Roman helmet he held under his arm.

'Clearly. We cannot hope to defeat them, and so we must persuade them to leave us of their own volition.'

'*Persuade*?' Sego gaped at his chieftain. The very idea that the great Cassivellaunus might be considering surrendering made his blood chill.

'Yes. This has all been a game of waiting, Sego. Of blocking, obstructing and demotivating. Do you really think I was planning to field an army against these people? Why then did we hound them all the way to the ford and back? Why did I throw our allies away at the river - where, by the way, you played your part admirably? With the exception of you and I and some of our more inspiring nobles, most of our people are absent. Have you not noticed?'

'I noticed that you moved our women and children to safety and made up the numbers here with the allied tribes.'

'Because they are expendable. The Catuvellauni are not.'
Cassivellaunus stood slowly and stretched before reaching down for
his huge, impressive sword. 'Look not to the burning granaries,
Sego. Look to the south rampart, where you will see their legions
marching to quash us.'

'What?'

'And that is where I have placed the Trinovantes in their bulk.
Those dogs can bark and yap at the Romans and die for them. We
have stretched Caesar to the limit and his army will soon break if he
does nothing, but we have also strung him out long enough to close
the door on another battle. At this point I simply intend to show
Caesar how serious I am.'

'But we *must* fight them!'

'Sego, you may join the Trinovantes at the wall if you wish, but I
would sooner not see you throw away your life for no benefit. When
the Romans are gone, we will have spent our allies' strength in the
process and we will be the strongest tribe in these isles. The druids
wish us to lend our support to our brothers across the water, but I feel
their time is done. We will build our power here to ensure that the
same fate as befell them will never befall us. But to do that we must
be all-powerful here. Do you understand?'

'Hardly, my chief.'

'Then come. Can you not hear the sounds of battle? Let us end it
and all will become clear.'

* * * * *

Fabius was laughing like a man possessed. Furius spared him a
glance and rolled his eyes. It was not the role of a tribune to leap into
the fray and bloody his sword. That much had been made abundantly
clear not only by the other tribunes of the Tenth, but also by Priscus
when he had expressly forbidden them from leaving the command
section and getting involved in the fighting.

And yet here they were, surging up the slope, dripping, viscera-
coated swords in hand, right in the thick of it. Priscus would berate
them later, but he would also envy them. Once a centurion, always a
centurion. It got into the blood and pushed you to become an
example to the common legionary, not a horse-bound spectator.

They had bumped into Centurion Atenos somewhere at the
bottom of the slope, where the enormous Gaul had been busy carving

218

a Briton into thin slices and the officer had bellowed something at them, but it appeared to be in his native language, so they had ignored him and pushed on. Carbo had caught their eye on the charge, too, but had wisely kept his mouth shut.

Again, Fabius' mad laugh cut across the battle, above the sound of killing. Furius turned in time to see him decapitate a Briton, his sword spraying blood across the advancing, struggling legionaries while his free hand lifted the head from the neck by the long, straggly mane.

One of the defenders pulled Furius' attention back to his immediate situation, leaping from the top of the rampart with an axe gripped in both hands and raised above his head. As his feet hit the ground, the blade already descending, Furius neatly stepped to one side. The axe continued to drop, gravity and momentum making it impossible to pull the blow, and it bit deep into the turf, the wielder becoming instantly unbalanced by the failed attack. Contemptuously, Furius kicked him in the side and paused only long enough to plunge his sword down through the man's back before tramping on up to the palisade.

Why were they fighting like this, the idiots? Any sensible commander would man the fence at the top and try to keep the Roman forces at bay below, but these lunatics were leaping over the defences and attacking them needlessly. It was almost mass suicide.

Another Briton lunged at him with a spear. Furius grabbed the shaft just below the head with his free hand as it passed his ear and yanked hard. The Briton, pulled forward and off his feet, tumbled away down the slope to be dispatched by the mass of legionaries pouring across the wide, shallow ditch.

It was madness.

Fabius was the first at the defensive line atop the slope, grabbing a panicky defender by the shoulder and head-butting him so that the bronze rim of his helmet cracked the man's skull. A warrior suddenly appeared at the timber fence and Furius locked his gaze upon the man. Here was a leader of some sort. He was well armoured in what appeared to be a stolen Roman mail shirt, somewhat tatty and with patches of rings missing but largely serviceable, and with a strange helmet that bore similarities to a Roman design but with a ridiculous bronze bird rising from the crest and two enormous horns from which ribbons hung. He was gesturing with his sword, and Furius realised at last what was happening.

The warriors were not eagerly leaping the barrier to bring battle to the Romans. They were being sent over by their masters. Furius knew enough of the opposition by now to realise what that meant. These poor bastards were yet more of Cassivellaunus' hapless allies thrown at the Romans to keep them away. Was this nobleman one of the Catuvellauni then? A leader of the locals?

Angling himself toward the new target, he clambered up the last stretch of the slope, batting away a pathetic attack and ducking a thrown spear. His foot hit the lowest tree trunk in the defences and he leapt forward, his free hand grabbing one of the upright timbers, giving him the leverage to climb. The Briton had not yet seen him, so intent was the man on sending the lesser warriors to their doom.

He would be useful. Furius would draw a few helpful answers from him before his head went sailing from his body. With a grin, the tribune clambered onto the top of the defences and threw himself at the man.

His sheer battle joy vanished abruptly in mid-air as his target vanished from sight. Furius tucked himself automatically into a roll and hit the ground, quickly coming up to his feet and turning to try and find out where his target had instantly vanished to.

His eyes found the Briton noble quickly enough, lying on the ground, spasming his last as a Roman pilum stood proud of his chest, thrown with such force that even part of the wooden stock had penetrated the battered mail vest. His eyes tracked back over the attack and narrowed at the sight of a centurion, arm still lowering to his side from the throw.

'He was mine!'

Pullo, senior centurion of the Seventh, shrugged. 'Thought I'd do you a favour. *Sir.*'

Furius' teeth ground, which only brought a grin from the other man. 'Best duck, sir.'

The tribune did so, all the more irritated by the man's easy manner. A Briton's sword that had been meant to take his head whistled through the air and trimmed the top off his crest.

'I don't give a flying, turd-burgling badger's scrotum what you thought, Centurion! That man was *mine!*'

Without looking round, he jabbed out behind with his blade and felt it bite into his attacker. Still facing the centurion, he twisted the sword and yanked it back, feeling the freedom as the man fell away in agony.

'My apologies, Tribune.'

'Furius! Look!'

The use of his name drew his attention and he turned to see Fabius pointing off into the settlement. Following his gesture, Furius frowned at what he saw.

A sizeable force had been committed against them here, while only a small group seemed to be dealing with the blaze off to the west, as though the granaries were not a great concern. But the majority of the place was empty space with scattered buildings, animal enclosures and the like. And in the centre, a party of riders was approaching at a casual walk, their horses stepping slowly and proudly as though at a parade rather than a battle.

'What fresh madness is this?'

'I dunno, but they've got their shields up over their heads. Reckon that means the same to them as it does to us?'

Furius shook his head in exasperation. 'They're surrendering?'

* * * * *

Caesar's white mare stood calm, tail flicking this way and that as the general studied the approaching party. Next to him, Priscus, Cotta, Trebonius and Roscius sat astride their own steeds, trying to look as noble and haughtily victorious as possible. The other officers gathered behind them in an arc of crimson and silver, while the reserve cohorts of the legions fell in to attention. The majority of the army was sweeping the Wheat Valley settlement, impounding goods, finishing off the wounded and taking prisoners.

The approaching riders were, as Furius' messenger had intimated, a party of four noblemen and a dozen burly warriors. They rode with their shields above their heads and weapons sheathed in a sign that could mean all out surrender, or perhaps just the desire to speak in a temporary cessation of hostilities. Accordingly, the Roman force continued to take full control of the settlement and was attentive and prepared near the officers.

'Which one of you is Caesar' asked a man with long red-gold hair, a golden circlet around his head, his arms covered with tattoos and whorls, his mail shirt extremely fine and costly and a strong, decorative sword at his waist.

'Cassivellaunus? Chief of the Catuvellauni?' Priscus responded with his own question.

221

'No' Caesar interrupted, raising an eyebrow. 'That one is a druid. Cassivellaunus is the one on the right weighing me up with his eyes, next to the boy who glares at me as though I had killed his pet.'

'Well done, general' the right-most Briton answered with an easy smile. 'This is Almanos - as you so astutely note, a member of that most sacred people.' He smiled and turned to the druid. 'Go to your people, Almanos, and thank you.'

The druid fixed Caesar with a long glare and finally nodded, turning to ride away. Priscus flicked a glance at the general that managed to carry the question as to whether he should intervene. Caesar gave an almost imperceptible shake of his head as the druid rode off.

'You play a strange game, chief of the Catuvellauni.'

'You seem unsurprised, Caesar? But then I hear you are a thinker as well as a leader. A player of the game.'

Caesar gave a light laugh that drew looks of surprise from his men.

'I could say much the same of you. You have led us a merry dance across your island only to give yourself to us so easily now?'

The chief of the Catuvellauni shrugged and glanced up at his shield. 'Would you mind if I lower this now? Symbolic it may be, but it is also as heavy as a roast hog.'

At Caesar's nod, Cassivellaunus lowered his shield and passed it to the young warrior with a Roman helmet and a perpetual snarl next to him.

'You speak exceptionally good Latin,' noted Caesar, 'and with little accent.'

'We have dealt with your traders for many years. A leader must know all the tongues of his enemies. It prevents misunderstandings.'

'It does.'

'And I want no misunderstandings here, Caesar.'

'Go on.'

'This is not a surrender.'

The Roman party sputtered their disbelief at the arrogance of the man, some even barking with laughter. Caesar ended the noise with a single swipe of his finger.

'You have the tone of a man who has just spotted the deadly opening in his enemy's formation.'

Cassivellaunus shrugged. 'I like to play games when I know I have already won, or at the worst forced a respectable draw.'

222

'I shall be interested to hear your reasoning for that statement.'

Cassivellaunus rolled his shoulders. 'What I offer you, great Caesar, is the chance to claim this idiotic foray into our island as a victory and leave with your skins intact.'

Several of the officers leaned forward and started to sputter their anger at once, but again Caesar cut them off with a slice of his finger.

'Tell me first why I have not simply won. I suspect I know, but I would like to have it confirmed all the same.'

The Briton rubbed his neck with his hand. 'In all this time, all I have done is throw valueless allies at you - simple chaff to keep you busy. The Catuvellauni are not to be found here, barring a few of us who opted to stay and command. You have won a glorious victory over the Dobunni; the Trinovantes; the Bibroci; the Cenimagni; several others who are but dogs at the feet of the Catuvellauni. If you wish to destroy our tribe, you will find it a harder proposition than the small victories you have thus far won. Even we are dispensable to our tribe and of little inherent value to you.'

'I thought as much. But we have time yet' Caesar added archly.

'Not much, if you wish to cross back before autumn. And you will, I fear, find your beach camp in some disarray. You may even find you need to repair your ships again.'

'Explain.'

Cassivellaunus shrugged with a smile. 'By now the Cantiaci and their other allies south of the great river will have launched an attack on your beach landing. They are not expecting a solid victory. They were to do as much damage as possible and then flee. I believe you are familiar with the tactic.'

'You have introduced us to it at length.'

'So you are tight on time to repair your fleet and return to your own shores. You certainly cannot afford the half year it would take to even bring my people to battle. And in the meantime your men starve.'

'We can take your grain now we are here' Trebonius pointed out.

'You could if we kept our grain here. But it is not here. You are in trouble, Caesar. You have a hungry - even starving - army a long way from safety and your time is running out.'

The general narrowed his eyes. 'You believe this enough to deter us?'

'Of course not. We all know of the great Caesar. A man of iron will, who achieves the impossible. No. I intend to sweeten the deal for you. You are in trouble, as I say, but I offer you everything you could wish.'

'Everything?'

'*Almost* everything' the chieftain replied with a wry smile. 'I will supply you with enough grain to keep your men alive and well fed until their return across the water. I will allow you...'

'*Allow?*'

'...to keep all the prisoners you have taken and I will give you a further hundred hostages and two hundred slaves, all of the Trinovante people. I will throw in even a little treasure you can claim as spoils of war. My men will show you to a place where a ferry operates that will allow you to cut down your return journey by at least six days. Does it sound sweet enough yet?'

'There is one thing I seek more than anything, chief of the Catuvellauni: I seek your solemn oath that you will not interfere in matters in Gaul.'

Cassivellaunus gave a laugh, filled with genuine humour.

'Nothing would please me more, general of Rome. I have absolutely no interest in your conquest and no exhortation by the silent white brotherhood will press me to sending my valuable kinfolk across the water to help a doomed people. Those people who treatied with your enemies in recent years are now the servants of the Catuvellauni and will cause you no further inconvenience.'

The group fell silent, the only noise the distant sounds of the legions taking control of Wheat Valley. It seemed odd to Priscus, sitting on horseback beneath the silvery glow of the moon and listening to a hairy barbarian dictating terms to the most powerful man in the world. And yet, he had to admit that the man offered a very tempting deal.

'I accept your terms, chieftain of the Catuvellauni' Caesar said suddenly and with a bright smile. 'In fact, I hope to seal them and arrange everything and be on our way by the time the sun sets tomorrow.'

As the Briton inclined his head gracefully, Caesar added with a sly smile 'I think it would be wise for us to put an ocean between us. I do not think the world is yet ready for a game played between two such men.'

Again, Cassivellaunus bowed, a curious smile playing across his lips.

Priscus heaved a sigh of relief. He had only been in Britannia for a few short weeks and already he was itching to be away from the place. Fronto had been right about the island in his gloomy appraisal.

Back to Gaul and to the endless rebellions…

* * * * *

Priscus scratched his head as his eyes bobbed around, following the motion of the vessels in the low water. Repaired on the beaches, the ships had only been run out into the water this morning - the morning of departure - to confirm their seaworthiness. To Priscus it seemed a little close to the event to check for leaks, but with the weather ready to turn at any time and twice experiencing the near-destruction of the fleet at the hands of Neptune, none of the officers was willing to risk leaving the ships floating at anchor for more than a few hours. Even then, the crews had stayed aboard in case they were needed.

'There are a lot less of them.'

Trebonius shook his head. 'Not really. A few perhaps. One benefit of taking down the fort is the extra timber for repairs. This past day another two ships were salvaged from the 'abandoned' pile. Given our losses there'll be plenty of room for the crossing.'

Priscus sighed and leaned on the post at the landward end of the temporary - rather flimsy looking to him - jetty that would be used for embarkation.

'Was this whole trip worth it?'

'In what way?' Trebonius turned with a frown.

'We've a guarantee that the most powerful tribes of Britannia won't involve themselves in Gallic affairs. From what I saw of that bastard Cassivellaunus, I doubt he would have involved himself anyway. I think he's trying to build his own empire here and sending his best warriors over the sea to help strangers would hardly aid that cause. Caesar think's it's a success, and so will the senate and the people of Rome, and the gods know most of the army think it's a success because they're getting out alive and they have slaves and a little booty. But the thing that irritates me is that I suspect the person it's been most successful for is Cassivellaunus. He's tightened his grip on his own land and essentially agreed a treaty of noninterference with Caesar. I have the distinct feeling we played into his hands from the start.'

'Doesn't matter if he's happy or not, so long as we have what we want. Now we can return to Gaul, get the legions in place for the winter and start preparing for your 'Gallic rising' that's in the offing.'

'I hope so. And I hope that we don't get back to find Gaul already in flames. You weren't here last year, but while the bulk of the army was across in Britannia, we had the shitty end of the sponge stick when the Morini decided they didn't want us any more. That was just one tribe and they're not even one of the more powerful ones, and the trouble they caused hardly bears thinking about. If people like the Aedui and the Treveri and the Arverni are in collusion we've got some real trouble on our hands.'

'First thing first' Trebonius sighed, slapping the wooden post next to him. 'Cross the sea again and reunite the legions. Then we can plan further. From what I've seen of Caesar, he probably has the next three moves in his game lined up.'

'Oh he's always ahead of the game. Problem is: sometimes he gets too far ahead for his own good. Fronto used to be able to haul him in and curb his more excessive ideas. I don't think anyone here these days can do that, so we just have to hope he knows what he's doing.'

He turned and scanned the camp with his eyes. Almost everything that labelled it a Roman military installation was now gone: the structures, the walls, the tents. Even most of the ditches had been backfilled. The men of the legions were gathered in their former camp sites, packing the last of their gear ready to fall in.

It was hard to see this as the site of a battle. Varus had taken command at the first sign of trouble and had done a good job keeping the attacking Cantiaci at bay. Of course, their attack had been a wary, careful one, more intent on causing damage and disruption than actually killing Romans, and yet still the casualty list had passed well into treble figures, with two centuries' worth of men dead. The charred site of their pyre was visible from here.

Priscus sighed.

It would be good to leave Britannia. And hopefully never come back.

Chapter Eleven

<u>**OCTOBRIS**</u>

Fronto staggered back across the peristyle garden and fell against the door to his father's 'special room', the strength in his legs buckling, hand shaking uncontrollably from the onslaught. Angrily, he pulled himself up next to the long-worn paint that warned he and his sister to keep out, and turned, reaching up to wipe away the blood flowing from his lip.

'You can't teach me like this! You cannot expect me to achieve the same skills as you. You're a decade and a half younger than me for a start; *and* you've been trained as a gladiator. I've been trained as a soldier. It's a whole different thing.'

Masgava bent forward and collected Fronto's fallen blade.

'This is pretty, but in the hands of the wrong man it is just an ornament.'

'Oh piss off. Yes, it's pretty. But it's a good, solid, military blade nonetheless. And I do know how to use it, and use it well. I've stuck one of those in so many Celts these past four years that I'm starting to see anyone with a moustache as a threat.'

'Then why this?' Masgava indicated the fact that Fronto was battered, bruised and slightly soiled and leaning against the door for support by pointing the fine blade at him.

'Because you've got me wielding the bloody thing in my left hand. I can barely wipe my arse convincingly with that hand.'

'Then you should learn.'

'Masgava, if I'm ever in the position where someone has taken my right arm off above the elbow, I won't really care about much other than bleeding out.'

'Short sighted view. You need to be able to use both hands, individually or together.'

Fronto sighed. He had to admit that Masgava's methods seemed to be having the right effect. He'd not been this fit since the last time he was in Hispania. His waistline was narrow, his arms muscular, his torso was beginning to mirror the bronze muscle cuirass he'd worn for years with lots of small muscular bulges instead of one large one below the diaphragm. Due to the Numidian's insistence on doing

227

everything outdoors he was actually achieving a healthy tan instead of the pasty paleness that had plagued him for decades and which Priscus had told him made him look more Celtic than the Gauls.

He was fit. He was strong. He was fast.

He was also still a dozen miles behind his teacher. No matter how heavy a weight he lifted, Masgava could lift him while holding it. No matter how fast he ran, Masgava was always waiting for him at the end. It was infuriating. And then there was the fighting. It was the only thing that Fronto felt he had ever mastered in his life, and yet he still felt like a boy waving a stick when facing the Numidian. The worst thing was that Masgava seemed to be taking a perverse pleasure in his student's failure and discomfort, while being paid for the privilege. Velius, the most infamous trainer the Tenth had ever had, was like a damn pussycat next to the big black-skinned killer.

'I just cannot get used to the left hand. I've had to do it a few times in desperation - in the heat of battle - but that's all taken care of by instinct and necessity and any success with it has been far more by luck than by judgement. In the legions the sword goes in the right hand and sits on the right hip. Not for me of course - officers don't carry shields, so our sword goes on the left hip, but it still doesn't matter whether the gods made you a rightie or a leftie, the sword goes in the right.'

Masgava's eyes narrowed. 'So you never used a shield?'

'Of course I did. When the situation both required and offered it.'

'So you have been forced to adjust your attack mode before.'

'Ye-es' Fronto replied hesitantly, not liking where this was going.

'So adjust again.'

'Easier said than done.'

'You've changed sword types easily enough. Even swung an axe with a certain sense that you felt natural with it. It cannot be much more difficult to train an off-hand with a familiar weapon than to train a regular hand with a new one?'

'Really? You think that?'

Masgava shrugged. 'I was trained with a knife in both hands before I grew hair upon my body. I can stitch a wound in my right arm with my left or vice versa. I have equal strength and speed in both, and only through training. By birth, I believe I was inclined to the left.'

'I won't tell you what my mother used to say about that. My great uncle Tullus was a leftie and he - well he enjoyed the company of pre-togate boys if you get my drift.'

'It matters not. The simple fact is that if I could unlearn and relearn, then so can you.'

'Your people were pretty tough by the sound of it. And anyway, you say you were trained with a knife in each hand. Well, a sword in both hands is a different matter entirely. It's not reliant upon my left alone, so compensation will be easier.'

The big Numidian nodded slowly in acceptance of the fact.

'Then we shall take two blades as our next step.'

Fronto stood, still breathing heavily from their most recent bout, and finally turned. Peering briefly at the faded words on the door, he crouched and scrabbled around in the flower bed, retrieving a key from some hidden location, which he inserted into the lock and turned, pushing open the door with a creak.

'Come on.'

The former gladiator, a fine sheen of exercise sweat covering his ebony skin, crossed the garden with an interested expression and followed Fronto into the gloomy interior. As their eyes adjusted, Masgava looked about in surprise. The room was only small, but well stocked. At the wall opposite the door four wooden torsos rested on stands, two clad in very high quality mail shirts, the other two in cuirasses of muscle-beaten bronze. A shelf above them on the wall held seven helmets of differing styles, some of which had gone out of fashion a century ago, and yet all were in perfect condition, polished and clean. One side wall held shelves that contained a variety of knives, swords and even two bows. But as Masgava took in the whole room with professional interest, it was to the fourth wall that Fronto crossed.

The bare plaster held only one item, hanging on a hook: a military style gladius, plain and business-like. Fronto unhooked it and brought it down, sliding the blade - nicked and well-used but also well-kept and in perfect condition - from the sheath, trying not to look at the inscription 'GN VERGINIO' embossed on the fine leather. Turning, he weighed it in his right hand, spinning it and twisting it.

It had been a while since he had held a normal military gladius, and yet it felt instantly natural; like an extension of his arm. The fine blade he had taken from a murderous tribune was theoretically no different, but its ignoble and grisly history made it feel more murderous than military and it would take a lot to right its wrongs. Besides, he'd had no call to wield a blade over the winter in the city.

He suddenly became aware that Masgava was watching him intently.

'Problem?'

'You have an armoury?'

'I do. Well, my *father* did. He felt it inappropriate to keep his military kit in the house, where the children could get to it, so he kept everything in this locked room off the garden - his stuff and that of various other family members. I never understood why he didn't just get rid of it all when he moved on from soldiering but this winter, now I've done the same, I think I understand why he liked to keep it around. It feels comfortable knowing it's there; like you've not properly left.'

Masgava wandered across the room and peered in the gloom at one of the cuirasses.

'This was yours?'

'My father's. The left hand one was mine.'

'Your father was a better soldier than you.'

Fronto blinked. 'I'm sorry?'

'There are fewer marks on his armour. You were hit a lot.'

'I stood in the press with my men. Dad just sat on a horse at the back. The same way I was always supposed to. You're a deadly man in the arena, but you've no experience of the army. In fact, I'd guess if you were little more than a boy when you were taken you've never experienced war?'

'I have fought a small army as part of a group at Carthage.'

'In the amphitheatre - with rigid organisation and rules. Carefully controlled. You've not experienced the chaos of war. You could put down any man I know, but facing me with a cohort at your back, I wouldn't wager a bent dupondius on you. It's a different game. You will always exceed me in your killing skills, but I could show you a thing or two about warfare.'

An uncomfortable silence fell over the courtyard, broken by a cough. Galronus had finished his bath and strolled out to watch the progress.

Masgava nodded in a business-like fashion. 'This sword means something to you.' A statement rather than a question.

Fronto looked at the former tribune's blade in the Numidian's hand. 'Yes. I told you. It killed-'

'No. That one.' A thick ebony finger gestured at the blade in Fronto's hand.

'Sort of. It belonged to a friend a long time ago.' He almost dropped the blade as Masgava tossed the other gladius over to him, forcing him to juggle for a moment with sharpened edges until he had one in each hand.

'Now you will show me how you handle two weapons and I will judge your left.'

* * * * *

Fronto lit the oil lamp in the tablinum and sank into one of the seats, reaching for the jug of fruit juice Masgava made sure he always had once he'd cleaned up from training. The room flickered with an orange glow as darkness took hold outside. With an aching arm Fronto tipped the juice into the glass beaker before him and stared at the deep red result. Galronus, at his side, smiled with startled surprise as he reached for the small snack bowls.

'Masgava?'

'I thought you trained well today. You deserve a treat.'

Fronto was too overcome with relief and gratitude to complain at being treated like a child.

'Besides,' the big man went on with a wide grin, 'since I've tipped the rest of your secret stash into the sewer, I thought you might want to make the most of your last jug.'

Galronus burst out laughing while the fires of ire flickered in Fronto's eyes, but he was simply too weary to fight now. That was a battle he would wage tomorrow when he felt fresh. He took a sip of the neat wine, savouring its thick, sweet, heady taste and sat back.

'Tell me how you ended up in the arena.'

Masgava fixed him with a dark look and then helped himself to a glass of the wine, watering it to a half and half mixture. 'Why?'

'Indulge me. There's only the three of us in the house for days on end and Galronus and I already know one another well.'

The gladiator's expression softened and he shrugged. 'It is not an exciting story.'

'And...?'

'There was a fight between my tribe and our neighbours when I was a boy. They won, and to make sure their mastery was complete they sold all the king's family and the tribal elders to Roman slavers. I had begun to learn the way of the blades and so Largus sold me on to a Lanista in Utica.'

'You were of a royal line?' Galronus asked with interest, reminding Fronto out of the blue that the Remi warrior was himself a prince of his tribe.

'Well I wasn't one of the elders.' He sighed. 'I was a distant sister-son. Peripheral at best, which is why I was sold off to die and not kept in case I was valuable.'

'Did the slaver teach you Latin or did you learn it in the ludus?' Fronto asked curiously. 'It's almost flawless, which is unusual for a man without his letters.'

'I was always clever. *Too clever*, my father used to say. But regardless, I knew Latin long before I was taken in chains; Greek too. You will find many ordinary merchants in Numidia that do so let alone nobles. The world is full of buyers for our kilim and other crafts, but there are few merchants operating south of the sea who are not Roman or Greek. They are the languages of trade.'

Fronto nodded his understanding. 'Starting tomorrow I'm going to teach you to read and write in Latin and Greek as well.'

'I may not wish to learn.'

'Then you're not as clever as you think you are.'

An uncomfortable silence fell across the room, broken finally by Masgava. 'Tell me about the army.'

Fronto frowned. 'Big subject.'

'You said this afternoon that as much as I could teach you about fighting, you could teach me about warfare.'

'Wait a moment. I'm paying you to train me, and I'm going to teach you your letters, and now you want me to teach you soldiering too? Just who hired who here?'

Masgava shrugged. 'I told you I don't care about reading or writing. Tell me about the army instead.'

'A whole lifetime of military experience isn't something I can pass on in a month.'

The big Numidian leaned back and relaxed into his seat. 'In the past ten weeks you have become a warrior again. You still have a lot to learn, but you no longer need to build muscle; now you have only to keep it - to train little and often. Now it is all about acquiring skills, and your regime should change accordingly. We will have more free time and you are house-bound anyway. Teach me.'

Galronus gestured with a glass. 'I can help too, Marcus. Might be fun, since we're both missing the life.'

Fronto frowned. It seemed like a waste of time and he had little idea of how to begin, but they were right, really. It was not as if they had much else to occupy them.

'Alright then' he said, placing his glass on the floor beside him with a clink and swiping the table clear of miscellanea, handing the various dishes and platters to the others. Dipping his finger in his wine, he drew two wavering lines across the table. 'These are the rivers Lureta and Trebia.' Swiping a handful of pine nuts he began arranging them on one side in piles. After some shuffling and apparently satisfied with the results, he scoured the nibbles Masgava had produced. Settling with a frown on a bowl of olives, he arranged them on the other side.

'Alright. We might as well start now, and this'll be good for you too, Galronus. Strategy is of prime importance in any military engagement and is harder to pick up than the technical side. We'll start with a cautionary tale. The olives are the Roman force of Longus. The nuts are Hannibal and Mago. This, gentlemen, is a cautionary tale...'

* * * * *

Balbus sat in the 'Grapevine Tavern' with his back to the cold brick wall, wondering why in the name of Vulcan the proprietor insisted on having a roaring fire going on one of the hottest days of the year. He had already removed his toga and sat in just his tunic and sandals, flapping the hem up and down beneath the table occasionally to waft air round his warmer parts. Beads of sweat trickled down his forehead from the sparse, greying hair.

For the past hour he had sat here alternating a well-watered dry Alban wine - a surprisingly quality find in such a place - with cups of barley water to keep cool and hydrated. Corvinia and Balbina were in the market doing the endless rounds of fabric stalls and jewellery traders. The effort had become too much for the ageing ex-soldier and after only a quarter of an hour or so he had removed himself to his favourite tavern in the subura, only a short walk from the forum, where Corvinia knew to find him once she had finished. It was a comfortable arrangement and one that had been going on for some time.

On the table before him, next to the nearly-empty cup, sat a coin: a denarius of Aemilius Scaurus. Issued in the year of the consuls Piso and Gabinius - the very year Caesar took the Eighth and marched them under Balbus' command into Gaul. Funny how it seemed so long ago now. It had been two years since he'd even served in the army.

His mind turned once more to the subject he'd been contemplating the past hour.

Fronto.

The man - along with Galronus and the pet gladiator - had been holed up inside the Falerii house on the Aventine for a month now. Occasionally the Gaul or the Numidian left to stock up on food and drink, but as far as Balbus was aware Fronto himself had not left the building at all.

Upon hearing tell of the endless string of accusations Pompey's people had leveled at the Falerii, and as the man's father-in-law, Balbus had taken it upon himself to visit Fronto as soon as possible. He had been met at the door by Galronus, who had explained in no uncertain terms that he was to visit no more. When pressed, the Remi noble - who had served with Balbus and considered him a friend - had explained unhappily that close association with Fronto in these trying times was a dangerous proposition and that Fronto wished to keep his friends at a distance for their own preservation. Balbus had argued that he could hardly appear disassociated given their familial connection, but Galronus had been adamant, apparently at the insistence of Fronto.

It had been a surprise to learn that Lucilia and Faleria had gone south to Puteoli and it was that more than anything that led to Balbus acquiescing and accepting Fronto's decision. If the former legate of the Tenth - a man who was no stranger to peril - felt the danger strong enough to send away the women, then Balbus should respect that.

But it had been a month! A *month*!

For the past few days Balbus had been toying with the idea of another visit. Despite the accusations leveled by Pompey, little was coming of any of them, most being disproved or turned aside by Galba and other cronies in the government of the city, and the general seemed to be losing some of his driving ire as the reality of

234

the situation settled on him. Though his anger had been earth-shaking, it had now in large part given way to grief and he rarely left his own house, echoing Fronto's lack of activity half a city away. The defamation of Fronto's character and that of his family continued, though now under the supervision of lesser men on Pompey's behalf. Soon enough it would end and things might be able to get back to normal.

Now might be the time to visit Fronto again and try and talk the recluse out of his square brick shell.

A surge of noise outside drew his attention for a moment. Though it was loud, it was some way off and merited little more than casual interest. It was a sad state of affairs in such a once-great city that civil disobedience and random acts of violence and unpleasantness had so become the norm that few men even looked up from their drink unless it turned into a riot. And riots were more common than festivals these days.

Too many thugs with gangs and too many power-hungry politicians pulling their strings. Rome had become a board for a massive game of stones that was played just to decide which would-be despot had the biggest balls.

'To Hades with the lot of them.'

'What was that?' asked a former legionary sat at the next table, still in his military tunic and boots.

'Oh nothing' Balbus replied. He'd not even realised he had said it out loud.

'Sounds like there's trouble' the veteran at the next table said conversationally.

'Isn't there always these days?'

'I'll drink to that. When I signed up the only fighting was against bearded Pontic and Armenian megalomaniacs.'

Balbus wondered for a moment why so little deference was being paid to him by a plebeian soldier, but remembered that he had removed his toga. A quick glance down confirmed that his own tunic was a mere plain green. He could as easily have been a pleb himself as a noble officer.

'You served out east? Under Pompey?' he asked casually.

'Lucullus. You?'

'Caesar. In Gaul.'

'Shit. You're lucky. At least you got green fields. They say Gaul's verdant. I was out in bloody Armenia. All mountains and dust. Like living in your own armpit, it was.'

Balbus chuckled and realised that the man was hovering over an empty cup. Reaching across with the jug from his table, he poured a healthy dose of wine for the soldier and slid his jug of water over.

'Cheers, mate. Got more cash, but it's at home. Only three streets away, but Milo's lot are out there today roughing people up and I'm buggered if I'm running that gauntlet for a cup of wine.'

'Milo?' Balbus frowned.

'Yeah. It's always either his or Clodius' men. Or occasionally both lots of bastards at once. Best to keep your head down and stay indoors. It's about time the big nobs sent those pricks off to fight in the wars. That's keep 'em busy.'

'I'll second that' Balbus agreed, taking a swig of wine.

'Sacred shit of Vesta!'

Balbus snapped up from his drink at the outburst from across the tavern. A bunch of lunchtime drinkers were staring at the door and pointing fingers. Following their gaze, Balbus saw a girl in a pale yellow chiton, covered with blood. As he watched, the innkeeper's wife ran across to the girl, cooing soothing noises that were somewhat spoiled by the desperate, panicked edge to her voice.

'Come, girl. Tell me what happened?'

The girl stumbled across from the door, her blood matted hair slapping against her face and leaving crimson trails. As she grabbed a table corner to straighten herself and fell into the woman's ample bosom, her hair fell away to the side.

Balbus felt his heart freeze.

'*Balbina?*'

'You know this poor tyke, sir?' the bar-woman asked, her gaze switching to the big old man with the strangely military bearing who was already rushing across the room.

Balbus said nothing. He was not ignoring the woman - even managed a faint nod - but his voice seemed to have dried up and died. His whole body had chilled to freezing point and his heart felt like a ballista ball, weighing down his frame.

The girl, perhaps concussed, turned to face him, her eyes glazed. She looked confused for a moment and then Balbus was on her, scooping her up from the woman, taking care not to put any pressure on her. She must be hurt. Her arms and legs seemed to move freely and in the right direction, but that confirmed only an absence of broken bones. Carrying her pressed to his chest, he returned to the table. The former legionary had swept aside his wine and was on his feet now, hurrying across to help. Balbus waved him away, so the man hovered close by, unsure what to do as he watched the distraught father cradling his daughter.

'Where are you hurt, baby girl?'

Still no sound issued from Balbina and, as gently as he could, her father prised her mouth open with his fingers, fearing what he might see. Her tongue was still there and intact and her neck had no marks. Shock or concussion, probably. Reaching up, he ran his fingers through her hair. Sure enough he found a soft, sticky patch on her crown. It was enough to hurt a grown man, let alone a girl of Balbina's age. But she seemed whole, if silent; just dazed. There certainly wasn't enough physical damage there to account for all the blood.

For the second time in a few short moments, Balbus' heart skipped a beat and gained a little weight. His cold body plummeted into an abyss of ice.

Corvinia!

The legionary had torn a piece from the hem of his tunic and was proffering it for Balbus to mop the wound. The old man suddenly seemed to register the soldier's presence, focusing on the rag. Turning to the man, he tried to speak, his voice only finding any volume on the third attempt.

'What's your name soldier?'

'Palmatus.'

'Look after her like she's your own!'

The soldier's eyes widened as the big man gently passed his daughter over, and Palmatus cradled her like a baby as she stared blankly at the ceiling. He stuttered out a reply to the effect that she would be his only concern, but the stranger was already gone, running out of the bar.

It was only after he'd gone that Palmatus saw the toga folded up on the seat next to where he had been sitting and the purse of money attached to a very fine military belt that could only belong to a senior officer. Swallowing nervously, the former legionary crossed to the other table and took Balbus' seat, keeping the officer's gear under close scrutiny.

Outside, Balbus was running. Tears filled his eyes and blurred his view of the subura's lower streets as he made for the forum and the source of all the noise. He didn't *need* to see clearly. He'd walked this route a hundred times and more to meet up with Corvinia and Balbina after their shopping trips.

There were, of course, a thousand explanations for the uproar in the forum. Just as there were so many possible causes for the damage his beautiful, delicate little girl had suffered. But even had he the time and the inclination to consider them at this point, he would inevitably have arrived at the same conclusion: Corvinia had been hurt, and badly. Badly enough for Balbina to run for the safety of her father even with a debilitating head wound. Many battle-hardened legionaries did not have the presence of mind and the inner strength to act so when dazed from a blow.

Little Balbina.

And Corvinia.

Rounding the corner of the tabernae nova, the former legate of the Eighth cast his gaze around the forum's open space. Crowds of bystanders had gathered on the steps of various buildings and in groups around the periphery, where they could indulge their ghoulish need to observe grisly events yet were far enough removed to be uninvolved and to disperse swiftly if necessary.

His eyes took them in only in passing as his gaze fell upon the focus of the forum's attention.

A small group of half a dozen folk stood at the corner of the temple of Janus, close to the building's south door. It was clear from their stance that they were gathered around something on the floor and with ice-cold certainty, Balbus knew what it was.

His feet, clad in very military style sandal boots, pounded across the flags of the forum, striking up sparks with the nails in the soles and he slowed only as he approached the concerned crowd.

Sensing something important and seeing the look on the big man's face, the men and women who had gathered opened up to allow the new visitor access.

A man crouched over Corvinia's body. He wore a long, loose-fitting grey tunic in a very Levantine style, an origin confirmed by the hair and beard that marked out the man as a Jew. Corvinia's head rested upon a folded robe of the same pale grey. Balbus tried to speak, but his voice seemed to have shrivelled once more.

Corvinia looked so peaceful. She might easily have been in repose if one saw her from only the diaphragm up. Balbus' eyes fell to the ragged hole in her front, just at the base of the ribs, and the blood that soaked her lower half, spreading out in a pool around her prone form.

One blow. Struck by a man who knew how to kill and do it quickly and efficiently.

Finally, his voice seemed to well up, buoyed on a tide of anger that was colder than the fear which had preceded it.

'Who did this?'

In a thick accent, the Jew - clearly a new arrival to the city - spoke as he stroked Corvinia's hair. 'No one saw. She was among the crowd.'

'*Someone* saw.' Balbus' gaze flicked up to the watching masses, narrowing. Deep in his heart he knew well enough that no one would admit to having seen anything. To witness a crime was to become involved, and the plebs and nobles of the forum wanted only their ghoulish look at what was going on - not to become involved. Besides, if the soldier back in the tavern was right and the forum had been the playground of Milo's men today, even a good and honest citizen would think twice before crossing such a gang.

'She passed very quickly and without too much pain' the Jew said quietly.

Balbus blinked and stared at him. 'The blood!'

'The blow cleaved the heart. Death was only moments in coming. She did not have time to speak, let alone to suffer; trust me - I trained as a physician. God's blessings shall be upon her.'

Balbus shook his head, tears starting to fall.

'She never hurt anyone.'

'An innocent is the hardest passing to bear' the man said sagely, drawing an angry look from Balbus. The urge to flail out at this calm man reciting platitudes passed as quickly as it came. Despite the pain, the anger and the fear, Balbus could still recognise a man doing his best - a man who had taken care of her even as she died.

Stooping, the former legate gathered his wife in his arms and rose with a grunt, Corvinia's lifeless arm swinging down loose until the Jew reached across and lifted it to fold it across her chest.

'For its worth, you have my sympathy. Though it is not my custom, I placed a perutah under her tongue. I trust you will not be offended by this?'

239

Unable to find a suitable reply, Balbus simply nodded curtly. For a long moment, he stared down at the calm face of his wife. The Jew had closed her eyes. The former legate was trembling lightly. As he drank in that peaceful visage, he felt himself torn in two.

On the one hand a good husband and father - something Balbus had always prided himself upon being - would take Corvinia to her home, collecting Balbina on the way, and care for the women, bringing friends and relatives in to help, calling upon physicians and priests. There would be so much to do - so many things to attend to, and the organisation of the household and any tasks associated had always been the responsibility of Corvinia.

On the other hand, despite his love for his family and his almost legendary calm, Quintus Lucilius Balbus was also a soldier - a warrior and a veteran, who had waded knee deep through fields of the dead and dying. Two decades had hardened him into a man who could detach from the horror of reality and surrender himself to the guided rage and the single-mind of purpose that was required to take lives without considering their value.

'What is your name?'

'I am Elijah of Beth Horon, sir.'

'Will you help me?'

'My hands are yours.'

As Elijah held out his arms, Balbus nodded his gratitude and gently dropped Corvinia into his grasp. 'I must find my daughter and take them home. Then I must call a council of war.'

* * * * *

Titus Annius Milo stood in the shelter of the doorway of the temple of Castor and Pollux and watched Balbus and the easterner depart from the north edge of the forum, toward the subura. Pinching the bridge of his nose, he shook his head.

'Did you see who struck the blow?'

His lieutenant - a dour Abbrutian called Servo with a crooked, broken nose - shook his head. 'Not one of ours as far as I can tell.'

'It matters not. The blame with land with us - with me. Do you know who that is?'

'An old, fat man.'

'He is an old, fat, *dangerous* man, who commanded the Eighth Legion across Gaul. Lucilius Balbus. A friend of Fronto's and a man of Caesar's.'

'Then it serves a good purpose in the long run.'

Milo turned to the Abbrutian. He was an able controller of thugs and a tough fighter, but what he had gained from the gods in strength, he had lost in sense.

'Hardly. War is not what we want. It's what we're likely to get, though, now. Shame really. I rather liked Fronto. Fought side by side with him a few years ago. Funny how things work out.'

He sighed and rolled his shoulders. 'Best report this to Pompey. He'll want to know.'

* * * * *

Gnaeus Pompeius Magnus sat in his tablinum, tapping his fingers on his knees. His face showed the signs of numerous sleepless nights and his unshaven chin was rapidly approaching 'bearded' status. Though he had recently become something of a recluse, beset by his grief, he had at least kept up his bathing and dressing as fitted such a powerful figure, rather than surrendering himself to slovenliness the way some distressed widowers did. A hard hearted man might say that having previously lost two wives to divorce and one to Elysium, he'd had some prior experience in these matters.

'Is it worth us making it publically known that we had no part in her death?'

Pompey shrugged and turned in his seat to face Milo. 'Doubtful. With the current political climate it is unlikely to make you look any less guilty, but it may give you an additional reputation for weakness and indecision. Better to be seen as harsh and wicked but certain than forgiving and weak. Given our recent political campaign against the Falerii - fruitless as it has been - and Balbus' closeness to the family, this will be seen as a personal attack by myself, whatever is announced in public.'

Milo nodded. He had come to much the same conclusion, though it was always best to allow the general to make the decisions. 'Then is it perhaps in our interests to pursue your campaign further.'

'Against Fronto?'

241

'Yes, general. Your pet politicians and lawyers have failed to push through any of their actions against him. Perhaps it is time to use force?'

Pompey shook his head slowly. 'For all my invective against Fronto and his sister, I will not commission *deaths* for my own gain. I am a master of Rome not a common criminal and, since you and your men are known to be solidly within my camp, I can hardly authorise you to move against the Falerii and their allies in any fashion. No. I need you to concentrate on keeping that weasel Clodius and his thugs busy. Since taking Caesar's patronage, the villain is proving far more resourceful than he ever was when he worked for me.'

Milo nodded again. Clodius' gang was a constant niggle. The man was wily and careful, never leaving the safety of his favourite haunts without a sizeable bodyguard.

'Leave me.'

Milo gave a curt bow and backed out through the atrium. Pompey waited a short while until he heard the sound of the enforcer and his escort being ushered out into the street. Another pause, as he listened to his heart pounding in his chest - a rhythmic noise that seemed to be the soundtrack to his life now that Julia had been taken.

'You can come out, now.'

A moment of silence passed before the hulking form of Berengarus the German appeared from the garden, where he had been waiting.

'You heard?'

The colossal man-mountain nodded.

'You may have caused me considerable trouble, you great northern oaf. Slaves do not perform tasks without their master's permission!'

'He friend of Fronto.'

'I realise, Berengarus, that for all your enormous size and prodigious strength, your mind is an under-developed muscle, but you really need to apply just a little thought from time to time, or at least listen to the wisdom of others.'

The big man frowned in incomprehension.

'I wished to visit upon the house of the Falerii my displeasure at their part in the death of my wife and child. While the physicians inform me that the infusion she took was not the *cause* of her death, they do suspect that it may well have weakened her enough for

242

nature to take its distressing course. In my heart I know that the beak-nosed pleb-lover Caesar put them up to this, but I can hardly reach out across the hundreds of miles to Gaul and strangle the man, and so I am left with Fronto and his witch of a sister.'

The frown stayed solidly in place on that big, blond Germanic brow. Pompey sighed and went on. 'Simply put: my wrath was directed at the pair for their part in it; not at their extended family or friends. I am not trying to wage war on half of Rome.'

Again, the big man simply shook his head.

'Are you truly too dense to grasp such a simple concept? Fronto and his sister. No one else. And even then, by acceptable, civic means. No murdering innocent women in the forum. I have no intention of sinking to their level. I'm of half a mind that even pursuing the pair of them is little more than a fool's errand, and I do not wish my name blackened in public by involvement in brutal unlawful killings.'

'Fronto must die.'

The general looked up at the barbarian. There was such a determined conviction in the big face, and the simple three-word sentence had carried such bile and venom that Pompey once again found himself picturing the vicious battle that had taken place four years earlier when the giant's family had perished: a wife scythed down with a cavalry blade; a son drifting, cold and blue-grey beneath the choppy surface of the wide river. For all their differences, were he and the barbarian really that different? The German sought revenge from the man he saw as responsible - or one of the men at least.

'The man is a soldier, you know? Resourceful and strong. He will be no easy target.'

'Must die.'

Pompey took a deep breath. 'I sought to ruin them, you know? Not to kill them. While I sympathise with your plight, I refuse to condone such actions. To have any man in my employ, be he freedman or slave, commit simple murder is unacceptable. Do you understand?'

With no sign of acknowledgement, the huge warrior simply stood and glowered.

'You truly desire nothing other than to destroy Fronto?'

A single nod.

'And you believe you can do it?'

Another nod.

'Then gather your things.'

This time, the big man frowned again and Pompey took a deep breath and sat back.

'You cannot be part of my household if you are to hunt and kill a Roman citizen. Gather your things and return here. I will have the felt hat brought out for you - to mark your manumission. Only a freedman will have the liberty to engage in such a hunt. I will have your status logged with the officials at the tabularium and gift you a small sum to help you on your way.'

Berengarus narrowed his eyes.

'For the love of Venus. I am freeing you, you big thug, so that you can do what you must. Now go and get ready!'

* * * * *

Fronto staggered back across the gravel, nimbly jumping the small pool in the garden's centre and landing on the far side, appreciating more than ever the growing strength in his previously bad knee.

Masgava was on him straight away, forcing him back among the plants, where he grasped the branches of a willow, using the trunk to keep the big Numidian at bay.

'Fronto!'

Shifting his eyes, his attention was distracted just long enough, and the flat of Masgava's blade rapped on his knuckles hard enough to make him drop the sword.

'Do not allow yourself to be distracted.'

Fronto glared at him as he rubbed the painful knuckles and then turned to the doorway into the garden where Galronus stood, waving an arm.

'What?'

'It's Balbus.'

'Tell him to go away. You know what to do.'

'I don't think so, Fronto.'

The former legate of the Tenth looked up past the shoulder of his Remi friend to see Balbus emerge from the shadows. The look on his face immediately alerted Fronto to the fact that something dreadful had happened. He was already rushing across the garden when

244

another figure appeared behind Balbus: a grubby, unshaven ex-soldier by the looks of him, who Fronto didn't recognise.

'Quintus?'

'They've gone too far, Fronto.'

'What?'

'Pompey. Milo. They've gone too far.'

'Quintus, what's happened?'

Balbus stumbled past him and out into the sunlight of the garden. Fronto frowned at Galronus, who simply shrugged. His eyes shifted to the retired legionary, who looked distinctly uncomfortable.

'What happened?'

The soldier took a deep steadying breath. 'The officer's wife. She was attacked in the forum.'

Fronto felt his heart skip. 'Corvinia? Is she alright?'

'Dead, Fronto' replied Balbus in a flat tone, turning in the garden. 'A single sword stroke to the heart. I thought for a while that Balbina had been attacked too, but Elijah says he believes she fell and hit her head while coming to find me. She won't talk, though. She's broken, Marcus. My little girl is *broken*!'

Fronto shook his head. 'Who's Elijah?' He shook his head. 'Doesn't matter. Ignore that. Are you sure it was Milo?'

'Who else? His men were all over the forum. It was no robbery, but an intentional death. They took my Corvinia, Marcus. I came here... didn't know what else to do.'

'Of course. We'll look after things' Fronto said quietly, reaching out to grip his friend's shoulder. Balbus pulled away.

'I'm not here for sympathy, Fronto. I'm here to recruit.'

'What?'

'Pompey wants war? Then Pompey can *have* war. You and I know soldiering, and between us we have money to hire enough men.'

'Quintus, don't be daft. I'm sorry. I know it sounds harsh, but Pompey's retreated into his house like a recluse. He's all-but stopped hassling me and Faleria, barring a few ridiculous suits that'll be bouncing around the courts for months yet. I was even considering calling the girls back from Puteoli. Things are settling down, so I'm not sure that whatever happened - however horrible - was Pompey's doing.'

Behind him someone cleared their throat, and Fronto turned to see the former legionary scratching his head. 'With respect, sir, I'm not sure that's the case. I'm pretty sure someone's watching you both.'

'What?'

'Well sir, I helped the legate here take the lady back to his house and we sorted things out with that Jewish feller and... well to cut a long story short, it was about two and a half hours before we set off over here. I can't exactly pinpoint it, but I've been in enough shitty situations in my life to recognise when I'm being followed. Someone was behind us all the way here. And when we got here this big heap of hairy shit about nine feet tall was standing on the far side of the street. He wandered off as soon as we arrived, but I'll tell you for free that he was watching your door.'

Fronto rubbed his chin, bristly and sweaty from his exertions. The description was fairly vague, but could only really be describing one person in Rome.

'This is getting ridiculous. I left service to Caesar because of all the mistrust, in-fighting, backstabbing and general lunacy and thought to retire back to Rome or Puteoli and get married and everything would sort itself out; become straightforward. Instead, it just gets all the more complicated and I start to find out that there are people in this city alone that make Caesar look like a paragon of virtue.'

With a deep breath and a shake of his head, he narrowed his eyes at the former legionary.

'You. I don't know what your name is, but take care of Balbus. He knows where everything's kept, though you'll be damned lucky if you find any wine. Keep him safe.'

The man nodded and stepped out into the garden. Balbus, his bleak face suddenly concerned, turned. 'Where are you going, Marcus?'

'A quiet word with the great Pompey. Galronus? Masgava? You two are with me.'

* * * * *

'The dominus is not accepting visitors.'

Fronto took a step closer until his nose was a hand-breadth from the doorman's face. 'He's accepting this one. Get out of the way.'

Behind him, Masgava and Galronus crept forward a pace, adding an air of menace. While the Remi chief was unarmed, there was still

246

an aura of violence surrounding him. The Numidian gladiator held a seven foot staff, shod with iron.

'Forgive me, sir, but I am not at liberty to flout my orders.'

A face appeared in the gloom of the entry hall, visible over the slave's shoulder. Pompey had a naked gladius tight in his grip as he stood calm and steady. His toga was immaculate.

'Step aside, Aeropus.'

The slave pushed the door wide and stepped behind it, revealing the entrance hall. As Fronto took an angry step inside the doorway, he became aware that other figures were moving in the shadows of doorways to the sides. While not as menacing as the two men at his shoulders, he counted at least six. Pompey took no chances; and being in a private residence and not on the streets they were not subject to the law against weapons. Blades flashed in the gloom.

'You've a nerve, Fronto.'

'Cut the horse shit, Pompey. You've been unravelling like a badly-woven blanket for more than a month now and I could see from the start that you were capable of some rough moves, but I need you to look me in the eye right now and tell me you aren't responsible for Corvinia's death.'

Pompey's face, impassive, shifted slightly into a sneer as he drew a deep breath to speak.

'And don't tell me you don't know who she is or hadn't heard' snapped Fronto.

'I was going to do nothing of the sort. I will place my hand - metaphorically - on the altar of Apollo and tell you that I am not responsible for her death. I wish the Lucilii no harm. I wouldn't waste the curse tablets - they all have your family name on them.'

'And Milo and his thugs?'

'Milo and his men were uninvolved. Indeed it was he who apprised me of the matter, fearing I would suffer culpability.'

Fronto peered deep into Pompey's eyes and was surprised to find no sign of duplicity. Suddenly unsure of what to do next, he paused, and then recalled the thing that had spurred him into the visit in the first place.

'And what of your big Germanic monster? Where is *he*, or have you still got him out spying on me?'

'Berengarus?' Pompey asked lightly. 'I'm afraid you'd have to ask him that. I logged his manumission this morning. He is a free man no longer attached to my house. But I do know that he has something of a personal grudge against you, so if I were you I would find a good stout cellar to hide in until you grow old and die.'

Fronto's eyes widened. 'You freed that animal?'

'Yes. He'd served his purpose. I suspect he's to his own agenda now.'

Masgava and Galronus were already backing away as Fronto stepped out of the door once more. 'You're insane, Pompey.'

'I anticipate news of your ending with relish, Fronto. Now unless you have other business with me, get away from my house and stop littering my step with your odious presence!'

Chapter Twelve

'I am reconsidering the disposition of the officers, Priscus.'

The legate of the Tenth rolled his eyes, sure that his lowered face hid the gesture from the general. 'A tough job, sir.'

'I am very well aware of that. I have spent the past hour closeted away with my lists.'

'The past hour?' thought Priscus. Since the army had arrived at the shores of Gaul the previous night and travelled uneventfully back to Gesoriacum to meet up with the Roman garrison, the general had spent the entire time in his headquarters, alone apart from occasional meetings that lasted but a few moments. Perhaps the general's voluntary solitude and his staccato attempts at organisation had something to do with the missive that had been awaiting them on their return and which still sat, furled but well-read, on the table before him amid the lists.

'Firstly, this matter with the Carnutes' Caesar announced, his grey-shadowed eyes roving across the map on the table. 'I am of a mind to send a single legion into their territory. Do you concur?'

Priscus nodded easily. News had reached Gesoriacum only the day before the fleet returned that the pro-Roman chieftain of the Carnutes - a man who had served well commanding auxiliaries and who had been supported in his bid for power among his tribe by Caesar - had been executed in the most appalling manner by his contemporaries. Though some flimsy excuse as to the cause had been bandied about, there was little doubt in either of the men at this table that it had been anything other than yet another piece being moved into place by the druids in their ongoing anti-Roman campaign.

'I think so, general. The chances are that the Carnutes are shifting away from allegiance with us, but there's no proof as yet. Sending in a legion for the winter will make a statement and should help keep things under control. It should hamper any efforts to raise the tribe further against us. Plus they can let us know the full situation and there will be other legions in northern Gaul and Belgae lands to move to their support if need be.'

He cleared his throat. 'In fact, general, given the likelihood that winter quarters will be quite widely dispersed this year, I think we would do well to make sure that every legion has another within at most a couple of days march for support.'

'Agreed.'

'Who are you thinking of sending to the Carnutes, general?'

'Plancus.'

'*Plancus*?' Priscus tried not to spit the name. He was in the general's tent after all.

'Yes. Lucius Munatius Plancus.'

'Are you sure that's wise, Caesar. He's not the most practical of men.'

The general gave a cock-eyed hollow smile. 'Perhaps not. But given the state of my officer lists, I would point out that he is now one of my longest serving legates and has had several years observing the state of the tribes in Gaul. He is perhaps not a stable battle officer but I believe in a more political role, he could prove his worth. However, the Fourteenth are not strong - not a veteran legion. I need to give him a battle-hardened legion against the possibility that things turn ugly. I think perhaps the Seventh. They've seen a lot of action, and their tribunes are unusually sharp and effective.'

Priscus nodded slowly, unhappily. 'If you say so, general. I worry about what Plancus will do to the Seventh. I hope you're right.'

'I appreciate your candour, Priscus, but while your tongue wags so, try to remember to whom you are speaking.'

'My apologies, general.'

Caesar nodded and brushed the conversation aside. 'To allay your fears, I will send a cavalry detachment with Plancus under the command of Varus. He will have all the support he needs. The next issue is the Belgae and the eastern reaches, toward the Rhenus and the Germanic peoples beyond. We have already had trouble with the Treveri this year. What is your opinion of them?'

'Easy, general. I would sooner trust a Syrian whore to be pox-free than any of that lot. We put your man back in control, but I wouldn't be at all surprised to find he's already been off'ed in the night and the tribe starting to rise. I'll bet there's a thousand Germans already in the Arduenna forest waiting for word to start eating Romans.'

'Agreed. We need to concentrate the army in the northeast. There have been few noises from the tribes of Aquitania or Armorica and we have limited resources. So we make sure to cover all the areas of known trouble.'

'If that's the plan, Caesar, then despite their past pledges to us, we should send a force to the Aedui lands. Dumnorix, before he died this summer, named his brother Divitiacus as a co-conspirator, and that puts the entire Aedui tribe into doubt. Also, given their size and power and that of the Arverni who are only a javelin-throw to the west from there, we'd be remiss to ignore them.'

Caesar shifted his wax tablets and peered at his map, spread across the table.

'You are entirely correct. Again: one legion. Roscius?'

Priscus bit his lip. 'The Thirteenth aren't as long-standing veterans as some.' He grasped the tablet with the legion lists. 'But then they are Gallic blooded. They might be more useful there than anyone else.'

'So' Caesar said, moving small markers with legion numbers etched onto their face across the map, 'Roscius and the Thirteenth babysitting the Aedui; and the man is a good officer with field experience so no need to support him. Plancus and the Seventh doing the same with the Carnutes, supported by Varus and his cavalry in case of trouble.'

Priscus nodded as he peered at the map. 'That looks workable. They will be close enough to support one another too, if trouble arises.'

'I intend to leave a third legion in Gesoriacum to maintain our port garrison and control over the Morini. They have proved duplicitous before and it would do no harm to have a legion within reach of Armorica.'

'Brutus' Eighth, sir?'

'The Eighth' Caesar confirmed, moving the 'VIII' marker to their current position on the map. 'I am, however, putting Brutus in overall command of the garrison, the port and the navy, as well as the cavalry contingent we leave there. That means I will need to assign a legate to the legion itself. What of the two men who arrived yesterday?'

Priscus cast his mind back to the two men he'd seen sitting in the mess hall, talking quietly. They had reached Gesoriacum only an hour before the returning force from Britannia and looked to Priscus woefully ill-prepared for the world of Gaul. The only two officers who had yet answered Caesar's summons, the older of the two - still little more than a boy himself - appeared to be a quiet, studious character with unruly hair and a squint. The other? Well the other, for all his youth, appeared to be focused almost to the point of being dangerously taut. That, however, was not what worried Priscus. The worrying thing was his lineage.

'The younger Crassus seems perilously eager. Brutus would have his hands full just keeping Crassus under control, I think. He seems to lack the discipline of his father or brother, and that very thought frightens the shi… worries me a lot, general.'

'So Gaius Fabius?'

'He's such a boyish, academic looking sort.'

'So was Crispus until Fronto got to work on him, and he turned out a fine officer.'

Both men fell silent for a moment at the memory of the poor, murdered academic. Priscus wondered whether Fronto had read his letter yet. Gods help Rome when he did.

'Fabius, then. At least he looks like he'll take Brutus' advice. The two should be able to work together and Gesoriacum will be safe. What will you do with Cicero if he's not commanding the Seventh?'

'I think: the Eleventh. Up here? Among the Nervii?'

Priscus nodded and watched as the 'XI' counter slid up to the north coast. 'At least he's solid and shouldn't need watching.'

'You may be correct, Priscus, in that he seems to have stopped exhorting me to change my mind every few moments. But just in case I think we'll transfer the two senior centurions with him from the Seventh. Pullo and Vorenus have kept Cicero at the top of his game so far. Let's let them continue to do so.'

Priscus frowned.

'You've a problem there from the start. Felix is the primus pilus of the Eleventh and has been since they were raised against the Helvetii. He's a good man. But Pullo's also been primus pilus for over a year - though he's been shifted from the Thirteenth to the Seventh already. You can't move him to the Eleventh and demote him, but you can't kick Felix out of the way either. You can't have two top centurions in the legion.'

'Felix?' Caesar tapped his chin. 'You mean Mittius? They call him 'Felix'? Yes, he is a good man. Did us proud back at the Tamesis in Britannia. Let us keep his lucky streak going then. I shall write up the orders to promote him. He can take the position of camp prefect for Cicero - the man probably could do with such a stable influence anyway. Then Pullo can maintain his primus rank in the Eleventh.'

Priscus sighed inwardly. With all the transfers it was a damn good job the legions were being dispersed, else all the centurions would be reacting to the calls of the wrong legions. It would be chaos. Caesar needed steady commanders and organised officers more than ever - it seemed that every passing month saw the army becoming more fragmented and complex. Indeed, the lack of experienced and trustworthy officers and the wide-spreading of forces was clearly starting to bother Caesar. Not only had the tic reappeared beneath his right eye - a mark of stress Priscus had come to recognise - but he had started to voice his private fears, albeit only to Priscus. Once more, he realised that this was exactly the reason that Fronto had been of value to the general. Not just as a senior officer or legate, but as a confidante and advisor. Priscus was doing a damnably good job standing in for him, if he did say so himself, but it was hard work.

'Where will you put Labienus, then? South, in Treveri lands? At the southern extent of the Arduenna forest?'

'Yes. With the Twelfth' the general confirmed, sliding a piece across the map. 'Again, he needs no supervision.' He looked down at the north-eastern stretches of Gaul. 'That leaves us an arc around the most dangerous region. We have hemmed the area in. Now let us populate it.'

He slid the remaining three counters across the map: IX, X, and XIV.

'We have two experienced legions and one relatively green one. And we have a number of experienced commanders left. I am inclined to place the two strongest legions at the centre of this entire web, on the western border of the great forest, where they can come to the support of most of the other legions in short order. That would be the Ninth and Tenth.'

Priscus nodded. 'My men will be ready and eager, general.'

The general rubbed his chin and sat back in his chair. 'I hope they can, Priscus. I'm moving you out again. You'll be coming to serve directly on my staff.'

Priscus stared at the map. 'Then who... no. No, no, no, no!'

'Yes, Gnaeus. Young Crassus will take command of the Tenth. I need you in your advisory and strategic role, much as you are now. Surely you must have noticed that I've been grooming you for the role all year. Only the lack of available legates kept you in command.'

'The lack of available '*experienced*' legates, you said, general. Crassus is a boy and one, I suspect, with a dangerous temper.'

'He is also the son of one of my two most powerful colleagues. With Pompey's grip ever on the increase in Rome, I might need Crassus' support at any time. To that end, I will grant his younger boy all the honours I can. The place he can do the least damage is with my best legion, who will not be swayed to stupidity. Especially since you will not be joining me until the spring. I want you to winter with Crassus and the Tenth and guide him into the role.'

'Is there no other way, general?' Priscus stared at the map and then grabbed the legion list and staff list and started to run his finger down them.

'What of the Fourteenth?'

'I shall be posting them to the far northeast, in Eburones territory. It's very much out of the way and not in an area of direct threat, so they should be safe enough. Besides, they being one of the weakest, greenest legions, I am hardly going to place them under the command of a green, weak officer, am I?'

'So who?'

'Cotta. Since Cicero has the Eleventh, Cotta will take the Fourteenth. And with him, Sabinus to keep thing stable. Given their somewhat distant position, I shall also assign a cavalry contingent to Sabinus.'

Priscus was still shaking his head at the bleak prospect of grooming that angry-looking boy to command his pride and joy, but something struck him as he peered at the map. 'Are you sure about this position here?' He stabbed his finger down at the point where Caesar had placed the XIV marker.

'We have had no reports of unrest from the Eburones. It will be very much a garrison to control the flank of the army.'

'It looks bloody cut off and dangerous to me, general. It's surrounded to the north and east by the Rhenus and beyond that are half a million angry Germanic monsters looking to rip off our heads and piss down our necks.'

'I am assured that the river there is far too wide for a force of any size to cross. If anything, it is a better defensive position than most of the others.'

'Still looks damn dangerous to me, general. You really interested in my advice?'

'Go on.'

'Either pull them back a way to the west or give them the support of a few veterans at the least. Maybe we can move the Ninth or Tenth up there and leave just one legion floating here?'

Caesar pored over the map for a while and finally tapped the position of Gesoriacum. 'This is the most stable region, and the Morini are now thoroughly cowed. We will spare half the garrison legion. Five cohorts of the Eighth under the command of their primus pilus can accompany the Fourteenth to their quarters. A few turmae of cavalry too. You approve?'

Priscus looked across the map, shaking his head. There were so many things of which he did not approve that it was hard to know where to begin. But the worst thing was that every moment longer he stared at the map, the fewer alternatives suggested themselves. It was like playing Latrunculi with Carbo. Despite the centurion's face, full of shiny, pink, open honesty, the man was devious as a snake inside a fox when it came to playing complex games. Every time they played, each new move further restricted Priscus until he reached the point where it mattered not what piece he planned to move, he could see why it would lead to him losing the game.

This map was the same.

He could move a commander to another legion, but in the end, each move left a weak legion with inadequate command, or an inadequate officer with a dangerous command, or a good officer with no one to command. It was hair-tearing. The legions could perhaps be better dispositioned, but only by splitting several legions into several-cohort vexillations, and that not only weakened each legion, but raised the number of commanders required. It seemed that Caesar had placed his pieces in the optimum positions no matter how little Priscus liked it.

Besides, something in the general's demeanour had changed following the arrival of his news and Priscus was far from sure that right now was a good time to start arguing with him. There was a strange feeling of tautness about the great man, as though touching him even with a feather might snap him. He scratched his head.

'While Balventius is going to curse me for sending his boys out there with the Fourteenth, sadly I concur, general. Shall I start to write up the orders?'

'Do so, Priscus. Thank you.'

With a weary sigh, the soon-to-be-ex-legate-yet-again turned and left the tent.

Chapter Thirteen

Titus Balventius, primus pilus of the Eighth Legion and pro-tem commander of the five cohorts attached to the Fourteenth, threw his gaze back and forth along the edge of the woods. Despite their veteran status, the men of the Eighth had been the first selected to scour the countryside and commandeer goods, cut timber and gather supplies - ostensibly because they were the most experienced and prepared for whatever might occur. Balventius had little doubt that in reality they suffered for their commander being subordinate to those of the Fourteenth.

Cotta's legion and its accompanying five cohorts had settled into their winter quarters only two days ago and already the tension was beginning to show between the two commanders, each of whom held the same rank and the same position as one of Caesar's staff, despite their specific assignments here. In a way, the allocation of supply harvesting to the men of the Eighth was a blessed relief, as it kept Balventius out of the constant arguments and disagreements in the command tent. While Sabinus held nominal seniority and Balventius was junior to both of them, the handling of his cohorts was still entirely his responsibility and out here, away from the now-fully-constructed camp, things were simple and military.

His gaze swept back to the fort in the distance and he could almost hear the 'frank exchanges of ideas' from here. The fortified winter quarters lay on raised ground some two miles from the river, several hundred paces from the small coppices and thickets that marked the very edge of the great forest of Arduenna. A steep incline away protected the north, but the forest still had to be cut back sufficiently to give a clear surround to the camp - and to supply timber for interior buildings - another thing that Sabinus and Cotta had argued over the necessity of.

The six centuries of the third cohort chopped wood, stripped the boles of their branches, topped and tailed the timber and then loaded the result into the wagons for transport back to the camp. Only one cohort at a time spent each watch out of the camp on such duties, rotating with the others on his orders, despite the urging of Sabinus and Cotta to speed up the process. While supplies were needed in short order, only a fool committed a third of his entire force to such duties at a time.

And so far Balventius had taken personal command of each cohort, barring his own First, leaving that one to his subordinate. Quite apart from the constant bickering between the commanders, which drove him to leave the camp at every opportunity, something about this place had made him uneasy from the start and Sabinus and Cotta were doing nothing to ease his fears.

And as his gaze made the latest pass of the trees it appeared that those fears had been borne out.

His eye stung from the constant squinting into the sun and the endless clouds of dust rising from the work, but he was alert constantly, regardless. Something first caught his attention on the slope of the low hill off to the copse's right. By the time he had rubbed his eye clear of the dust and focused, he could count more than a dozen figures cresting the hill. Alerted by some unknown sense, he spun only to see other figures rounding the edge of the woods to the far end.

An instant appraisal borne from near five seasons of fighting in Gaul labelled them Germanic. They could be one of the Belgae tribes, but their mad, almost raging scramble toward the fight was symptomatic of those violent tribes from across the Rhenus. They lacked the pomp of the proud Belgae that Balventius had experienced: the carnyx blaring its tortured goat sounds; the waving boar and wolf standards of the Celts; the flanking cavalry that was such a strength of the Gallic tribes that Caesar had been adopting them for years into the Roman force. If they were Belgae or Gauls, they were wild ones, almost as crazed and vicious as the Germanic peoples.

'Ad Signa!' he bellowed. 'Fall in to the standards. Enemy in sight!'

The reaction from his veterans was gratifying. The individual centurions, standard bearers and signifers immediately relayed the orders and started gathering their men into formation. Would they have time to beat a retreat to the walls of the fort? Would there be few enough of the bastards for a single cohort to face? The latter question was answered first as the number of men approaching along the flanks increased and he began also to pick out shapes in the woods ahead.

Retreat or die, then. Only an idiot put the honour of the legion above its survival.

Glancing over his shoulder, he could see the ramparts perhaps a quarter of a mile away up a gentle rise. A routing run would be suicidal, but a standard orderly falling back would be equally fatal. If they ran, they presented open targets to all comers, particularly missiles and cavalry. If they formed into a shielded formation and began a step back retreat, keeping a solid front to the enemy, they would go so slowly they could easily be flanked by the enemy.

A quandary - and one that lasted in Balventius' head for only a blink of an eye. This was why a legion or vexillation needed one commander and not two: decisions needed to be made at the snap of a finger.

After all, if democracy worked, Athens would now be master of the world, not Rome.

Turning, he bellowed the orders for the cohort to form up in a single block, loose at the centre and shieldwall tight at the edge. It was a formation he had used a few times before in similar circumstances - a formation not to be found in any military treatise but devised by he and the legate Balbus. The best in flexible protection and speed.

In two dozen heartbeats the 'box' - as Balbus had called it - was complete.

No retreating shieldwall in a standard formation could hope to achieve the 'full pace' in ordered retreat without becoming entangled with the other lines of men. Barely could they hope to match even the standard military pace in those conditions. The 'box' however, called for a single line of men to create a shieldwall in a square, the rear and right sides of the formation facing in the direction of travel and the front and left still facing the enemy in retreat, so as to provide shield-facing on every front. With only a single line of men, the shieldwall could retreat without danger of colliding with their fellows and this way the entire square could maintain the full pace which would see them back at the ramparts in around the count of three hundred.

The beauty of the formation was that while the shieldwall was extremely weak with only a single line of men enforcing it, the interior of the square was open and loose enough for officers and men to move to wherever they were most needed, even at a run, and react to any pressure on the unit. Moreover, the standards could be kept at the centre and well away from the enemy.

As the cohort began to move - each centurion was now shouting their orders - Balventius eyed the enemy pouring out from the edges of the woodland and appearing among its sun dappled centre. Just over four hundred men formed the 'box', with over a quarter of those - two centuries - in the external shieldwall and the rest jogging loosely in the centre, ready to react, swords gripped tight - pila had not been brought on the foraging mission. Balventius had already estimated about twice that number of barbarians just on the northern slope, let alone those at the far side and those coming through the woods. If the enemy numbers were evenly split it would come down to a six-to-one fight. He had done well to instigate the fall back. Despite the weariness of men who have been at manual labour for over an hour, the cohort was retreating at speed and every shield and weapon was raised and ready.

At his estimate, they would cover over half the distance to the camp before the enemy were upon them, unless they suddenly produced cavalry from some gaping orifice. Briefly, he wondered whether Sabinus and Cotta had stopped arguing long enough to set up the artillery.

One hundred. At the centre of the square, in the most open space and close to the signifers, Balventius took his eye from the ground, risking the rabbit holes and undulations of the gentle slope in order to take in the general situation.

He had underestimated the speed of the enemy. The Germanic warriors were almost on them already.

'Second century to the front, Third to the rear, Fifth and Sixth to left and right respectively. Prepare to repel.'

As the men at the centre of the box reordered themselves to face the incoming threat, Balventius glanced once more at the charging enemy. Were they crazed? There could be as many as three thousand of them out there, and certainly no less than two thousand. Even if they had the support of a cavalry unit as yet unseen, while there were clearly enough warriors in the band to swamp his cohort, they must be out of their minds to attack them this close to the legion's winter quarters. Just a few hundred measly paces back up the slope lay a fortified position manned by over seven thousand professional killers, all well-equipped, rested and dug in. Yes, the Germanic lunatics could cut off their cohort, and might just manage to do so before they reached safety, but they must be aware of the danger so close. The chances of them managing to leave the scene of their small victory were miniscule. Were they really so blood-crazed as to throw away their lives to destroy a cohort?

Still, the *causes* for the attack were moot at this point. What mattered was the battle itself.

'Ready the shieldwall on the left flank. Here they come!'

Balventius cast up a short, sharp and fervent prayer to Mars and Fortuna. The tactic that he and Balbus had prepared for such a situation was a serious gamble and untried against such a sizeable foe. He was about to either buy them a few more paces and cripple the initial attack, or hand the cohort's heads to the barbarians on a platter.

'Ready! Three... two... one... give!'

The timing was perfect, which was a necessary factor in the manoeuvre.

As the front wave of warriors threw themselves at the shieldwall in a group of perhaps twenty five men - ahead of the main bulk of their force - determined to batter down the defences and open the box, every third man in the line put all his body weight into his shield, leaning outwards even as he marched. The men to either side of him withdrew from the shieldwall and fell in behind, opening huge sections of the line to the enemy.

Surprised at the wall they were about to hit opening up the warriors howled triumphantly, some of them smashing into the one-in-three men still in position and coming up dead against their immobile shields. The rest ran, stumbled, tumbled and even fell through the line and into the interior of the box, where the legionaries of the Fifth century awaited them, swords at the ready.

As the surprised and apparently victorious warriors staggered around trying to right themselves and choose a target, they were already being systematically butchered by the legionaries awaiting them. Behind them, the left flank shieldwall had already reformed, sealing them in, the legionaries who manned it bracing themselves as they moved against the attacks of those still outside.

The primus pilus smiled with satisfaction. Still performing his three hundred count, he realised he'd not even passed twenty numbers between the shieldwall opening up and every interloper being downed. By a count of twenty more the formation - which had never paused its run - had moved on, leaving the dead and dying barbarians on the grass in their wake, the rear line of legionaries taking the opportunity to stamp on them with hobnailed boots as they passed.

No time to check that flank once more. He'd have to leave that to the centurions there. The right was about to come under pressure. Had the enemy there seen the manoeuvre? Most likely not - a square of Romans had obscured their view.

'Ready the shieldwall on the right flank. Prepare to receive!'

The same prayer was offered up once more to the two deities who would be watching the fight.

'Ready! Three... two... one... give!'

The back-stepping right flank mirrored the actions of the left, stepping in and opening great holes in the shieldwall to allow the barbarians ingress. As unprepared for the tactic as their brothers had been, the nearest warriors of the barbarian force leapt at the shieldwall and found themselves miraculously and unexpectedly falling through it and into a forest of steel blades awaiting them within. Precious few managed to turn with the hope of fleeing the trap, only to find the wall shutting behind them.

By the time Balventius passed two hundred and ten on his count, a fresh swathe of forty or so bodies littered the slope behind the mobile box.

The problem was that the tactic would not work again. Now, the barbarians were coming at the shieldwall more carefully, not charging headlong. Ever-increasing blows rained down on the shields from warriors running alongside, free to attack without thought for their neighbours.

The killing began.

Unable to keep up the pace and fight back, the majority of the legionaries were forced to merely shift their shields fractionally to take the blows as best they could, no opportunity presenting itself to actually attack their foes.

This, of course, was where the unusual 'box' tactic fell down. Balbus' original plan had called for the men in the centre to now keep the attacking enemy at bay with regular casts of their pila. Due, however, to their nature as a foraging party, the retreating cohort lacked their throwing weapons. There was the faint possibility that the interior defenders could deal with the worst threats through judicious use of the gladius, but even to attempt that was to put the formation in peril, men interfering with the shieldwall and trying to fight through it endangering the stability and pace of the outer line.

Two hundred and fifty three.

The turf rampart with its timber palisade was tantalisingly close now. The square was making for the gate at the centre, directed by the centurion at that side. They would make it, but they would lose a few men. Indeed, the cries of pain were on the increase and a simple glance around was enough to tell him that the shieldwalls were on the verge of collapse. Every fifth or sixth man was falling to barbarian swords, axes and spears and every count of three he saw another body drop into the square's interior, to be instantly replaced by one of the running soldiers within.

Better that than standing and fighting at the woods, though. Twenty percent casualties would be high for the number of kills they made, but had they stood and taken the attack, there would be precious few left at the end to tell the tale.

Why were the ballistae and onagers at the camp not firing?

Surely they were close enough now for the Fourteenth and the rest of his own men to be launching a counter attack? What were Sabinus and Cotta thinking? *Were* they thinking, or just gainsaying one another in the command tent?

The gate in the defences was still resolutely shut and, while the number of men at the rampart was increasing with every heartbeat, preparing a defence, there was no sign of missile attack and no sign of the legions opening a way into the camp for them. Were they to be sacrificed for the safety of the rest? Surely not?

The call to halt from the leading centurion came, echoed down the line along both sides. Balventius glanced past him to see that they were now only a few dozen paces from the closed gate.

'Contract the square; three lines.'

Around him every other man stepped back and the square closed to half the size, second and third lines taking position behind the shieldwall, forming a more traditional defensive unit with much less open space at the centre. Suddenly, the attacks of the barbarians were causing far fewer casualties and, now immobile and free to fight, the men in the wall began the butchery that was the Roman legion in open ground facing a rabble.

Again, Balventius' gaze wandered around. He itched to get stuck in to the hairy, disorganised bastards that were slaying his boys, but the situation was not yet apposite. He had to be on hand to modify the cohort's tactics, depending on the changing status of the fight. At least the standards were all secure and safe. Even if the entire cohort fell, the enemy would never get away with them, with a camp full of legionaries looming above them.

Again, he wondered why that camp was so still. Why the ballistae were not firing? They would have a job to miss the enemy at this range, so densely packed.

His answer came even as he pondered on the next possible move. Over the din of sword on sword and sword on shield, the rumble was the first hint. As he felt his pulse quicken, the ground began to tremble, the turf responding to the pounding of hooves.

'Have at 'em lads!' he bellowed, as the cavalry rounded both corners of the camp, having issued from the gates along those sides, undetected by the enemy. At least the two senior officers had put *some* damn thought into it, then.

Only a tiny portion of the cavalry forces available in Caesar's army had been assigned to this location, of course. The cavalry these days - mostly Gallic auxiliaries - numbered almost as many men as the legions. But even the fifteen turmae of Bellovaci horsemen with three years' experience in the Roman military, now eschewing much of their own gear, armoured in Roman mail shirts and with lances and shields, presented a frightening sight. More than two hundred riders appeared from each side, smashing into the outer edge of the Germanic force, picking off the rear ranks and then riding away, having landed a heavy blow to the attackers. Riding off along the turf away from the fight, they wheeled. Those whose spears remained intact and in hand prepared for a second charge; the rest drew their own traditional Celtic long swords and prepared to sweep them low and take heads.

The attack faltered. Like the ripple of a stone dropped in a pool, word of the cavalry attack on their rear swept forward through the mass and finally reached the men hammering down blows on the shield wall.

'They're breaking!' Balventius bellowed. 'Give 'em a good reason!'

With renewed vigour the legionaries, given heart by the change in their fortunes, started to kill with the viciousness and fury of wronged men.

The cavalry managed another harrying strike on the outer edges, their attack forcing the barbarians to turn and provide a second front. Most of their spears were now broken and used. The rest of the cavalry swords now came out and the horsemen turned, urged on by their Belgic chieftain officer yelling something in his own guttural tongue - something that was completely incomprehensible to Balventius yet was clearly some sort of biological curse involving male body parts. Roaring, they made for a third charge.

That attack barely connected.

The barbarian warriors had broken and were already running for the trees. Despite their numerical superiority in a direct attack, they could not maintain the fight on both fronts and their morale melted away under the scornful gaze of the legionaries at the rampart.

One of the centurions somewhere on the side facing away from the camp had to bellow the order to stand fast as his men surged after the departing barbarians. Long moments passed while the enemy flooded away from them down the slope toward the woodland where the Eighth had so recently been cutting timber.

From his vantage point - and given his natural tallness - Balventius could see the carnage along the slope. Close to their position lay perhaps a hundred barbarian bodies, mostly dead, but with the odd badly wounded man writhing in agony among them, gripping his gut to hold in his bowels or clutching a stump of a limb that fountained crimson on to the churned turf. Beyond that, the slope told a different story, four of every five bodies wearing the mail and red tunics of legionaries. The butcher's bill for this would be high, but all-told the action had been a success. Had they stayed, most would have died long before the cavalry reached them.

The men stood, still in formation, panting and groaning, stretching worn muscles and watching the last of the fleeing figures melting away among the trees. There looked to be considerably less leaving than had initially arrived, which felt good when balanced against the steel and crimson on that slope. The cavalry had pulled into their turmae to either side, their commander having called them in and prevented his men from pursuing, showing the restraint that those auxiliary natives had attained after serving with the legions for years. Good man.

Even as he watched, the last enemy figures disappeared from sight. His wandering gaze, attuned to danger, immediately caught sight of what could be a fresh threat.

Off to the right, at a tangent, a second group of men had crested the hill. This group, however, bore all the hallmarks of a Gallic force - signs that he'd failed to see among the first. A group of two dozen riders in gold armbands and jewellery, armoured in bronze and dressed in fine wools, accompanied by the ubiquitous carnyx and boar standards. Behind them came a small force of warriors on foot, presumably the noble or chieftain's personal guard.

'What in the name of Juno do this lot want?'

* * * * *

Quintus Titurius Sabinus, Lucius Aurunculeius Cotta, and Titus Balventius, the commanders of the forces encamped in what had quickly become known as 'shitty valley' stood on the rampart by the gatehouse as the remaining men of the beleaguered cohort and their cavalry saviours poured through the gate and into the camp to safety.

Across the open ground, the Celtic riders had reined in and now sat some seven hundred paces from the defences, their carnyx issuing 'deflating pig' noises. Cotta, frowning, leaned across to a lesser officer who stood close by at the palisade.

'Optio? Your men are Gauls. You know what that signals?'

The optio turned to face the commander and shook his head. 'Not me, sir. Born twenty miles north of Rome me, sir.' Ignoring the irritation on Cotta's face, he turned to a legionary with an unfashionable drooping light brown moustache.

'Aegidius? You're a Gaul. Know that tune?'

'It's a call for talks, sir.'

Cotta nodded, his irritation fading. 'Do we assume this lot are the Eburones, then?'

'Seems likely' Sabinus agreed. 'Shall we go meet them?'

Cotta shook his head. 'My senior tribune is the man who Caesar used to send to them as an ambassador. Assigned him to me specially against just such possibilities.' He turned to the small knot of tribunes standing at the far side of the gate.

'Junius? You know him?'

'It's either Cativolcus or Ambiorix. Possibly both, sir. Can't see at this distance.'

'But you've met them before?'

'Yes sir. The twin kings of the Eburones. See, the nation's split into two half-tribes and...'

'Enough of geography lessons, Junius. Take Arpineius and a half century of men as an honour guard and go speak to this king. Find out if he was involved in that mess and what he wants.'

Junius and his junior tribune swung up into the saddles of their horses that stood tethered near the gate with the rest of the officers' steeds, called a centurion across and gathered half a century of the tidy, undamaged Fourteenth. Opening the gate, they rode and marched out of the camp and across the wide swathe of body-strewn grass toward the royal party.

Balventius stood watching as the parties converged and fell into calm negotiations with a minimum of the gesticulation that seemed traditionally necessary for a Gaul to express himself adequately. Gritting his teeth, the senior centurion closed his ears to the sound of Sabinus and Cotta disagreeing on some new matter. He could hardly influence the decisions of his superiors, so it was safer not to become involved in the first place.

Almost a quarter of an hour passed before the Roman ambassadors turned and made their way back to the camp, passing beneath the gate just before it shut tight. As the soldiers returned to their assigned positions the two tribunes clambered from their beasts and up the slope to the rampart top.

'Report?' Sabinus ordered.

'It is Ambiorix of the western Eburones, sir. He was trying to reach us before any harm befell us but as he neared the camp, he discovered us under attack, so he stayed out of sight in the woodlands until the battle had resolved.'

'Brave man, then, this Ambiorix?' Sabinus sniffed.

'With respect, sir, he has perhaps four dozen men. He could not have hoped to come to our aid.'

Cotta nodded. 'But what did he have to say?'

'He came to warn us, sir, that the Germanic tribes are crossing the Rhenus.'

'He might be a little late for that.'

'He claims there's a lot more than that, sir. He reckons it was an advance party out looking for him that accidentally found us. Apparently King Cativolcus has sided with some big conspiracy of chieftains against the Romans. They're drumming up support from all over the place and even invited the German peoples across the river to come and join in pushing us all the way back to Rome.'

Sabinus nodded. 'Priscus' general revolt he's been warning was coming. Caesar seemed to think it would be held off until a new campaigning season. Seems Priscus was right to be concerned.'

'It's a little worse than that, sir' Tribune Arpineius chipped in.

267

'How so?'

'If he's right, this Ambiorix claims it's not just the eastern Eburones and the Germans, or even the Treveri and Ubii and Nervii and several others we'd not heard of. He reckons it's half the tribes of northern Gaul. They're planning to rise up simultaneously and take all the winter garrisons at once, while we're all spread out so that we can't come to each other's aid.'

'Then why is he here and telling us this?' Cotta narrowed his eyes. 'If the legions are about to be annihilated and half his tribe are the chief instigators, why put himself in such danger and not join in or at least sit back and watch us die. He can't be that loyal. No one's *that* loyal.'

Junius shook his head. 'Ambiorix has always been one of the staunchest, sir. I've met him a dozen times and more over the past three or four years. Half his oppidum speak Latin. They have our traders among them. He wears tunics embroidered in Mediolanum and cloak-pins from Magna Graecia, sir. He's as pro-Roman as they come. Even makes the Remi look like savages.'

Cotta looked unconvinced but Sabinus nodded.

'So what is he intending to do about it? Is he here seeking sanctuary with Rome? Seems short sighted if we're about to be wiped out.'

'He's fleeing west and south, sir, into the heart of Roman control. It's too dangerous for him here now, since he's known to be one of Caesar's strongest supporters. He hears that Cicero's legion is a couple of days southwest. He's taking his family that way and begs you to bring your legions with him.'

'I'll bet he does' Cotta laughed. 'With half the Germanic peoples nipping his backside and only two score warriors I'm quite sure he'd quite like to have seven thousand legionaries around him. I think we'd best bolster the defences and wish him luck.'

Sabinus shook his head. 'Hang on, Lucius. If he's right, the only hope for the army is to consolidate our forces. We could be back with Cicero in two days at a run, if we travelled light. Then we'd have twelve thousand men. Better odds, I'd say.'

'*If* he's right. It's a lot to bet on the fidelity of a barbarian' Cotta snorted, unaware of the angry silence forming among the soldiery around him, the majority of whom were of pure Gallic blood, albeit southern.

'What's your opinion on this, Junius? You know the man.'

268

The ambassadorial tribune pursed his lips. 'He's never played us wrong. He's been Caesar's man in the northeast, keeping an eye on the lower Rhenus for three years now. He's supplied riders for our army and grain for the men. He's a man who prides himself on his honour and honesty. I cannot believe he would betray us.'

Sabinus spread his hands. 'See? Your problem, Cotta, is that you still think of all the Gauls as barbarians. Look around you. Who do you see manning these walls, for all their Roman kit? Who sit astride those horses? Gauls. All of them. We may not be able to trust the Germanic tribes, but you have to be able to look at the Gauls and see allies as well as enemies - Labienus has been hammering that into us for years now. He thinks this entire situation can be diffused without resorting to war. He believes the Gauls are ready to become a client state with Roman funding and support. Men like Ambiorix are the pins around which all of that turns. We have to keep them on-side.'

'I don't like it. His arrival at the same time as those Germans was too convenient.'

'They were *looking for him*, Cotta. Of course they were close.'

'Listen. We can get word to Cicero by rider in less than a day, so in two days we can have word *from* him. That means that in four, he could have contacted Caesar and we could have word from the general. Just four days! Less if the couriers take changes of horse and ride like the wind. It would be not only a breach of our orders to abandon this position, it could be suicidally dangerous if that man on that horse is not telling the truth. The chances of the entire nation rising up and managing to take out all of the garrisons within the next four days are ridiculously small. We would have had word of more than just this. *Priscus* would know - the man's been investigating this Gallic uprising for a year. Let's just sit tight and wait for word from Caesar.'

Again, Sabinus shook his head.

'If we sit tight and they're close enough that their front ambushing forces are already on us we could be facing half the population of the tribes across the Rhenus by tomorrow morning. I for one have no intention of making a glorious last stand here just to stick rigidly to our orders. We need to start trusting our allies, Cotta.'

He threw his arms out expansively. 'If the whole of Gaul is catching fire as Priscus believes, then there's no reason to doubt this man's word when he brings us tidings of rebellion, and we all know it would take precious little nudging to push the Germanic tribes against us. They've been itching to chastise us ever since we hammered Ariovistus all those years ago, let alone for our forays across the Rhenus last year. The king's only giving us the information Priscus has been expecting. If he tells us that Gaul is rising and we need to uproot, then we should listen to him.'

Cotta turned and gripped Sabinus' upper arms in a way that drew an angry glance from the commander.

'It is precisely *because* of the general rising of which he warns us that we *cannot* trust him. Don't you see? I have nothing against the Gauls' he added, glancing round warily at the legionaries who were exuding an unhappy silence. 'In general I would like to offer trust first until betrayed, but with what we believe to be happening, we just don't have that luxury. We need to dig in and send to Caesar for orders. That is what the general would want!'

Balventius opened his mouth to speak, unhappily wondering whether the time to interject had come, but Sabinus waved a dismissive hand and spoke, his voice raised enough to carry to most of the men nearby.

'You can stay here and dig yourself in all you wish, Cotta. You will find that when the barbarians come we will be cut off. Seven thousand against half a million. They would not even need to fight us. They could just starve us. We have no supply train in place, our foragers have not managed to bring in more than a week's rations, and we will get no supplies from allied tribes while under siege by them.'

The legate of the Fourteenth Legion was becoming horribly aware that he was losing the support of the men, who were falling easily to Sabinus' words. 'But...'

'No, Cotta. You command the Fourteenth, but I have seniority here. At dawn the army will move out back to the west. We will accompany this King Ambiorix at least as far as Cicero's camp and consolidate forces with him while we send missives to Caesar. We will travel light, taking only the quick horse carts. No oxen. We will have to leave the ox-carts and the artillery here, along with a quantity of the supplies if we want to travel fast. We take the most important weapon and ammunition supplies and light personal goods and leave everything else, right down to the tents themselves. I want this army moving back to Cicero's position as fast as a legion can really hope to.'

With an angry glare, Sabinus turned to the two tribunes.

'Go back to the Eburones and tell their king we will accompany him at dawn. In light of the situation, however, he will have to make camp more than a spear's throw from our ramparts until that time, lest he draw a pilum or two from our men.'

The tribunes saluted and scurried down toward their horses.

Sabinus' angry glare scanned the faces of those nearby, searching for any sign of argument. When all remained silent, he turned away and stamped down the bank and off toward his quarters. Cotta and Balventius exchanged a look.

'I know you tried not to overstep, Centurion, but I would have welcomed just a little support there.'

Balventius ground his teeth. 'He might be right, sir.'

'He might. But he's not, is he? You know that as well as I. If you had seniority, would you really lead the legions out of their nice safe defences and off into the wilds? On the say of a possible enemy?'

Balventius struggled with his answer. In his entire career he had never openly disobeyed a command in the field, and certainly never taken a contrary position - Fronto and Balbus didn't count, to his mind - and it came with difficulty.

'He might be wrong, sir. I very much fear he is. I would sooner put my trust in these earthen banks than in a man who could very well be harbouring druids and grudges. But Commander Sabinus is the man Caesar placed in command, and he's one of the longest serving and most experienced men in the army - one of very few left these days.'

'Gods, I hope he's right, Balventius. I really do.'

As Cotta strode off to deliver the orders to his legion, Balventius looked out over the parapet to the two tribunes and their guard of legionaries converging on the party of Gaulish nobles.

'So do I' he agreed, quietly but emphatically.

* * * * *

The early morning sun streamed along the shallow valley from the army's rear, glittering off mail and helmets, the reflections dancing and leaving yellow-purple shapes in the eyes of the men. The cavalry rode at the front of the army, some hundred paces ahead, acting as a van. Then came the five cohorts of Balventius, behind whom the officers and their accompanying Gallic party rode along with the standards and musicians, high above the dust cloud kicked

271

up by those in front. Behind them came the Fourteenth, followed by the rear-guard and the faster moving carts pulled by horses.

The primus pilus of the Eighth was striding out on foot with his legion, despite the opportunity to ride with the officers as the nominal commander of a large vexillation. In addition to the discomfort caused by the constant wrangling of the two senior officers and a foot-march being his natural place in things, Balventius was doing everything he could to avoid the accusatory looks Cotta kept slinging at him whenever Sabinus asserted his authority, which he was doing with worryingly increasing regularity. For all the fact that Sabinus had a great deal more field experience in command than Cotta, it was hard to see him now as anything but a petulant child endangering everyone in order to prove himself right.

Not for the first time, Balventius glared at the shapes of the Eburones nobles back there, throwing all the weight of his irritation into the glare.

But this time something was different.

With astonishment, he saw that the entire party of Gauls were departing up the slope of the valley through which they travelled, casually and freely.

'Tapapius? Keep the men on track but be ready for anything. In fact, have the men unstrap their shields and get them on their arms ready.'

'Sir?'

'Just do it!' Transferring his discomfort and irritation onto his own officers was less than professional, but this entire situation was starting to ache in his belly like an old wound. As Tapapius gave out the orders, echoed by the other centurions and optios, Balventius turned and jogged back along the line of his cohorts, failing to acknowledge their questions or comments, his good eye fixed on the party of Gauls nearing the crest of the hill.

Finally, he reached the level of the officers and had to waft the dust cloud aside to see Sabinus and Cotta.

'Sir?'

Both men looked down at him. Sabinus had an air of haughty superiority and rode casually with his head uncovered, his helmet in the carts at the rear. Cotta, he noted, was as battle ready as his own men of the Eighth, and showed the signs of fatigue and sleeplessness in the grey beneath his eyes and the cold sheen of his complexion.

'Yes?' Sabinus asked in a business-like tone.

'Respectfully, sir, where are the Eburones going?'

'To get their bearings, Centurion.'

Balventius blinked. 'Sir, shouldn't we send our own outriders and scouts for that?'

'They know their own lands better than us, Centurion.'

'Then they shouldn't need to get their bearings, sir. Something here stinks.'

Cotta was nodding 'He's right Quintus. It's wrong.'

'Do you really think...' Sabinus' eyes narrowed. 'Where did they go?'

Balventius turned with a sinking feeling, horribly aware now of the fact that Ambiorix and his party had vanished at the point when the valley narrowed and deepened into a worrying defile.

'Call the men to arms, sir.'

Sabinus was shaking his head. 'I don't think...' Beside him, Cotta leaned forward in his saddle. 'Tribune Junius: have the men unshoulder shields and prepare for trouble.'

As the command echoed along the line accompanied by the sounds of thousands of shields being pulled from their carry straps and gripped tight, still in their leather covers, Sabinus opened his mouth to berate his fellow commanders, but fell silent at the sudden commotion.

'What in the name of Venus was that?'

Balventius didn't have to look - a good thing, since he was a third of the way back along the line and his vision was obscured by the dust cloud. 'That, sir, is the sound of horses in pain and men under attack. I would surmise that the van have come across anti-cavalry pits dug across the valley.'

Without waiting to hear what Sabinus would say next, Balventius turned and ran back along the line of his men. He was not half way when the first man shouted a warning. A quick glance confirmed the cry.

Along both sides of the valley, hundreds upon hundreds of men were appearing at the crest. While the majority began to descend, coming to rest on the upper slopes - still out of comfortable pilum reach so high up - behind them came the archers, the slingers and the javelin throwers.

By the time Balventius reached the front of his cohorts, the army had come to a halt. The Bellovaci cavalry who had come to their rescue so bravely and effectively only the previous day were already

273

half gone. A wide swathe of the valley had been decorated with covered pits disguised with thin turf on a lid of interlaced sticks, interspersed with scattered caltrops. Fully a third of the horsemen had collapsed into the pits or fallen foul of the caltrops, horses lying shuddering half in and half out of holes, others with broken limbs or intact but trapped and screaming in terror. Their riders lay mostly mangled among the equine wreckage.

The rest of the cavalry had been forced around the edges to escape the trouble, only to encounter the enemy warriors running forward with long spears - the perfect anti-cavalry weapon. The attack terrified the surviving horses and many, in a blind panic, ran straight into the mess of pits, caltrops and bodies. Driven back by the spear men with their hedge of sharp points, the cavalry were useless, being herded into the men of the Eighth Legion, who had drawn up and stopped to prevent themselves being crushed by panicking horses. Even as events started to unfold, the remaining horsemen were pushed by the spearmen into an ever-tightening circle in front of the legion. A few of the attackers fell to javelins cast by the riders and one or two enterprising legionaries who had anticipated the command to throw.

A command decision had to be made.

Balventius ground his teeth. There were perhaps a hundred horsemen left from the four hundred or so that had formed the van. They could be saved, drawn back into the fold, but only at the expense of the infantry. Already missiles were starting to rain down from the heights. To open the ranks and allow the horsemen to retreat behind them - safely away from the spearmen - would prevent any effective defence from missiles, and Balventius could not afford such a move. The cavalry would have to be abandoned; sacrificed to give the rest a chance.

'Shields up. Tighten those lines!'

As the cohorts pulled into a more compact unit, well-protected by the large, squared-oval shields with their bull emblems, Balventius ran past them. It looked from here as though little was being done with the Fourteenth toward the rear. If Sabinus and Cotta didn't do something soon, the valley would become one mass Roman grave.

As he jogged alongside, the doomed cavalry, having run out of places to go, hurtled past him, back down the valley. As they rode, several were picked off by well-aimed arrows, spears and sling bullets. There was nowhere else for them to go but straight at the enemy, either into the hedge of spears - which their horses would refuse to do - or up the slopes where they would be at the mercy of the bulk of the enemy. And so they rode to the rear. Desperate and foolish. If the Eburones had planned to halt the van and pour in at both sides, it was pretty certain that they had also sealed in the rear.

'Dismount and join the legions!' he bellowed at them as they passed, the only hope for their survival being on foot. None paid any attention in their panicked need to get away.

The five cohorts of the Eighth Legion were now fully shielded all along the valley, swords drawn and ready to take anything the enemy could give. Balventius noted with approval that the centurions and optios had had them discard their pila, jamming them, butt-spike first into the ground. With the gradient of the slopes there was no point in even attempting a pilum volley. Every man's attention was better focused on keeping their shield in the way of falling missiles and having their sword ready to deal with close attackers when they finally came.

Conversely, as Balventius passed the last ranks of his men, the Fourteenth seemed to be in chaos. Sabinus was nowhere to be seen, but Balventius could hear his voice, loud and angry, bellowing orders toward the back. No one seemed to be paying any attention to him. The men of the Fourteenth had at least had the presence of mind, despite their officers, to form a shield wall for protection against the missiles, which were coming in increasing force as the number of archers, slingers and spear throwers at the valley sides increased.

It took a moment of searching before he found any sign of Cotta. His dappled white mare danced around riderless among the command section while two musicians, their curved horns over their shoulders, tried to steady it and prevent it bolting. Cotta himself was struggling to rise from the ground. Striding over, Balventius reached down and helped an over-burdened signifer who was trying to pull the legate to his feet. Cotta surrendered himself to the pair and they lifted him easily to his feet, where he reached up to his helmet twice - missing it entirely the first time - and undid the strap letting it fall to the ground. As it did, Balventius noted the enormous crease in the bronze from a sling bullet that was still wedged in it. The metal had buckled inwards and cut through the felt cap inside to slice into

Cotta's forehead just below the hairline. Blood was running down the side of his face.

'Legate?'

Cotta swayed a little and took a moment to focus on him.

'Hmm?'

'Legate, can you hear me?'

'Yes, Centurion.' The signifer let go of his commander and Cotta immediately staggered to the side until he regained his grasp. 'Sorry. Head hit.'

'Yessir!' Balventius replied. 'Can you still command?'

Cotta let go of the signifer and staggered a little before regaining his stance. 'I think so. Damn that was painful. My ears are ringing like bells at the Bacchanalia!'

'You need to pull your legion into tight formation so we can protect against missiles and start to break out of this situation.'

'What of the carts?'

'Piss on the carts' Balventius said, forgetting his composure for a moment as he heard Sabinus yelling conflicting orders that would only be making matters worse.

'You're right, Balventius. To Hades with the carts.' He turned to the musicians and signifers. 'Sound the call for both legions - Eighth and Fourteenth - to combine into a defensive circle.'

Balventius nodded, despite his disapproval - A circle was good to defend against a mob of barbarians, but precious little use against falling missiles. 'I'd best get back to my men, sir. Are you alright here?'

'Yes, Centurion. Let's show them a defensive wall while I try and find Sabinus and see what he wants to do.'

Balventius shook his head in irritation as he turned and started to jog alongside the column once more toward his men at the front. As he ran, the cornicen began to blast the call for the new formation, relayed by waving standards, centurions' whistles and optios' shouts.

The falling missiles were becoming steadily more troublesome as the attackers found their range and settled into their shots. Worse yet, now that the army had come to a complete halt, a large number of scruffy barbarian lowlifes and womenfolk had joined the missile troops, throwing rocks of all sizes from pebbles to boulders down the slope. To begin with not many were striking home, but it would not be long before they, too, found their range, and even a small pebble could blind or incapacitate in this situation.

Balventius found he was still grinding his teeth.

They had consolidated to minimise the damage, but not a single barbarian was suffering, while every count of ten found another Roman falling with a scream to a pierced limb or a shattered face. It was, quite simply, a disaster. If they didn't do something soon a legion and a half would die in this valley. In an uncharitable moment, he found himself wishing that Cotta had died from the head wound. Then Balventius would have had no compunction about taking command and shouting out the orders. He'd disagreed with Cotta on the formation, since it simply saw them settle into a position they could hardly maintain. As soon as the legions were in formation, they should start to pull out of the valley. A quarter of a mile back they would be safe from overhead attack, with the valley sides so much lower. And perhaps two miles back was the abandoned camp.

Now, with the huge oval formation, leaving would involve detaching a few cohorts at a time in smaller defensive units, forming essentially giant testudos and heading at a good, solid pace back east for the safety of the camp. The further they got from this valley, the safer they would be. Oh, they would have to fight the enemy that were blocking their rear on the way, but then at least they would be doing something other than cowering behind shields and hoping not to be hit with anything.

It irked him almost to breaking point that even now, when his men's lives depended upon the command decisions, Cotta would not attempt to move until he had discussed it with Sabinus, who seemed to be doing his best to get everyone killed.

Well the pair of them had best sort it out quickly, before the entire Roman force went to Hades hand in hand.

Chapter Fourteen

The first Balventius knew of Sabinus' presence was when the men he was busy yelling orders at snapped to attention and ignored him entirely, their gaze rising over his left shoulder. Dreading the ensuing moments and knowing what the men were reacting to, the veteran centurion turned, coming to a salute before he even faced the officer.

Sabinus sat astride his horse amid the legionaries like a well-dressed haughty rock in a muddy puddle. The common soldiers would see only a senior officer who demanded respect by his very presence. Balventius - used to the company of such commanders - saw the tell-tale signs of a man on the edge. Despite his apparent demeanour, Sabinus' eyes were wild and staring: the look of a man watching his world falling apart and knowing that he is directly responsible.

'Centurion: We need to break out of this valley!'

Balventius felt his irritation smooth over somewhere deep down inside. Despite his panicked and uncontrolled beginnings, the commander had finally grasped the vital need of falling back.

'Definitely, sir. We'll form an arc with a testudo roof and provide rear-guard. We can keep them off you while the Fourteenth…'

'I think you misunderstand me, Centurion. I need you to take a cohort and break out to the front, driving a tunnel between those spearmen so that we can continue west toward Cicero.'

Balventius blinked.

'Sir?'

'Do you have a hearing problem, Centurion? Break me out forward!'

Balventius gripped and ungripped his free left hand repeatedly as he stared at the commander, his voice coming out as a low, angry growl.

'Sir: that would be foolish at best; suicidal at worst. The land in front of us is covered with pits, caltrops, thrashing horses and corpses. We'll have to clamber over and around everything, all under missile attack from both sides, while the enemy poke us with spears.' He looked up and around the valley. 'And those infantry are ready to pour down on us the moment we move.'

278

'Are you refusing an order, Centurion?'

Balventius felt his fingernails bite into the palm of his hand. Once in his career had he deliberately disobeyed an order - the arrest of Paetus three years ago - and that had been under extremely unusual circumstances. For a centurion to actively refuse to carry out an order in the heat of battle was unheard of and unforgivable. If he refused he could face any punishment - and looking at Sabinus' expression, crucifixion seemed likely.

'Of course not, sir. I was simply pointing out...'

'Let me repeat myself just once, Centurion. Take a cohort and forge me a path west.'

'Yes sir' Balventius replied through grinding teeth.

As Sabinus turned his horse with difficulty among the press of men and rode off back toward the knot of signifers and musicians, Balventius eyed the situation. There was no way he could see that any attempted break out west would succeed. Back to the east there was no stretch of pits and caltrops, just enemy infantry who could be fought through. There was a good chance that - with heavy losses admittedly - a breakout back east toward the camp would be a success.

With a deep breath, he called to the nearest pilus prior - the centurion commanding a cohort.

'Lucanius? Get your lads ready for a push.'

'Sir?'

'You heard me. I want them tight and well-shielded. We form a wide wedge and stay as close to formation as possible, driving ahead down the valley, opening a path for everyone else.'

Lucanius stared at his primus pilus, but the expression on Balventius' face said it all, and he gave a professional nod.

Balventius watched for a few heartbeats as the centurion gave out his instructions. The other centurions and optios and signifers listened in disbelief, occasionally ducking and diving, one optio too slow and taking an arrow in the neck as he opened his mouth to object. The man disappeared into the press with a gurgle and a spray of crimson.

'Form!'

Balventius stepped forward, falling in toward the rear of the formation, where the optio who had just crossed to Elysium would have been standing, goading the men on with his stick. The soldiers cast fearful glances at him, more terrified of doing something wrong in the close proximity of their primus pilus than of facing the forces arrayed before them.

The moment the last shield thudded into place, a single thump lost among a cacophony of sounds, Lucanius blew his whistle and the other centurions and optios in the formation began to bellow the commands. Balventius remained silent, preferring to watch his officers at work rather than take his place in the command structure. He was here not to command but rather because no senior centurion should send his men into a situation he himself was not willing to face.

The force began to move and Balventius was immediately impressed with Lucanius' level of control. The cohort formed a rough wedge but with a flattened tip. Their primary concern was not to punch through the spear men at this point, but to make sure enough men got past the wreckage of the cavalry and the pits and caltrops to reform into a wedge at the far side. *Then* they would punch through the infantry.

Gods willing.

Through reliance on his lesser officers playing their part perfectly, Lucanius did not begin to move at the standard pace as was customary, but fell straight into the full pace that came just before a charge. Despite the move from stationary to startling speed in an instant, the formation held tight, every officer shouting and directing the men under his command.

The blunted wedge moved into the field of death, the remaining cohorts of the Eighth closing up the huge oval in the valley behind them and contracting the edge to create a good, solid shieldwall.

Despite the best efforts of Lucanius and his men, the formation began to break up as they reached the anti-cavalry defences. The necessity of skirting pits both empty and occupied, of clambering over the bodies of horses and men, combined with occasional soldiers falling away as their foot was impaled by the iron spike of a caltrop that had eluded his careful gaze all took their toll. It was remarkable really that Lucanius managed to keep *any* semblance of formation, and Balventius found himself moving forward through the chaos, passing the struggling legionaries.

Every pace forward brought him and the insane charge closer to the far edge of the defences and the waiting spearmen, who had reformed to block the valley beyond, having driven off the cavalry. Sadly, the breakup of the wedge formation had destroyed the tight testudo roof around the periphery and now the missiles of the Eburones on the hillsides were having a devastating effect. No matter what direction Balventius turned his head, he saw a man vanish, an arrow plunging deep into the soft flesh between the chin and the neckline of a mail shirt, rupturing organs and entering until only the flights protruded, a slingshot smashing so hard into the side of a helmet that the man was literally spun around before he fell, his brain damaged by the deep crease in the helmet punching through his temple, a spear striking so hard with the fall from above that despite being unable to penetrate a mail shirt, it threw the man from his feet and deep into one of the horse-trenches.

Men were dying so fast Balventius could hardly count them falling.

In a vain attempt to distract his attention from the grisly numbers, Balventius' gaze rose to the hillsides only to bring him fresh hopelessness. The Eburones' infantry at the western end of the valley sides were now pouring down to come to the aid of the spearmen and prevent the cohort from achieving anything.

Perhaps he could have bent the rules and sent the cohort up the slope instead of along the flat? But that plan would have brought its own difficulties and would likely have been no easier. None of it made any real sense.

His gaze fell ahead again, trying to locate Lucanius so that he could apprise his centurion of the fresh threat, but he could see the pilus prior already glancing back and forth at the two incoming forces. Half a moment later came the command for a charge. Such a headlong run in this mangled wreckage of bodies and deadly traps was little more than suicide, but it was also their only hope to take on the spearmen before the rest of the Eburones managed to descend the hill and reinforce them.

The shrill blowing of whistles and accompanying shouts echoed the order and a moment later the already fragmented wedge descended into chaos, all hope of a shielded formation gone, every man running for his life to reach the waiting spearmen.

With the determination of the professional soldier Balventius locked his attention on the waiting enemy, refusing to allow himself the luxury of worrying about those men falling to traps and missiles as they ran, concentrating on hurdling bodies and dips, avoiding the evil spiked caltrops and reaching those spearmen, his mind running through the standard manoeuvres of infantry close-combat and everything he knew of Gallic tactics.

And then, suddenly - his attention so riveted - he was out in the open. It took him so much by surprise that he almost ran straight into the enemy. He had moved so fast in his singularity of purpose that he was now among the leading men of what had been the wedge, Lucanius only a few paces away to his right. The white-haired professional centurion leading the attack began bellowing more orders and the men arriving between the last few pits began to fall into position.

A swathe of grass perhaps thirty paces long was all that separated the spearmen from the arriving Roman cohort. Missiles were falling with considerably less regularity and accuracy here, so much further along from the archers' positions and too close to their own forces to risk too many wild shots.

The rest of the tribe, descending the slope, were almost here already and Balventius weighed everything up as the new, sharp, Roman wedge began to form in preparation for a punch through that bristling hedge of iron and bronze points.

There was a very good chance that they would break through the spearmen only to find the rest of the tribe on foot gathering beyond.

But there *was* a possibility now. Against all the odds - and despite his shock at Sabinus issuing the order in the first place - it seemed that the wedge had actually survived the worst stretch and might be strong enough to drive a gap through the enemy. They could *do it*. They had lost probably near half the cohort already to the traps and the missiles in that crazed run, but half a cohort could still do it.

Lucanius seemed to be having the same thoughts. The wedge was still forming as he gave the order to advance. Speed was now of the essence. The other men would have to run and catch up to fall in.

'The Fourteenth 'as seen!' A legionary close to Balventius shouted. 'Sir! They're comin' in support!'

Balventius strained to hear over the din and became quickly aware of commands being blasted out on cornu and buccina back at the main force. It made sense. There was a chance now, but the rest of the army would have to leap on it. They should already be moving forward to take advantage of his cohort's sacrifice.

He blinked and shook his head in disbelief at what he was hearing.

'Either you need your ears cleaning out or to relearn your orders, soldier. That's the damn recall!'

Lucanius had heard and was staring at him in shock.

'Sir?'

'Yes I heard it too. What are they thinking?'

'What do we do?'

Balventius turned to look at the enemy. The cohort, advancing as they had been, were now a mere ten paces from the points of those spears. Retreating into that killing zone again would be a disaster. It was also orders. They could continue on their attack - by all rights that was exactly what they *should* do - but with no support coming, they would have nowhere to go. Tired and unfamiliar with the territory, they would be dead within the hour.

'We fall back!'

'Sir?'

'I said we fall back as ordered!'

The cohort stumbled to a halt without the order needing to be given, every man disbelieving what he heard.

'Rally on the left!' bellowed Balventius. 'We're going up the slope a little and running around the defences. Their main infantry have come down to join the spearmen, so it's the quickest and easiest route.'

'We'll be at the mercy of their missiles!' Lucanius shouted.

'Just follow my orders.'

The Eburones, shouting in triumphant glee at the sudden halt of the Romans, began to surge forward in the attack, the spearmen hungry for blood, newly-arriving warriors from the hillside filtering in among them.

Balventius chewed the inside of his cheek. Speed was important, but so was protection. A testudo, then.

'Every man of the Eighth! Rally to me and form testudo. Centurions, optios and veterans to the rear, facing the enemy.'

It would be costly on the best men in the cohort, but it was the only real option if they wanted to escape with their lives. The testudo would face back east and skirt the edge of the cavalry defences, running for the army at full pace. Hopefully they would be able to maintain the shields as they ran. It was extremely difficult at speed - which was why Balbus and he had invented the 'box' - but without speed they would fall to the infantry and without a testudo's shield-roof they would fall to the missile troops.

Damned if you do…

Centurions and optios and veterans to the rear was appalling tactics. They would have to fight off the pursuing infantry and back-step at full pace in line with the testudo. There was a good chance they would lose most of the officers and veterans, but they were the only men who stood a chance of pulling it off.

The trouble they were in made itself all the more evident as the first blows from spears and swords struck even as the testudo was forming for the retreat.

As soon as the last shield 'clonked' into position, a shout from a helpful legionary at the front brought the command to move and the entire formation began to retreat back toward the army, jogging at speed up the lower slope of the valley's southern side, skirting the pits and caltrops. The going was more than a little difficult and it gave Balventius a sense of immense pride even at this horrendous moment that his men were so professional and well-drilled that they kept a uniform pace and the shields in place despite the gradient and the rabbit holes and more that threatened to ruin their retreat.

Balventius' world shrank to that of a testudo soldier: a hot, sweaty, stinking metallic world mostly of darkness, with cracks of light between the shields and one single slit ahead at eye level through which he could see the spear points of the Eburones continually lunging at the formation, trying to hit the gaps and take out the men.

Half his concentration was taken up with walking backward at the brisk pace and managing not to separate from the rest of the formation or trip over them and bring the whole group down. It was a credit to the Eighth how well the veterans and officers were coping with the near-impossible manoeuvres.

The downside was that that left only half their attention for the following Eburones.

As they neared the range of the missile weapons once more the sounds of stones, slingshots, arrows and the occasional cast spear cracked, smashed and pinged on shields everywhere, Every ten heartbeats or so there was a squawk as a spear punched through a raised shield with the added weight of gravity and pinned the wielder's shield to his arm and his arm to his torso, or a stray arrow or sling shot hit between the cracks and maimed a soldier, felling him among the press of men, who had no option but to walk over him and on to the east.

The rear rank began to find the going all the harder as they were forced to step backward over their fallen comrades.

And then the first disaster struck. One of the Eburones chasing them swung a huge decorative axe which bit into the shieldwall, almost severing an optio's arm. As the warrior yanked the weapon back it ripped two of the shields from the line, along with a sizeable piece of the forearm. The spearmen around the axe-wielding warrior immediately leapt on their opportunity and jabbed with their weapons, striking home again and again into the bodies of the two men whose shields had gone, inflicting a dozen horrendous wounds to each man, ripping ragged holes in necks, faces, chests, groins, bellies and legs. The optio and the veteran disappeared with screams, lost in the ranks of howling Gauls as the testudo moved on, two of the men from the middle turning to try and take their place.

But the damage was already done. Two enterprising Eburones cast their spears into the gap and one replacement legionary fell while turning, bringing down his closest companions. The formation foundered and slowed.

Across the right side of the line a lucky or very well-aimed spear thrust punched through a shield and when hauled back yanked the shield out of the line, the legionary behind it finding himself pulled bodily from the formation and onto the ground before the enemy.

As the formation began to reform and fill the gaps to move on, Lucanius suddenly howled - a sound of sheer anguish and horror that drew Balventius' gaze. In shock, he watched the senior centurion who had led the entire engagement cast his shield aside and fall out of line. Lucanius lunged toward the figure of the unfortunate legionary, who was now being hacked to pieces by another axe man.

Something triggered in Balventius' memory and he remembered disapproving of Lucanius pulling strings to transfer his son into his own century. It never did a man good to be serving in the same unit as his family, as was evidenced by the terrible scene now unfolding. Forgetting his duty to the entire cohort, the panicked Lucanius ran at the enemy in a vain attempt to save his son.

It was stupid.

Clearly the lad was already dead. His neck was half severed from a single axe blow and his head lolled to one side as it sprayed a torrent of crimson across the man busy cutting off his other limbs with the half moon blade.

'Shit!'

285

It was almost as bad as Lucanius's own stupidity, but Balventius was already out of formation himself, shield held high to ward off the spears as they thudded toward his face. Jamming his sword into the handy little crack in one of the shield struts that he'd cultivated for just that purpose, Balventius reached out and grasped Lucanius' wrist as the man raised his sword.

'Not now!'

The centurion was beyond reason, however, and simply pulled himself from Balventius' grasp, throwing himself at the hedge of spears. He never landed a blow. The first spear caught him in the armpit, throwing him back and to the ground, catching in his mail. As Lucanius' sword fell from his grasp, two of the Eburones grabbed his legs and started hauling him into the mass of howling barbarians.

Balventius watched in impotent horror as the centurion disappeared, screaming, beneath the mass of enemy warriors.

The second disaster was, by his own actions, Balventius' fault. He'd broken the rules in trying to rescue Lucanius in the same way the short sighted father had done in an attempt to save his son; and just the same as both of them, Balventius now paid the price for his breach of discipline.

A spear thrust slammed into his right thigh just above the knee, severing muscles and ripping free of the side of the leg in a shower of flesh and blood. The primus pilus staggered and almost fell, a hand grasping his shoulder and hauling him back into the formation. Just as he limped and lurched into the line, raising his shield against other attacks, another spear thrust smashed into his left thigh, close to the hip. His legs vanished beneath him, fiery pain coursing through his system, neither leg having the strength now to support him.

Balventius felt himself fall; felt the searing agony of his severed muscles. He felt hands grasping him.

Idiots!

If they didn't leave him they wouldn't be able to close up the line. They had to drop him. Summoning up all his strength, he threw his shield at the enemy, yanking his blade from its place as he did so. Lucanius never had the chance, but Balventius would take a few of the bastards with him. With the last of his strength, he wrenched himself free of the grasping legionaries and felt his legs fail; felt himself falling again. His hand remained tight on his sword ready to jab at anything that came within reach.

Something struck him on the head and he had the faint impression of his brains leaking out of his head as they ran, liquid-like, down his face and into his good eye.

Blackness descended to escort him to Elysium.

* * * * *

Cotta was watching the worst military debacle of his generation unfold before his very eyes. Sabinus had ordered Balventius to take a force out west, which was clearly a move destined merely to sacrifice a sizeable force of veterans to the enemy. He should have stopped the mad bastard issuing that order and still he'd stayed quiet. And yet, the one-eyed old bastard who led the Eighth had been on the very verge of achieving the unachievable. He'd been about to break through the Eburones and open the way to leave the valley.

And Sabinus had panicked.

The reforming of the Eighth after a cohort's departure had left the western edge of the Roman formation loosely manned and they were coming under increasingly heavy attack. Deciding that the lack of Balventius' single cohort was endangering the rest, Sabinus had sounded the order for that advance to fall back into position again.

Cotta had been speechless.

If he had been Balventius, chain of command or not, he would have kept pushing on to the west and tried to get to safety. It certainly didn't bear thinking about what the scarred veteran would say to his senior commander if they lived through this. He might well kill him. Cotta wouldn't blame him; might even hand him the sword with which to do it.

And the astounding thing was that, despite the fact that a successful fall back from that awful advance was impossible, again, Balventius and his men seemed to have carried it off. From his mounted vantage point, Cotta had watched as the advance force reappeared around the edge of the cavalry defences in a testudo formation and returned to the Eighth's ranks. When he found the old centurion later he would not have the words to put over how impressed he was.

Moreover, it had steeled Cotta's resolve.

This mess had gone on too long. Sabinus may be the man in command, but he was becoming increasingly useless. Panic and desperation were now informing his orders rather than reason or

287

pride. He was issuing conflicting commands and the army was being steadily battered into submission by missile attack throughout.

His gaze fixed on Sabinus, sitting tall and proud.

Wheeling his horse, he pushed his way through the mass of despairing legionaries to the senior officer. Sabinus turned as he approached.

'Yes?' A barked, harsh single word.

'Are you going to order the general retreat?'

'Don't be an idiot, Cotta. We...'

'We are in the shit up to our necks, Titus. It's retreat or die. If we can make it back to the camp, we might have a chance. Only a small one, but a small one's better than none at all.'

'I will not...'

Again, Cotta interrupted. 'Then I will.'

'What?'

'I am assuming command. You are not in a fit state to order these men.'

Sabinus started to splutter, his face turning a puce colour in rage. Ignoring him and feeling finally at peace with a decision he should have made an hour - or even a day - ago, Cotta turned away from him and pulled himself up in his saddle, clearing his throat to address the legions as loud as his voice would carry.

The order never came.

A lucky sling bullet smashed into Cotta's face, striking just between the nose and the right-hand corner of his mouth. In shock, the legate tumbled from his horse, shattered teeth embedding themselves in his tongue and the roof of his mouth, pieces of jagged jawbone driven into his throat.

He gagged on blood. The pain was indescribable.

Three legionaries stooped to help him up and he looked in agonised astonishment to see Sabinus peering at him with a look that spoke of both satisfaction and pleasure. Paying him no further heed, Sabinus began to bellow out orders again.

Cotta struggled. He seemed to be able to grunt and gurgle and nothing more, and every attempt felt like he was gargling with broken glass while the lower half of his face burned as though in a furnace. A capsarius was suddenly next to him trying to reach into the ruins of his mouth. Cotta, agony making it hard to concentrate, batted the man aside. This was too important. He tried to tell the man he needed something for the pain, but it came out as a wavering gurgle.

'Your teeth sir? I need to pull the shards.'

Gurgle. Cough, grunt, howl, gurgle - *just stop the pain*!

'The jaw will mend, sir.'

Oh for the love of Venus!

'I think he wants some pain killer' a helpful legionary butted in. Cotta nodded emphatically, glancing briefly at Sabinus, who was busy elsewhere.

The capsarius looked at his patient for only a moment before reaching into his satchel. Selecting the small glass vial of viscous liquid formed from henbane and mandragora mixed with honey and grape mulch, he tipped it slowly and with painstaking care, trying to measure a dose into a wide, flat spoon. Seeing the look in the officer's eyes, he hurriedly unstoppered the vial and tipped more than two doses' worth directly into the ruined mouth - possibly even three or four. It was dangerous in such concentration and high quantity, but at least it would hit his system quick, particularly entering his blood through the wound.

By the time the capsarius had scurried off to treat another wounded man, Cotta was already starting to experience a strange calm. While he could feel a rising wave of nausea, his pulse seemed to have slowed and the pain was receding at a rapid speed. He could feel himself starting to drift...

Damn the bloody physician. He'd overdosed him!

Somewhere through his drifting fug of calm, Cotta realised the missiles were no longer falling and the sounds of battle around him had ceased.

Spinning round in a manner that made him dizzy and raised the nausea to almost unbearable proportions, Cotta tried to focus. Something was happening on the hill. Two figures that swayed and blurred were moving in front of the others. He had the feeling one of them was speaking, though all he could hear was his own blood thumping.

Grunting and mumbling, he tried to ask the helpful legionary who was still holding his shoulder what was going on. Something in his face must have conveyed the question. The legionary swallowed.

'Their king is offering us terms, sir.'

King? What king? Terms? He mumbled something.

'We're to lay down our arms and the killing will stop' the legionary added, a note of desperate hope in his voice.

Cotta shook his head - a movement that caused him to cough up a hefty pile of vomit. His mouth no longer hurt at all, but he was so sick and dizzy and couldn't think! Couldn't work out...

Lay down their arms?

Cotta's mind filled with images of an enslaved legion at the mercy of the druids that were supposedly behind all of this. The very notion made him sick again. *No. They mustn't! It would be suicide!*

Shaking his head, he began to make urgent noises at the legionary, trying to tell him what must be done. The order must not be given. Must *not*!

Somewhere in the awful woolly mess that was his head facts started to sink in. The shape of Sabinus stepping his horse out, the tribunes behind him.

No!

Cotta, vomit still dribbling from his mouth and mixed with the constant flow of his blood, clawed at the legionary's arm. He had to stop it! He mumbled and grunted and wheezed at the soldier, but it was too late.

Sabinus must have given the order. The front ranks of the army lowered their shields and cast their swords and pila to the grass. Cotta shuddered in disbelief at the stupidity of the man. Had he not already been fooled once by this treacherous Gaul? Idiot!

Sabinus dismounted as he approached the party of Gaulish nobles on the middle of the slope.

Cotta tried so hard to concentrate - it seemed his mind was becoming more fluffy and fuddled with every passing moment. The damn capsarius had *ruined* him. He was too drugged to function. It took every last ounce of concentration just to focus on what was happening.

The Gauls - there were a small forest of them. No. He was counting some of them twice. No. There were a dozen? A score? They were on foot. Sabinus and the four remaining tribunes approached the king. Sabinus was offering his sword in surrender!

Cotta tried to shout something. He wasn't really sure what it was any more but that hardly mattered since it would be unintelligible anyway.

Ambiorix - that was the traitor bastard's name - reached out and grasped the handle, accepting the ornate hilt of the expensive

290

officer's sword with a nod. He gripped Sabinus' upper arm in the traditional warrior's gesture of brotherhood even as he drove the point of the blade deep into the commander's chest.

Cotta felt his body surrendering to the fluff. He was suddenly aware that he had collapsed and only the legionary next to him was stopping him from falling to the grass in a gelatinous heap.

There was a cry of dismay that rose from the entire army as Sabinus and the tribunes were executed on the slope. A man in a long grey robe - a druid, clearly - took his own blade to the collapsing figure of Sabinus, who was still choking out his life around a mouthful of his own blood. As two other Gallic warriors held the dying officer up, the druid used the long knife hilt to smash his ribs to fragments and then with a butcher's skill cut out his heart and held it before the legions.

A second tumultuous roar rose from the Fourteenth as the husk that had been Sabinus was discarded to the earth and his heart was offered up to the sky.

Before they could even grasp their shields as the centurions were now ordering, the missile attack began anew, felling men in droves, their only defences lying on the grass in front of them, discarded on Sabinus' orders.

Cotta felt sicker than he had ever been.

The Fourteenth were doomed - that was clear - and with them, half of the Eighth. There was no chance of a fighting retreat now. A tenth of the remaining force was systematically felled by arrows, rocks and sling shots in that opening volley.

Desperately, aware that he was fighting off unconsciousness with every beat of his heart, Cotta tried to make himself understood to the legionary.

Shields up. Defensive formation. Every century form a testudo. Each century to run east as best they can and try to reach the relative safety of the camp. It was hopeless, but better to die trying than surrendering.

Hopeless... like his attempts to communicate. The legionary couldn't understand what Cotta was trying to tell him. The mangled face worked madly with grunts, whines and gargling noises but the officer was too far gone to be comprehensible even with the help of gestures.

The Fourteenth was collapsing in on itself, no shield wall raised against the missiles. Cotta spun around to the far side to see the warriors starting to pour down the hill toward them.

This was it. The legion was about to be massacred. An ignominious defeat and - this particularly rankled - the first casualty of Priscus' damned predicted uprising.

When the sling stone caught Cotta in the eye and ploughed through the orb, shredding a line all the way through his brain and rattling against the back of his skull, he fell into a white cloud of bliss. There was no pain - the capsarius had seen to that. He felt the blow in every last detail, but with fascination rather than agony. The fact that he was dying seemed to be a blessing. He tried to gesture even as he fell, begging the legionary to place a coin under his tongue. He had family he hoped to see in Elysium.

The world went blessedly, painlessly, black.

* * * * *

Balventius awoke with a start and instantly wished he hadn't.

At first he thought he must be blind, but as shapes began to resolve around him he realised that the sun had gone down and it was dark, a thick blanket of cloud hiding both moon and stars and turning the land into a deep blue-black world of shadow.

The pain was the second thing that hit him, hot on the heels of the darkness. Feeling the ground shaking beneath him as though in the midst of a tremor, he tried to struggle to his feet only to realise that there was not an ounce of strength in either leg. Both had severed muscles and tendons and neither would respond to his attempts to move them, let alone lift his weight. The spear blows had crippled him and the pain was intense and unrelenting.

Indeed, it had been the pain that had awakened him.

The idea of becoming one of those legless crippled ex-soldiers that filled the sides of Rome's streets begging for a coin frightened him more than any enemy he had ever faced,

Slowly he became aware that the ground was not shaking after all. Despite his immobility, it was him that was moving. His head snapped round and he realised that he was being dragged, his feet bumping up and down with every rock, dip or undulation of the ground. He was surrounded by battle-weary legionaries; perhaps a score or three dozen from the shapes moving in the gloom. He could smell the blood and the urine. The smell of a defeated army.

Where were they?

Even as his feet bounced and before his dry, unused throat attempted to find his voice, he recognised the severity of his injuries. He had been wounded so many times in his career that he had lost count a decade ago and had suffered a score of wounds to the legs alone. His experience made it abundantly clear that his right leg was now beyond help. Even had it been salvageable following immediately on from the battle, how many hours had passed since their early morning disaster that it was now dark? The leg was lost to him, which made him an ex-soldier whatever happened. There was the very high likelihood that the left was in a similar state too.

Both legs!

Balventius spat his anger at the world.

'You awake Centurion?'

Somewhere deep in his chest, Balventius' voice came out a wheeze. He tried again.

'Just' he croaked. 'Where are we?'

'Nearly back at the camp, sir.'

Balventius nodded. Just as it should have been in the first place. How had he been unconscious for so long? He remembered the leg wounds and collapsing...

'I was hit in the head?'

'That was Mittius, sir. You wouldn't let the lads save you, so he had to clout you to stop you struggling.'

Balventius almost laughed at the absurdity of it. Legless and defeated, what made them think he wanted to be saved? Bleeding out his age-old life in a Roman gutter begging for scraps was no way for a soldier to go.

'The cohort's retreat was successful?'

Another voice - a familiar one - laughed. 'It was. Damnedest thing I ever saw!'

Balventius focused on the source of the voice: Petrosidius, the eagle bearer, with his precious burden still held tight and shining over his shoulder. Lately of the Tenth, the man had become something of a legend after last year's landings in Britannia. If anyone other than Balventius could hope to be a focus and a beacon to the defeated legionaries it would be him.

'What happened?' he managed.

'Your lot got back nice and safe and then that donkey-prick Sabinus surrendered!'

'*What*?' Balventius almost lurched out of his escort's grasp.

'Led the tribunes out and threw down his weapons. Gave the order for a general disarmament. Soon as the shields were down, some druid bastard gutted him and they opened up their missiles on the men.'

Balventius tried to picture the scene, but it left a sour taste and he moved on, shaking away the image.

'Cotta? Didn't he argue?'

'No one knows. Disappeared about that time and no one's heard anything of him since. Doubt he got out alive, though.'

'Shit. So they massacred the men? Didn't anyone rally the legions?'

'The centurions of the Fourteenth did. Their primus pilus tried his best. To his credit we fought on for three hours, until the sun was high in the sky. Last I saw of the Fourteenth in bulk there were maybe two hundred of them left, fighting hard up against the abandoned carts.'

'And you ran?' Balventius tried to put some invective and disapproval into the statement, but he found he had none left. What man would have stayed voluntarily for that? Any survivors would be turned inside out and used as a wall decoration by the druids.

Petrosidius was suddenly next to him, staring deep into his eyes.

'Did they run? The veterans of the Eighth? Are you mad, Balventius?'

'Sorry.'

'They beat a fighting withdrawal. Half a cohort managed to get out of the mess and made it up the hill. We kicked the snot out of a couple of hundred archers and slingers until their reinforcements found us. Then one of your older centurions gave the order to pull back to the camp. Good on him. If he hadn't, I would have. We fought off a good few hundred of the bastards, but by the time we got clear of the field we'd lost most of the men. Last count we had thirty one, but that was at the sunset break. I reckon we've lost three or four to wounds since then and there'll be more coins for the boatman before the sun rises.'

Balventius shook his head. 'Wait. It was only two miles or so to camp. How...?'

'We took a slightly circuitous route. We've been in the Arduenna forest for most of the time. The Eburones seem to be everywhere and we're in no fit state to fight so we've kept out of sight as we moved slowly. To be honest, I'm not sure what we'll do when we get back to camp, but it was something to make for. A focus. I'm the only officer left, y'see. Apart from yourself, of course.'

Balventius sighed.

'More than seven thousand men. A massacre. It's the worst loss Caesar's had in his career, I shouldn't wonder. The old man's going to be a mite angry when he hears about this.'

'*If* he hears.' Petrosidius rolled his shoulders and switched hands with the eagle. 'Bear in mind this might not be an isolated incident. What happens if this has hit every encamped legion in Gaul?'

'Then our occupation is over and Gaul is for the Celts again. They'll have won.' He shook his head. 'But Jupiter won't let that happen. Caesar's still there. I can feel it like he's watching us. No. We got hit because we're the most remote. I reckon we were a test of strength, resolve and readiness and we've proved to be about as tough and dangerous as a bag of grapes. That'll just give them the confidence to do it again and maybe even on a bigger scale.'

He blinked away the sweat, blood and grime. 'We need to get a message to Caesar - to tell him about this; about what happened.'

'Seems unlikely' Petrosidius replied calmly

'Bet you wish you'd stayed with the Tenth' Balventius grunted hollowly.

'They might yet be in even deeper shit.'

Someone shouted something inaudible out of Balventius' arc of vision.

'What was that?'

'They've spotted the camp defences. We're nearly there. Couple of dozen heartbeats and we'll be in what we might laughingly call 'safety'.'

Balventius shook his head. Not from *his* point of view. The rest of the men were facing the way they were going, eagerly - even hungrily - eying the imagined security of the camp. Not so: Balventius. Being dragged by the shoulders by two burly legionaries, he could not see the ditches and mound of the winter quarters. What he could see were the figures emerging from the treeline some few hundred yards behind them.

'I think we're out of time' he breathed, causing Petrosidius to turn and pick out the figures.

'Thought we'd lost the bastards. Oh well. Looks like we'll go down fighting after all.'

The two men tried to make a rough mental estimate of the numbers of the Eburones flooding from the treeline toward them. It was not a good number. It spelled certain defeat even for a full, fresh century, let alone half a century of tired, badly-armed and wounded men.

The officers looked at one another as the men bearing Balventius bounced him painfully down the first ditch and then up the slope before dropping down into the second.

'Halt!' he bellowed.

The legionaries, their endless drilling bringing them to a dead stop with the command despite the situation, glanced back the way they had come. One of them said 'but sir... the barbarians?'

'They'll be on us any moment' Balventius snapped. 'We're dead men walking...' he snorted at the irony of the phrase as his two carriers pulled him upright. He looked at Petrosidius. 'You thinking what I'm thinking?'

The aquilifer rubbed his brow. 'I guess so. Using the ditch?'

Balventius nodded. 'You'd best start running now.'

The standard bearer shook his head. 'Bollocksed if I'm going to be the one who carries this news to 'eagle beak'. Besides, you can't stand up. You need a good helping hand here.'

Balventius began to splutter his argument but to his irritation, Petrosidius ignored him entirely and turned to one of the legionaries nearby - a man who was still fully equipped and whole and who appeared of an age to be a reasonable veteran. 'Nasica? You're in charge.'

The old soldier frowned. 'In charge of *what*, sir?'

'In charge of the survivors. Take the two best men and this.' As the legionary watched in surprise, Petrosidius wrenched the silver eagle from the long, smooth staff and thrust it at him. 'Wrap it up and keep it safe. Head south through the forest and try to get to Labienus. He's about three days' march away, but you'll be slowed by the forest. Stay out of sight of everyone. All that matters is that you find Labienus and tell him what happened here. And make sure that if you do get caught, you bury that eagle deep first. That thing never gets into the bastards' hands, alright?'

Nasica nodded, reverently coddling the eagle.

'Get moving. Follow the ditch round to the far side of the camp and then break for the trees and don't stop until you find that other camp.'

Even as Nasica turned and grabbed two of his fellows, running away along the deep ditch where the enemy would not be able to see their departure, Petrosidius turned and grinned at Balventius as he drew his blade.

'Idiot.' Balventius grunted. 'You should have gone.'

'And miss this?'

* * * * *

Lucius Nasica wrapped the precious eagle of the Eighth Legion in his spare tunic. He'd long since taken to the habit of carrying his spare tucked discretely into his shield cover, just in case. He and his two closest comrades eyed the dark, threatening gloom of the sacred forest of the Treveri's Goddess ahead. It was said to be haunted and protected by flesh eating spirits. The very idea of spending probably four or five days traversing it and then trying to locate another Roman camp in enemy territory was heart-in-mouth stuff.

But Nasica had served in the Eighth too many years for comfort. He would sooner twist off his own head than see that eagle fall to the Eburones or their allies. And, of course, news of this disaster had to be brought to Caesar.

The three men took a deep breath and leapt up from the camp's outer ditch, running for that forbidding forest.

Halfway across the long stretch of open ground, the veteran glanced back.

Just once.

The fight was beginning at the far side of the camp and the sheer numbers of the natives that were pouring across the grass to the ditch made the result inevitable.

It was over before they reached the 'safety' of darkness beneath the boughs of Arduenna's great woodland. Nasica cast up a quick prayer for the departure of Balventius and Petrosidius, and never looked back again.

Chapter Fifteen

NOVEMBRIS

Balbus strolled slowly out of the bedroom, closing the door carefully and shaking his head.

'Still nothing?' Fronto enquired soothingly.

Another shake.

'She had a shock that no little girl should have. It's going to take her a while. Your Jewish friend is convinced it's all in her mind, though, and there's no physical damage.'

'She's my little girl, Marcus. I'm going to gut someone for this.'

'I think you need to calm down again, Quintus. Every time you look at Balbina you start to boil over. If you go mad off the leash and start chasing that big Germanic killer, they'll be mopping you up off the street. Masgava's the only one of us who would stand a chance against that thing. I think we're all agreed that we need to deal with him carefully, with prior planning.'

'I don't care how it happens, but he needs to be removed from this world for what he's done, Marcus.'

Fronto nodded. 'No argument from me. For now, though, we need to deal with the dice as they've landed. It's been nine days, and we should already have arranged the funeral rites and feast for tonight. I'll grant you've been a little preoccupied with Balbina, but for Corvinia's sake it still should be done. I'll ask Galronus and Palmatus to head to the markets and bring back the supplies. I think even Masgava might relent on the free-flowing wine tonight.'

Balbus nodded slowly. The entire group had now spent over a week closeted away in Fronto's house. The Jewish physician and the retired legionary seemed to have become an almost constant fixture, only occasionally returning to their residences to deal with their own affairs. He was starting to wonder what he would have done without the pair.

'The rest of the family should be there, Fronto - at the feast.'

'All the random cousins and uncles can mourn in their own time and ways. It's more important that she is remembered by those of us who were close. It's a shame that Lucilia won't be here, but...'

He fell silent, aware that he'd just dredged up yet another worry for his friend. Balbus had been putting off writing the letter to his daughter, and Lucilia was still blissfully unaware of events.

'Anyway' he went on, 'we'll have to take wine to the mausoleum. We'll have to be damn careful this evening that we don't fall foul of Berengarus somewhere in the back streets. On the bright side, with you and me, Galronus, Masgava, Palmatus and Elijah I very much doubt the German bastard will try anything. One against six would be suicide even for him. And I think those of us who held military rank should go in full uniform. The swords will have to stay covered until we're out of the city, but we'll be armed and armoured. Should be enough to put off any potential attack.'

'Let him come' Balbus growled.

'Everything in good time. First thing's first: we pay due honour and respect to Corvinia. Then we have to decide what to do about the girls down in Puteoli and how we handle Pompey's pet killer.'

A knock at the front door echoed around the atrium in which they stood and Fronto frowned. The six people who had any business in the house were already here, Palmatus and Galronus sparring with Masgava in the peristyle garden and Elijah watching them from a bench where he was poring through Lucilia's collection of texts on plants and herbs.

Balbus shot him a look, his hand going to the gladius at his waist that had only been removed in the last nine days to facilitate sleep, and that had come in only short and disturbed bursts. Fronto's eyes dropped to the hilt and the fingers caressing it. Several times over the past week he'd had to hold his tongue against expressing his disapproval of the old man being armed in the house, but now, at that single knock, being armed suddenly seemed a good idea and his mind's eye roved back across the garden with its sparring warriors to the storehouse of his father with the swords hanging inside.

'Be ready, just in case.'

As Balbus nodded, Fronto padded barefoot across to the front door, catching sight of himself in the long bronze mirror Lucilia had installed in the entrance hall to adjust her clothing before heading out into public.

He cut a very different figure to the man who had stood here and complained about the cost of the enormous mirror. Gone was every ounce of fat, replaced with rippling muscles of the sort he'd not had since the days he served in Hispania. His stance was straight and tall, not the slightly curved and leaning posture of a man with a cripplingly painful knee and a tender back. His eyes were bright, missing the pinkness that was their customary shade. He'd even taken to shaving more than once a week. He had to admit that he looked a decade younger.

Lucilia would hardly recognise him.

A second knock reminded him of where he was and he turned and opened the door with a quick nod to Balbus at the side of the entrance hall.

Fronto's first reaction to the figure standing on the step outside was one of unleashing pent-up anger. His hands twitched as they reached up and out toward the man's neck, but he stopped them with a great effort of willpower and lowered them back to his sides.

Publius Clodius Pulcher!

The man was becoming something of a recluse at the moment. While his gangs were still prowling the streets and causing mayhem, occasionally clashing with rivals, the man himself had taken to staying at his palatial and secure townhouse much of the time, only venturing out into the streets when required, and then with a sizeable bodyguard. While his reputation seemed to have lost some of its former tarnish through his close ties to the peoples' beloved Caesar, he was still well-despised by a number of the more important figures in the city - including Pompey and Milo - and his life may well be endangered should he let his defences slip too far.

And now he was standing not three feet from Fronto - a man who had more reasons than most to wring his scrawny neck.

The bodyguard were there, though.

While Clodius stood defenceless and easy before Fronto, the street behind was filled with his killers, leaning against walls and doorways, watching every space intently. He must feel damn certain that Fronto was no impulsive killer.

It was touch and go whether the man was right.

Fronto glanced once back at Balbus, whose blade had slipped a few finger-widths from its scabbard. He wondered for just a moment how much good it would do the city just to nod and let Balbus go to work. The older ex-officer was usually too reasoned and honourable a man to even consider such an act, but recent events had robbed a lot of that reason and his eyes were those of a man prepared to take lives.

Besides, the old man had been one of the voices instrumental in separating Fronto from Caesar, and this creature on the doorstep was Caesar's man in both body and soul now.

'What do you want?'

'And good morning to you, Fronto. Might I come in and take a few moments of your time?'

Fronto tried to put the full extent of his feelings into his look.

'I try not to let rats nest in my house. I say again, what do you want?'

Clodius smiled, but not like a rat. It was strange and oily, like a snake smiling.

'I need to speak to you, Fronto, and what I have to say is not for any wagging ears in the street, or even for your noble friends inside. This is for you alone. I would speak in private, man to man.'

'Man to mollusc, perhaps! After everything you've done, you expect me to actually invite you into my house.'

'My bodyguard will stay outside, Fronto, and I am entirely unarmed.'

The former legate of the Tenth turned and looked at Balbus, back in the hallway. The older man shrugged.

'I will spare you a few moments,' he replied, turning back again, 'but bear in mind that I have a number of trained fighters in this house and if I don't like what I hear I might just let them get to work on you. It would, I'm sure, be a benefit to all mankind.'

Clodius' snake-grin widened. 'Thank you for your generous and charming acceptance. Shall we?'

Fronto stepped to one side to allow the toga-clad nobleman entry, loading his gaze with threat as he cast it around the various thugs in the street outside. Clodius nodded amiably to Balbus and strode into the atrium, where he stopped and looked around appreciatively. Behind him Fronto closed the door on the bodyguards and tried not to think how easy it would be to do away with one of Rome's most dangerous and hated men right now.

'I see your builders have done an excellent job reconstructing the house. I am pleased. Very unfortunate what transpired here a few years ago.'

'Unfortunate?' Fronto snapped as he re-entered the atrium. 'As memory serves, it was your doing.'

'The ebb and flow of politics in Rome are unpredictable, Fronto, and sometimes some unpleasant silt and debris is carried in to shore.

301

I most profoundly regret what happened and assure you that I hold no ill-will toward you.'

Fronto blinked in disbelief. '*You* hold no ill-will toward *me*?'

The man continued to smile and Fronto felt the distinct urge to knock his teeth down his throat. He also noted that a statement of regret was hardly the same thing as an apology.

'Can we step into somewhere private to talk?'

Fronto frowned at the voluminous toga. 'Keep in mind that I'm fast these days. Any concealed knife is unlikely to get as far as my skin before your nose gets broken.'

'I told you I was unarmed.'

'If I told you your presence didn't offend, would that necessarily be a truth?'

Clodius laughed lightly, a sound that merely heightened Fronto's irritation. 'You are a piece of work, Fronto. I can see why the general valued you so.'

'Caesar and I may not be on the best of terms at this point, Clodius, but he has at times commanded my utmost respect. You, however, rate little more than something I scrape off my boot. Come on. Let's make this quick. Every moment you spend under this roof threatens to make me vomit.'

Ignoring the look of genuine humour on the man's face, Fronto directed him to one of the unused bedrooms, where they could speak in private. As Clodius strode across the floor and sat primly on one of the twin chairs by the desk, Fronto simply closed the door and leaned against it.

'Talk, then.'

'I come with an offer, Fronto; a one-time offer.'

'There is nothing you can offer me that I could want.'

'Don't be so sure.'

Clodius reached into his toga, causing Fronto to flinch momentarily. Despite the man's words, he half expected a knife to emerge. What actually appeared, however, was a rod around a foot long, wrapped in a leather strip that was wound around it in a long spiral.

'You know what this is?'

'It's a scytale. Caesar used to use them to transmit coded messages.'

302

Clodius smiled. 'He still does. This one's all ready.' He handed it to Fronto, who took it gingerly and turned it slowly, reading the words picked out by their position on the baton.

RECRUITOFFICERSURGENTLY

He passed it back and leaned once more.

'Recruit?'

'Caesar needs good men. He is facing a great deal of difficulty in Rome, for certain, with Pompey's ties now severed and Crassus absent, as I'm sure you are well aware, and the death of his daughter has hurt him on such a level that he has not even brought himself to mention it since hearing the news. I fear he still denies the truth of it.' He sighed. 'It also seems that your old comrade Priscus has uncovered something that threatens Caesar's position in Gaul. I am to recruit, as you saw - and urgently. Implied is a fairly open mandate from the general, but he also had some specifics for me in another communique.'

'You want me to run back to Caesar?'

'It has come to my attention that you are rapidly building a group of dangerous enemies in the city. You need the support of the powerful and a level of security that you cannot yourself provide for your friends and family. Caesar can supply the former. I can supply the latter in his name.'

Fronto snorted and folded his arms.

'Even if Caesar would have me back, you are deranged if you think for one moment that I would place my family in your devious hands.'

'Caesar has mentioned you by name in one of our many missives. You angered him when you turned your back on him last winter, but he is a reasonable man, and a brilliant one. He knows your value and would make this offer himself were he here. But it is, as I say, a one-time offer. Neither he nor I can afford to waste a great deal of time securing your support. He needs you in Gaul more than he ever has, but if you are not ready to take this deal, then I have others to approach in his name and I cannot afford to tarry for games. Time is of the essence.'

Fronto frowned, shaking his head slightly. It was a surprising offer and despite the fact that he would trust a snake sooner than this man, there was little doubt that he spoke the truth. After all, it must be irking Clodius to have to come here with such an offer after the trouble Fronto had dealt him in the past. And to have to enter this house unarmed was a tremendous risk. Caesar must not have asked him to do it; he must have demanded it.

'I am not unaware of the value of the offer, Clodius, and you can transmit to Caesar a genuine apology that I cannot accept it, but there are matters that need to be attended to here before I can even consider any future moves, and while I would still consider serving Caesar again, I will not ever, in the world of men, place the wellbeing of my loved ones into your treacherous, wicked, devious hands. If it is a one-time offer then I regret saying no, but no it must be.'

Clodius straightened.

'Sad that your anger blinds you to possibilities. Your distrust of me is greater than your need to stand in the field once more? To conquer the barbarian? To avenge your friend Crispus?'

Fronto stepped away from the door for a moment, his arms unfolding.

'What?'

'I can believe that you detach yourself from the deaths of so many unnamed comrades at the hands of those Gallic savages, but I am led to understand that young Crispus was a close friend. Have you not the urge to chastise his killers?'

'Crispus?' Fronto snapped, stepping forward again. His mind filled with flashes of the young legate, his fresh, boyish face at odds with the uniform he wore. In another world, Crispus might have been his son. He was actually of an *age* to be, and yet was as good a friend as Balbus in the next room.

'Crispus is dead?'

Clodius' face became a picture of surprise and Fronto narrowed his eyes. The man appeared to be genuinely taken aback.

'You haven't been informed? Strange. He fell to a treacherous Gaul some months ago during an attempted escape by an Aeduan prisoner. His ashes were brought back to the city and will be interred in the family mausoleum by now.' He stood slowly. 'I do apologise for breaking the news so suddenly. I assumed you knew. I feel bound to make one last plea on behalf of our mutual benefactor. Caesar needs good men in Gaul and he recognises you as one of them. Will you go?'

Fronto turned and pulled open the door he had been leaning against. His eyes were cold and flinty. 'Tell the general in your next letter that I am truly sorry to decline and that in the future, when circumstances allow, I would reconsider, but for now I must look to my family.'

Clodius nodded.

'Then I had best leave. Perhaps Caesar will extend his generosity in future times. I would rather we served the same master than meet as enemies.'

Fronto's glare hardened further. 'If I ever return to Caesar, it will be to serve *with* him, not to serve him and, whatever the future might hold, you and I will never be less than enemies. Pompey and Milo may be mutual adversaries, but the divide between you and I is uncrossable, Clodius Pulcher. Thank you for your offer but now you must leave, and you are no longer welcome in the house of the Falerii.'

Clodius simply smiled his snake smile again and walked calmly past Fronto and out into the atrium. His host followed and paused for a moment in the doorway. Balbus now had his gladius unsheathed and was running the fingers of his left hand over the point in a decidedly threatening manner. A few paces away Galronus stood, arms folded, blocking the way out toward the garden, his face sour yet unreadable.

Crossing the atrium, Fronto opened the house's main door once more and waited as the unwelcome guest passed through and into the street. Clodius turned on the step to speak, but the door closed in his face as he began.

Turning back from the portal, Fronto peered into the atrium and walked slowly back toward the two men there.

'Crispus is dead.'

His eyes narrowed as Balbus stepped back, this fresh unpleasant news managing even to break through the shell of obdurate and implacable emotionlessness that the older man had worn since the death of his wife. Galronus, however, looked distinctly uneasy.

'You knew?'

The Remi nobleman nodded slowly.

'How?'

'A letter from Priscus. It came for you a week or so ago.'

'And you opened it?'

'You had a lot on your mind, as did Balbus. I saw no harm in it, but when I read the news...' he sighed. 'Well, I hardly thought that this was the time to burden you both. After all, he didn't fall in battle, but was killed in cold blood by a rebel. You were in no fit state to hear that then. I thought perhaps in a month or two, when things had calmed down...'

Fronto's hand came up threateningly as he took a step angrily toward his friend, but Balbus was suddenly between them.

'He's right, Fronto. It's just added misery and another step on the stairway to Hades. Don't know about you, but I'd rather not have known. We'll mourn him tonight with Corvinia, and tomorrow we'll start work on revenge. First the Germanic monstrosity who killed my wife, and then we'll look to the sons of Celtic whores who killed our friend.'

Fronto stood for a moment, his gaze swapping back and forth between the two men.

'I want to see that letter, Galronus. Whatever your intentions, don't keep things like that from me again. I want you and Palmatus to go down to the markets and fill a cart with everything we need for a proper send off for Corvinia and Crispus. And don't stint on the wine. Get a lot - good stuff too.'

'I will, Marcus. But there's something else you need to see, first.'

Fronto's brow creased again at the strange tone of his friend's voice.

'What?'

'In the garden.'

* * * * *

For the second time that morning, Fronto stopped dead at a doorway, surprised by what he saw.

On the gravel walkway around the small fountain, which was now missing a number of pieces of decorative stonework following their regular sparring sessions, stood Masgava and Palmatus, each with a drawn sword - one a notched gladiatorial sica and the other a well-used military gladius. Both blades' points were hovering a hair's breadth from either side of their prisoner's neck.

Fronto took two more steps out into the garden, Galronus at one shoulder and Balbus at the other, and shook his head in bemusement at the surprises the day was bringing.

'Paetus? What in the name of seven stinking latrine demons are you doing in my garden?'

The former Camp Prefect of Caesar's army, betrayed by both Clodius and the general, presumed dead on a Belgic battlefield and now back in Rome vowing revenge on his betrayers, smiled coldly.

'It's been a long time, Fronto. Could you have these two raise their blades, you think?'

Masgava and Palmatus kept their weapons hovering over his jugular.

'I don't think so.'

Galronus kicked something across the floor and Fronto looked down to see a bronze dagger with a wide crosspiece moulded straight to the blade and tapering slowly to an almost needle-point. A Parthian weapon, if Fronto was any judge.

'This yours?'

Paetus nodded fractionally, aware that too much head movement could draw blood in his current situation.

'You know I have no grudge against you, Fronto. Jove, I've even saved your life a couple of times.'

'No quarter offered, Paetus, until you tell me what you're doing armed in my garden.'

'Can't you guess, Marcus?' He sighed. 'Missing an opportunity is what.'

Palmatus pricked the very tip of his blade into Paetus' neck, drawing a tiny bead of blood. 'This piece of shit was lurking on the roof, looking down into your atrium, Fronto. Masgava knocked me back to the rear wall when we were fighting, which is bloody lucky, else we wouldn't have seen him at all.'

Masgava nodded.

'You're after Clodius?' Fronto asked quietly. 'I assumed you'd given up or gone to ground. I've not heard a word of you for over a year.' Shaking his head, he gestured to the two men beside the prisoner. 'You can let him go. He was here to try and kill Clodius. Can't blame him for that - I felt the urge myself, frankly.'

As the two men lowered their swords, Fronto bent and picked up the eastern knife.

'Not over-keen on you attempting to murder a prominent politician under my roof, though, Paetus. I'd prefer it if you could keep your private war out of my house.'

The former prefect rubbed his neck, looking at the smear of crimson on his finger as it came away.

'You've some good men here, Fronto. Quick and steady.' Stretching, he shrugged. 'I've been itching to get to the slimy piece of crap for over a year, but he's permanently protected. I've come close three times now and even managed to get into his house once, but every close call just makes the man more paranoid and draw another level of armour round him. I almost couldn't believe my eyes when he walked unescorted into your house. He doesn't even visit his own clients without an armed guard.'

Fronto tossed the Parthian blade into the air, watching it twist as it rose and fell and then catching it by the point and proffering it to Paetus, who took it and sheathed it at his belt.

'So you took your opportunity?'

'You'd be surprised how easy it is to get onto your roof unseen. You might want to look at that, given the number of enemies you have, Fronto.'

'I'll manage.'

Paetus nodded toward the small table by the stone bench where the Jewish physician had furled his scrolls and was watching with interest. On the table sat a bowl of fruit.

'May I?'

'Be my guest,' Fronto replied, 'since you apparently are anyway.'

Paetus reached out and took an apple, shining it on his tunic and then taking a bite and savouring the taste.

'I miss fresh fruit.'

Fronto simply raised his eyebrow questioningly. Paetus grinned. 'Sadly, my family's few remaining funds ran out during the winter and I was forced to seek employment in order to fund my ongoing campaign to bring down that monster and his master.'

Since Fronto remained silent and questioning, Paetus took another bite and shrugged again.

'I've signed on with Annius Milo.'

Galronus and Balbus were suddenly next to the man, three blades wavering at him as Galronus cracked his knuckles. Fronto smiled unpleasantly.

'Milo has no friends here, Paetus. I think you've just outstayed your welcome.'

'Come on, Fronto. Milo holds you in surprisingly high esteem, no matter what Pompey might do. And I'm no Pompeian myself -

they're just a means to an end. If anyone other than me stands a chance of gutting Clodius it's him.'

'Still, I think it's time for you to go.'

Paetus smiled and chewed on the apple. 'By all means. But I think it only fair to warn you that you might want to think about leaving too.'

'Milo doesn't scare me, Paetus.'

'It's not Milo to whom I refer. Pompey has given us strict instructions that we are not to lay a finger on you. I suspect he worries that any further interference will damage his political standing in the city. No... there's others that *you* need to worry about.'

Balbus' blade touched Paetus' breastbone, forcing the man to step back almost into the pond.

'Berengarus the German? His time is almost up.'

The former prefect nodded. 'He's a big one, but I can see how you lot would have no fear of him. Yet I still think you need to reconsider.'

'Why?' interjected Elijah, leaning forward from his seat and grasping a plum from the bowl. 'What has changed?'

Paetus rolled his shoulders. 'Yesterday we escorted Pompey to the Carcer.'

Fronto had a flash-memory of the unpleasant, dark prison with its animalistic denizens shuffling around behind the bars; the wraith that had addressed him when he visited.

'The carcer?'

'Yes. The great Pompey, in a moment of magnanimity, ordered that all the inmates he had interred there be freed.'

Fronto squeezed his eyes shut. 'And Berengarus was there too, I have no doubt.'

'He was in the street out the front, yes.'

'Did you hear anything more?'

'Sadly, not. We were simply escorting the general. Beyond hearing the initial order I was kept busy, but I think I can extrapolate on what's about to happen. As, I note from your expression, can you.'

Balbus turned his head sharply. 'Fronto?'

'There are some wicked, horribly dangerous men in there, Quintus. Or there *were*. Freed and on the streets, they'll have had

309

nowhere to go, but I suspect the big German has a job or two for them.'

Paetus smiled. 'As I said, we were told not to harm you, so that's exactly what I shall do. We weren't told the carcer visit was a secret, though, so there you are. Consider it a friendly and timely warning, for the sake of the old days. You've a bad history of getting the shit kicked out of you in this house. Run away, Fronto, while you still can.'

Fronto pinched the bridge of his nose and gestured with his thumb over his shoulder toward the atrium. Masgava and Palmatus escorted Paetus from the garden. There were no goodbyes but, as the man disappeared into the darkness, he said 'Run, Fronto.'

He opened his eyes to find Balbus staring at him.

'What?'

'We can't run, Marcus. The monster needs to die for what he's done.'

'I don't disagree, Balbus, but we're not talking about one man now; we might be talking a dozen, and they're mostly going to be very experienced killers. I cannot imagine what was going through Pompey's mind. He's unleashed a plague just to get at me.'

Balbus took a step forward. 'Don't tell me you're actually thinking of running away, Marcus.'

Fronto shook his head and heaved in a deep breath.

'Not as such...'

'Marcus, I have to see this through. Even if you run, I cannot.'

'I don't want to run, Quintus, but we're just hopelessly unprepared to deal with this. Alright there are six of us here right now, and even though I'm sure Galronus will stay with us whatever happens, Palmatus and Masgava are free men. They are entitled to leave. And the good physician over there? Well it's not his fight and even if he decided to stay, he's hardly a bred killer! Two years running now I've fought for my life in this place. It's not lucky. Fortuna's gaze doesn't fall on this house no matter how much I pray to her, and you heard how easily Paetus found it to get in.'

'You are?' Balbus snapped. 'You're thinking of running away.'

The two men glared at one another for a moment and the tension rose even with the return of the two warriors from the doorway into the garden.

A cough finally broke the silence. Both men looked around to see Elijah rise from the bench.

'What?' snapped Fronto, somewhat unfairly.

'May I interrupt?' When neither man argued, the swarthy medic reached up and scratched his chin.

'It seems you are being offered both a problem and an opportunity.'

'Explain?' asked Balbus sharply.

'I have not been privy to all of your discussions, obviously, gentlemen, but I do believe that you, master Fronto, wish to see your family safe so that you can look to your future career. You, master Balbus, seek revenge for your lovely wife, and while I cannot condone such a course of action, I can entirely understand it and sympathise. Neither of you feel this is the correct time and place to fight them. You are, by your own admission, unprepared, and you worry about the family you have back at your villa in Puteoli.'

'That's not an explanation.'

'If these people are as bad as you say, staying here and fighting, master Balbus, would leave your families unprotected so many miles away, and these may be the sort of people who would enjoy causing you pain by bringing violence against those you love? Witness the death of Corvinia.'

Balbus' face drained of colour.

'He's right, Fronto. They've been loose since yesterday. What if they're not coming for us? What if they're already half way to Puteoli?'

Fronto nodded, appearing calm, though his eyes had taken on a worried wideness.

'Precisely' the Jew replied calmly. 'I am given to understand that you are familiar with the land there?'

Fronto nodded slowly, his eyes narrowing in comprehension. 'I spent much of my life there.'

'And while these unpleasant murderers may well be overly familiar with the streets of Rome...'

'They will be totally *un*familiar with Puteoli' Fronto finished, turning to Balbus. 'He's right. It doesn't matter whether they've gone or not and whether the girls are there or we send them somewhere secret, *we* should go there. Get the bastards into *my* world. I'm sick of spending all my time reacting to problems caused by others. I'm always either struggling to make Caesar's more impetuous plans work or stumbling around in the dark trying to avoid dying at the hands of some piece of shit like Clodius or Hortius and Menenius. It's time I started to take a bit more control.'

Balbus sheathed his sword, suddenly all urgent business.

'Time is of the essence, though, Fronto.'

'What of the funeral feast?' Palmatus asked quietly from the doorway.

'To Hades with tradition. The girls are more important.'

'Of course.'

'What's the fastest way to Puteoli?' Balbus asked Fronto, wiping his sweaty brow.

'About two and a half days by horseback riding every available hour. We can shave off maybe half a day by taking a change of horses with us.'

'Not so, gentlemen' the Jewish physician smiled, twisting the half-eaten plum in his hand.

'How so?'

'A liburnian vessel with a good captain can cover the distance by sea in less than a day and a half if the weather is right and the ship unburdened.'

Fronto turned to the man. 'How do you know such things?'

'You think I walked here from Judea? I am a veritable fount of knowledge, good sir.'

Balbus nodded. 'It'll cost a fortune if we want the ship to ourselves without a cargo.'

'We can pay it, Quintus. And even if those murderers are on their way already, we might be able to get there first. If not, we'll have time to prepare for them.' He scowled. 'Of course it'll take me half a day to stop bringing up my stomach contents when we get there, but it's still worth it.'

He spun around and looked at the others.

'None of you owe us anything.'

'You're still paying me' Masgava replied with a half-smile.

'Well, if you're paying?' added Palmatus with a grin.

'Thank you. But you, Elijah, I think we are parting ways.'

The physician pursed his lips. 'I will not take part in your fight, I'm afraid, no. Hippocrates himself bade those of the medical profession pledge to keep all from harm and, while I can see the need for a judicious bending of that rule, I will not break it to kill outright. But I have a duty to care for the young girl until such time as she

312

sees fit to grace us with her light once more. I presume you are not amenable to leaving her in my care in the city?'

Balbus shook his head vehemently.

'Then I will have to join you on your journey, if only for her sake. I can keep her and the ladies company while you soldiers of Rome fight the good fight.'

Fronto nodded, his face serious, reflecting that of his older friend. 'In that case, Palmatus, consider yourself on a retainer. You do a good job and you can name your own damn wage… same for you Masgava. Medicus? I'll leave it to Balbus to make any arrangements with you, but I'm grateful for your help. And you Jews are supposed to have a direct line to some powerful god if I remember rightly. I'll take it kindly if you'll throw a word in with him for us, since mine seem to be suspiciously absent these days.'

The physician smiled indulgently.

'Palmatus: take the good medicus here down to the emporium - he seems to know about the journey. Don't come back until you find a ship's master with a fast vessel who'll take us to Puteoli without cargo. Passage for seven people and seven horses plus personal belongings. Pay whatever you need to but try not to let him know that's the case! At least make an *effort* to look choosy.'

The former legionary nodded and crossed to the Jewish physician.

'Galronus and Masgava? Start packing up everything we'll want to take with us. We don't need anything we can't fit on horseback. I want *both* my swords, though.'

The two men, without bothering to acknowledge the order, moved across the garden toward the armoury.

'Balbus: I suggest you get yourself and Balbina ready for the journey. I'll deal with the beasts. Bucephalus is in Puteoli and we've only got a couple of nags in the stable here, so I'm going to go and see a man about a horse. Six horses, in fact.'

* * * * *

'We go for Fronto. Break house. Kill men.'

Berengarus' piercing green eyes almost boiled with the desire to cause harm as he glared at the man standing before him, the other's wisps of wild, white hair only reaching up to the big German's chest.

313

'You are impatient, my gargantuan friend. I understand, but impetuousness carries dangers. We cannot afford to be so impulsive that we leap into the pit without checking for wolves first. All things in good time. When I took your coin you agreed that I would do the thinking.'

'Think faster.'

The grey, flickering tongue licked the lips in the parchment-skinned face as Tulchulchur, the Monster of Vipsul, smiled. 'Vengeance is best appreciated slowly and laboriously, else it is over too fast my friend. And vengeance completed is a hollow victory. When Fronto lies skinned and broken before you, you will have no idea what to do next. Achieving such a goal robs a man of his ongoing purpose.'

'What you know?'

Tulchulchur laughed - a sound like a hundred tomb gates creaking. 'The first man I ever killed was my own father, for what he did to me. It took him nine days to die and he screamed for merciful death every moment of every hour of every day. I was quite distraught when he finally passed. I had such plans for each day of two weeks and missed out on the opportunity to test some theories as to the body's limits. Fortunately, though robbed of my young life's goal, I found my purpose in those nine days. I discovered the one thing that made me whole - the one thing at which I truly excelled. Those remaining dozen tests were carried out again and again as I found new meat worthy of my knives, and the astounding thing was that I discovered there is no limit to possibilities. Every month until I was incarcerated I discovered a new way to cause agony.'

He grinned. 'Fronto will die, but I fear that so will you when you no longer have him to focus upon.'

'Hurry' was all the enormous German said, turning and stamping away into the next room.

The monster of Vispul watched his 'employer' leave the room and shrugged nonchalantly. Berengarus was still young. He would learn.

Tulchulchur - a Demonic appellation he had given himself upon abandoning his birth name - had heard some fantastic estimates of how many men he had killed during his decades-long spree up and down the lands of Etruria and Latium. Some said two thousand, even.

He knew better.

314

Though he had long ago lost count, he could still attempt a good estimate. Never more than one person a month - until now, but then he had some time to catch up on - and never within fifty miles of the previous victim. One a month was enough; sometimes he could make them last three weeks and more, anyway. To some extent it irked him that he had become infamous for sheer volume. It was the *quality* of the work that mattered, not the *quantity*, and he was a master. Quantity would always come if you had the time.

He turned back to the poor, broken thing on the table. He was rushing this, and that rankled as much as anything else. Berengarus' impatience was causing him to hurry when he should be savouring. But then this victim hardly fitted his usual profile. It felt strange to be carrying out his art on such a man, but then this was business - not pleasure.

The slave gave a whimper as his remaining eye noted the tormentor turn toward him again. The only other figure in the room stepped forward into the lamp light: a youngish man, scarred and worn. An ex-soldier, clearly, but with a leer and hungry eyes that send a shudder up the spine of all that beheld him, the young man gestured at the slave.

'You really believe he knows anything else? He would have sold out his mother and his children by now.'

Tulchulchur tutted and waved his hook-pointed knife back and forth in an admonishing fashion. 'He knows more yet. I can see it in his eye - that's why I left one. And when he has divulged his last secret, even that is not necessarily a reason to stop. Any skill requires regular practice or one becomes rusty. I have languished in captivity for some time. I have already made nine mistakes.'

'Mistakes?'

'You are young; a novice - you do not recognise mistakes. I nicked a major blood vessel in one of my early cuts. I tied it together with the skill of a surgeon, you know? But something is not quite right with the repair. He will bleed to death into his own belly in less than half a day. Had I kept in practice that would never have happened. I missed my knives in the carcer. Had I still had them, Berengarus would have fewer recruits, but I would be in better practice.'

He gave a chuckle like a cold wind blowing through a catacomb.

'Would you like to help, legionary Modestus?'

'Don't call me that.'

Five feet away, strapped to the table at wrists, ankles and neck, Nestor - Balbus' Greek body slave and a close and respected member of his household for more than two decades - tried to speak. He wanted to say '*no*'. He wanted to say '*please, for the love of mercy, let me die*'. Unfortunately it had not taken long for the evil wraith to discover that he could write in four languages and that had been when his tongue had gone, and then his teeth one by one. Even that had been individual agonies - not the whole extraction he had once had for a rotten tooth, but each one broken carefully off at the gum line.

He had wanted to die now for two hours, but the wraith would not let him.

'Your eye tells me you know more. Let us recap and then we will discuss what else we should hear.'

Nestor felt his mind reel with the possibilities of what might come next. He had tried to free his arms from the stone table in the kitchens of Balbus' town house, but the bastards had secured him so tightly he could hardly breathe, let alone move.

'Your master and Fronto, along with their pet Gaul and some others about whom you are realistically vague - including what appears to be a black-skinned gladiator - have left the city by ship and are bound for villas above Massilia - the ones I see the construction plans of in the office - with all the supplies they need to wait us out. Their remaining family members are there.'

The creature wafted close, bringing with it the smell of stale sweat, halitosis and decay, and peered with pale, rheumy eyes down at the terrified slave's face.

'No, no, no, no, no. No, my Greek friend. I do wish you would cooperate.'

The wraith sighed as the hook point of the knife caressed the cheek and hooded lid below Nestor's remaining eye.

'I don't kill *Greeks*! I am, despite my reputation, very particular, you know? I only ever killed Romans, the way any good Etruscan would if he be true to his heritage. You should, by rights, be standing as I, over the body of a putrefying Roman, exploring his innards and making him wail and shriek for every hour your land has been under his boot.'

Tulchulchur heard the legionary behind him cough meaningfully and realised he had drifted into reverie.

316

'Oh, don't get me wrong. I do what I do for the love of doing it. If I had slit the last Roman from balls to brain, I would find a new culture upon which to prey, but I do like to add levels of meaning to my work. It gives it a sense of completeness.'

Nestor scribbled something desperately on the slate by his left hand with the piece of chalk. The Monster of Vipsul peered at the writing, somewhat messy due to the level of constriction of the hand.

'I don't think so. You see, you know your master as well as any man, and your lies might fool me, were I hunting Balbus. However, you do *not* know Fronto, and you have no idea how to lie convincingly about him. You'll have to do better than that. For that, I think I will have your nose.'

Nestor tried to scream, but the blood-soaked rag thrust into his mouth muffled the sound. Not that it mattered. Berengarus and the other seven former prisoners had dealt with every other living soul in the house and no sound would be audible from the street.

Reaching down to the small table he had set next to the stone slab, Tulchulchur picked up a set of shears - slightly rusted iron things; heavy and solid. Leaning over Nestor, he went to work, placing them around the slave's nose. With a smile, the tip of his tongue protruding from the corner of his mouth, the Monster of Vipsul snipped half the Greek's nose from his face, the protrusion flicking into the air and disappearing into the shadows of the kitchen floor somewhere.

Modestus dropped to the floor to collect the grisly souvenir and, rising again, pushed a hole through the nose with a needle, threading it onto the body-part necklace he was making.

Tulchulchur waited a few moments for the fresh screaming to die down.

'Before we get to anything new, something you said already is not right. I wish you to write it all down for me again.'

Leaning over, Tulchulchur wiped the slate with a damp rag and replaced it beside Nestor's hand. The fingers twitched but did not move.

'I am certain you do not wish me to start removing your lips, though I am very good at it. Write.'

Tears streaming from his remaining eye, blood and ooze from the socket of the other, Nestor reiterated everything he had told them in sharp scribbles.

317

As the chalk fell away from the tablet, the wraith swept it up and peered at it closely, his clouded eyes running back and forth along the lines of messy, agonised text.

'This. This is where you lie: Massilia. You see, along with my years of experience in causing exquisite pain, I have become - through collateral means - a true expert on several other things: thievery, espionage, scouting... acrobatics, even. Mostly, though: truth-seeking and medicine. In the same way a man has 'tells' when he lies - one can check by watching his reactions and his eyes - writing can hold the same warnings. The very stress you feel when you deliberately mislead is visible in the strokes of chalk. And here - where you have written Massilia - is where your writing shows unusual stresses. This is where you lie.'

He smiled and reached for the sharp, short knife with the serrated section of blade.

'And I see that despite everything, you still do not take me seriously. So before I issue any further threat, I shall take your lips to show you just how serious I am.'

The following fifty heartbeats of sawing, slicing and screaming drew the hungry young Modestus to where he could see more clearly. The now almost skeletal face of the Greek shuddered at the agony, the exposed teeth stubs gnawing helplessly at the crimson rag between them.

'Now without pushing me to make any further gestures of my sincerity, I would like you to replace 'Massilia' with the truth.'

Smartly, he used his rag to wipe the place-name from the slate.

Nestor cried genuine hopeless tears as he wrote the name of Fronto's home town on the slate. He had done all he could... no one could expect any more.

'And now you will tell us what else you are holding back.'

Nestor's eye widened. There *were* other things, of course. Fronto's knee history that might be exploited. Balbus' heart condition that could easily be made to work for them. The directions to the villa he had been given and the name of a local merchant in Puteoli he could contact to move goods to them if needed. All sorts. Nothing critical anymore, but every tiny fragment he gave them would make it worse for the master and his companions. And if he did not, this monster would go on hurting him for many more hours.

He was choking!

The blood from his ruined nose was running down into his throat and, given the constriction of the bindings, he could do nothing about it. He finally smiled a broken smile. He was going to die. Blessed Aphrodite, he was going to die and be saved further agony.

'Tut tut tut.'

Awareness flooded back into him and he realised with horror that his tormentor had loosened the neck restraint and raised his head to clear his throat. He was going to live. He could feel life-giving oxygen returning. No! *Nooooo!*

'I am no amateur, my Greek friend.' Turning, Tulchulchur nodded at Modestus, who put his grisly necklace down on the small table and wandered over.

'Hold his head up so that he can breathe while I clean my instruments. Then we will uncover the rest of his secrets.'

Nestor felt the former legionary take the killer's place holding his head up while the wraith went back to his knives.

The man's fingers probed the back of his hair, feeling the sticky blood matted into it. The sick ex-soldier was caressing his blood-soaked hair! And that was when Nestor had his idea.

Modestus was busy fondling the hair, rather than holding the head, when the Greek slave slammed his head back against the stone table with the audible crack of a skull breaking. Modestus stared down in surprise at his blood-slicked hands as Tulchulchur turned, his face a mask of abject fury. Before the former legionary could stop him, Nestor lifted his head again, leaving a pool of blood and hair on the surface and brought it down once more with another crack.

Modestus leapt in to stop the man's suicide, but he was too late. When the Greek's head came up again, brains were on the slab. The third thud was final, and the light passed from his remaining eye in moments, a rattle in his throat.

The legionary stood, stunned, staring at the body.

'I... I'm sorry.'

Tulchulchur drifted, ghost-like across the stone-flagged floor. 'You fool. Can you not perform even the simplest of tasks?'

* * * * *

Berengarus turned as the Monster of Vipsul entered the triclinium, wiping the last of the blood from his forearms.

319

'Well?'

'Fronto, Balbus and four others including a gladiator and a physician took ship this morning for Puteoli, which is a town in Campania over a hundred miles down the coast. Their womenfolk are there and Fronto knows the place intimately. I would have had a great deal more information, but the idiotic soldier boy let him die too soon.'

'Modestus?'

'He will not be joining us. He has been contributing to his own necklace. I would apologise for the depletion of your force, but I fear he is no great loss. Come... let us uncover what we can of Puteoli.'

'We go book ship.'

'No. We are not prepared. I wish to know everything about the place before we leave. Fronto knows the ground, and so he has the advantage. We would be foolish to move without nullifying that advantage first. Modestus was a soldier. He would have told you all about tactics were he not so rash and foolish. You are an expert killer, my German friend, but sometimes it is worth learning from the military, especially if you are meaning to face them, and at least two of our quarry are experienced officers.'

Berengarus' lip twitched angrily.

'Do not worry, my friend.' Tulchulchur grinned as he handed him a hook-pointed knife. 'We will soon flay their hides from their bones.'

Chapter Sixteen

Titus 'Felix' Mittius - camp Prefect and former primus pilus of the Eleventh stared down at the enemy. A veritable sea of Gauls and Belgae spread out across the wide valley to every side of the winter quarters, their armour and weapons glinting in the early morning sunlight as they prepared themselves for the next stage of the assault just out of ballista range. Six days now. Every morning the same sight. For six days.

Felix turned, cursing once again his ill luck in having been promoted to the position of camp prefect with full responsibility for the winter quarters' defences and construction just in time to have them tested to the limit by an unexpected army. He also kicked himself for not paying more attention to the grumbling of Priscus months ago about some great Gallic rebellion. He had - at the time - chided Priscus for jumping at ghosts and spreading panic about some mythical revolt.

It looked considerably less mythical from this angle.

Behind him, a party of the wounded from yesterday's brutal assault were busy tying sudis stakes together to form jagged barricades to bolster the wooden palisades where they were weakest. No one was being given rest - not even the crippled. Cicero had had a go at him for that, and even Pullo and Vorenus had expressed their displeasure at the badly wounded not being given adequate downtime. But Felix was determined to take his role seriously and he knew the legion better than anyone. The camp had to hold - forever if necessary - and the Eleventh were up to the task.

Cicero himself stood on the rampart at the west gate some thirty paces away, leaning on the crutch the medicus had given him. He did not look well - each day ravaged him a little more in fact - but still nothing stopped him from taking his place on the walls.

The Eleventh Legion had settled into the pleasant wide valley two weeks ago now and spent the first of those weeks on supplies and construction. The camp was a work of art, even for a legionary fortress. Felix had leapt on the chance to prove his worth in his role and, despite the fact that no trouble was expected, had set the rampart at almost twice the standard height, gates with fighting platforms, a triple ditch with 'Punic' style slopes on the outermost - a steep drop from the exterior and a gentle inner slope, allowing for easier missile attack of the foundering enemy within it - and standard 'V' ditches for the other two. The interior buildings were of good solid timber and the central, most important ones had roofs of tiles formed from the mud of the nearby river and baked solid. Others were thatched in the native style for ease until more tiles could be manufactured.

But then, seven days ago, such manufacturing became an impossibility.

The Second cohort had been on logging duties across the river when a sizeable force of Nervii had poured from the heart of the woodland, screaming and hacking. Felix hadn't been there, of course, but he'd heard the story a dozen times now and, despite minor embellishments with acts of individual heroism from the tellers, the tale was fairly uniform. The cohort had abandoned their tasks instantly at the calls from the centurion and followed the signals that told them to cross the river in their own way and form up on the far bank. A few men had been lost during those initial clashes, but the barbarians had been unwilling to cross the river in dribs and drabs with a full cohort forming up waiting for them. The moments that bought them allowed the Roman force to pull back to the camp with little harassment.

By the time the enemy leaders had arrived on the scene and driven their men across the river, the Legion was safely behind Felix's solid defences and on the alert. Bless that centurion for having the foresight to abandon protocol and let the men cross the river however they felt best and form up on this side. It had been a combination of that decision and the enemy's reluctance to cross into Rome's waiting arms which had saved the legion, giving them time to prepare.

That first day had been as fierce a fight as Felix had ever experienced - every bit as bad as the most brutal actions of the past four years. As soon as it became apparent that they were not facing a small-scale uprising, but a push on a major scale, Cicero had made the decision to inform Caesar. The small force of native cavalry that served with the Eleventh - including a surprising number of Nervii - had confirmed that not only were the force outside members of that self-same local tribe, but also the Treveri, the Eburones, the Centrones and half a dozen others. And that meant an organised, region-wide rising against the Roman presence.

322

As the enemy had drawn up their lines on the south and east, Cicero's couriers had issued from the north gate and raced for the treeline on horseback, hurrying to deliver news of the attack to the nearest of the other legions: the Tenth. The legion had then settled in to weather the storm and await relief. The initial assault on the walls had come dangerously close to success a few times, the Gauls apparently riding high on a wave of self-belief, but as night fell on that first day it became apparent that the Eleventh had the strength to hold them off.

The legion's proud satisfaction had received its first knock that evening as the first Gallic campfires burned away the shade of the night, illuminating a grisly spectacle: Cicero's courier riders, each bound and nailed to a cross in the Roman style. The next few hours had involved an object lesson in how serious the rebels were about removing Caesar's army from Gaul. A few legionaries had managed to put a pilum into the suffering, tortured messengers to bring them an easy, early death, but several of them had lingered until the moon was high.

Cicero, Pullo and Felix had immediately gone into conference and decided that the only thing they could do at that point was to strengthen the defences. As that first long night dragged on, the men of the Eleventh had constructed twenty four towers at regular intervals around the ramparts using the stores of timber that had been destined for barrack blocks. The men sacrificed their comfort for their safety, remaining in their tents for the time being.

The Romans had made their move in the game of siege craft, strengthening the defences and placing their few scorpion bolt-throwers atop the towers. The morning saw the reply of the Gauls, their force having almost doubled in size when the first glimpse of the sun brought with it half a dozen more tribes eager to put an end to Cicero's occupation.

The second day had been, if anything, harder than the first. The smaller tribes who were considered more expendable - or possibly had more to prove - came forward under the missile attack of the legion and began to fill in the ditches for their stronger compatriots, who would then launch another attack on the walls.

And that became the norm for the week: by day the Gauls would expend their weakest men in an attempt to neutralise the Roman defences as far as possible, and then launch a vicious attack against the walls. Each time they were driven off, but the damage was

323

worsening each day. More legionaries were sent to the medical section or laid out ready for burning each evening, leaving an ever-reducing force. And while the losses of the Gallic army were horrible and outstripped the Romans' each day, their numbers never seemed to diminish as new small groups joined their cause daily, appearing from the woods with the pomp and splendour of the Gallic elite - all goose-honking horns and dragon banners.

And then each night the Romans slept in rotation while every man - soldier or officer, crippled or healthy - dug out the earth that had been dumped in the nearest ditches and repaired the walls and towers for the next day's assault.

By the fourth day stakes with fire-hardened points had joined the defences, as had lilia pits with sharpened sticks, sudis barricades and every trick the engineers could come up with. They needed it. The onager ran out of ammunition that very morning.

It had been the fourth day, too, when it had become apparent that Cicero was not well. He had been briefing the officers when he had staggered back and almost fallen. Righting himself, he had become worryingly pale. Despite the urging of the men, he had refused to halt the briefing and had finished up before allowing the medicus to speak to him. The physician had confirmed that the legate was suffering with a fever and should be confined to his cot, though Cicero had told him in no uncertain terms what he thought of that idea.

And so the commander had continued to play his part each day, though every shift he took clearly further weakened him and he now occasionally forgot where he was or mixed up his words in the simplest of sentences. The senior centurions Pullo and Vorenus had wordlessly defaulted to delivering their questions and requests to Felix to alleviate as much pressure on the legate as they could.

'Looks like they've got some new men again' noted Vorenus, strolling along the rampart's walkway. Despite the arch looks Felix kept giving him, the second most senior centurion in the legion consistently failed to address Felix by his new title. However, since it was clearly because Vorenus still saw him as a colleague of equal ability, Felix had let it slide. Vorenus was a good man.

'This lot are from down south some way, I reckon. There's a lot of Roman kit there that's unavailable from merchants up here' Felix nodded toward the fresh group who were gathering just out of missile shot to get their first look at the hated legions. 'Those mail shirts are definitely ours. I dunno whether they've been buying our kit from enterprising Roman merchants down Vesontio way or looting bodies, but they're well-armed and armoured for Gauls.'

'They'll get their arses handed to them the same as the rest' shrugged Vorenus. 'Hello, what's this?'

Felix followed his gaze and frowned. A small group of Gauls on horseback were approaching with their shields over their heads - noblemen judging by the expensive clothes, armour and gold accoutrements.

'Well I think the chances they're surrendering are pretty small, so I guess they want to talk.'

'I'd be tempted to invite them as close as we can and then stick a few ballista bolts into the hairy turdbags myself.'

Felix smiled. Vorenus had a curious habit of voicing whatever thought was currently running through Felix's head.

'It'd be nice, I have to admit. But we do things by the manual. Go tell the legate.'

As Vorenus dashed off along the parapet, Felix clambered down the steps on the inside of the bank and gestured to the aquilifer and the standard bearers who were busy shifting grain sacks from the edge of the camp into the centre, away from danger.

'Get the eagle and all the standards over to the gate, and call the musicians across too. We're going to speak nicely to the hairy bum-holes who've been trying to kill us for the best part of a week.'

Reasoning that they would have a few moments and that it would do the Gallic bastards good to have to wait, Felix swung by his tent and picked up his plumed helmet and crimson dress cloak, shaking out the dust and fastening it over his shoulder with his bronze fibula brooch. Best to look his intimidating best.

By the time he reached the gate, half a dozen of the most senior centurions and standard bearers clustered around Cicero, his tribunes and the silver eagle.

'Sir?' Felix said quietly as he approached the legate. Cicero had a waxy sheen to his skin and was pale and sweaty, his left eye flickering constantly and his stance that of a man who would have fallen to his knees by now without the crutch under his arm.

'Prefect?'

'Sir, it might be better for you to observe from the gate platform?'

'Thank you, Prefect, but I'm just ill, not incompetent. It's my legion, so I'll hear what this man has to say in person.'

Felix nodded, despite his disapproval. At least the equisio was bringing the officers' horses around. Cicero, his tribunes and Felix would ride out to meet the enemy party, the standards and a century of the best men accompanying them on foot.

He waited patiently as the horses arrived and then pulled himself up into the saddle with surprising ease. Though not a natural horseman - riding was hardly a required skill for a legionary centurion - he'd had cause to use a horse a few times in his career and managed to sit astride the beast without looking out of place. Riding in a cuirass was taking some getting used to, though. A mail shirt moved with the horse's gait and allowed for all sorts of jogging. A cuirass simply bounced around badly and bruised him in soft and giving areas.

As soon as the party was mounted, the signal sounded and the gates swung open, revealing the mass of Gauls just beyond missile range, the party of nobles out front at the far end of the causeway across the ditches, their carnyx horn bleating impatiently like a goat being slowly and painfully abused.

Felix eyed the party carefully as they approached. It was clearly formed of the leaders - kings even perhaps? - of the more major tribes present. He was sure he recognised one or two from previous negotiations or councils. Despite the gathering of high nobility, though, it was clear that one man had precedence. The noble at the centre sat with the ease and confidence of a senior Roman officer, for all his Gallic blood - a comparison that came easily to Felix's mind, given the fact that the man wore a cuirass clearly looted from a Roman. No merchant sold such goods. The embossed body armour was of the highest quality and had obviously been hand-made for a rich Roman. As they closed on the party, he realised also that the helmet beneath the Gaul's arm was also a fine Roman one with the military plume or crest removed and replaced with some native eagle design.

'Watch that one, sir' he whispered as he leaned toward Cicero who was himself also leaning, though for entirely different reasons.

'Hmm?'

'The leader. He's looted a senior Roman officer, sir. And he's proud of it.'

326

Cicero squinted as he tried to make out details that should be clear at this range. His illness was robbing him of his faculties. Felix hoped he wouldn't fall off his horse unconscious during the negotiations - it would be horribly inappropriate.

The legate, however, held up his hand, halting the small Roman party as they sat between the middle and outer ditch, the latter currently partly filled with muck and clutter. The Gallic group sat some fifteen paces away.

'Quintus Tullius Cicero - Legatus of the Eleventh, lieutenant of Caesar and his representative in the lands of the Belgae. Who dares to raise arms against the forces of Rome?'

Despite a slight quiver in his voice, the statement was delivered with aplomb and gravitas, and Felix couldn't have done a better job himself of setting the groundwork for the meeting on Roman terms.

'I am Ambiorix' the Gaul said in passable Latin, with an accent that placed him among the Belgae.

'That means nothing to me without a tribal name' Cicero said flatly.

'Of the Eburones' added the Gaul with a flicker of irritation.

Cicero shrugged theatrically and turned to Felix. 'Heard of them?'

The prefect hid his smile behind a hand raised as if to grip his chin while pondering. They all knew of the Eburones, of course. Every tribe in these benighted lands was marked on the military maps back in the headquarters. They were a sizeable group - the farthermost tribe northeast, by the Rhenus at its lowest reaches. Sabinus' winter command...

The smile of satisfaction at the irritation in Ambiorix's eyes died away as he pieced the two names together and realised whose armour and helm the Gaul was proudly displaying.

'The Eburones is some collection of piss-poor little barbarian hovels up near the Rhenus, sir' he replied, trying to keep the anger of his realisation from his voice.

'Oh, up by the motherless Germanics, then?' Cicero smiled. 'You'd do well to go back there and take care of your farms, chief Ambiorix.'

'*King* Ambiorix' the Gaul snapped. 'Do you not even recognise the spoils of our war?' He slapped the bronze cuirass with the Pegasus embossed across its chest angrily.

327

Cicero squinted. He genuinely couldn't see clearly enough through the fever. It was a good thing, really. If he could, he might have lost his composure in his current state. Felix stepped his horse forward and to the left a pace to make himself the focus of enemy attention, trying to shield the ailing legate from their attention.

Best he take the reins now…

'I do. I trust that Sabinus and Cotta loaded you with curses before they passed to Elysium.' He felt the other officers beside him reel as they took in this piece of information and processed what it meant. A legion and a half had already been defeated somewhere east of here. Before anyone could react, however, Felix went on. 'I trust you are not expecting us to faint and wail like professional mourners because you have had a lucky encounter with an unfortunate Roman force. You will not find all legions such easy pickings.'

'Prefect?' Felix heard the legate behind him and recognised a certain steel in his voice, despite the illness. Cicero stepped his own horse out again, taking the fore.

Ambiorix spat toward them.

'Romans always think they are indestructible. Be sure you're not! I obliterated a legion larger than this a week ago and with a force half the size of the one I have now.'

Cicero had elected not to wear his helmet as they rode out, partially because the weight and heat of it was causing him a great deal of discomfort in his condition, but also because a bareheaded officer gave the impression of fearlessness. He reached up and scratched his head as though considering his next words carefully. Felix had the horrible feeling for a moment that the legate had drifted off once more and forgotten where he was, but suddenly Cicero leaned forward in his saddle and cleared his throat.

'I am not concerned with the failure of other officers to deal with a disorganised rabble.'

Ambiorix was so surprised he actually blinked a few times and opened and closed his mouth trying to work out this hopelessly arrogant Roman. Quickly, though, the ire rose and brought out a flush on his cheeks.

'I will not waste any more time with you, Roman. I came to give you an offer and I will still deliver it, despite your words. If you surrender yourself and your men to our care, we will consider…'

Cicero swept a hand dismissively in front of him, again surprising the Gaul so much that he stopped mid-sentence.

'I have a counter-proposal' Cicero said in his haughtiest voice. 'You and your ten thousand pig farmers can lay down your weapons and walk away now, go back to abusing their wives and marrying their own children and I will not see every last head in this valley atop a spear by the end of the week. Do you accept my terms?'

Two of the tribunes failed to hold their composure and barked out a laugh, drawing a disapproving look from Cicero, who swayed as he turned to silence them, almost unhorsing himself. Felix felt a swell of pride in his new commander. Crispus had been a young and untried legate, but had proved his worth and been adopted by the Eleventh. He'd been worried about the new posting - Cicero was a man with his own command habits and the word among the centurions had been that he was not one of Caesar's strongest. It was, however, hard to imagine any other legate pulling off such a breathtaking parlay while suffering the way Cicero was.

Ambiorix began to splutter, his anger simply too strong to grant him audible words. In the end he snapped something in his native tongue, spat once more at the Romans and turned, riding off among his own men.

Cicero smiled as he swayed again.

'Well that went as well as could be expected. Shall we get back to the camp before they decide to cut us to pieces here and now?'

Felix allowed himself a chuckle as the party turned back, despite the memory of Sabinus' armour on that Gallic runt. Ambiorix would pay for that little display.

* * * * *

Felix watched the equisio leading away the horses. Cicero was back on his crutch, skittering this way and that as he fought both fever and weakness of the bones to reach the rampart and a clear view of what was happening.

'Are they lining up to attack?' he asked as he struggled with the lowest step of the rampart climb.

'I haven't the faintest idea what they're doing, sir' Felix said, scratching his head as he turned back to look over the Gallic army arrayed before them.

329

He had half expected to charge back into the camp, dismount and clamber up the rampart just in time to see the entire collection of motherless sons of a septic sheep running at the ditches and walls screaming death curses at Rome. Instead, he had stood the past few moments waiting for the legate to join him and watching strange manoeuvres being carried out - like some sort of slow, laborious dance designed for a thousand men at a time. Whole tribes appeared to be de-camping and moving a few hundred paces in order to set up exactly as they had been in another spot, while a huge force disappeared into the woods. Another group had opened up huge square areas devoid of both men and gear. It was the oddest thing to watch. The most immediately disturbing thing was how the entire force had pulled back another fifty paces from maximum missile range as though they thought the Romans might find a sudden extra burst of power. It created a wide cordon all around the camp, beyond which they were still entirely surrounded.

He watched, fascinated for another quarter hour as Cicero and his tribunes climbed the rampart, the latter helping the ailing legate as much as possible without making him feel useless. In the meantime, Pullo came along the rampart from the south gate, frowning.

'What do you suppose they want timber for?'

Felix rolled his eyes. Of course! That was what the bunch had disappeared into the woods for. He'd wondered whether they were trying to reposition their forces without his being fully aware, but it did seem farfetched, and they hadn't taken all their gear with them either. Almost as if in answer came the first sounds of axes striking trees. Logging on a fairly impressive scale, given the number of men who had gone to carry it out. As many as Felix had sent into those very woods to gather lumber when they'd first arrived.

'Well it can only be two things, surely' he replied. 'Attack or defence. Are they building their own enclosure or some sort of siege machine? Do the Gauls really know siege craft? It's not something I've heard of.'

Pullo shrugged. 'Me neither, but they've had four years or more of watching us. If they've been observant, they'll have learned a few things. Jove, a few of them probably served with us at times.'

Cicero slumped against the palisade and rested his elbows on it to keep him supported in relative comfort.

'They're building a wall.'

'Sir?' Pullo and Felix both turned to the legate.

'They don't want anyone to escape. There's been no news of Sabinus' defeat and we're the closest legion encamped to them. That heavily suggests that no one got away. They made damn sure they didn't let any of our messengers get away, so they intend to do the same to us. They *fadh*....'

The two listening officers lurched forward as Cicero slumped almost to the floor, the strength in his legs giving up totally. With their help he pulled himself upright again.

'You have to go rest, sir. The medicus was right.'

'I have to stay here. Help.'

'You'll be no help if you kill yourself, sir.'

Cicero studied his officers' faces for a moment and finally nodded. 'Alright. I'll do that. But keep a close eye on them. They want us contained and to kill every last one of us. That means they're working their way through the camps, obliterating one at a time.'

Felix nodded. 'At least that means the others are safe as long as we still stand. They can't move on until they've dealt with us.'

Pullo pulled a face. 'It also means we're doomed. There's no way they're going to let a single man live and they won't give up and run. They can't. And they're getting strengthened after each loss. We need to get a message out whatever else we do.'

'I just don't see how' Felix sighed, looking back over the rampart.

A wall. They were going to surround the camp with a rampart. No escape. Something would have to be done.

But what?

* * * * *

The sun rose on the eighth day to reveal a breath-taking sight. Even Felix, a battle-hardened veteran centurion with decades of experience and a fatalistic approach to life was taken aback by what the night had wrought.

It very much appeared that the Gauls had learned more of Roman siege craft than any of them had anticipated.

Already the circumvallation of the Roman camp was complete in its early stage. While not as neat or well-constructed as a Roman rampart, the raised earth bank that surrounded the winter quarters of the Eleventh was twice the height of a man and in places a good timber palisade was already being completed. There was no need for a ditch, of course, as they had left only a short berm before the rampart, making use of the Roman ditches - enough to gather an attacking force. Gates in the Gallic rampart faced the solid sections of Roman wall and the sections of ditch outside those had been filled during the darker hours.

There had been a few incidents during the night as the sentries watching the Gauls' progress had decided that they were coming a little too near and picked off the front men busy shovelling earth into the dip, only to come under attack in turn from Belgic archers, though the winds had gradually picked up through the hours of darkness, making arrow shots difficult to direct.

Felix's standing orders during the night were only to attack or raise the general alarm if the enemy reached the inner ditch. In their situation, with no end to the siege in sight and no way to send for help, ammunition was as precious as food and water and should not be expended on anything less than a major attempt to breach the walls.

But it was not the surrounding ramparts that drew the breath and much of the remaining hope from the Roman watchers. It was what had occurred in those strange empty squares to the rear. In the distance, unseen during the night among the chaos and the campfires of the Gauls, some clever devil with a good knowledge of Roman techniques had constructed three siege towers - shorter than usual, but high enough to overcome the Roman defences - as well as a number of Vineae - rolling roofed enclosures to protect attacking troops. With an almost superhuman effort, the enemy had managed to complete their builds during a single night and already they were starting to move forward from the construction grounds.

It seemed that the Gauls were serious now about their mission.

'Time for a short, sharp prayer to Mars, I'd say, sir.'

Felix turned to see Pullo standing at his shoulder, shielding his eyes with his hand as he viewed the scene unfolding before them.

'It's our best choice,' the prefect agreed. 'Fortuna's clearly abandoned us.' He frowned and rubbed his neck. The short sleep he'd managed had done nothing to refresh him, but had given him an irritating crick in the neck and the howling winds buffeting at him were doing nothing to improve it. 'What's your professional appraisal of the situation?'

Pullo rolled his shoulders.

'We're in trouble. Our best chance now is to take enough of them with us that they can't present a serious threat to any of the other legions - to declaw them with attrition.'

'Arrows!' bellowed a legionary just along the wall and Pullo and Felix ducked instinctively.

'What in Jove's name are they doing? It's too windy for arrows. They'll have trouble hitting anyone.'

Pullo raised his head to peer over the palisade top. 'Not if they loose enough of them.' He ducked down again. 'I don't want to ruin your day any further, Prefect, but you won't believe what I've just seen.'

Felix narrowed his eyes and rose to peer over the top. A shower of arrows were pattering against the wood and humming over the ramparts to fall into the camp's interior. But Pullo was not worrying about the small lethal missiles. Felix instantly picked up on what had drawn the centurion's attention.

'Oh shit.'

'Think they looted them from the Fourteenth, then?'

'Where else?'

Both men rose again to watch the Roman ballistae and onagers being moved into position along the Gallic ramparts. The bastards were laying a Roman siege almost by the manual.

'They won't have trained artillerists so the shots will be fairly random, I reckon' Felix said, though his voice held an underlying note of uncertainty.

'They certainly won't be of a Roman skill with them' Pullo agreed. 'But it's *that* which worries me.'

Felix focused on the subject of Pullo's pointing finger. The Gauls were bringing up braziers and carts of flammable missiles. Even as they watched, the Gauls began to load the weapons and ignite the ammunition.

'It's going to take them a while to find the range. Even a Roman engineer would take a shot or two. *They'll* need half a dozen. And it's at least clear there's no expert doing it, else they'd be using rocks to range-find, not precious burning pots.'

Pullo nodded. 'That said, we've a lot of timber and straw buildings. Best organise the water chain parties.'

As the primus pilus dropped back down from the walls to issue the commands, Felix watched the siege engines preparing their first shots, the towers and Vineae moving up to the gates ready for the assault.

At least if they were following Roman techniques, they wouldn't actually send in the men and the towers during the artillery barrage. Not that the thought was much consolation.

* * * * *

Lucius Vorenus, centurion of the Second century, First cohort, turned and bellowed to the line of walking wounded who ferried buckets of water back and forth from the barrels near the granary. As soon as it had become obvious that the enemy's fire attacks were aimed at the straw roofed structures, he had ordered all supplies moved out of them and into the tile roofed headquarters building and commanders' quarters.

Even as he reprimanded a legionary for carelessness, slopping too much water from his bucket before he reached the blazing former granary, another flaming bundle smashed through the straw roof, this time taking with it enough ceiling timbers to bring the whole roof down in a fiery mass. The granary was an inferno. Vorenus ground his teeth as he made the decision: no point in wasting any more water trying to save it. He gestured to the men and bellowed at them.

'Stop there. Save the water.' His eyes took in the nearby buildings. The armoury - also now emptied of goods - stood too close for comfort. Already, with the strong winds, sparks were leaping across to its roof and smouldering in the straw, and beyond that building were three others that still stood full of salted meat, water barrels and other goods.

'Tear down the armoury. I want that building nothing but rubble by the time I count a hundred!'

The wounded legionaries immediately placed their water buckets on the ground and scurried across, picking up mattocks and axes to hack at the walls and pull down the timbers before the fire could spread too far. This wouldn't do. They could hardly just sit here and watch as the camp was burned to the ground around them.

Behind him, a particularly lucky shot smashed into the wall of the building that served as quarters for both the legate and the camp Prefect. Luckily, Felix was at the wall and Cicero in the makeshift hospital, but as their building exploded in a blazing morass Vorenus realised that most of the officers' gear was gone in the conflagration.

334

Whether the Gauls realised what they had hit or simply registered another good shot, a roar of triumph rose from the masses beyond the walls. Vorenus turned away from the duty he had assigned himself and looked at the south wall. Most of the shots had been coming from the north and east, while the siege towers and Vineae were manoeuvring out of the gates of the enemy rampart to the south and west.

His gaze caught the unmistakable shape of a siege tower looming close to the south wall. The bastards had managed to fill in a causeway across the triple ditch remarkably fast.

His eyes narrowed and he turned back to the mess behind him as legionaries dragged the already burning mess of the armoury to the ground. His gaze moved from the fiery wreckage to the onager nearby. All the smaller artillery was kept on the walls. This onager had kept up a valiant attack for several days, dropping hefty stone balls onto the massed ranks of the enemy outside, but the ammunition had run out on the fifth morning and the beast had stood silent since then. Bolts and small stones for the ballistae had been abundant enough, but the legion had only amassed so much stone for the onager and were unable to leave the camp to fetch more.

His eyes strayed across to the near-a-hundred walking wounded serving as a fire-control team.

'Anyone here an engineer?'

Three of the men paused in their work and turned, raising their hands. Vorenus grinned. 'Can you use that thing with any accuracy?'

The men nodded. 'Be sure' he reminded them. 'You need to hit spot on, first time, despite this wind. Can you do that?'

Two of the men looked at each other nervously, but the third stepped forward with a nod.

'We can, sir.'

Vorenus' grin widened.

'Alright. You!' he shouted, pointing at a random legionary. 'Go tell the commander of the Third cohort to pull back from the ramparts. Keep the men well away from that siege tower!' Turning his predatory smile on the engineer who still stood saluting, he cleared his throat. 'Here's what I want you to do...'

* * * * *

Pullo tapped Felix on the shoulder, unable to attract his attention over the tumultuous noise of the battle and the cheering of the Gauls beyond the ditches. The prefect turned in surprise.

'What do you suppose Plutius is up to?' the primus pilus mused, watching as the Third cohort began to pull back from the south-western quadrant, leaving the defences unmanned as the nearest of the siege towers closed on it implacably. The wind ripped at the centurion's horsehair crest, bending it back as he gestured.

Felix frowned as he watched. 'He'd better have a good reason, else when I get hold of him, I shall tear him a new arsehole.'

The pair watched the tower as it crept over the filled-in remnant of the closest ditch and then blinked as a blur of molten gold appeared from nowhere, streaking through the post-dawn air and suddenly turning the impressive siege tower into an exploding inferno of fiery destruction.

A dozen flaming bodies hurled themselves from the walled platform at the top, dropping into the ditch, breaking arms, legs and necks as they sought to escape the conflagration and roll around on the ground, trying to extinguish the agonising flames.

In a couple of heartbeats the top half of the tower was gone, the rest roaring with flames as the wind carried a roiling column of black smoke off to the east, choking the mass of warriors gathered with ladders and waiting to accompany the tower.

As Pullo and Felix stared in wonderment the Third cohort returned to the walls, jeering at the Gauls. One legionary even paused on his way along the rampart to display a naked backside at them. He should be disciplined for such an act really, but all Felix could do was laugh. The pair followed the rough trajectory of the fiery missile to see the onager - out of action for days now - being turned toward the other siege towers while legionaries carefully manoeuvred a mass of flaming material to load it as soon as it was in position. Roughly halfway between the artillery piece and the two watching officers, Centurion Vorenus was striding toward them grinning from ear to ear.

'Taste of their own bloody medicine' he declared as he mounted the stairs.

'Nice' Felix replied, nodding. 'Bought us a little time. Question is: to do what?'

'We're doing an excellent job of holding them off' Pullo agreed, looking at the ladder men as they retreated in confusion once more.

They were temporarily discouraged, but already the Gallic leaders were moving forward, urging their forces to rally and attack. Ambiorix and his cronies were shrewd enough to recognise that despite the failure of the first siege tower and the likely fate of the others, they had enough momentum now to get men onto the walls and to allow their men to retreat and panic would destroy any advantage they had.

'Problem is: we can't hold them off forever. The leaders are turning them round already. We could have done with a bit more discord flowing through their ranks first.'

The two centurions looked at one another and grinned.

'You always thought you should have been the first to reach primus pilus' Pullo said with a raised eyebrow. 'Care to prove it?'

Vorenus laughed. 'With respect to your rank, my friend, I could fight my way through that lot before you even got your sword unsheathed!'

'Come on then.'

Felix shook his head. 'That's suicide.'

'Never underestimate a Sardinian, Prefect. Tough mountain men, we are.' Vorenus grinned as he drew his gladius.

'Has to be done' Pullo nodded. 'We've got to give them something to think about - something that'll frighten them and make them think we're too dangerous to attack. I don't know whether you're aware, Prefect, but we're almost out of ballista ammunition, and the reserve pila are already at the walls. You know as well as us that if we run out of both of those it's only a matter of time until they get over this wall, and then we're dead men.'

Felix nodded. 'You're right, of course. And maybe - just maybe - if you can cause enough trouble, we can get a messenger through and out to Caesar.' He tapped his lip. 'In fact, this might be the time to start doing something underhanded and devious. You two get your centuries formed up and ready to sally. I'm going to find Vertico and his cavalry.'

As the prefect descended the steps, the two centurions looked at one another.

'He thinks you meant to take the men with you.'

'That's 'cause he's never seen a Sardinian fight. Besides, we need a nice little gesture to put those two tribunes of the Tenth in their place.'

337

* * * * *

Felix looked back at the couriers as he approached his customary position on the south rampart. It was one of the most unpleasant aspects of command, to send a man knowingly to his death, and this was worse than most. The nine men gathering by the west gate were doomed not only to death at the hands of the Nervii, but likely a most agonising, gruesome death by torture.

Well, eight of them.

Once again, he peered at them - eight men in light armour, four on horseback and four on foot, each ready to issue from the gate, fanning out in an attempt to make it through the enemy lines and to the open ground beyond to carry their sealed messages to the general. None of them would make it, and they likely knew that but brave as they were, they were prepared to try, for the survival of the legion.

And hovering in the shadow of the gate, close by, was their only true hope - and a damn dangerous hope it was too.

The last messenger of the nine was one of the auxiliary natives under the command of Vertico the Nervian. He was of a blood with the men outside the walls and dressed identically.

As the messengers dispersed and made their own attempts to make it through the army, the Nervian would disappear among his own people, able hopefully to make his way through and to the safety beyond. Felix's main worry was not for the man's survival, but for his loyalty. He prayed to Fides - a Goddess he rarely bothered with - that the man didn't simply discard the message and join the besiegers.

A roar went up from the legionaries on the southern defences, signalling that the two centurions had launched their attack. Simultaneously, the west gate jerked open and the eight Roman couriers rode and ran through it, making for the enemy rampart sections where the palisade had not yet been raised. Behind them, just as the gate shut, a figure in Gallic trousers and cloak emerged and disappeared into the ditch.

'Divine Fides watch him. Mars shelter him. Mercury grant him wings.'

Turning his back, he climbed the steps to the southern palisade to watch the advance of Pullo and Vorenus and the first two centuries of his legion - men he had personally commanded as their centurion

338

until this winter. He was totally unprepared for the sight that greeted him.

* * * * *

Pullo was faster than Vorenus remembered. It was a rare occasion these days when the two men - both natives of Feronia on the north-east Sardinian coast - had a chance to fight side by side, and certainly not without having to busy themselves with the command of a century of men apiece.

Having leapt from the top of the palisade, the two centurions had hit the embankment already curled and rolled to a halt on the narrow berm before the nearest ditch.

The sheer audacity of the move had taken the crowd of Gauls gathering in the Gallic gateway for the next attack so much by surprise that the pair had climbed the far side of the first ditch and dropped again to the middle one before any enterprising Celt decided to loose an arrow at them.

As they hurtled across the bottom of the second ditch, struggling to keep the shields they had borrowed from their men in position and not bouncing on the uneven turf, Pullo was already hefting his precious pilum ready to cast as he reached the rise at the far side of the ditch.

Vorenus shifted his grip as he put on an extra turn of speed to catch up, preparing to throw his own missile.

This time the Gauls were ready and half a dozen arrows were released as Pullo and Vorenus suddenly emerged over the lip of the middle ditch.

Fortunately, they had cut across at an angle and the arrows, released reflexively, went wild, aimed at the place the two centurions had been expected to appear.

As Pullo - first to crest the top - reached the surface, his arm came forward, releasing the pilum with careful aim. The seething mass of Gauls hardly required a great deal of care, but Pullo had marked his target before even leaving the walls. After all, they had to do enough damage to frighten the Gauls. The pilum caught a man at the fore - clearly one of the tribal leaders - bare-chested and waving a spear angrily, hurling him bodily back into the crowd. The Gauls barely had time to register the blow before Vorenus' own pilum disappeared among the press, piercing another Gaulish nobleman and

339

drawing an agonised squawk. In response, the Gauls suddenly closed on the two wounded and downed leaders, shields coming up in a defensive arc.

More arrows flew - this time on target - only to whistle through thin air as the two men dropped into the outer ditch. Once again, they angled their approach so that, as they reached the far side, they appeared at an unexpected position. Their movements were carefully planned, despite appearances: as they clambered up the far side, they had arrived at the gentlest area of the slope, next to the Roman causeway that led directly to the south gate.

Pullo was still in the front and his sword came out with a rasp as he crested the rise and charged the Gallic army like some demon of the night.

Vorenus topped the slope a moment behind, just in time to see Pullo take a spear throw to the front. His friend's shield was already in the way, but the heavy Gallic weapon punched straight through the leather and wood, hurling Pullo backward onto the ground. As Vorenus leapt forward, the Gauls were already rushing to envelop the fallen Roman. The junior of the two centurions felt a wave of relief as he saw Pullo struggling, the spear jammed through his discarded shield and wedged between the bronze plates of his belt, prevented miraculously from a death-dealing blow by a narrow strip of leather. Even as Pullo struggled to free himself of the constriction, his sword was flashing out defensively against the oncoming Gauls.

By the time Vorenus was at his side, there were near a dozen Gauls lunging and thrashing at them with spears, swords and axes. Pullo's discarded shield was preventing them from getting to his undefended side - a hindrance due to its size and bulk - but any moment the pair would be swarmed over by angry, vengeful Gauls.

Screaming Latin obscenities, Vorenus launched himself at the Gauls, using his shield as a battering ram and knocking back and aside half a dozen men in a single leap, his sword flashing out again and again, biting into flesh, slicing arms and once severing a man's jugular. The spray of arterial blood washed over the entire scene, blinding half the combatants and making it difficult for anyone involved to see what was happening. A man appeared above Vorenus and lunged down with a sword, only to be struck by a well-thrown pilum from the camp's walls. He disappeared backward with a shriek.

Angrily, Vorenus shook his head, blinking away the crimson veil, only to lose his footing to an animal warren's entrance. With a curse, he fell forward, his own shield slipping his grasp and disappearing off to the side. A roar of victory went up among the front ranks of the Gauls and some of the lesser warriors found themselves pushed roughly aside to allow the greater nobles to reach the fallen Roman - not the two leaders they had pinned with their pila, though.

Vorenus rolled to avoid a spear thrust which jammed into the turf where his chest had been but a moment before, lashing out with his gladius and feeling it catch flesh in the sudden press above and around him. He felt something wet and rubbery slap across his cheek and a fresh splash of crimson washed his vision. A thrust blade ripped a few links from his mail shirt and bounced along his ribs. He hardly noticed, so intent was he on avoiding the rest of the iron and bronze points lunging down at him.

Again, a Gaul was plucked from his feet by a carefully placed pilum from the camp walls and Vorenus almost laughed as the sudden gap in the surrounding enemies trying to kill him filled with the frenzied form of Pullo, who had finally extricated himself from his predicament.

'We've got to go!' he yelled at Vorenus as he slammed his blade into the neck of the Gaul to his left, stamping his nail-soled boot down on the foot of another man.

'So soon?' he managed to shout back with a manic laugh.

Pullo's reply went unheard as Vorenus concentrated on keeping two lunging spearmen off him, knocking the weapons this way and that with his sword so that they could not manage a straight thrust at him. As one spearhead slammed into the turf, pushed aside from its intended target, Pullo was suddenly next to him, lifting him with his free arm while his sword continually slashed at the enemy.

Vorenus felt his own blade come out of his grasp, his fingers numbed by the scrape of a spear head along the knuckles. Involuntarily, he yelped and then, irritated by the unmanly noise, shouted something to the effect that the spear-wielder's mother had known her brother in most unfortunate ways.

Something grazed his leg as he stumbled away, drawing blood and leaving a hot score-mark across the back of his thigh.

Suddenly they were in the open again, making their way onto the causeway and back to the gate in the camp ramparts, which was already creeping open for them.

Celtic warriors chased them, leaving the safety of their lines and trying to get close enough for a good spear throw, only to find themselves in range of the scorpions in the towers that protected the gate. The nearest two Gauls were impaled in a heartbeat and knocked back, encouraging the rest to stay at a safe distance.

Stray arrows and sling stones began to track them and as they ran they zigged and zagged across the causeway, presenting the most difficult target they could. Pullo was spun sideways as a bullet clanged off his helmet making a sound like a bell and Vorenus had to grab his arm as they ran to keep him heading the right way. An arrow thudded into his own shoulder, the mail shirt taking most of the power out of it, but the blow still slamming him forward. He could feel the wound beneath the links burning and throbbing.

And then they were inside the gate and the timber leaves were closing behind them. Vorenus fell to his knees, gripping his painful shoulder and coughing up bile. Next to him, Pullo wrenched off his helmet, noting with dazed interest the dent in it and feeling for the matching dent in his skull from which a trickle of blood ran. He shook his head to try and clear the fug of the bell-ring that had robbed his senses.

By the time the pair had pulled themselves upright and stood recovering with deep breaths, Felix had descended the ramparts and was wandering toward them, shaking his head in baffled wonder.

'You two are absolutely out of your minds. You know that?'

'Just a bit of exercise, Prefect.'

Felix laughed.

'They just did a headcount on the wall. Comes out differently each time, but we can be fairly sure you killed or badly wounded at least eleven of the bastards, including three nobles. Not a bad rate for two men. I was expecting more of a major assault, but you might just have given the messengers the distraction they needed.'

'If Fortuna hasn't *completely* abandoned us.'

* * * * *

The evening brought a calming of the winds, which was a great relief to the men on the ramparts. Following the crazed activity of the two centurions, the Gauls had surged against the fort walls with renewed anger, though their outrage at what had happened served Rome well, driving them into frenzied, chaotic attack, rather than the carefully planned siege that their leaders were obviously favouring.

Still, the day had brought too many deaths for comfort. Felix stood watching the numerous campfires of the Nervii and pondering on the butcher's bill he'd just been delivered. The legion was now down to less than three thousand men. Still a strong force by headcount, but little more than half that which had manned these walls a week ago, and that included a large number of wounded.

Each day now would go further the way of the enemy as the strength of the defenders waned ever more.

The reason for the small camp fires that had been lit on the Roman side of the Gaulish ramparts had confounded he and the other officers for a short while, but it had not taken him long to recognise that there were eight of them and piece together their meaning.

It had caused outrage and despair in roughly equal quantities along the wall when the eight Roman couriers had been raised on their crosses above the flames, each man beaten and cut but alive enough to appreciate the agony of a slow death by burning from beneath.

He refused, despite his rising gorge, to take his eyes from the sickening, horrifying sight. *He* had condemned them to this - he could hardly turn his face from them now.

'Just give the order, sir and we'll put them out of their misery' mumbled an optio nearby.

Felix felt the muscles in his jaw twitch. 'No. That's what the bastards want: a waste of ammunition. We have less than two hundred pila left and only thirty or so shots with the scorpions. We can't even afford to waste eight. Those few missiles might buy us an extra hour.'

The optio saluted and turned, stalking off along the rampart unhappily. Felix could hardly blame the man. No one should have to see this.

The question was: where was Vertico's man? Was he off in the woods somewhere, or was he brandishing a burning stick from lighting one of those fires?

The future looked bleak.

* * * * *

343

Ariogaisos clutched his side as he staggered through the woods, worrying about the quantity of blood that smeared his hand as it came away.

He had made it through the army surrounding the Eleventh Legion's camp through the judicious use of bravado and speed. He'd had the ill luck to have come up from the hidden ditch among a crowd of the Pleumoxii, who immediately distrusted the sudden arrival of one of the Nervii among them. Only by bluffing had he made his way through them, discovering on the way that the Nervii were based on the far side of the army in their entirety, scuppering any plans he'd had to rely on passing as one of them.

Instead he had kept his head down and his voice low and muffled so as to hide his heritage and try to pass as one of any of the numerous smaller tribes involved in this siege.

He had known that the Romans did not trust him, despite having had to rely upon him. They had little reason to trust, really. Surrounded by his tribe, why would they give their confidence to a man who could so easily turn on them? His master Vertico - the chief of a sizeable oppidum to the northeast - had given his oath to support Caesar in much the same way as the other Nervian leaders. But unlike they, who had formed an ignoble alliance through the druids to eject Rome from their territory, Vertico considered his own word to be of far more binding importance than his allegiance to that secret sect, however sacred they may be. How could a man devote himself to the gods and their druidical followers and not hold dear the great Celtic principle of a given oath being binding?

Ariogaisos had almost fallen among the last tribal group through which he had passed when they demanded to search him, suspicious at his passage away from the centre of events, and he had refused. A knife had been drawn and had cut him below the bottom rib, but he had managed to stagger away and into the woods.

He had a rough set of directions to the next winter quarters, given by the Roman commanders, and he knew enough of the territory to reach the boundaries of Nervii land safely. Whether the Tenth Legion - the next closest camp - would believe this stray wounded Celt was another matter. The message he carried should be proof enough.

'Halt!'

344

Surprised by the sudden Latin command so far from the legion and deep in the woods, Ariogaisos pulled himself upright and looked around. A figure stepped out of the undergrowth. He was Roman, dressed in their standard tunic, and yet unarmoured, still pulling up the breeches the Romans had adopted from the Gauls as he gestured with his blade. The reason for his presence became clear as the Gaul looked past him and saw a dozen or so other Romans gathered in a small clearing, encamped for the night. The one closing on him narrowed his eyes.

'You speak Latin?'

The Celt nodded and then, realising how stupid that was, cleared his throat. 'I am Ariogaisos, shield man of Vertico of the Nervii, bound on a mission for the legate of the Eleventh Legion.'

'Really?' the Roman replied disbelievingly. 'What's his name, then?'

Ariogaisos blinked. He'd never thought to ask that. As far as he was concerned, he got his orders from Vertico, who served the legate.

'I... I don't know' the Celt said quietly.

'Get in that clearing.'

As Ariogaisos staggered forward, clutching his bleeding side, the legionary urged him on with the point of the blade.

'Well well' commented a man in centurion's kit as they entered the clearing. 'What have you found, Nasica?'

The legionary padded over to a companion and retrieved something wrapped tightly in red cloth, hugging it to his chest as though it were his precious child, while two other legionaries pointed their swords at him.

'Only Nasica could go for a piss in the woods in the middle of nowhere and find a damn spy!'

'I am no spy' Ariogaisos replied. 'I serve under Vertico, the Nervian chief in the Eleventh Legion.'

As the other soldiers' voices rose in disparagement, the centurion waved them to silence.

'I remember Vertico. Where are you bound?'

Feeling a sense of relief flood through him, Ariogaisos reached into his shirt, drawing urgent gestures with the two swords, but producing a small folded piece of parchment, sealed with wax and the bull stamp of the Eleventh Legion.

'I am bound for the Tenth Legion to bring tidings of war.'

'There's a coincidence' mused the centurion. 'The Eleventh are in trouble?'

'Yes, Centurion.'

'The Nervii?'

'Yes, Centurion. And others.'

The officer nodded. 'Ambiorix and his Eburones. They've already obliterated the Fourteenth, and now they've moved onto Cicero's lot. Give me that.'

As the Celt passed over the parchment, the centurion cracked the wax seal and perused the contents. After a moment, he straightened and gestured for the two guards to sheathe their swords.

'Are you badly wounded?'

'It will heal' Ariogaisos replied.

'Are you feeling brave?'

The Gaul nodded, a dread feeling that he knew what was coming sinking into his gut.

'Can you get back into the camp?'

Yes - that was it. He nodded again.

'Then I'm going to give you a reply. You take it back to Cicero and Felix and tell them to hold. Help is on the way.' As he scrabbled for his stylus and the wax tablet he kept in his pack, he gestured to the legionary coddling the wrapped object. 'Nasica?' Put that thing down for a moment and get yourself back in armour. No more napping, anyone. We ride day and night now until we find the Tenth.'

Chapter Seventeen

<u>DECEMBRIS</u>

Fronto stepped onto the jetty and beheld his hometown with apprehension for the first time ever. When he came home it was invariably after a summer of campaigning and for rest and recovery over the winter months, down here where the climate was comfortable and more conducive to relaxation. Puteoli and its surrounding area were renowned for their dry, hot summers and their mild, if often damp, winters.

It was the place he automatically associated with family and friends - even though none of the latter would be in the area at this time - with wine and frivolity, with walks and swimming, hunting and days out to Pompeii and Neapolis.

In short: his happy place.

And now he was bringing all the troubles born of his past few years back home with him. Would he ruin Puteoli for the family the way the previous two winters had ruined Rome for them?

The sailing had been less rough than he'd expected this time of year and they had made good time, though he had still spent the requisite half the time at the railing adding his stomach contents to the treasures of the deep. It would be a few hours before he felt able to eat or drink, but he was becoming so inured to the sea-sickness these days that he was able to seal away and ignore the after effects to some extent - enough to concentrate on matters at hand, anyway.

To some extent the solitude he'd had at the ship's rail had been a cathartic time, if he was honest with himself. The news of Crispus' demise had come as a tremendous shock to him and the group's troubles had immediately expanded to fill all their waking thoughts, leaving him no time to ponder or grieve until aboard the ship and watching the gulls and the grey water in silence.

The thought that Crispus had been sent to Elysium in Gaul cut him all the more with the deep personal fear that, had he not severed his ties with Caesar and returned to Rome, he could have been there to stop it. It felt as though he had abandoned his friend and thus indirectly caused his death.

By the time the ship had reached Puteoli, he had finally come to terms with the loss, though a funeral feast and libations were overdue, and he would move the world itself if he had to in order to arrange a night with Priscus and Varus and the others.

A clatter as a bag was mishandled onto the dock drew his thoughts back.

As the others disembarked and the ship's crew unloaded the horses and their bags, Fronto looked along the jetty at the port - one of the busiest and most impressive in the Roman world - and then back to the city beyond, all narrow maze-like alleys and twisting vertiginous streets. Rome was a place of wide avenues and well-ordered streets - well, in the wealthier areas anyway - but almost none of Puteoli was designed like that. The city dated back to the days of the Greek settlers, before Rome's influence had reached this far south, and it suffered the design flaws of that artistic and disorganised people.

Despite the presence of the low-lying port and the sea-front part of the civic area behind, much of the city rose on high cliffs and spurs and from the jetty created something of the impression of looking up into the seats of a giant theatre arcing across before them.

'Where do we go?' Balbus asked, his voice catching. The man had been uncharacteristically quiet throughout the journey, more with nerves born of the news he carried for his daughter than the pain he himself felt.

Fronto nodded to himself. He'd forgotten that Balbus had never been here before.

'We'll have to make our way up through the city. From here, just past that bloody great arcaded building and to the right of the baths' cistern - that great square thing past the white roof - you can just see the curved top of the amphitheatre. We head up to there and turn right just past it. The road from there leads out toward Neapolis and we stop about a three quarters of a mile along the cliffs. If we'd come in from the southern direction, I could have shown you the villa. You can see it from the sea.'

He realised he was starting to enthuse, despite everything, and Balbus was in no mood to hear of Fronto's love for his home. Instead, he turned to the others. Elijah held Balbina by the hand. The girl's eyes were unfocused, unseeing - almost glazed, but the Jewish physician never let her spend a moment alone or uncared for, acting more as a brother or uncle than a medicus, comforting her and encouraging her to interact. It wasn't working, but something needed to be done.

Galronus, Masgava and Palmatus were in conversation about fighting methods, as seemed their norm. They made a strange trio - a Roman born, a Belgic chieftain and a dark-skinned Numidian - but they seemed to have settled into an easy friendship, and one that was equally extended to Fronto and Balbus.

'When we get to the villa - assuming all's normal - it might do us some good to look around it first with an eye to its defence' Fronto announced. 'We can deal with returning to the ladies afterwards. I would be happier if we at least scout the place out first and decide how we're going to approach the coming storm.'

The three warriors broke off their conversation and looked over at him. 'First,' Galronus replied 'we need to make sure the ladies are safe and whole.'

Balbus turned to face them all. '*I* will go and see the womenfolk. I need to speak to Lucilia and give her the news, and I would prefer to do that before you all settle in there; with a little privacy. You all see to the defence plans - you don't need me for that.'

'Nor I' added Elijah. 'With your permission I will bring your daughter.'

Balbus nodded and managed a weak smile for his blank-faced child. Elijah strolled over to join him as the porters loaded their bags onto the horses' flanks and settled them in place. As soon as all was ready, the six men and their young charge mounted up, Elijah lifting Balbina into position in front of him.

Without exchanging a word the group set off, clattering along the jetty and into the streets of the city. Fronto spent most of the first few hundred paces trying not to vomit again; to keep his insides where they belonged. Balbus rode with a singularity of purpose, his brow low and eyes burning with loss, anger and the fear of the coming exchange with his daughter, keeping his horse close to Fronto and Galronus, both of whom knew the way from the port and rode easily and confidently.

Behind them, Elijah, Palmatus and Masgava chatted amiably as they rode, their gaze slipping around them to take everything in.

Slowly, the cavalcade of six horses and their riders wound their way through the city and up the slope toward the rolling skyline of volcanic hills. Strangely, though they felt the need to hurry against the possibility of their enemies reaching the villa before them, this last stage had seen them slow, their reluctance to deal with what they might find and what they knew must come bringing hesitation to their every step.

Within the next quarter of an hour they had passed the amphitheatre, its arcades silent on this day without games, and turned on to the Neapolis road. A short, silent ride further, during which the new visitors took in the impressive scenery, and the group turned off the main road.

'We're heading back toward the sea?' Palmatus enquired.

'Yes. The villa's a cliff-top one.'

'Seems surprisingly sparse out here' the former legionary noted. 'I'd have thought that with the climate *all* these slopes would be covered with vines and villas.

'Puteoli region's not over welcoming of strangers' Fronto said with a wry smile. 'The ground smokes, bubbles and moves in places. Only long-term locals or brave adventurers sink their money into villas here. We have tremors in the land every few years, too - some are quite bad. Parts of our villa have been repaired three or four times before now and a few years ago we had to rebuild the barn.'

'Delightful' Palmatus noted, the news of the terrain drawing his attention toward what looked like a forest fire in the distance to their left - a haze of white smoke wafting up into the grey sky. 'The ground smokes, you say?'

Fronto turned and looked off to the north-east at the haze rising from the rolling hill tops.

'That's Vulcan's Forum. Never stops. The more superstitious call it Hades' Gate - they think it's the way down into the underworld. Personally I think it's the very ground rebelling against us cultivating it. As I said: not welcoming, although the mud and steam's supposed to be good for ailments. Lucilia's dragged me up there 'for my health' before now and we used to play up there as children.'

'Delightful' Palmatus repeated, eying the haze suspiciously.

'There's the villa' Fronto announced, reining in his horse on the crest of the slope. The others peered ahead at the Falerii's family holdings and Masgava whistled through his teeth.

The villa proper consisted of a surprisingly large double-storeyed main building with north and south wings embracing a courtyard garden that was enclosed with just a low wall, a single simple gate allowing ingress from the road. Beyond, and connected to the villa by terraced walkways were a low, wide building that could only be a bathhouse from the smoking chimneys, a large structure reminiscent of rural warehouses and farm stores with a squat quadrangular building attached, and a small porticoed structure facing the sea. The land all about was cultivated with vineyards and vegetable plots and dotted with occasional small sheds, and a herd of goats roaming a slope, contained by a low fence.

But it was not the sizeable and wealthy villa, nor its cultivated surrounds, that drew the gaze of the new arrivals; it was the terrain.

The buildings had been constructed on terraces gradually stepping away toward the sea, connected by stairways and paths, and beyond the final grassy lip, simply open air all the way down to the crashing waves far below. Puteoli centre was visible off to the right as a distant, low-lying mass by the water, so far down it gave the impression of being part of another world. Baia and Misenum watched jealously from across the water.

Palmatus swallowed noisily. He pictured a man rolling down the slope beside that house. If he picked up enough momentum and failed to grasp one of the terrace edges in his descent, he could quite simply roll past the entire complex and then out over the cliff and into nowhere.

The very thought of the drop he couldn't quite see beyond that grassy horizon made his backbone shiver.

'Your family picked a magical place for a villa. Hope none of them ever sleep-walked!'

'Not the surviving ones' Fronto replied with a straight face, and Palmatus could not decide whether or not he was being serious.

Figures moved around the courtyard garden, going about their daily tasks and the sight was instantly reassuring. Clearly they had beaten their enemies here and things were running normally. Balbus turned. 'You all do your planning. Elijah, Balbina and I will go inside and meet with the ladies. Give me half an hour.'

Fronto nodded and clasped his friend's arm. 'Fortuna go with you Quintus. Be gentle.'

He and the three other warriors watched the two men and the girl descend to the courtyard, where they were greeted by one of the slaves. Fronto deliberately paid no further attention to them. Some things had to come first, given the trouble heading their way, and this would hardly be a happy reunion.

'As you can see,' he announced to the others 'it's quite defensible in some places, but hopelessly open in others. Peaceful

351

area, you see. Never expected to have to defend it, so it's a residence with no thought for martial security.'

Masgava nodded. 'What are the buildings?'

'Come on. I'll show you.'

Fronto kicked his horse into life and took them off to the west, skirting the built up area on the city-side. In the same fashion as most rural villas, the outer faces of the Falerii's home were plastered in white with small windows at regular intervals, their shutters thrown back to allow in the light. Both storeys of the main building were of uniform shape and construction and the roof was of good red tile. As they passed around the side, they could see the arcaded portico that ran along the rear on the ground level, an entrance in it allowing access to the path which forked and ran down to the next terrace and other buildings.

'The main house is far larger than it ever really needed to be' Fronto noted. 'This villa doesn't come from the Falerii you see - came from my great grandmother's side. She was from a rural family of modest equite rank but with an almost bottomless purse. She and her brother believed that half the battle for acceptance into the elite was having an impressive house. They failed, of course, though her daughter married my grandfather - who was insufferably noble but low on available money. It was a marriage made in social-climber's heaven. So we ended up with a pleasant and rather over-sized country estate and everyone was happy.'

'Just the two entrances?' Galronus enquired.

'Hardly. Three off the central courtyard - a main public one, a private one into the apartments, and a servants' one. There's two at the rear, out onto the portico, too - one for the family and one for the slaves, but the portico has only the one way in or out, so I guess you could call it one.'

'Not easy to defend' Palmatus observed. 'One man could hold the portico entrance, but an agile warrior would just climb in through the arches. So to be sure, you'd need a man at each inner door. That would leave us with three for the front. That's just one for each door into the courtyard. A man at every entrance but no reserve.'

'There will be other men. But you don't think we could hold the perimeter wall to the garden?' Fronto enquired, already convinced of the answer, but seeking confirmation.

'Wall's too low and too feeble. Even if you stockade it or build it up, the whole thing was covered with vines. Looking at how well-tended and neat they were, they'll have been there a long time and they'll have screwed the stonework. A well placed shield barge would probably bring down a section of the wall.'

'So that *would* be all of us with one door each' Masgava frowned. 'Rather thinly spread. Can we discount the house for defence and concentrate elsewhere, or do you have plenty of other guards?'

Fronto shrugged. 'There should be a small army of hired swords if Posco's done his job right.'

'That makes things easier, then.'

'Perhaps' Fronto said, kicking his horse forward again. 'But present company excepted, I'm no believer in the quality and loyalty of hired swords. The sort one might hire in port cities are not the finest to be bought, loyalty-wise, and despite having plenty of money and his heart in the right place, Posco's no judge of a fighting man. Until I've looked them in the eye and seen them at the palus, I'll reserve judgement.'

The cavalcade veered to the right, descending the slope toward the cliff between the edge of the nearest vineyard and the bath house that clung to the terrace, resting on vaulted substructures. The baths were bigger than any such private establishment any in the party had laid eyes upon - almost as large as the main villa building.

'Big baths' Palmatus noted, trying not to look too closely at the cliff edge coming ever closer at the bottom of the slope.

'Got its own pool for swimming and more than one of each bath. While my great grandmother was one for glory and ostentation, my grandfather took his bathing rather seriously.'

'Only two doors there?'

'Three. But I've had bad experiences fighting in bath houses recently. I'd rather avoid that. Besides, it's quite dark in there apart from the natatio, which has windows big enough for someone to climb in.'

'So we rule that out' Galronus nodded. 'What's that place?'

Fronto looked ahead to the small porticoed structure on the lowest terrace.

'My mother's sun house. Just three small rooms and a portico. Three windows; one door. Only real way of accessing it is from the cliff side.'

Palmatus swallowed noisily and eyed the edge. 'Has no one ever thought to put up a fence or a rail?'

'Why?'

'I dunno. To stop some poor bastard rolling off it onto the rocks?'

Fronto smiled. 'No. But the sun house is probably the most defensible place. The only other buildings out at the other side are the barn and stables. Too many arches, doors and windows there. Or there's the caves, of course.'

Galronus and Masgava looked at one another and the big Numidian raised an eyebrow. 'Caves?'

'There's a small system under the grass off toward the left. There are stairways down into them from two of the small sheds you keep seeing in the fields, and three holes in the cliff side about a third of the way down.'

Palmatus shuddered. 'Doesn't sound good. Hate to be trapped in them.'

Fronto scratched his head. 'Good fall back position, though.' He scanned their surroundings and his gaze fell upon the bulk of the main building, towering above them higher up the slope. Behind it, he could see the distant haze of the steaming ground in the vast crater of the Forum Vulcani. Slowly a smile spread across his face.

'Of course it doesn't have to be *anywhere* in the villa.'

'What?'

'Well we've just been thinking how to defend the villa. What if we just quit the villa and drew them somewhere different? Problem with the villa is we think too traditionally and we have to consider what to do with the women and the slaves and servants, and everything else. We're very constricted - like being besieged in a fort. And if everything goes wrong, there's no way to escape.'

Galronus shook his head. 'And if we plan to meet them elsewhere and they come here first, what if they ransack the house?'

'I don't think they will if they know we're not here. These people are murderers and killers - and probably rapists - but I doubt they're thieves. Thieves would be too careful to sign themselves up on something like this. Besides, Pompey and Berengarus will have selected the more brutal prisoners to set on us. I think they'll be intent on blood, not robbery.'

'So what do you think?' Palmatus asked, trying not to let the relief at the possibility the cliff side may no longer be involved show on his face.

354

'The Forum Vulcani... the door to Hades. I know this is going to sound stupid, but I know the place like the back of my own hand. My friends and I used to sneak away as children and play there against the wishes of the elders.'

'You think it would be better?' Masgava asked.

'I think so. There are a dozen hazards for the unwary thrown in by nature, let alone anything *we* do. Admittedly, the dangers tend to change from time to time, so we'll have to familiarise ourselves with the place as we prepare, but I think it might be just the thing.' He grinned at Masgava. 'You put me back on the right track, my friend, and you've taught me a few things, but now we need to marry your ingenuity and adaptability with my experience at strategic defence. I think we might be able to spring a surprise or two on them.'

'And what of the women and servants?' Galronus asked quietly. 'You can't put them in the same danger, and you can't leave them in the villa, in case you're wrong and the killers come straight here to rummage around.'

Fronto nodded as he kicked his horse into life again. 'Our family has associates all around the bay. Most of my actual friends are in Rome or serving in the military or on the staff of various governors, but their parents will look after the family for us. We'll send them with most of the hired blades off to the Sennii over in Baia or the Tineii at Cuma. They'll be safe and totally out of the way, which will allow us to concentrate on our work. What do you think?'

'I think you're perfectly mad' Palmatus grinned. 'Let's do it. Just us four and master Balbus? Or do you want to bring any of the hired men?'

'Just a few. Too many would be more of a hindrance than a help, given their likely unfamiliarity with the land - I'll pick four of the most violent looking ones. Now, I think we need to see the women and settle in for a few hours, and then I'll take you up to the Forum Vulcani and show you around while there's still enough light. Has it been half an hour yet?'

As the small party rounded the far corner of the villa and made their way back toward the entrance, they became aware of the sound of raised voices.

'Perhaps we should do another circuit first' winced Palmatus.

As they approached the front, Balbus was blocking the courtyard wall's gateway. Fronto caught sight of Lucilia standing in the middle of the garden. She had a sword in her hand - Balbus' probably,

355

looking at the blade - and was gesturing angrily at her father. The Jewish physician stood behind her, by the door to the villa, holding Balbina's hand and looking on with a concerned expression.

'Get out of the way, father.'

'Be realistic, Lucilia!' Balbus snapped. 'Where will you go? You think to hunt a pack of murderers? I've always been proud of your self-assurance and strength, but on this occasion it's misdirected. You're being a foolish girl!'

Fronto winced at the comment and Lucilia stepped forward, the gladius point coming up unwavering at her father's chin.

'Don't be childish, Lucilia.'

In a move quicker than Fronto could have expected, Balbus reached out and snatched the blade, wrestling it from her hand. Lucilia threw herself at him, her fists balled and hammering on his chest. Calmly, with more emotion showing on his face than Fronto had seen in over a week, Balbus tossed his sword aside into a flower bed and wrapped his arms around the girl, who continued to pound his chest angrily even as he pulled her tighter into his embrace.

Fronto worried that his heart might break as he watched the fight pass out of her. He had never seen Lucilia surrender to anything before. He was becoming used to being the one who would have to do the giving in at any situation but, as he watched, the pounding stopped and Lucilia went limp in her father's arms. As Balbus coddled her, her face buried in his tunic, he reached up, releasing some of the strength in his grip and stroking her hair.

Lucilia began to shake as the sobs wracked her.

By the time Fronto was off his horse and at the gate she was all but a mess in her father's arms. Balbus spotted Fronto approaching and gently but firmly stepped back, holding Lucilia up and away in his strong grasp.

The young woman looked at him in befuddlement for a moment and then noticed Fronto. He held out his arms and opened his mouth to speak. Nothing came out; he had no idea what to say, though it appeared that hardly mattered. Lucilia almost fell into his arms and her embrace tightened, restricting his ability to draw deep breaths. For a long moment she squeezed tightly, expressing her loss and her grief and her need all in one crushing embrace.

He took a shallow, shuddering breath and gripped her in return.

* * * * *

Lucilia tapped the wagon and peered at the horses tethered to it. In the back, the two women of the Falerii, mother and daughter, sat along with the strange Jewish physician who seemed to be a rock to which young, silent Balbina clung.

'Nothing I can say is going to persuade either of you, is it?'

Fronto and Balbus, side by side in the villa's garden gateway, shook their heads.

'I'm no soldier, I know, but I'm strong and clever and I know which end of a sword goes in my hand and which goes in the enemy.'

'I've lost enough already, Lucilia' Balbus said flatly. 'I'll not lose you, and I know your husband is of the same mind.'

Lucilia sighed. 'How will we know when it's over?'

'When we come and get you. Lucius Tinneius will keep you all safe, and you've got more than a dozen guards with you.'

'And what if you *don't* come and get us?'

Fronto smiled as reassuringly as he could. 'Can you imagine anybody standing up to Masgava? And I'm not the feeble fleshpile I was back in Rome, Lucilia. I'm back at my peak. Gods, I'm above the peak and looking down, now. And as well as us five there are four more of the guards staying with us. That's nine. And we're all better than any simple murderer.'

'Just be careful.'

With a last hard look at Fronto and her father, Lucilia turned and mounted the wagon, taking a seat opposite the two Falerii women and next to her sister and the Jew, her back to Posco on the driver's bench. The large party of hired muscle settled their blades in the sheaths and stretched muscles before nodding at the driver.

Posco turned and smiled unhappily at Fronto.

'Fortuna, Domine.'

'Hope she's with you too, Posco. Keep them safe.'

'With my life, sir.'

Fronto stood statue-like, trying not to let any of the nerves he was beginning to feel show in his face as the cart creaked and began to roll away toward the city proper and the road that would follow the curve of the bay past some of the world's most astounding places and up to the great acropolis of Cuma, where the Tineii had their villa, nestled close to the entrance of the Sibyl's cave. Behind them, the force of mercenaries trod the road in the chilly breeze. As the cart

357

and its escort disappeared out of sight around the curve, Fronto turned to Balbus.

'They'll be safe in Cuma. No one would expect them to be there and we're the only people who know where they are. Let's go.'

Balbus stood for a moment, watching the empty road and the bend around which his daughters had disappeared, and nodded. For the first time since Corvinia's death in Rome, Fronto noted something of the determined positivity of his old friend returning to Balbus' eyes.

'Show me the killing ground, Marcus.'

* * * * *

The 'Forum Vulcani' was well named - a mortal could quite imagine the great blacksmith of the gods at work here.

As the party of nine warriors crested a rise covered with scrub grass and a few sparse scrub bushes, they received their first view of the place that was to be their stand against the killers from the carcer. The five friends gathered in a small knot, the four hired swords waiting respectfully and patiently to the side to hear their orders.

The sky was bright, if grey - the wind fast and cold, whipping along the high blanket of cloud at a remarkable pace, and yet the gate to Hades was still shrouded in clouds of its own.

A crater perhaps half a mile across had been scooped out of the land by the hand of some ancient Titan, leaving the most astounding depression. Despite the greenery of the surrounding hills and even the scrubby vegetation on this slope, everything below the lip in that wide bowl was unearthly and desolate. The whole crater glowed with an unnatural yellow-white colour and the ground was chalky and pale, spotted by patches of darker grey and rocks coloured yellow through to orange.

Smoky steam sat in the hollow like low-lying cloud, the product of bubbling pools and jets issuing from small cracks and crevices.

Galronus shuddered. 'Pleasant' he said with a snort. 'And what in the name of precious *Taranis* is that smell?'

'Get used to it' Fronto said quietly. 'It's the smell of the very ground and everything that comes from it.'

'Smells like Hades has a stomach complaint to me. But the steam could be useful' Balbus noted. 'Particularly if *we* know where we're going and they don't.'

'That's only half of it, Quintus. The central area - you can see where it's lower and darker - is where most of the steam comes up from. The whole area's a maze of narrow tracks you can walk along surrounded by bubbling pools of mud. You slip into one of those and you'll be wishing someone had stuck you with a gladius instead. One of my pals when I was a boy got his leg in one of them. Had to have it removed at the knee. Nasty, it was.'

'So you get lost in that mist and don't know the ground and you're buggered' Palmatus whispered. 'Not sure my memory's up to that.'

'That' Fronto replied, 'is why we'll all be bringing a good stout walking pole with us to test the ground in front of us. We should have time to familiarise ourselves, but I'd like to avoid any accidents.'

'Me too' the former legionary added fervently, peering down at the unearthly mist.

'Tell us about the place then' Masgava said, pointing down into the crater. 'What can we use? What benefits does it give us?'

Fronto nodded.

'Well Balbus and Palmatus have spotted the first thing. And the worse the weather, the better for the cloud - if it rains the steam gets worse and you can hardly see a thing down there. We find a nice defensive spot in that central area and they'll have an evil task getting to us. Hopefully they'll lose a few in the process.'

'Agreed. Not enough to rely upon for a victory, though.'

'No. I'll show you what else there is. From here we have about the best view to plan it all; that's why I brought you the way I did. When the enemy come, they'll follow the track straight from the villa and appear on that ridge over there.' He pointed.

'You haven't said yet how we're going to get them here' Galronus noted, folding his arms.

'Isn't that obvious? Someone is going to have to stay at the villa and be seen. He'll then have to outrun them to the Forum Vulcani - lure them in.'

The rest of the group spent a few heartbeats glancing at one another. None of them relished the opportunity.

'Relax' Fronto smiled. 'It would have to be Quintus or myself. Has to be someone they know by sight and who's important enough to them to devote their attention to. They wouldn't bother chasing the rest of you... and I'm afraid, Quintus, that despite the fact you're about to volunteer, it has to be me.'

Balbus opened his mouth to object but closed it quickly. Fronto was right and they all knew it. He was the very centre of Berengarus' attention - the man the enemy had been assembled and set to kill. He was the only one who they would definitely follow en masse. Moreover, with the exception of Masgava, Fronto was now the fittest man, sporting muscles long unseen and capable of a turn of speed unusual for his age.

'I will bring them over that lip. I'm the one here most familiar with the crater and I'll lead them a merry little dance. Now...' he peered around the crater, cradling his chin in his hand. 'As well as the mud pools, there are two or three other things we can make use of.'

He pointed to the northern slopes.

'See that low building there?'

The group nodded as they peered off toward the incline of yellow-grey scree from which half a dozen small jets of steam issued. Nestled up against the slope was a single-room building, perhaps eight feet across in both directions, with no windows and a single low door that was currently shut. The room was pierced all around just below the flat, flagged roof with small holes, each of which threw out a continual jet of steam.

'That's the Laconium - the sauna room. Lucilia's taken me in for my health. It's as hot as Vulcan's scrotum in there and almost suffocating. Smells ten times worse than this too. I can't stay in there even a moment when they shut the door. Some people stay in for maybe a count of a hundred with the door closed and the vents open like they are now. The standard treatment, though, is to leave both the vents and the door open and stay inside for a quarter of an hour. Longer than that just isn't safe.'

'I think I see where you're going with this' Balbus smiled grimly.

Fronto nodded. 'Some poor sod on a health visit from Neapolis a few years back went in there with the door shut and a random tremor in the ground dropped the lever and sealed the vents. They found him an hour later and he'd been cooked. Quite literally. Horrible way to go. Since then, there's been a safety catch on the vent system and the city ordo removed the catch from the door. Pretty sure we could put them back as they were, though.'

Galronus shuddered, imagining being stuck in the dark in that hell of boiling steam. It didn't bear thinking about.

'What else' Balbus nudged.

'There's the steam jets at the east end, just down there.'

They followed his pointing finger to see an area of the lower slope where narrow jets of steam shot high into the air with tremendous pressure from the ground. As they watched, their eyes widened in fascination as the jets altered. Some died away and vanished while new ones burst from the ground in unexpected places.

'This place is full of lovely surprises' Palmatus boggled. 'How does *that* happen?'

'I've no idea, but it's been doing it forever. Thing is, while the jets change all the time, there are two or three safe routes through it. I know them by heart - stupid and dangerous games kids play, eh? Could have been flash-boiled a hundred times when I was eight. Fortuna's always been my lady, though. I *can* tell you that if one of those jets actually gets you it'll be like having burning pitch poured over you in a siege. I've heard horror stories of other boys who got the routes wrong.'

'Anything else?'

Fronto continued to cradle his chin as he scanned the crater, musing over what he could remember.

'There are a few other surprises it holds, though we'd have to work out how best to use them to our advantage: hot water springs that boil continually, yellow rocks that burn to the touch - that kind of thing. I'm sure Masgava's devious mind will come up with some inventive uses.'

'So' Galronus said, sitting on a smooth boulder and scanning the crater before him, 'what's the plan? You're going to lead them here from the villa and then basically draw them into the various traps? That means that we'll have to have men ready everywhere to spring them?'

'Pretty much, yes. Although it might be nice if we can split them up as soon as we get them over the lip. Lure some off to the steam jets, one or two maybe to the sauna and others elsewhere. Then we can gather at the mudpools in the centre and use it as our last stand - watch them fall as they get near us and then we'll hopefully only have to fight a hardcore few who manage to get to us. We don't know how many men they'll have. There can't have been too many in the carcer, but there's every possibility that Berengarus has been hiring lowlifes off the street too.'

He turned to the four hired swords. 'I think you four can cover the steam room vents and...' he frowned in deep thought. 'Any of you good with a sling?' One of the men nodded and another shrugged. 'I can shoot a bow pretty well' he said.

'Good. Well, that's you men sorted then. We'll get you two in good positions. Might even be able to use some of those burning-hot rocks with the sling. The other two can take the steam room and then come and join the rest of us when you're done.'

Palmatus cleared his throat meaningfully. 'There is one problem you've not mentioned.'

'Go on.'

'We're going to have to set all this up without you.'

Fronto frowned. 'Why?'

'Because you need to be at the villa for when they turn up. You can't sleep or rest until they do any time you're on your own, else they might just arrive and gut you in your bed and never come near this place.'

'Shit. Never thought of that.'

Masgava shrugged. 'We'll all stay at the villa during the night and sleep in shifts. Then everyone but you can spend the daytimes getting used to this place and working out where everything is. We'll spend the rest of today with a wax tablet or two marking all the paths through the mud and the vents. Maybe we can actually mark them on the ground with coloured rock or something. Once we know the safe paths, we can do the rest without you. You'll just have to twiddle your thumbs and keep yourself busy at the villa while we wait for them.'

'What if they don't come?' Palmatus frowned. 'What if they never hear about this place?'

'They'll come' Fronto said. 'Even if it weren't for the fact that half Rome's nobility know where the Falerii come from, I can feel it in my bones. The bastards are coming. And they're coming soon.'

* * * * *

Four days had passed since the wagon had carried the ladies and their escort from Puteoli and the spectacular family villa up to the equally luxurious house of the Tineii at Cuma, north of the bay, on the west coast. The first three days had been torture for Lucilia. Faleria and her mother seemed to have achieved a stoic calmness that was at odds with the general situation and were going about their life as though on a vacation, chatting with their hosts and strolling in the gardens, visiting the great acropolis and the forum, talking of a trip to consult the Sibylline oracle... Lucilia shuddered; no help there - she'd met the Sibyl before.

But for Lucilia it was imprisonment and nothing less. Her husband, for whom she cared more than she would ever admit publically - and without whom she could not even imagine a life - was preparing for a battle against a most brutal and unpredictable enemy. Her father was with him, too - her father who had a weak chest and had been close to death already once in recent years. The exertion alone might kill him. Galronus, soon to be her brother in law, was there too. Lucilia was still not sure how to deal with Galronus. He seemed as Roman as any of them, yet there was something about him that threw her expectations occasionally - a Celtic nobility that seemed to leak through his façade of Roman civility. But she would hate to lose him before she came to understand him.

Three men she cared about - as well as others her husband seemed to regard as good friends - all facing a threat of unknown intensity and danger. And leading that enemy was the man who had murdered her mother and apparently unhinged her younger sister's mind, no matter what Elijah might say about her chances of recovery.

It was simply too much to bear; too much to *expect* her to bear.

She had argued that they could be a part of it, of course. Even if the menfolk wouldn't let them bear arms and take an active part in the fight, they could keep watch or even perhaps throw stones. Posco would not hear of it though and, despite the fact that he was a slave, he had Fronto's full authority to do what he must to keep them safe. Besides, neither of the Falerii women seemed to believe involvement was a good thing. But then *they* had not had their mother murdered by the swine.

She had finally given up the argument the previous evening. Her dreams during the night, however, seemed to be directing her to disobedience and to fleeing the safety of their hosts in order to take a role in the defence that their men were planning. She had contemplated running, but in the end she knew deep down that her presence would merely distract Fronto and her father from their business and that could be a fatal mistake.

And so she had settled for keeping herself as busy as she could. The sun - such as it was - a pale watery orb behind a bank of high cloud that constantly threatened drizzle, was at its apex as she descended the drive from the villa's main doorway toward the road into the centre of town. The house of the Tineii was actually only a short walk from the thriving heart of Cuma, but the walk was mostly through gardens and orchards belonging to the villa.

At her belt was a purse of money that Posco had warned her to keep hidden against the possibility of thieves and criminals in the forum, and over her arm was the handle of a shopping basket. An hour or two at the forum and the two markets would distract her from her interminable incarceration in that luxurious prison. The eldest daughter of the Tineii had offered to make her a new dress if she chose the material and some accessories, and that had leant extra purpose to her shopping trip.

'This is a foolish decision, if I may be so bold.'

Lucilia snapped her head round sharply at the voice. Elijah, the Jewish physician, stood on the path a few paces back, folding up a cloak and draping it over his shoulder in case the weather turned the way it threatened to.

'Everyone knows where I'm going. No one complained.'

'They were labouring under the impression you would be taking some of the guards with you, young lady.'

'I'm only going to the forum and the markets, Elijah.'

'Even here it is not necessarily safe for a young lady on her own. This may not be Rome, but cities are cities and all forms of life are to be found here, including the lowest.'

'If I *must* have an escort, feel free to join me' she replied in a snippier fashion than she truly intended. The Jew had been nothing but accommodating to her and her family and friends over the few days she had known him, and - as far as she was aware - for no recompense. He seemed to be trying to help her sister out of the goodness of his heart. A rare thing - especially from a Jew, if all the tales the ladies of Rome told were true. His race's focus on one god alone was said to blind them to possibilities and make them insular and unfriendly to Romans. It was hard to see such a description fitting Elijah.

'I was hoping to take Balbina for a wander in the gardens before the rains came, but I daresay she will manage another few hours. I hear the herb and spice stalls in the markets here are well stocked, so perhaps I can pick up some useful medicine components.'

Falling in alongside her, he smiled easily.

'They will be fine, you know?'

'Your god told you, did he?' Mean and unworthy, she knew, but the day was starting to annoy her again.

Elijah simply nodded as though it were a straightforward enquiry. 'Jehovah watches over even those who deny him. He is a forgiving god.'

'Fronto only believes in luck and vengeance - Fortuna and Nemesis. I've heard him tell the other gods that they don't exist, even while he's pouring wine on their altars. Struck me as particularly funny, that. I do believe he thinks that if he denies them they won't affect his life. Strangely, it does seem to work for him.'

'Luck and Vengeance alone would make for an empty soul. I suspect that your husband is considerably deeper than he would like anyone to know.'

'He is a simple man and a complex one both at the same time' Lucilia agreed. 'Every day I learn something new about him - and some of those discoveries make me grind my teeth - but he is a good man.'

'Of that I am in no doubt. Your father also is good, and Jehovah watches over the good with special favour.'

Lucilia felt herself begin to relax as the two strolled down the path and turned onto the main road with its uneven slabs worn and rutted through centuries of feet and hooves and cart wheels, the gravel periodically thrown over it to ease travel had simply settled into the gaps and all-but disappeared. A few other folk strolled the street - more and more as they neared the centre of town.

As they walked, she began to quiz Elijah about his homeland and his people, and was surprised to learn how ancient their culture was. He was able to name kings who had ruled Judea when the city of Rome was still a dream of future glory in the eyes of Romulus. It seemed that Pompey's conquest of their land had done nothing to dent their pride in their past or their sense of self-worth.

The more the pair walked and talked, the more Lucilia came to appreciate the soft spoken physician and his gentle acceptance of everything around him, and by the time they passed into the busy forum and moved around the stalls set up at its edges, she had decided that she might like to visit his home one day.

'What brought you from your land, Elijah?' she asked, the question having only just now occurred to her.

The Jew smiled as he regarded the mass of people ahead, and there was something of an age-old sadness in it. Momentarily, Lucilia regretted the question but he began, undeterred.

'Rome has had her sandaled foot on the throat of my people for almost a decade and nothing eases - the voices raised against her just increase with each passing season. Interference and control by Rome has raised a great deal of anti-foreign feeling among my people.' He turned his sad smile to her. 'I am - as you know - a physician, and my own work relies upon the knowledge and learning of other great thinkers, be they Greek, Roman or Egyptian. My house became a target for scrawled messages of xenophobic hate. In the end, God sent me a message in the form of a Roman merchant who bemoaned the lack of good medici in the capital. It seemed a fortuitous meeting, and within the week I had sold my home and carried a bag of money to Rome to sell my services. I had only been in the city less than a week before master Balbus found me with your mother's...' he paused and smiled weakly. 'I am sorry. I should not have brought that up.'

'Don't worry' Lucilia replied quietly. 'Your god seems to have sent you to us at just the right time. I wonder whether it is *your* god's work or *ours* that you are here.'

Elijah smiled.

'Lucilia, you are a remarkable girl, and Fronto is a lucky man.'

The western end of the forum was busier than elsewhere and as they made their way between the stalls, the girl poring over the goods for sale, they found themselves jostled from all sides. Lucilia, mindful of Posco's words of warning, cast her eyes around the folk among the stalls, her hand dropping to her purse and clutching it tight. The forum of Cuma was filled with men and women of a dozen ethnicities, from Punic immigrants to Greek traders to Syrian slaves to huge blond Celts.

A strangled gasp caught her ear and she turned just in time to see Elijah fall back into the crowd, the spray of crimson from his neck fountaining up into the air like a grisly monochrome rainbow. Lucilia's eyes widened in horror. The Jew grabbed for his throat and clamped his fingers over the ragged slash that had dug deep through windpipe, muscle and arteries. Before he hit the floor he was already going pale.

Lucilia screamed something.

She wasn't sure what it was, but it seemed to attract entirely the wrong sort of attention. A big, muscular ham of a hand clamped itself over her mouth as another arm went round her front, pinning her own limbs against her side and an enormous torso. The crowd were shouting a hundred different cries now, but no one seemed to be trying to help her. As her constricted airway choked the consciousness from her and her world slipped into a grey fog, she felt herself being hauled backward through the crowd.

* * * * *

Tulchulchur stood in the deep shadow at the rear of the warehouse, his ghostly, pale, scrawny shape barely registering in the light that glinted off his favourite eye-spoon.

'I am in two minds. On the one hand, Berengarus, I have to admit I would love to see Fronto's face while I peel her slowly in front of him. It would be something to savour. On the other hand, I can see Acrab's point. Just keeping her around complicates matters - perhaps we should just kill her now.'

Berengarus shook his head vehemently. He was starting to become seriously irritated with all the delays. They had resupplied in Rome before taking a ship south - and even then the ghoulish Tulchulchur had insisted they embark at Ostia, not Rome and sail to Cuma, not Puteoli in case of a watch being set on the port. The crazed murderer was thorough to a tee, but now had to be the time to move.

There had been a dozen of them by the time they left Rome, and the wraith had brought another six on board in Cumae, delaying a further two days to make enquiries as to the identities of the most vicious lowlifes for hire in the city. Certainly the new additions would add to Berengarus' small, brutal army, but that was enough now.

Still, had they gone straight for Fronto and his friends at Puteoli, they would not have been passing through the forum when the Jew and the girl strolled past talking openly and loudly about Fronto and Balbus. Idiots. And even if the names were not enough, it had taken only a momentary glance for him to recognise that pretty little woman who had accompanied Fronto to Pompey's house on occasion.

Whatever Tulchulhchur thought, Berengarus had no intention of killing the girl now - it would hurt Fronto, but not enough. Fronto had led a *legion* against his people by the river Rhenus. His men had severed Aenor's spine with a blade and driven young Gerulf into the river to drown while dragging him off in chains. Nothing was too painful for the Tenth's legate, including being held tight while watching his wife being peeled.

'Acrab not in charge' Berengarus snapped. The way Tulchulchur raised an eyebrow suggested that he believed *he* was the commander of this little war band. The big German had deferred to the 'monster of Vipsul' for planning and organisation, but he was in no way relinquishing his control of the group. The only reason these *things* - and to him they were little more than animals - were out of their incarceration and walking and breathing was because he might need them to put Fronto down. After that had happened, he might break Tulchulchur in half himself. It would feel good. It would be his leaving present to his Roman hosts when he headed north once more to his refreshingly cold and verdant homeland and the rest of the Roman bastards that had murdered his family and people. Caesar and the others would pay in time.

'Acrab led an army against Pompey in his Syrian homeland' Tulchulchur replied, snapping Berengarus back to the present from his reverie. 'He is a forward thinking man with a shrewd mind. It is foolish to brush aside his wisdom through sheer lust for blood.'

'Girl lives until Fronto watch her die.'

Tulchulchur shrugged. It *would* be fun to ruin that milky white skin and those pretty eyes. He twisted his favourite eye-spoon in the lamplight and grinned.

'Very well, but we will not take her with us. We will find somewhere to keep her until we have Fronto. One of the others can stay with her.'

Berengarus narrowed his eyes suspiciously, but the wraithlike killer radiated an air of honesty in this matter. Finally, he nodded.

'The first thing, though,' the Monster of Vipsul added 'is to wake her and find out everything she knows about Fronto and the rest. Prior knowledge is half the battle.'

Berengarus continued nodding. He was hungry to begin, but to extract information about the size and disposition of Fronto's force was worth another small delay.

They would all die soon enough.

Chapter Eighteen

Priscus tried for the third time in a row to tie the Hercules knot around his midriff and this time gave up and knotted it in a fashion that would likely have to be cut to be removed. As a symbol of command at a high level it was a necessity in order to display his rank but, no matter what he did, the ribbon always gradually slipped down his cuirass until by midmorning it rested on his hips, looking somewhat deflated and ridiculous.

As legate of the Tenth, he'd only bothered to put it on when he was likely to be in the presence of the general, but he was damned if he was going to saunter around the camp of his beloved legion that now served under young Crassus without a reminder that he was still the senior man here.

His fingers tensed and his knuckles whitened as he pulled the ribbon tight, his temper once again darkening at the thought of that young lunatic in charge of his legion.

It was an unworthy thought and he knew it. His image of young Crassus had been heavily influenced by previous contact with his family: his elder brother, whose harsh and violent approach to military command had produced great results but had also caused almost as many problems as it had resolved. And of course his father, a notoriously avaricious and pompous man who had risen to become one of the most powerful men in the republic through his dubious amassing of wealth and a willingness to overlook the ethics of any action.

The younger Crassus scion appeared to be nothing like his brother, though. Though there was only less than two years between the pair, Marcus Licinius Crassus appeared more than half a decade younger than his brother, fresh faced and with an almost childish enthusiasm.

What irked Priscus most was the fact that, while this Crassus had enough personality and passion to inspire a legion - he was eminently likeable and easy to deal with - he clearly had not even a fragment of his brother's talent for military strategy. They were as unalike as could be. Publius could have crushed an army twice his size, despite bad terrain, though his legion would resent his rule and the after effects could be wicked. Marcus would never manage in the face of terrible odds, but the Tenth would look after him. They had already adopted him as one of their own, yet still looked to Priscus for their orders.

That last, at least, suited him... but for how long? When would Caesar call him away and leave the Tenth under this pleasant and well-meaning young fool?

The military knot slid down to rest on his waist and he sighed and hauled it back up to his diaphragm, reaching out for a piece of the honeyed bread on his table - a noon meal that had sat there untouched for a number of hours - and dabbling just enough honey on the sides of his cuirass to anchor the ribbon in place. The front drooped a little, but he straightened himself, satisfied.

For a moment, he wondered whether to wear the helmet with the high black plume, but decided against it. He didn't need to stand out as an officer - they all knew him - he just needed the touches that placed him above Crassus.

With a last look at himself in the small, undulating bronze mirror that made his face misshapen, he nodded and stepped outside his quarters.

The sun was low, just brushing the tips of the trees and threatening to vanish in the next few moments, and legionaries went here and there with their fire-tools, lighting torches and lamps against the coming night.

'Glorious evening, isn't it?'

Priscus started and swung round to see young Crassus standing to one side of his quarters, his commander's armour and accoutrements impeccable. *The bastard.* Crassus sniffed the air deeply and stretched as though he'd just risen in the morning.

'I don't know about glorious' grumbled Priscus. 'Feels bloody chilly to me.'

'But the sun is shining and the grass is dry. There's a bite to the air, but just enough to make it refreshing.'

'If you say so. Probably the filter of youth. When you get to my age, you'll see it as far too bloody cold and threatening to snow. What are you doing loitering around outside?'

Crassus grinned.

'Preparing for manoeuvres, of course.'

Priscus pinched the bridge of his nose. The headache that had seen him retreat to his room for much of the afternoon was returning, and it was bringing with it a cohort of other pains and irritations.

'I assumed you would be staying in charge of the camp, as their legate. I was only taking two cohorts out.'

Again, Crassus stretched, looking irritatingly supple, alert and enthusiastic.

'I think that, as their commander, it would be a good idea to at least observe these night time manoeuvres? If I didn't know better I would say you kept trying to shield me from the real action in the legion.'

'*If only you knew*' Priscus thought as he nodded in fake appreciation. Instead, his voice came clear and friendly and supportive. 'Very well, legate. We shall leave your primus pilus in command and take the Fourth and Fifth cohorts out.' A mean streak somewhere deep inside surfaced. 'Perhaps you could take the Fourth ahead and set up the ambushes and I'll bring the Fifth into them?'

Crassus' lively grin should have faltered at the immense pressure such an opportunity might put on an untried commander, but he simply grinned as though he'd been given a gift. Priscus sighed inwardly.

'Just be careful and don't go more than four miles. We've only got a picket cordon in a five mile radius.'

* * * * *

Crassus' attempt at an ambush was considerably better than Priscus had expected. Oh, he still saw the first scouts a long time before the Fifth cohort stood any chance of walking into it, but it was not a bad first effort. Likely the veteran centurions of the Fourth had given him a few pointers, but credit where it was due: it was a worthy first attempt.

'Matrinius?'

'I see 'em sir. Ambush ahead. Heavy to the right, so we need to watch out for missiles to the left.'

Priscus nodded. His men were good. Ought to be, really - between him, Velius and Atenos, they'd been trained by the very best the army had to offer.

'Hello. What's this, sir?'

Priscus followed Matrinius' gaze and frowned at the group of horsemen cantering along the forest road.

'Part of some clever trap?' the centurion mused, his arm going up to stop the column without the need for orders, whistles or trumpets.

'No' Priscus said quietly. 'The Fourth cohort only had Crassus' horse with them.'

In instant response, Matrinius' arms made half a dozen silent gestures and the officers of the cohort behind him began to respond, forming a four-man wide column in the open trackway, shieldwalls raised at all four sides, pila up for casting at the front.

Priscus peered into the darkness. It was simply too gloomy to pick out any detail.

'Who in Hades are they? They're armoured in mail - I can hear it - but that doesn't help.'

The commander nodded in satisfaction as the riders closed on the waiting cohort and he could just see figures slipping from the treeline behind them, forming a blockade across the track behind. Sharp thinking on behalf of either Crassus or the centurions of the Fifth cohort.

His tension eased as the figures on horseback became more distinct and he could pick out details that labelled them Roman: the russet-coloured tunics and cloaks; the crest of a centurion; the formation of the riders. Then the tension heightened once more. Why would any other group of Romans be out here, especially riding in from the east.

'Matrinius: have the courier ride back to the fort and place the entire legion on high alert.'

'Sir?'

'Romans from the east means trouble from the east. Especially when they ride in fast at night. Get the Tenth ready to move on my order.'

Leaving the cohort's senior centurion to it, he turned back to the approaching riders. There were less than twenty of them. Two contubernia with some officers and hangers-on by the looks of it.

'Halt!' he bellowed.

The group slowed and the horses came down to a walk, the centurion pulling out ahead.

'Baculus?'

The grizzled centurion, primus pilus of the Twelfth Legion and a veteran of the years of Gallic campaigning, nodded and threw out a weary salute to Priscus as he slid from his horse.

'Thank Mars and my swollen, bruised, saddle-sore behind. Priscus of all people. Sorry, should that be *Praetor* Priscus, sir?'

Priscus swept the comment aside. 'What in Hades are *you* doing out here?'

'Bringing news of the shittiest kind, old friend.'

As the two clasped arms, Priscus turned to his senior centurion again. 'Matrinius: send someone to call Crassus and his men out of the trees. I think we're about to rush back to camp.'

'What happened?' he asked as he turned back to his old friend.

Baculus gestured over at the motley collection of men behind him. 'Representatives of two legions, Priscus. The rest of the Twelfth are on the march north through the great Arduenna forest. By now they'll probably be about where the Fourteenth used to be.'

'And where are the Fourteenth *now*?' Priscus asked tensely, images rising forth from his memory to remind him that Petrosidius and Balventius were stationed among that legion now.

'Here' Baculus said flatly, pointing at his escort. 'They now number three. We've got their eagle safe, but they all fell to a rising of the Eburones. All the officers are gone, including Sabinus and Cotta. Labienus decided to go try and track them down and make them pay, but he'll have his work cut out. It's a slow job negotiating that godsawful forest.'

Priscus felt his stomach churn. Balventius? The man had always been an immortal: one of those centurions that could never fall in battle. Like Baculus, in fact. Like Priscus...

'Anything else we need to know? Like where the bastards might be by now?'

'Yes. We were most of the way here when we stumbled across a Gallic auxiliary who was sent to find you to warn you that Cicero's Eleventh are under siege and in trouble. Sounds like the Eburones have gathered a few more tribes to them - probably the Nervii for one - and moved west. Labienus ordered me to pull in any reinforcements I can get and keep passing word until I find the general.'

Priscus nodded - everything was starting to pan out very much the way he'd been fearing, though he'd not thought it would come to a head quite this fast. 'Perhaps this mysterious Esus I've been hearing about is one of the Eburones.' He straightened. 'Time's of the essence, then. The general is in Gesoriacum with Fabius, Brutus and the Eighth. They're about the only other legion within reach -

Trebonius' Ninth are too far west and the Seventh and Thirteenth are off down south. I would suggest that you race for Gesoriacum and get the general moving. If you and he are quick, we could meet up on the road near Cicero's camp. If the enemy are strong enough to keep the Eleventh pinned, then we'll need a sizeable force to break the siege.'

Baculus nodded. 'I sent the Gallic scout back to the camp to tell Cicero to hold and that we'd be coming soon. We'll ride on through the night and mobilize the Eighth straight away. We could be there before noon tomorrow.'

Priscus could hear the sighs of dismay from a couple of the weary riders behind his friend.

'There's a tiny shit-hole of a place called Turnaco on the main route to Cicero's camp' he replied, 'just a native slurry pit, really, but we've used it as a muster place before. Have Caesar, Brutus and Fabius meet us there as fast as they can. From there we're only a few miles from Cicero.'

Baculus nodded. No attention to rank or deference - just all business, the way Priscus liked it. He gestured to the riders. 'Those of you from the Fourteenth: you stay with us.'

As Baculus turned and rode off with his men, the three horsemen indicated trotted over, saluting. One of the legionaries was coddling a bundle that made the act somewhat troublesome.

'You' Priscus pointed at him. 'You seem to have been looking after that well. Congratulations... you just made standard bearer. Get that eagle on top of a pole as soon as we get into camp. Your two mates can gather whatever kit you need. While we're there I'll transfer a few men from the Tenth. Just half a century or so, but until the Fourteenth can be reconstituted, you're it. Make sure you stay alive and that eagle stays up. I'm thinking you'll want to use it to smash the brains out of whoever killed your mates, and I intend to give you the chance.'

As the hoof beats of Baculus and his riders retreated into the distant darkness, a fresh single set echoed on the road as Crassus reined in close by and slipped from his saddle.

'Trouble?'

'You could say that. Time to stop playing soldier now and prove yourself, young man.'

* * * * *

Ariogaisos, shield man of Vertico, held his breath and crept lighter than any man had ever done, the balls of his feet barely grazing the earth with his passage. Around him the Nervian army seethed even at night, drink flowing freely, accompanied by song and humour. The gradual crushing and starvation of the Eleventh Legion was a balm to the Gauls encamped outside and, with the exception of the pickets and sentries, ninety nine percent of the Gallic army relaxed and spent the hours of darkness drinking in celebration of their situation and then sleeping off their intoxication.

They had, after all, little to do.

By day they assaulted the Roman defences, which was dangerous work, yes, but far from the peril it had been early on. The Romans had run out of missiles for their engines and few spears remained. Each night they managed to manufacture a few more, or hack the cross piece from their marching poles and sharpen the end to create makeshift spears, but the tide had turned and now few Gauls were falling with each push, while swathes of Romans died each day.

Ambiorix had given his men a week. The Gauls and Belgae raised against Rome had fought hard and won gloriously over the Fourteenth, obliterating them to the last man - so they believed - and they now had the Eleventh trapped and almost extinguished. The army had run far and fought hard and it was doing morale a great deal of good to spend a few days at a more relaxed pace while they whittled the Romans down. By the time of the new moon in a few days, however, Ambiorix would make an end of the fraught defenders and move on to the Tenth.

In the meantime, the Nervii were actually *enjoying* the siege - especially at night while they caroused and drank the wine they had looted from the Fourteenth's camp.

Ariogaisos nipped quickly between two tents, past a camp fire where a small, compact Gaul was crouching, his face contorted as he blasted out a musical fart for the edification of his friends.

Just a hundred paces to go and then he would reach the Gallic gateway and look out over the dead-strewn ditches to the beleaguered fort.

He drew a deep breath and looked up at the spear tip that wavered in the moonlight above him, his breath frosting in the chilly night air. Winter had been late leaving the land this year, but it

376

seemed to be late returning, too. The silvery point dipped and he kept his eyes on his message tied to the haft just below the spear head and tightened his grip on the shaft.

It was suicide, of course.

There was no hope of him getting back into the camp as he'd told the centurion he would. Even if he managed to get through the Nervii - and the ones near the gate would be alert - the Romans would stick him before he ever got close to their wall. After all, why would they allow one of the enemy to approach during a siege.

And so he had decided - resigned to the high probability of an imminent death - to try a different approach. He had no knowledge of the markings the Romans made on their parchments, even though his spoken Latin was not too bad, but he had drawn a fairly unambiguous picture. A small towered square that could only be the fort was surrounded by a circle of figures that could only be the Gallic army. Off to one side a group of men with crests and square shields ran toward them. Without knowledge of their 'writing' or anyone to help, it was the best he could do. He just had to hope they would understand and hold on. If they gave up or attempted to leave somehow, they would just hasten their fall and the relief would get here too late to help

His eyes locked on the gate. The Gauls' confidence was so strong that the gate stood open, half a dozen inebriated warriors sitting in the gap, laughing.

Tutting, he angled away and slipped between the tents toward the next gate, eyeing the top of the rampart as he went. There were men on the parapet and they looked more serious and alert than the drunks at the gate. Better the latter, then.

The next gate along provided no easier option, with half a dozen men playing a game throwing daggers at a target. With a resigned understanding, he returned to the original gate. It was his best chance. At least they were drunk and that gate was open.

Nearing the aperture once more, he began to pick up speed. As he passed a camp fire a voice called out in consternation, but he ignored it and ran. At this point there was precious little value to stealth.

His breath coming in gulps, his legs swinging, feet pounding the earth, Ariogaisos passed out of the encampment, into the opening in the Gallic defences. The inebriated warriors struggled to their feet, drawing swords and spears, but he was too fast for their befuddled

377

brains and before they were ready to stop this strange attack from within their own camp, Ariogaisos the Nervian was out into the open killing zone between the two armies.

His fast, pounding gait carried him across the causeway and he started to wonder whether he might make it.

The thrown spear hit him squarely in the back, slamming into his body and sliding between his ribs, punching through organs and gristle and then bursting from his chest in a fountain of blood, the droplets black and shining in the night.

Ariogaisos fell but, despite the agony that was coursing through his body as his life attempted to flee its fleshy prison, he pulled himself upright and hauled his shaking arm back. Taking a deep, agonising, shuddering breath, he cast the message-bearing spear.

He never saw where it went.

The second thrown spear from behind hit him in the midriff, tearing out his bowels as it burst from the front, and an arrow sank into his neck as he fell.

His eyes were glazing over before his head even bounced on the sodden muddy turf.

Ahead and above him, his own thrown spear with his daubed message of hope quivered for a moment where it landed, stuck into the side of a tower on the Roman defences - just one among a number of others. Figures were appearing on the Roman parapet, trying to see what was happening out in the night.

None of them looked up at the spear.

* * * * *

Turnaco was little more than a village, without a rampart or stockade, sitting atop the slope above a wide, glittering river. Some quarter of a mile from the native settlement stood a manually-flattened plateau where the legions had camped and mustered more than once before during the campaign. The now half-disappeared ditches and mounds that marked a camp large enough for three legions were still just about visible, and Priscus gave the order to have them raised and excavated and a new stockade put up, even if they were only likely to be here for a few hours. With what was clearly happening in the north of Gaul, only the suicidally unprepared would not take every precaution.

378

Turnaco was one of those places scattered around the north where a small Romanised presence was permanently maintained, partially as a link in the ever growing supply network, partially as a reminder of the existence and power of the legions in Gaul, and partially to house couriers and pass on messages, aiding the legions whenever they mustered here. Cita had begun the operation a couple of years ago, but Priscus had turned his fluid system into a web of small permanent almost-mansios where messages could be left.

He snapped the seal on the wooden box as he strode through the dip that represented a future gate in the rising defences, and flipped open the leaves to peruse the message held on the wax within.

To Gaius Julius Caesar, Proconsul, from Titus Atius Labienus.

Greetings.

Priscus ground his teeth at the memory of how much he'd had to argue - even wearing his senior officer's drooping knotted ribbon - to get the courier to hand over a message destined for Caesar. It wasn't until he'd had the young legionary by the testicles, quite literally, that the tablet had been handed over.

The message had arrived here on its way to Gesoriacum the evening before the Tenth Legion hoved into view, and as soon as Priscus had learned that a courier was present bearing a message from Labienus to Caesar he'd been determined to read it. The message would after all almost certainly have a bearing on his own decisions in the next few days, and must have been sent just after Labienus had sent his primus pilus to bring the news. His eyes skipped to the next line with a sinking feeling in his stomach.

I hope that my centurion Baculus has already delivered news of the Fourteenth's fall. I set out with the Twelfth to pursue the Eburones and chastise them this morning, but only three miles from the camp and before I even entered their sacred forest we stumbled across what appears to be the entire Treveri nation under arms. Their numbers are immense and I declined to meet them straight away, unprepared and in the field.

I have therefore returned to camp with the legion and prepared to deal with them here. We are well stocked and provisioned and

379

should be able to handle them. My apologies for my absence in the field against the Eburones, general, but I feel that to flee the region and join up with the Tenth and the Eighth would be foolish, leaving the south-eastern flank of the army open to Treveri attack.

I will send further single mounted couriers with any developments as long as the way remains open to them, but I cannot risk dispatching any more small parties of seasoned soldiers as I may need them here. I await confirmation of your approval of my decision or your further orders.

Regards.

Your servant and commander of the Twelfth.

Priscus nodded to himself. It was far from good news, but Labienus was absolutely right in staying there and keeping the Treveri occupied. If the east of Gaul was rising, better to keep them separate and busy while putting out whatever fires could be found. The most irksome thing of all was that Priscus had - earlier in the year - been completely on top of this revolt situation, unwrapping the layers of conspiracy one at a time, until the expedition to Britannia had intervened. Had he been left in Gaul with a couple of cohorts at his command, he could have had all this predicted in advance and been ready for it.

The important thing now, though, was to save Cicero and hammer the crap out of the Eburones, the Nervii and their rebellious friends. That seemed to be the main thrust of the revolt. If Baculus and his men had ridden hard and Caesar, Brutus and Fabius were equally swift and efficient in breaking camp and marching east, then there was every likelihood that the Eighth Legion would arrive in the morning. Then they could look at giving the rebellious bastards a good kicking.

* * * * *

Cicero staggered out of his doorway and felt a spot of cold rain on his forehead. Despite his feelings about the Gaulish weather, this particular spot was surprisingly welcome. His fever had finally broken during the night and he felt better than he had done since they had first set up camp here. The spot of rain felt like Aesculapius pouring a libation to his recovery from Olympus on high.

He spread out his arms to take in the next few droplets.

His positivity was about to take a knock, he knew, but it was still welcome at this particular moment. Walking slowly and carefully, aware that he was still far from strong and his muscles were tired and underused, he made his way across the fort, noting the burned remains of the buildings and the makeshift shelters and tents that housed the legion as he approached the steps up to the rampart.

Felix was in his habitual place, watching the enemy as though by careful scrutiny he might find a way to simultaneously burn them all to the ground.

'Prefect.' he greeted the man as he hauled himself wearily up the stairs.

Felix turned and smiled as he saw his commander. It was the first time Felix had smiled in several days, but it was a hollow pleasure to see the legate up and about.

'Good to see you back in colour, sir.'

'Thanks. Now I just need to regain enough strength to wield a sword and then we're sorted.'

The two men smiled at one another.

'Looks bleak' the commander noted finally, succumbing to the need for truth and efficiency rather than coddling himself and ignoring the trouble they were in.

'Very' Felix replied, clearly in a similar mood. 'We're out of nearly everything. The men are on quarter rations and even that'll run us dry in a day or two - if there's anyone left to starve, of course. And missiles are gone. I've got a few men managing to hammer out metal from broken swords and armour and make a few javelin heads, but we're just about down to flinging our own shit at them now.'

'Lovely.'

'There's no denying we're in trouble, sir.'

'What's the damage? The butcher's bill?'

Felix sighed as he shrugged. 'Last count we were down to a little over seven hundred men, including the walking wounded.'

'Jove!' Cicero whistled through his teeth. 'A tenth, maybe. Six thousand or so dead in so little time.'

'If it's any consolation, sir, we've taken at least double that of them. Maybe even treble.'

'It's not. They get reinforcements every morning from yet another stinking tribe who think they can do it this time. I don't think there's any less men out there this morning than there were when they arrived. More, possibly. I suspect I know it, but give me your honest professional opinion.'

'We're buggered six ways from market day. Royally shafted with the wide end of a pilum. Made to...'

'I get the metaphors, thank you, Felix. What's next then?'

'Pullo's just reorganising the men on the walls and looking at a possible last defence redoubt we could make from the ruined granaries for when the walls finally fall. At least we can hold that long enough to bury the eagle and keep it out of their grubby hands. I've sent Vorenus out to collect every used missile they can find. I suspect that this morning will be the last one. 'King' Ambiorix is about ready to wipe us out now.'

Cicero nodded. 'Then we'll have to make him work for every foot of ground they take, eh?'

'Definitely, sir.' Felix pursed his lips. 'What annoys me, sir, is not knowing whether they caught and skinned your messenger or whether the miserable little bugger just offed and joined them out there.'

Cicero nodded glumly. It had been too many days now for hope to hold out.

The pair looked out in silence over enemy forces that were already shuffling into new positions, mobilizing ready for a new day's action. Neither saw Centurion Vorenus until he was almost next to them.

'You'll never believe this, sir.'

The two officers turned to look at the weary centurion, who was covered with blood and grime and gripping spears in both hands, half a dozen short shafted ones in his left and a long, Gallic cavalry affair in his right.

'Well done, man. That'll keep us going for a moment longer, eh?'

'No, sir: this.'

Vorenus stacked his javelins against the parapet and pointed at the tip of the long spear.

'What is that?'

'Parchment, sir. Good quality parchment. And I reckon it's Roman, sir. Never seen these hairy arse-scratchers writing anything down, leastwise.'

Frowning, Cicero reached up and undid the strange item from the spear, lowering it and unfolding it in view of the others.

The three men stared.

Felix barked out a sharp laugh. 'That has to be your man, sir.'

'Does it mean what I think it means?'

'Can't see anything else it could mean. Men with crests and square shields on their way? I wonder how long this bloody thing's been stuck in the wall?'

Vorenus shrugged. 'A few days, sir. One of the lads remembers a commotion a few nights ago when some mad Gaulish bastard ran out front and threw a spear at him. The attacker was put down by his own men - only reason he remembers it so well. Could be that spear.'

'Whoever threw it and whenever it came' Cicero grinned, 'I think we can be certain of its meaning.' He pointed with a trembling finger above the seething mass of Gauls. The other two men followed his gesture. A dust cloud the size of a small city rose above the distant horizon. 'Only one thing raises a haze like that: a multi-legion army on the march.'

He turned to Vorenus.

'Go find Pullo. Tell him to forget the last-ditch redoubt and concentrate on keeping those walls in our hands. Caesar's about five miles out!'

* * * * *

Caesar reined in his white horse, his red cloak showing dark spots as the first spit of rain fell upon them. Around him Priscus, Crassus, Brutus and Fabius hauled on their own reins and took in the wide valley ahead.

Some four miles distant the camp of Cicero, well placed with good open ground all around, appeared to be almost submerged in a sea of Gauls. Their initial question - and the reason the five senior officers had ridden out ahead of the column - was answered even as they watched. The sea was moving, individual waves of men lapping around the sides of the camp as they withdrew west like a tide retreating down a beach.

The siege was being abandoned as the Gauls turned to face a new perceived threat.

'They're coming, then' Brutus noted with an uncertain mix of satisfaction and nerves.

'It would appear so' Caesar replied. 'We do not have a great deal of time to prepare. What would you say of the numbers?'

Priscus shaded his eyes, spots of rain pinging from his hand. 'Gotta be fifty or sixty thousand I'd say. A dozen tribes at least. No wonder Cicero was in trouble.'

'And we have?'

'In terms of fully-ready fighting men: a little over fourteen thousand, including the few auxiliary missile units and the cavalry.'

'Four to one then' Caesar mused and tapped his chin with his finger. 'And I do not believe we can rely on any support from Cicero. After this length of time his men will be low on equipment, exhausted and seriously reduced. It's down to us, gentlemen. We need to bring those odds more into our favour,'

'We could hit them and run a few times' Fabius hazarded. 'Keep drawing them west. Trebonius and his Ninth cannot be more than three days away. That would help.'

Caesar shook his head. 'We cannot rely on the Ninth being here. Remember what happened with Labienus, after all. And we put ourselves at too much of a disadvantage if we keep moving. We need to consolidate.' His brow wrinkled. 'Half a mile back, where we left the column, there was a good deep valley with a stream at the bottom. You remember?'

Crassus nodded. 'It was something of an obstacle.'

'And would be for them. They know where we are now and they're coming. We return to the army, set up camp atop the far side of that valley and then we have the slope to our advantage and the river at the bottom to slow them. There were a few gullies and small woods that we might be able to use as well.'

Priscus pursed his lips. 'Do you think they'll really try and attack us up that slope? It would be tactically *moronic*!'

'I suspect they will for two reasons' Caesar smiled. 'Firstly, we are a much smaller army and if we play the panic gambit they may try to take advantage of it.' He rose in his saddle. 'And secondly, they will know that I am with this force. If they are intent on driving Rome from Gaul they will not miss an opportunity to put me down

384

personally. To that end I need to make myself as open, obvious and tempting as possible. I will take personal command of the cavalry.'

He peered at the mass moving slowly west from the fort a few miles away. 'They are disorganised. That will buy us extra time. Their leaders will want to pull them in together first before they consider an attack. Crassus and Fabius: look to your legions. Brutus: take command of all the auxiliary missile units. Priscus, you have camp prefect duties again.'

Priscus rolled his eyes. Sometimes it seemed his military career was up and down like an Aegyptian's underwear.

'I need you to work some magic for me, Priscus. I want the fort to be feeble and easy to dismantle from the inside but to look powerful and defensive from without. Can you do that?'

Priscus nodded.

'Good. Come, then gentlemen. Let us engineer the end to this revolt.'

* * * * *

The valley was better than Priscus remembered and it seemed the Gauls were giving them more time than they could hope for. By the time the first scouts from the enemy force appeared on the crest across the valley, almost three hours had passed.

A man can do a lot in three hours: win his freedom in the arena; watch a godsawful Aristophanes 'comedy'; spend good money in one of the better brothels of the Subura; or, if one was a legionary, dig out several paces of defensive ditch or construct the same amount of rampart.

Priscus had been given a luxury.

He had been given the best part of eight thousand men purely to construct a largely fake fortress. The ditch was real - that was the strongest defence and a necessity, as a proper ditch is almost impossible to fake. A ditch on a thirty degree slope was a new challenge for Priscus, but the men seemed unfazed and managed with aplomb. Behind the ditch however, while the rampart *looked* high and impressive, it was actually loosely laid - not compacted and solid - and was thin and high rather than wide and backed with a solid revetment. There had been no time to cut timber for a stockade, and so a defensive hedge of pointed 'sudis' stakes had been strung out along the top of the rampart. But against procedure, the stakes were

385

only laid against one another and propped up, rather than bound with ropes into a troublesome pointy hedge. A quick flick of one stake could collapse a whole section to the ground.

It had the appearance of one of the strongest forts he had ever set up, despite the lack of a full palisade.

In reality, it had all the defensive strength of a leather legionary tent.

Essentially, the impressive military structure that brooded over the valley was a fiction. What the general had in mind Priscus could hardly imagine, but the man was an intuitive leader and a lateral thinker and - with the odds as they lay - if the man had a plan, it was not worth questioning.

'Can you cut some spare turf and leave it stacked behind the walls?' the general mused next to him.

'Of course, general. Could I venture to question why?'

'You could' Caesar smiled as he turned and walked across to where Aulus Ingenuus - the commander of his Praetorian guard - sat astride his horse with the ease of a veteran cavalryman. As he approached the young officer, Caesar smiled. 'Repeat your orders, Ingenuus. Let us be clear.'

'Engage the enemy repeatedly - in skirmishes only - at the stream in the valley bottom and keep retreating back up toward the camp. Never enough to bring them up with us, though. May I ask why, sir?'

'You may' nodded Caesar. 'Suffice it to say that I want them to be twitchy and ready to leap on us by the time I show my face.'

The young commander nodded. 'How will I know when to cease the skirmishes, general?'

'You'll know, Aulus.'

'Yessir.'

'Now get going. Let's taunt them into the first tussle while they're still arriving at the valley.'

* * * * *

It seemed strange to Ingenuus. He'd begun his career fighting in the Helvetii campaign five years ago and won Caesar's praise and an astounding promotion, had taken his role as the head of Caesar's bodyguard very seriously and had practiced and trained and drilled both his men and himself constantly over the years, yet he had rarely seen any real combat action. If Caesar's bodyguard were seeing action, things were going wrong.

And so it was very odd to suddenly find himself not only commanding his guard in a combat situation, but also commanding the auxiliary cavalry escort, which brought his unit to almost a thousand men in all.

What was most surprising was how naturally it all came, despite his four year absence from active service. As he wheeled his tired horse in the drizzle half way up the slope, he raised his arm to prepare his men for another charge and realised that the limb was crimson past the elbow and trickles of blood - sped by the addition of rainwater - were running up his inverted arm and into the armpit, staining his white officer's tunic. The iron taste as he licked his lips told him that his face was also spattered with the blood of the enemy - at least, he was pretty sure none of it was his.

Around him, the cavalry also turned, a few of his Praetorians among them in fine Roman leather-backed mail with shoulder doubling, large shields bearing not only Caesar's bull but also an image of Venus - the general's family deity, and long swords of a Celtic design. The rest were Gallic auxiliaries in rough basic mail and with spears and swords, shields among them painted in whatever design the warrior favoured.

For over an hour now, the cavalry had been harrying their opposite numbers among the Gauls. Above, the Romans had watched from the ramparts while the Gauls continued to arrive and amass across the valley.

The lowest reaches of the slope to both sides and the grass on both banks of the stream were now treacherous in the extreme, littered with corpses and the shuddering, whinnying bodies of horses and the screaming shapes of wounded men. There was little green to be seen among the russet colour that had become the valley bottom's norm from a mix of churned rain-softened mud and spilled blood.

It was almost impossible to tell which bodies belonged to which army, particularly given that more than ninety five percent of the whole lot were Gauls of one tribe or another. Indeed, in the press of it at the bottom, Ingenuus had rarely known whether the men he was shouting orders at were his or the enemy. It was only when they raised a weapon and made for him that he knew to defend himself. And yet, with every pull back up the slope - and there had been many

- his force had diminished only a little, while the enemy seemed to be suffering heavy losses.

But then, they had so many more to lose.

In only a few more hours the sun would begin to sink behind that hill crowded with Gauls. Whatever Caesar had planned would have to happen soon. The cavalry were close to exhaustion and soon they would start to make mistakes. Then the dying would begin in earnest.

Dropping his arm, he kicked his steed into action, racing down the hillside, praying to Epona and Mars that his horse would not lose its footing on the steep slope, made slippery and treacherous with the constant low drizzle. Around him, the heavily armoured Praetorians - intermingled with the Gallic irregulars - raced into action once more.

As with the previous five charges, Ingenuus selected an opponent roughly ahead, angling himself so as to encounter his enemy on his left, where his shield could take the spear blow and knock it aside while he raised his own blade to strike.

The intervening space narrowed in mere heartbeats and suddenly the fight began once more. The Gaul lowered his long, bronze-tipped spear and kicked his horse forward, lunging with the weapon. Ingenuus, his shield held back slightly to entice and draw the attack, suddenly slid his arm forward, the large oval shield coming in at an angle.

The spear tip scored a line across Venus, disfiguring her exquisitely-painted chest, caught for a shoulder-jarring moment on the lip of the bronze boss, and then flicked out and bounced off harmlessly into thin air.

The Gaul tried to pull his own slightly smaller shield up and into position, clearly having been surprised with how easily his own attack had been turned aside. It had been no surprise to Ingenuus, given how many times he had done just this in the past hour.

Before the Gallic shield could come up to block, Ingenuus swung downwards with his raised sword, across his chest and down. The blade bit into the Gaul's neck, just above the collar of his mail shirt. Scything through two braids of red hair, it cut the tendon, causing the Gaul's head to snap back in the opposite direction, further opening him to the blow that continued down smashing his collar bone, half-severing the head and leaving him dying soundlessly, his windpipe caught in the slice, a fountain of crimson spraying out to the side. Ingenuus turned his face away, not at the sight - he had seen worse deaths this day - but to avoid being blinded by the spray at a critical moment.

He was lucky. Had he not turned, he would not have seen the other spear driving toward him. With the speed and dexterity of a born horseman, he dropped to the horse's neck, the spear head slicing through the open air above his head.

When he came back up, his shoulder knocking the spear shaft aside, he realised he could not bring his sword up into play in the tight space. Desperately, aware that he was temporarily vulnerable, he tried to make his horse step back a few paces but something was suddenly in the way. In a blur, a gladius lunged out past him and sank into the armpit of the Gaul who was desperately attempting to haul his spear back for another strike.

Ingenuus looked around into the eyes of his saviour and blinked in surprise.

Caesar smiled at him as he jerked his blade back. Behind him the three survivors of the Fourteenth Legion sat astride horses, their eagle gleaming wetly, their blades singing out, taking revenge for their fallen comrades.

'Think I've got their attention?' the general laughed.

Ingenuus looked past the general at the rest of the melee. There was, he could see, a sudden urgency among the press of Gauls. Caesar had joined the fight and the news had spread like fire through the enemy. The great oppressor of Gaul was suddenly theirs for the taking.

'It would appear so, sir!' he said, marvelling at this foolhardy move while a few paces away, Nasica used the prized eagle of the Fourteenth to stove in an enemy rider's bare head. Had the general discussed the plan with Ingenuus in advance, he would have had to stop his commander. It was the job of Caesar's chief bodyguard not only to protect the general from the enemy, but also from himself should he need it. Such was almost certainly the reason Ingenuus had been kept in the dark about the plan.

Too late now, anyway. All that mattered now was getting the general back to the camp intact.

'I'm afraid you cannot stay in the field, general. We must pull back. I will set a cordon...'

'No you won't, Aulus. This will not be an orderly fall back, but a general panicked retreat. I want this cavalry back up that slope as though the snapping jaws of Cerberus himself were at their

389

backsides. And try and persuade a few of the auxiliaries to shout panicked things in their own tongue.'

'You're drawing them uphill, sir?'

'Indeed.'

Ingenuus thought to question the logic of pulling back to a fort that was little more than a fake show of strength, but already the general was wheeling, shouting the retreat orders in a desperate voice. The sudden appearance of their ever-implacable senior commander bellowing a panicked retreat and turning to flee had an electrifying effect across the whole field. The Roman force disintegrated, each man wheeling his horse and bolting back up the slope in their own panicked fashion, some falling to the enemy as they turned.

It was a rout.

The Gauls, taking advantage of the sudden failure of their enemy, whooped and howled as they kicked their horses into life to give chase, the bulk of their cavalry leaping the stream to join the action and seek the head of the man in crimson and white fleeing up the slope.

Somewhere at the point where the low gradient gave way to the steeper upper slope, as the fleeing Romans slowed through necessity, Ingenuus managed to pull alongside his general.

'I do not understand, general. All we have done is draw their cavalry. We can hardly turn and fight, and they will retreat as soon as they see the defences - unless they realise those defences are a sham?'

Caesar smiled as he hauled his mount this way and that to navigate the slope.

'I want them to get a good look at the defences - to see how well we have constructed them; how afraid of them we are. See the blockages?'

Even as they closed on the gate that would separate them from their pursuers, Ingenuus could see the legionaries blocking the gates with turf sods.

'General?'

'They will let us pass through and then seal it all up tight. I want the enemy to think we're trapped and afraid.'

'We *will* be, sir.'

The general simply laughed and pushed his horse forward and through the gate into the flimsy fort's interior.

* * * * *

'This won't hold against them for long' muttered Brutus, peering at the blocked gate. Priscus and Caesar, standing nearby, nodded - though only the latter smiled.

'It is an illusion' the general declared, 'as much as the rest of the camp. A single sod of turf thick. The only question now left in my mind is whether the enemy will buy what we sell. Will they test us and discover our weakness or have we tempted them just enough to make them commit blindly?'

Priscus stepped up to the blockage - so flimsy that, close enough up, he could actually peer through the gaps between sods and see the valley beyond.

'I think your question's just been answered Caesar. The cavalry have pulled back half way down the hill, but it looks to me like the whole damn lot of them are crossing the river and preparing to attack.' He took a deep breath. 'I hope you're right about this, general.'

Caesar gave him an enigmatic smile. 'The day that I cannot beat a simple rabble of barbaroi, Priscus, you can retire me in peace to a pretty little island. But that day is not today.'

* * * * *

Cativolcus of the eastern Eburones, king and son of kings, overlord of more than a dozen chiefs and joint commander of the army, pulled his horse alongside that of his brother king, Ambiorix.

'They will not surrender. Romans do not surrender.'

'I think you forget our first great victory' Ambiorix laughed, slapping the decorative Roman cuirass he himself had unbuckled from the corpse of the Roman general Sabinus.

'*He* was an idiot. *This* is Caesar. Caesar is *not* an idiot.'

'Then we will kill them all. Just get it over with.'

Cativolcus nudged his horse out ahead of the mass of their men, peering with distaste at the Nervii who formed much of the forward edge. He personally would have preferred not to have the Nervii with them - they were notoriously fickle in his experience. The huge army sprawled across the slope below the Roman camp, which stood glowering above them, impressive in its defences. The cavalry had

391

scouted it out briefly and confirmed that it was sealed tight, even the gates blocked with turf. The Romans were going nowhere and they would not surrender, whatever Ambiorix thought. It would be a long fight, then, akin to the one they had just left. Perhaps he could persuade his fellow king to throw everything they had in a constant straight attack and finish it quickly this time?

Some paces out in front of their army - which had stopped half way up the slope and massed ready for the assault - Cativolcus turned his steed side-on to the Romans. He had some small command of their tongue - a rigid and ordered thing with no emotion or colour, much like its speakers - and had spent a few moments formulating the speech as best he could.

'Romans!' He paused to make sure he had their attention. The general noise atop the slope died away as the defenders behind their high ramparts listened. At least this time they only had these stick barricades and not walls and towers. Perhaps they would fall fast after all.

'Romans, I give three hour. You come to me by three hour, I let you live. Past three hour: everyone die.'

He was entirely unsurprised when three Roman javelins arced up over the wall and converged on his position. Even as he pushed his horse on out of the way, he was impressed at their accuracy. He had thought the army well out of the range of their weapons. He had been mistaken. Why then were they not launching their javelins? Fear? The knowledge that they might need to conserve their ammunition?

It mattered not. He had given his ultimatum as the two kings had agreed, and the Romans had given their reply by a simple act of violence.

He looked over at Ambiorix, who nodded.

'Sons of the Nervians - children of Taranis - you have the first taste of our final victory. Cross their ditches; tear down their ramparts; smash their gates. The Eburones will flank you and move to envelop them.' He contemplated exhorting the other tribes to victory, but it was hardly worth it, for their numerical contributions were dwarfed by the masses of the Eburones and the Nervii.

For a moment he wondered whether the treacherous Nervii were going to argue. It was glorious to have the main assault he had given them, but it was also dangerous and costly. When all of this was over and the Romans piled in decaying heaps, the Eburones would be strong and drinking their toasts to the dead. The Nervii would be glorious, but few: just how he would like them to be. Perhaps when Rome was gone, the territories of the Nervii would look good under the rule of the Eburones.

To his immense relief and satisfaction, the mass began to move forward - slowly at first, as though uncertain as to whether they were doing the right thing, but soon the blood lust fell upon them. That was the one thing you could count on with the Nervii: when the lust fell and the desire to fight filled them, they were hard to turn aside. It was motivating them to start with that was the trouble.

But now the Nervii were howling as they raced up the slope, waving spears and swords and axes. A few of the less intelligent paused in their run to throw their spears up at the ramparts or loose an occasional arrow or slingshot despite the fact that the height, distance and gradient made it all-but impossible to even hit the defences, let alone pass them.

At a wave of his arm, the Eburones began to move up the slope beside their allies, his own subjects on the left flank and those of Ambiorix on the right. Here and there he could determine signs of the lesser tribes whose chiefs simply selected where they wanted to be, having been given no specific commands.

Victory moved slowly up the slope with them. Caesar's blood was almost close enough to taste.

At a shout from their king, the Eburones put on an extra turn of speed. Just as the Nervii began to fill in the ditch and then climb the rampart and dismantle the defences, the Eburones would swoop around the sides and seal off any chance of flight, waiting until the Nervii rabble had done their job and shattered the defences before moving in themselves to finish the fight.

Gaul was almost free. There were more legions to deal with yet, of course, but the rebel kings had utterly destroyed two, and two more were about to fall along with the man who led them and kept them here. The rest of the task was simple 'mopping up'.

So why did Cativolcus feel so unsure?

* * * * *

Caesar stood on the low rampart behind the scant defence offered by the sudis barricades. The enemy had committed. They had *all* committed. And now they would learn that victory could not always be assured by superior numbers, even as much as four men to one.

He smiled and waited three dozen heartbeats until the first of the Nervian warriors crested the far side of the ditch and clambered across it, reaching up to claw at the turf bank of the rampart. The fools had not even questioned why the legions were not throwing their pila.

He turned his smile on the officers beside him as he squared his shoulders.

'Now.'

* * * * *

There are many reasons why a battle is won. Weight of numbers can be a decisive factor, but only if all the other facets are in equal balance. Terrain is often a heavy factor and has ruined many a great commander's day. Morale can be crucial and sees off even supposed conquering armies. And surprise can swing the tide of a fight in a heartbeat.

When all three of these others come together in a single moment, the effects can be cataclysmic.

Cativolcus, king of the Eburones, was not a young man. He would have liked to have been the man to take Caesar's head, but he was also wise enough to recognise his advancing years and the negative effect they were having on his skills as a warrior.

And so he sat ahorse at the periphery of the field, on the high slope some hundred paces from the action, watching as events unfolded. He couldn't see the man, but was fairly certain that Ambiorix - despite his relative youth and vigour - was probably doing the same at the far side, past the seething mass of Gauls and the fort of the Romans.

Cativolcus watched the weight of numbers bringing him an assured victory.

And, as he watched, he saw with shock the Roman gates fall inwards as though they had been blocked with leaves and then blown in by a giant. He blinked in surprise as the sharp, wooden fences across the fort's perimeter simply collapsed as though a wind had blown them over.

In two heartbeats the Roman fort was all-but gone, barring a ridge and ditch around its edge.

394

He realised in those two heartbeats just how badly they had been duped. The pointed stakes that had been their only defence were suddenly weapons, the men who had dropped the fence casting them like heavy spears into the mass, where they had a surprisingly brutal effect. As they hit the warriors they did little damage other than the occasional broken bone, but the terrain took them then. The slope was too much for men battered with stakes, and the victims toppled backward, bringing down a dozen men around them who - in turn - brought down dozens more until a significant portion of the Nervian attack was tumbling back down the slope toward the stream, causing chaos and shouts of panic and consternation to rise from the rest of the army.

But that was a simple opening salvo.

As the gates vanished and the fences disappeared, they revealed not a panicked, trapped force of Romans scurrying around like rats in a granary caught when the door is opened, but a mass of tightly packed soldiers bearing a solid shieldwall that was already advancing into the face of the suddenly-panicked Gauls like some implacable steel monster. Far from terror, the Romans were chanting something in their own language in time with their uniform steps.

A voice shouted an order and two thousand arrows rose up into the air, the drizzle not having had time to ruin the strings on the previously-covered bows, and descended like a grey cloud of death into the massed ranks of Gauls, punching through eyes, necks, torsos and limbs, pinning men to the floor and killing them in droves..

Even before the solid shieldwall and its five-man deep support smashed into the Nervii sending them scattering down the slope, two other shieldwalls unfolded at the wings, hinging on the corners and coming out to face the advancing Eburones on the flanks. Those who were unlucky enough to be beyond that sudden clash found themselves facing that Romano-Gallic cavalry yet again, who swept forward despite their exhaustion, bellowing curses, to take the Eburones' heads.

Cativolcus saw utter defeat in those half dozen heartbeats.

He knew they were beaten.

Ambiorix had persuaded him to throw in his lot in this crazed mission. He should have listened to the damn druids who had been trying to persuade them to wait. *It was too soon*, they had said. *It would fail*, they had said. They had been right, but Cativolcus had been swept along by the words of his brother king. He had tried. They had failed.

As he wheeled his horse and rode for the woodlands where he knew he could lose himself, he found himself cursing a man over and over, but it was not Caesar. The Roman played the game well and he had won with his great talent. Never again would Cativolcus disbelieve the rumours that the Roman general was descended from their gods - he was clearly favoured by the divine.

No. The man he cursed and would curse until he died was the man who had wrought this disaster: Ambiorix.

The revolt of the Eburones was over.

The future of Gaul was now in the hands of the druids and their Esus.

Chapter Nineteen

Priscus stood on the ramparts of Cicero's camp and shook his head in exasperated wonder. For the last hour, as the Eighth and Tenth legions had scurried around putting things right at the ravaged winter quarters, and while the scant remnants of the brave Eleventh had rested and eaten freshly delivered rations in peace, Priscus had prowled the battlefield like some restless spirit, trying to take in the enormity of what had happened here.

It clearly *was* the uprising he had suspected, that he should have been able to prevent.

And yet something nagged at him and made his scalp itch. Though Ambiorix and Cativolcus had both escaped so he could hardly prove it, none of the captives they had found had ever heard of 'Esus' even when questioned by Blattius Secundus and his evil knife. That, and the distinct absence of any druidical influence found among the enemy - both dead and captive - prompted Priscus to believe that this was something somehow disconnected from his discoveries; that worse was still to come.

The dead were being carried off and dumped in piles for burning, the records of the legion being checked against the corpses' identity tags. Priscus knew from experience that near a tenth of the men would not be found or identified, but at least this way the ferryman could be paid for most of them and stones set up in their memory.

Somewhere back across the camp, he could hear Caesar's voice raised in praise, delivering a public address to the Eleventh and thanking them for their bravery and fortitude, promising them bonuses and loot from the smashed Gallic army and their tribal lands - once punishment was delivered upon them.

The Eleventh weren't cheering, but no one expected that. The poor brave bastards had fought for weeks against insurmountable odds with no hope of relief and with a commander who had apparently been laid low by an almost fatal fever.

It was a feat just to have survived this long. There would be tales written and songs sung about Cicero's siege. He had succeeded on a level more pronounced even than Sabinus' failure.

Priscus tried to block out the sound of the general's words.

397

No druids. No 'Esus'. Just two big tribes and a lot of smaller ones riding in their wake, raised against Rome. It felt like a war of opportunity, not the grand-scale revolt he had been finding rumours of with every Gallic stone upturned. Even with the troubles down among the Carnutes - which had presumably caused no issue for Plancus - and with the resistance Labienus was meeting in the lands of the Treveri, this was less than nothing compared with what he'd been *expecting*.

No druids. 'No Esus'.

It wasn't over yet.

This was a prelude.

One of the things that had bound Priscus to his commander - Fronto - in their early days together had been a shared heritage in the great lands of Campania to the south. While Fronto hailed from the seaport of Puteoli and serious lineage and money, Priscus had been raised inland at Nuvlana into an unpopular branch of an old family, with faded glory and heavy debts.

But the one thing they could both recount was the tremors that habitually swept through their homeland. No child of the region had lived to adulthood without feeling the shaking of the ground more than once. And sometimes, when there was to be a big quake - one that sheared marble columns and toppled weaker buildings - there were warning signs in the hours to its approach that a native could watch for: Faint trembles; cracks appearing in walls; even the birds leaving the trees in droves.

That was what *this* felt like.

It was a first rumble. A crack in the fabric of Gaul. A warning of the earth-shaking to come.

With a sense of foreboding, and wishing for the thousandth time that his old friend was here to share his fears, Priscus turned from the rampart to tend to the business of command.

* * * * *

Caesar pushed the lists and maps back across the table.

'I think that is all we can do.'

Priscus peered at the map and its markers. 'The Eighth back in place. The Tenth and Eleventh to Samarobriva. What of the Ninth? Trebonius will likely be here tomorrow.'

'The Ninth to Samarobriva as well. It was a tactically sound idea to spread out the army, but we've learned a painful lesson, Priscus. Now let us have a strong central force that we can take to any trouble spots. Samarobriva is within a week's march of almost anywhere it could be needed.'

Priscus nodded. 'With the Eighth back on the coast, and assuming that Labienus is still in position and not wiped out, we have a reasonable grip on the land. I'd like to hear word from both he and Plancus before things are set in stone, though.'

'Agreed. We will send fast riders in the morning to determine their status. With changes of horse, they should be able to being us news within a week.'

Priscus rubbed his eyes wearily. He really needed to sleep.

'Are you staying with us until all the reports are in, general? The weather is still unseasonably mild for travelling south.'

Caesar leaned back in his chair.

'More than that, Priscus: I will be wintering in Samarobriva with you and the main force.'

The veteran officer blinked in surprise. The general never wintered with the army, with political and familial commitments elsewhere. Illyricum sometimes; Cremona and Cisalpine Gaul on occasion. Even Rome for some months. But never the far flung Belgic lands.

'Caesar?'

'We both know Gaul is far from settled, Priscus. Anything could happen in the coming months and I do not intend to be sitting sipping mulsum in Pola while Gaul bucks and churns and attempts to dislodge us.'

'General? Your administration? Your family?'

Something passed across Caesar's face and Priscus found himself leaning back away from the great man's suddenly frightening dark eyes.

'The administration of a province can be carried out without its governor, Priscus. Only those skimming a dangerous sum from the takings need to supervise it personally. And with my parents and children gone, I am freed of personal entanglements in Rome.'

Priscus felt as though he'd been hit with a brick, such was the force of whatever passed between them in that simple, dead, shocking statement. He sat silent for eight heartbeats, not knowing what to say to his commander, and with a strange suddenness the cloud passed and Caesar stretched, his demeanour switching seamlessly back to the casual military officer

'Then if that it all, Priscus, I think we should call a general meeting and brief the others, yes?'

Priscus could only nod.

In a year that had brought Rome's control of Gaul to the brink and threatened their very existence, it seemed that crises and disasters were not limited to the army. With a second nod - this time to himself - he stood, wishing the army had not fragmented so much this past year.

'With respect, Caesar, I fear you need to look to the command system again and promote a few good men to senior positions.'

The general gave him a strange, quirky smile.

'The matter is in hand, Priscus. Upon our return to Gesoriacum, I enlisted the aid of an old friend. Call the rest in and we will plan ahead for the winter.'

Chapter Twenty

Fronto sat atop the courtyard wall in the early morning sun - watery and pale thing that it was. The drizzle had died away just before dawn, around an hour ago, when the rest of the villa's occupants had left for the great crater and their daily wait.

Despite wiping the wall dry and having laid out an old cloak from the servants' quarters to sit upon, the stone was still cold, damp and uncomfortable and he kept returning to the tales Posco had told him of how such activity was a major cause of piles. 'Bum-grapes' was the last thing he wanted right now, just when he had shaken off two years' weight and indolence and hit a physical peak he'd not have thought possible the previous year.

He sighed and kicked the wall with his heels, rearranging for the twentieth time the sheath that contained the decorative gladius he'd taken from the murderous tribune the year before.

This was now the fourth day he had spent sitting and waiting and he was starting to worry about being foolish. What if they weren't coming after all? What if they were waiting until some unspecified event? Would Fronto and his friends be forced to repeat the procedure every day for months?

Grinding his teeth, he shuffled his backside to try and find a better position. There *wasn't* a better position. He could wait anywhere, of course, but the main gate wall was the obvious spot. It would be where the enemy arrived, supplied the best view of the surrounding approaches, and was also the very best spot from which to run for the Forum Vulcani.

Squinting into the grey, hazy brightness, Fronto first saw the arrivals as a shapeless blob on the horizon where the road crested a low rise, and he had to strain his eyes to discern their numbers. He was expecting at least a dozen - probably more - and so it came as something of a surprise to spot only three figures.

His mind raced. Was this all that were coming? Had he seriously over-estimated their numbers? It seemed unlikely. They had the resources to drag in every killer from the carcer, and quite possibly others along the way. Three could not be the whole force.

And that begged the question: where were the rest?

His mind raced in the way his body should be doing. Did he run for the Forum Vulcani, or was it wasting an opportunity just to draw three men into the crater? Perhaps the rest were a few moments behind? If so, could he afford to wait? The longer he waited the less chance he had of staying ahead of them.

Irritated at his own lack of foresight and planning, failing to account for such changes and form contingencies, he smacked his fist down painfully on the cloak-covered stone and slid from the wall.

No. It *was* worth it. He had to run and lead them off, because the shapes were now resolving into more than simple figures: they had become *identifiable*. The left one his keen gaze easily picked out: Berengarus - huge and bulky, a long blade in his hand and a single-minded expression of malice. The figure at the right hand side was equally unmistakable: a wraithlike figure who drifted across the ground as though not quite touching the floor, its robes tattered and frayed, its wild hair floating and whipping about in what should not be a strong enough breeze for such activity.

His feet rooted to the spot as he recognised the figure between them.

Lucilia?

How in Hades had they got hold of Lucilia?

Panic flooded through him. What could he do? As the figures came closer, he could see that Lucilia's arms were bound behind her back with a leather thong, the other end of which was held tight in the wraith's left hand; in his right: a curved knife.

'Run!' his wife shouted at him, and was rewarded with a heavy cuff around the back of the head that send her staggering forward before being jerked back painfully by her tied wrists.

Fronto felt his knees begin to give in to the panic. How could he run now?

But what else could he do?

Setting his jaw firm, he took a few paces forward toward the two killers and their prisoner.

'Let her go and I'll give myself to you.'

The giant's step faltered and Fronto realised that he was actually considering the offer. However, next to him, the wraith gave an unpleasant smile and yanked on the cord, pulling Lucilia in front of him. His curved knife came up to caress her throat.

'We will have both, young Falerius. I had hoped to tie you down and make you watch as I slowly dismembered and peeled this pretty young thing, but now that we have arrived at our destination, I am of a mind to simply end her now and concentrate on you instead.

Fronto's eyes widened as the wraith's left hand released the cord in order to grab Lucilia's brow and turn her head, raising the face so that her neck was presented clear to the blade. His right hand twisted to prick the gleaming point into her throat just enough to draw blood.

Fronto felt his world fall away.

He wanted to close his eyes and hope that all of this went away like some childish nightmare, for he knew the wraith's mind from his eyes and his stance. This was not a man who bluffed or procrastinated, and this was no threat to cause anguish. The wraith simply meant to kill her and to do it now.

He started forward to intervene as his eyes watched the blade move in for the final, slicing blow, and his heart skipped a beat as Lucilia's foot rose and then slammed down with a strength born of desperation on her captor's foot.

Fronto was too far away for such a small noise to carry, but he imagined well enough the sounds of most of the bones in the man's foot smashing. Lucilia's sandal was only light, yet her blow was anything but!

The wraith gave an unearthly howl, his sharp blade scoring a fine red line on Lucilia's throat. Fronto watched in panic as the pale flesh bloomed red and waited a single heartbeat for the arterial spray to begin.

It never came. Instead, as the wraith reacted too late, the throbbing agony in his foot clouding his senses and interrupting his reactions, Lucilia ducked and came up in front of the blade that had been at her throat.

'Run!' Fronto bellowed, realising that she was trying to grasp the man's knife in her bound hands. The killer was wounded, but not enough to relinquish that blade to her. If she did not run now, he would recover soon enough and then she would die.

Lucilia took to her feet.

He had not told her *where* to run - had not had the opportunity to think that far - but Lucilia knew Puteoli and the villa almost as well as he after two years of growing familiarity, and she would find somewhere to cut her bonds and hide.

Berengarus turned his head almost nonchalantly to watch the girl run. His expression revealed his thoughts clearly enough: he would have liked her to die, but she was at best peripheral to his plan. With Fronto alone and only twenty paces away, he was hardly going to concentrate on a meaningless woman now.

The barbarian came on with a mean sneer, the wraith hobbling close by, looking over his shoulder regretfully toward the retreating shape of Lucilia, who disappeared down the grassy slope toward one of the sheds that gave access to the cave system below. She would be as safe there as anywhere until Fronto had dealt with the situation.

If he *could*.

Watching the two men close on him, Fronto waited until Lucilia had gone from sight and then turned and ran through the courtyard and into the house.

* * * * *

Diotimus sat beside a heavy, man-sized boulder of yellow-white rock and spat on his sling, rubbing the liquid into the leather to remove some of the interminable white dust that seemed to settle on everything here within a quarter of an hour. Next to him, Cadurcus was struggling to bend his shortbow tight enough to slip the fresh string over the end - the drizzle this morning had slackened the original. Habitually, he carried half a dozen spares in his pouch.

Balbus - Fronto's old army friend who seemed to be in command when their actual paymaster was absent - had visited them just now to make sure all was well, and had then moved on down toward the mudpools at the centre.

Both men were well positioned behind three large rocks on the south-eastern ridge of the crater - just about the best place to watch the approach from the Falerii villa, maybe two hundred and fifty paces away. Nearby was a small pile of hot yellow stones that they had ferried up carefully in a leather bag that now lay scorched and burned nearby.

They had found three such good observation points and occasionally rotated to another for simple variety, but this was the best and their favourite.

Cadurcus said something in his native Gallic tongue and Diotimus grinned, watching the cursing Salluvi mercenary struggling with the string before returning his attention to the Puteoli approach.

The first thing he knew of the attack was when a hand clamped around his forehead while the blade was being drawn across his throat. He tried to scream out a warning, but his windpipe was severed along with his arteries, and even as he realised he was dying and all that was coming out was a bubbling hiss, the pain from the wound finally reached his brain.

Next to him, Cadurcus slumped forward, a knife handle sticking out of the base of his neck. A pair of empty hands reached down and grasped the bow, easily looping the string over the end and testing it for strength.

* * * * *

Eurycles and Picentus fiddled absently with the vent control, bored beyond belief with their lot. They clearly had the easiest initial job of the crater's defenders - they had no task other than closing the vents and closing and bolting the door. Until that time they simply had to stay hidden and wait for the fly to drift into their web. After all, despite all the unpleasant features of this stinking place, the only actual structure was this building. What attacker would not send men in to check it out?

'When this is all over, I will have to bathe for a week to get this stench out of my skin. I smell like a bad fart.'

'You *always* smell like a bad fart. If anything, I'd say this place has improved you.'

'Piss off you inbred Greek.'

The two mercenaries grinned at one another. Only moments ago Balbus had dropped by to make sure that everything was as it should be and had found them engaged in a farting competition. His reprimands had been half-hearted: it was not he who was paying them and they were mercenaries who could walk away any time they liked. Moreover, he knew how excruciatingly tedious it was waiting day in and day out, hiding behind a building and waiting for an attack that they were starting to think was never coming.

'You staying on after this if Fronto keeps the pay up?'

'Might do. Don't see why he'd need us then, but you know these patrician nobs. They never seem to plan ahead. I've heard there's good money to be made in the capital. Pompey's hiring again they say, and paying well.'

'That old has-been? He must be ancient by now. 'Bout time he and his cronies moved aside and let someone younger and brighter have a go at bullying the senate.'

Picentus grinned. He knew damn well Eurycles' views on the senate and Roman government. The Greek never passed up an opportunity to rise to that bait and argue the ineffectiveness and unfairness of Roman government compared with the ancient glory days of his native Athens.

Silence greeted his verbal jab. Picentus let go of the vent lever and turned, frowning.

Behind him, Eurycles fought desperately against the grip of the two men who had him by the arms and the hand stuffing a rag bundle into his mouth. The Greek's eyes were wide in terror, but Picentus only gave him a passing panicked glance. His gaze instead locked on the olive-skinned thug before him, wielding a heavy wooden practice sword, raised and ready to strike.

''Ello' said the big killer with an unpleasant, nine-toothed smile just as the heavy, lead-cored wooden sword fell and cracked Picentus across the skull, dazing him and driving out his wits.

When he awoke, to the urgent shoving and desperate shouts of his Greek friend, he at first panicked that his captors had blinded him, so utterly black and featureless were their surroundings. Then he finally spotted the misty-hazed thin white crack in a square that marked out the position of the door.

Oh shit.

Already the air was almost unbreathably hot and sulphurous. He could feel the sweat literally running from him in torrents. His clothing was as soaked as if he'd thrown himself in a pool, though only a pool of almost scalding water.

'Help!' he bellowed.

'No use' wheezed Eurycles. 'They've gone.'

'*Someone* will hear' he replied desperately, struggling to his feet despite the flashing lights in his brain and the thumping of his battered skull. 'Someone will come.'

'No they won't' the Greek said quietly. 'They're expecting someone to be in here and screaming, remember? Unless they're close enough to hear the words they won't even blink. We need to escape.'

Picentus felt the icy fingers of fear grip him despite the unbearable heat. Eurycles knew as well as he that there was no way out. The two of them had been the ones who had checked each individual vent and the door lock and frame and hinges, Everything had been reinforced. The bastards had even propped something heavy against the door as was now obvious from the area of darkness blocking the feeble line of light at the base of the door.

They were going to boil to death. If they were lucky they would pass out from the heat and fumes first.

For the first time, Picentus cursed the pleasant Falerii family who had hired them and paid above the odds. Nice bunch, but no amount of nice would balance this.

Something somewhere deep in the earth shifted slightly and the billowing cloud of sulphurous steam burst into increased life, filling the room with a fresh wave of tortuous heat.

* * * * *

Balbus, finishing his bi-hourly tour of the crater to check its defensive status, nodded in satisfaction as he reached the fumaroles. The jets had moved, of course. Every time he came here the steaming columns of deadly heat were in different positions. But much to his satisfaction, the paths that they had marked with darker grey stones were still safe and clear. No matter how often he came here, every time he expected them to be obscured by a new jet.

With an unintentional indrawn and held breath, he stepped onto one of the four paths and took a dozen or so steps into the maze of steam jets, his eyes constantly shifting between the infernal environment around him and the path ahead.

With a skipped heartbeat he stopped dead in his tracks, realising that he had almost stepped away from the trail. Some new sliding of scree or shaking of the ground had dislodged a few of the grey pebbles and they had rolled off to the side.

Balbus stared at the errant rocks and weighed up the importance of them. There was a horrifying possibility that he would bend to move the rocks back into place and a jet would open up beneath him and flash-boil his hand. He did *not* relish that possibility. But then, there was also the possibility that if he did not move them back, he or someone else in the heat of battle would do exactly what he'd just almost done and walk off the path and into an unpleasant death.

With another held breath, Balbus dropped sharply to a crouch to move the stones back into their correct position.

It was only the suddenness of the move that saved his life, as two arrows and a sling-propelled sulphur rock whizzed through the air where his head had been and clattered off among the rocks and steam vents.

The sounds were barely discernible over the pop and hiss and crackle of the fumaroles and the pounding of his own heart, but Quintus Lucilius Balbus had spent much of his adult life in command of a legion, and he knew the sound of arrows and sling stones as well as he knew the map of pronounced veins on the back of his own hand.

He knew before the missiles had skittered across the rocks that he had come within a hair's-breadth of death. He also knew that the missiles had come from his rear right quarter and at a raised angle, which put them on the crater's slope where no one should be.

His instinctive strategist's mind kicked in and he made himself as small as possible, little more than a ball of human being curled up on the ground. He was a reasonably tall man and, standing, he had been visible above the bulk of the steam, apart from the stronger jets. At ground level, hopefully the roiling whiteness would hide him from view. It was a gamble, but one worth taking, given his exposed position.

He counted ten heartbeats - certainly long enough for a halfway-competent archer to nock and release another arrow. No further missiles came.

He was invisible in the steam. There was the possibility he would be suddenly betrayed as the vents shifted, though, and so, crouched and in a tight, small shape, he began to shuffle as fast as he dared along the path.

After another twenty heartbeats he heard a curse in Latin and a sliding section of scree. He was being pursued - someone had been following him on his rounds, probably. He wondered momentarily about the others, but quickly his attention focused once more on his predicament. He did not have the leisure to worry about the others.

More cursing and shouts and a name: Acrab? Not a name he knew, but a Syrian one, he believed. The directions made it clear that they *had* been following him, or at least had seen where he entered the steam. They were following the trail the same as he.

With a malicious smile, he decided on another gamble. If others were coming down here after him, the chances were good that the archers and slingers would not loose their ammunition for fear of hitting their own.

Swiftly, he rose and started to walk slowly forward, kicking the grey stones off to the right, changing the apparent course of the trail. After a few extra feet off track they would peter out, of course, but by then...

He had almost emerged from the far side of the steam vents when he heard his nearest pursuer scream.

* * * * *

Acrab - 'The Scorpion' - had been left in charge of the main force by his employer and former cell-mate - the enormous, unhygienic Celt - due to his knowledge of tactics and his ability to deal with sudden turnabouts in enemy forces. In his native Syria, he had taken good gold from the Parthians for continual disruption and trouble-causing to the Romans. He had fought well and evilly until that bastard Pompey had finally captured and imprisoned him.

He knew how to position his forces according to terrain and enemy numbers, and the information the Fronto woman had given them seemed to be holding up. She seemed to have known the terrain here like one born to the area, and had told them of the eight men who would be in the crater - four hirelings and four soldiers.

Fifteen men split into three groups. Five had gone for the shed to deal with the two men hiding there; five had gone to disable the archers, and the other five were with him. He had not given the signal until they had watched the leader - this 'Balbus' - visit all his defensive positions. Then, when they knew exactly where the meagre defenders were and what to expect, he had set his two other groups to their work and led the third down to the steam vents to take down the commander before he could re-join the others at the centre.

But then somehow things had gone wrong here. Through sheer ill luck, his three archers had missed the old man and lost him in the steam. In response, he had told them to train their weapons on the far edge of the roiling haze and watch for his reappearance. At the same time, he took the other two men - he in the safe, rear position - into the steam. It immediately leapt to mind that the old man might move the trails of stones and kept his eyes carefully on the ground, but that had apparently not occurred to the morons in front of him.

The fumarole had boiled Quadratus before their very eyes, turning him bright pink and searing his flesh, raising blisters and pustules. The most horrifying thing - and little sickened Acrab these days - was watching the man's eyeballs soften, blister and then burst in the length of a single heartbeat.

The second man in the line - Euphrillos - had panicked in that brief moment and instead of standing right where he was or carefully backing up the way he had come, he spun to flee, lost his footing on the rocky scree and vanished sideways with a shriek into the steam. At least Acrab hadn't had to watch that one!

With deliberate, slow care, Acrab stepped back onto the original path and began to wend his way back to the entrance. There was no point in pursuing the man further and risking emerging from the far edge only to fall foul of his own archers. As he emerged from the steam, he gestured his intention to the missile troops and skirted the area of dangerous fumaroles, heading for the far edge where presumably the old man would emerge.

* * * * *

Galronus looked round at the sound of the scream and nudged Masgava.

'Hope that wasn't Balbus.'

'It wasn't. But that means they're here. And since the signal wasn't given, they didn't come from the villa approach.'

'Do you think Fronto...?' Palmatus hissed the unfinished question.

'Fronto can take care of himself' Galronus stated flatly. 'We need to deal with our own problem right now. Do we stay here and wait or do we try to leave the mudpools and find them?'

'We stay' Masgava replied. 'If we leave, we might run straight in to them, and we certainly negate all the advantages we chose this place for.'

'Then Balbus is on his own' Palmatus sighed.

'Balbus also can take care of himself' snapped Galronus.

'Can you see something?'

The three men peered into the haze of steam surrounding them, rising from the mudpools and reacting with the cold air. After a moment there was a distinct humanoid shape some twenty paces away in the mist.

'He's close.'

'He's buggered' replied Palmatus, nodding in that direction.

Almost as if to illustrate his point, the figure disappeared with a shriek and there was the muted sound of some sucking glutinous murk. A blood-curdling scream suddenly rent the air and wailed constantly, going from strength to strength as the man who had slipped into the boiling mud floundered, his legs coated with liquid fire. No matter how much he rolled around it was not putting out the burning in his flesh.

More figures began to emerge from the mist, grey and ghost-like as they moved ever closer, inching slowly, horribly aware of the dangers. The very fact that they were so careful and attentive spoke volumes to the defenders. The newcomers had known about the place before their attack, and that meant they must have done for Fronto, as he was the only one who wasn't here and who knew all their plans. And, of course, he had not arrived with them on his tail.

Despite all their pre-warning and care, two more men fell foul of the bubbling, boiling mud before they came close enough to do any real damage, and the screams of three men were now forming some sort of disharmonious chord through the steam cloud.

'Seven. Three of us: seven of them' Palmatus whispered.

'Yes. I almost feel sorry for the poor bastards' Galronus laughed, and a dazzling white grin split the ebony face of Masgava.

Palmatus shook his head. 'You lot are crazy.'

* * * * *

More than half a mile away, Fronto skittered across the marble flooring of the summer dining room and out to the building's rear portico, ducking to the side of the door as he emerged into the arcaded walkway.

It had felt almost cowardly running from the two men now that Lucilia was safe, but he was also shrewd enough to know that even with his fitness at an all-time high, taking on a giant and a murderer - both of whom were masters at the craft of death - in an open fight was nothing short of suicide. Divide and conquer. He had to split them up somehow.

Now, leaning against the house's rear wall, he paused only long enough to remove his hobnailed boots and drop them over the arcade into the flower bed beneath. The initial run had relied on speed to put

411

distance between them and also announce his direction of movement to the enemy, laying an audible trail. Now that the pair would be prowling through the rooms of the villa searching for him, he needed a little more stealth, and hob-nails on marble was less than stealthy.

With bare feet, unencumbered by armour or heavy toga, he felt light and lithe.

Strangely, despite everything he had done to bring this fight onto his own ground instead of ending up running through his house and fighting for his life as he had for *two damn years now*, he had ended up through ill fortune doing exactly that. The house was different, sure, but the situation was almost the same as when Clodius' thugs had attacked the house on the Aventine, or when the murderous tribunes Hortius and Menenius had hunted him through his own bath house.

But not quite.

Something was different this time.

Fronto was smiling.

Instead of being a put-upon physical wreck being assaulted on his own property and trying to stay ahead of the enemy, he was as prepared as a man could be. He felt confident and strong. Perhaps for the first time in years, both Fortuna and Nemesis were watching him on his home ground and nodding their approval.

He was no fugitive or panicked defender this time. For all that he had run from them outside, it was in truth a planned move to gain him enough distance to remove his boots and to undertake the next step. He was in control of this fight. Berengarus and the monstrous ghoul that accompanied him had picked the wrong man to mess with this time.

With a quick rub of the Fortuna pendant he'd picked up on his return to Rome last year he took a deep breath and crouched, launching himself upwards. His hands grasped the lintel of the roof and with a dexterity he'd almost forgotten about, pulled himself up and onto the tiles of the portico roof, the sheath of his sword almost catching, forcing him to adjust mid-manoeuvre.

He could, of course, have easily run up one of the two internal staircases to the upper level, but the stairs were of creaking, noisy wood and he would easily have been heard by his pursuers. Instead, they would have heard him run through the house in his nailed boots and know that he was still on the ground.

More fool them. With a gentle slap of flesh on the wooden boards, he dropped through the upper floor windows and into one of the many unused rooms. Pausing, he could hear the pair clumping around on the ground floor in their heavy boots - well, he could hear the giant German thumping around and a strange dragging sound that denoted the movements of the wounded ghast with his damaged foot.

The latter first.

With a smile of personal satisfaction, Fronto moved through the room, mentally tracking the scraping of the broken foot. He nodded to himself as he heard the very slight change in tone when the ghoul stepped from the delicate patterned marble of the tablinum to the plain stone at the base of the staircase. Few would be able to discern the difference, but Fronto had played games reminiscent of this with his friends in his youth and had come to know every corner and crevice of this place and even the sounds of the floors.

His brow creased as he moved to the landing above the wooden staircase and he almost sniggered. Moving around to the opposite end of the staircase from the top step, he reached out to the bust of his grandfather. It really was surprisingly ugly. He didn't remember the old man having a misshapen strawberry for a nose or such drooping baggy eyelids. The sculptor of this memorial bust should have been beaten senseless for crimes against art.

Fronto cleared his throat - a sound more reminiscent of a laugh than anything else.

Just as he'd predicted - just as Lollius had once done aged seven and received a cup of urine on his head for his efforts - Tulchulchur, the monster of Vispul appeared at the bottom of the stairs, his face turned upwards, leering as he brandished his curved blade.

The marble head of Lucius Falerius Draco hit the killer at the hairline above his left eye, smashing his skull and driving fragments of bone into his brain.

Fronto watched for a moment as the strange old wraith gently folded up like some wooden apparatus, brains and blood leaking from his head as the marble bust bounced off across the stone floor, covered in gore and clumps of hair.

Tulchulchur lay on the ground, one foot shaking wildly as his system fought to control his body despite the fact that a sizeable portion of his brain had been mashed and invaded by bone shards. Incredibly, as Fronto peered down, he saw one hand reach out and grasp the step, using it to pull the twitching body up to a seated position.

How could such a frail old thing still be alive after that?

And yet the smashed, crimson head turned upwards, the rheumy eyes refocusing slowly on the face looking down over the banister.

'Yeeee-ooooo-uuuuu. Dhhhhh-iiiiieeee' it hissed, spittle on its lips mingling with the blood running down its face. Fronto had a horrible feeling as the thing began to pull itself to its feet that the Monster of Vipsul was more than a mere man. Was it one of the *Lemures* - shades of the wicked departed that wandered the world carrying only malice?

The crushed foot shuffled forward to the step and, ignoring the pain and the pulping of its own brain, the wraith began to climb, slowly and laboriously, parchment thin knuckle skin whitening with its grip on the wicked curved, razor sharp knife. The right eye was fixed on Fronto, while the left one, slightly dislodged from the blow, rolled a little in the socket, not quite able to follow.

Fronto shuddered. He could see pink-grey brain matter through the crimson gloop on the thing's skull.

'Beerrrrrrengaaaarusssshhhhh' the thing called out to its companion. 'Up sssstaaaaaiiiirssss!'

Fronto felt a coldness in the pit of his stomach. He had expected that to end the wraith, but now it seemed to be coming for him still.

* * * * *

Balbus ducked from the far side of the vapour jets but stopped, crouched, at the edge. Another trail of dark stones led back in only a couple of paces away. Keeping low in order to remain obscured by the steam, he moved along to the next path and disappeared into the white fog once more. Just as he ducked back inside, he saw a figure emerge from the edge - someone had skirted the entire area to try and catch him and had missed his re-entry by a couple of heartbeats.

Very carefully - making sure of the efficacy of his trail - the ageing commander moved along the path as fast as he dared. He had trod these tracks more than a dozen times each morning over the past few days and knew exactly where the trail emerged.

He smiled.

With a pop and a bubbling sound one of the jets near his right side suddenly died away and, sure enough, a moment later a new jet burst through the scree a few paces away.

A shield. He could have done with a shield, but it was sitting at the last defence point in the centre of the mudpools with the other three. All he had here were his mail shirt that seemed to weigh more every day he donned it, his sword and his pugio dagger.

It would have to be enough.

Like all soldiers, Balbus did not have a nebulous and all-encompassing fluffy equal favour for all the gods. He *respected* them all, of course, but a soldier's piety was a small and powerful thing - it had to be carried on his person into battle - so compact and tight it was a shining diamond of belief. Soldiers tended to devote their worship to one god in particular; often it was all they managed - who had time to invoke a pantheon facing a hail of arrows?

Balbus had always reserved his prime prayers for Jupiter - he was 'Greatest and Best' after all - but prolonged contact with Fronto and the peculiar habit of devoting his piety to the less invoked Fortuna had rubbed off, and he found himself asking the divine lady to watch over him for the next few moments.

The trail of darker stones ended a few paces ahead where the cloud thinned and Balbus squinted to see through the steam.

Fortuna was with him after all. And perhaps Jupiter and Mars too.

The three men with the missile weapons who had shot at him had come down to the lower levels and now sat by a low flat rock perhaps ten paces off to his left watching the far edge of the steam - entirely the wrong direction. Better still, the slinger had his leather weapon hanging loose in his hand and was facing away, speaking to the pair of archers whose weapons were primed but pointing away.

Reaching down, Balbus drew both his blades. Momentarily he weighed up the chances of hitting one of them if he threw the pugio, but quickly dismissed the idea. The standard military blade was not well weighted for throwing and he would almost certainly miss. The result would simply be one weapon less with which to fight.

He could feel his heart pounding away in his chest and felt a momentary worry that it was fighting too hard and that he might suffer the same illness he had fallen to against the Veneti two years ago. But no. It was excitement, pure and simple!

With a grim smile, and acknowledging the fact that after two years of enforced retirement, he felt he was back where he should be, doing what he should be doing, he burst from the steam at a run.

Should have had a shield.

The first arrow whizzed past his ear and narrowly avoided ending him mid-run. The second smashed into his shoulder, hitting the doubled section of mail with the extra leather-backed layer. The protection was entirely adequate and the arrow slammed into him but then fell away. The blow knocked him back and to the side, and would bruise badly, but did nothing to stop him.

Ten paces can pass quickly when running into battle. While the archers had only needed to turn toward him and release, their bows already primed, the slinger was still only just reacting with a turn of his head when Balbus hit him. Reserving his weapons for the archers, the older soldier simply used the slinger as a springboard, his nail-soled boot smashing into the back of the man's head and driving his face forward into the rock as the former legate leapt at the other two.

Balbus saw the expressions in the archers' faces change in that single heartbeat where he - airborne - descended on them. Desperation turned to sheer panic and dread. He was aware that he was grinning like a child opening a gift - he must look peculiar.

The archers had managed to discard their bows and reach down to their blade hilts but there had been no time to draw the weapons before Balbus hit them with unerring accuracy. His gladius slid into the notch at the base of a neck, through a windpipe and on, pausing briefly with the resistance of the spinal column before punching through and out the back of the man's neck. His spine severed, the archer's astonished, open-mouthed head lolled around loosely, the tendons fighting for control over it. Finally it flopped back almost facing to the rear, leaving a gaping second mouth of liquid crimson filled with steel.

The dagger plunged into the other archer's eye socket. A pugio's blade was wide - wider than an eye socket, anyway - and the blade jammed gratingly against the bone with only a third of its length in. Balbus let go of the hilt and it stayed where it was. The archer began to issue a high-pitched keening noise as he reached up to grip the hilt of the blade jammed in his head, eye-humours and blood running down his face, his mouth opening into a tragic theatre mask.

416

Turning, Balbus scanned the scene. In return for a single bruise, he had killed one, incapacitated another and left the third stunned and shaking on the floor. No others around. And Fronto kept telling him he was getting old!

Casually, he ripped the gladius from the dead man's neck and strode over to where the slinger was crouching, trying to stop his world spinning before attempting to rise.

He would never rise again.

Balbus grabbed his hair, lifting his head to face upwards and then calmly cut his throat from ear to ear. The man wheezed and bubbled as the blood fountained out onto the dusty earth and the older soldier let go and stepped back, trying not to become coated with any more gore than necessary.

All three. With a nod of satisfaction he turned, ignoring the wailing of the man who was still trying to dislodge the dagger from his eye. With a shrug he consigned the pugio to the 'lost' category and stepped a few paces down the hill.

Squinting, he tried to focus on the far side of the fumarole-strewn ground. It was with a mix of satisfaction and regret that he spotted the man who had tried to circle and entrap him running for the Puteoli road and accelerating with every pace. Acrab - the Syrian? - was leaving just in time.

The only activity remaining - barring the screaming of the wounded man behind him - was a vague shape of men deep in the central mudpool area. The others were fighting off the rest, then.

With a deep breath, Balbus shifted his grip on his sword and strode toward the low-hanging white cloud.

* * * * *

Masgava was comfortable with his lot. Three men *was* a challenge, but not an insurmountable one. He had once killed five in one fight in the arena at Thuburbo Minus, and had come away with only three stitched wounds. His two companions he wasn't so sure about. While they were good men and clearly fighters by trade and experience, a soldier was not trained the same way as a gladiator. They were taught to rely on formations and the support of their comrades.

The big Numidian parried a clumsy sica thrust with his own longer sword and brought his short-handled axe up, twisting it to trap the enemy blade. With a quick jerk downwards he used his two weapons to shatter the man's sica.

The move left him open to the others, but they were predictable - unimaginative fighters. As the pair lunged at him he sidestepped, driving his bulk into the warrior with the broken sword, and the other two narrowly avoided driving their weapons into each other. Content that he was in control of the fight, Masgava risked a glance sideways at the others.

Palmatus was struggling, but still in control. He had managed to force one of his opponents to drop his small circular shield - looked like he'd broken the man's arm - and the warrior was fighting on half-heartedly, but the other was still in good condition and seemed to be pushing the former legionary backward.

Galronus was faring little better. The two men on him were working concertedly, taking turns to force the Gaul onto the defensive while the other made a lunge for some unprotected part. The Remi noble was managing to fight off each attack and had even managed to draw blood on them in a couple of places, but he was clearly tiring.

A movement out of the corner of Masgava's eye caught his attention and without even looking round, he lashed out backward with his foot, catching his would-be killer in the crotch and making him double over.

A blade slashed his upper arm - just a decorative line among the network of scars - but Masgava stepped back to reposition. Served him right for getting distracted.

The man who wielded now only a stub of jagged broken sword had gripped it in both fists in an overhand position and raised it in front of him, looking for an opportunity to drive it into any ebony flesh that came available.

With an almost negligent laugh, Masgava turned and swung the axe, rear facing. The air rushed along the blade as the leading edge - a two-finger-width haft of ash - slammed into the broken blade end on. The man's hands and the weapon in them were slammed back and the rounded pommel of the broken sword smashed into the man's forehead with an audible cracking noise. The killer's eyes turned humorously inward and he dropped like a stone.

Masgava instinctively ducked from the waist as a blade whistled through the air at chest height. Turning, he grinned at the two men facing him who took a nervous step backward, one of them still gripping his aching crotch with his free hand. The pair looked at one another, perhaps for support, and then shifted their grip on their weapons and took a single deliberate pace forward. Masgava hooked one of his boots into the dry mud and dust at his feet and waited. Sure enough, the two men leapt at the same time. The Numidian brought his foot up and showered them both with choking, blinding dust and mud.

As they floundered and fell forward, coughing and blinking, the gladiator casually chopped down with his axe and cut through the neck of one. The blade was not quite large enough to completely sever the appendage, but the body slumped to the ground with the head at an odd angle. The remaining man backed away, wiping his eyes desperately.

Once more, Masgava took the opportunity to check on his friends. Both were down to one opponent, and both the enemy were wounded, but Galronus' left arm was hanging limp at his side, blood coursing down it in torrents from the shoulder. Palmatus' right leg was shaking, almost buckling, and soaked a dark red with blood from some fairly unpleasant wound. He would have to be careful else he might end up prone.

Well, when he was finished with this cretin, Masgava would go and help the others.

He turned back to the remaining man only just in time to jerk his head to one side. The man had thrown a dagger and Masgava felt the blade scrape along his temple and skull before it disappeared off into the distance with a muddy splat.

By the time he had recovered from his sudden unplanned defensive move, he turned back just in time to see the man running at him, shoulder first, intent on knocking him flat, sword back and ready to swing once the big Numidian was unbalanced.

Masgava almost laughed as he simply stepped aside and let the man's momentum carry him on and into the mud pool beyond where he tipped, yelling, into the boiling gloop. The third man had been dealt with, but Masgava had not the leisure to watch the poor fool boil. Instead he looked down at a sudden pain only to realise that the man had actually succeeded with that swung blade as he passed. With a grimace and biting down on his lip, Masgava dropped his weapons, reached down to his belly and gripped the bottom lip of his wide wound with his fingers, pulling the sheared flesh up to contain the loops of bowel that were sliding around ready to fall out.

419

Damn it!

With the single-mindedness of a man who had cheated death a hundred times, and with gritted teeth against the agony of the wound, Masgava lifted the flap of his stomach flesh outwards and peered into the hole in his gut.

He smiled. Miraculously he could see no real internal damage. It had simply been a lucky glancing blow. With grinding teeth and tears of pain welling in his eyes, he pulled the lips of the wound together and held his innards inside.

There was a scream nearby, but he could not spare the time to check what was happening with the other two.

'Jove!' said a wheezy, tired voice. The big Numidian looked up at the invocation to see the blood-spattered figure of Balbus striding toward him with sword in hand.

'Lucky blow.'

Balbus shook his head. 'A belly wound.' His face was a picture of concern. Such wounds were usually the worst for a warrior. It could take days to die and the pain would be intense the whole time. Masgava took a deep, shuddering breath.

'I need your help.'

'You have it.' Balbus glanced at the others but seemed satisfied with what he saw.

'I will open the wound and I need you to run your hands along the tube and look for cuts. I think it is intact, but I need to be sure.'

Balbus went pale. '*What?*'

'Check for interior damage. If my gut is whole it will heal and I will live. If not, I want you to give me a warrior's death here and now. I do not want to live out my final hours on a table stinking of blood and shit and writhing in pain. Will you check?'

Balbus stared and then nodded. What else could he do?

'And then' the big man added, 'I will need help pinning the wound together.'

Behind them, Galronus and Palmatus, the latter limping and staggering, the former with a swinging useless arm, closed together on the one remaining man. The criminal turned to run - a fatal mistake.

* * * * *

420

Fronto backed away from the stairs, listening to the creepy drag - thump - drag - thump of the wounded wraith's feet on the steps. Distantly, he could hear the clatter of Berengarus' own passage through the building and up the wooden staircase at the house's far side.

He had perhaps a count of a hundred before the big barbarian found him, and that meant a count of a hundred to deal with the living-dead thing that was rising up the staircase to find him.

Tulchulchur was a murderer rather than a warrior. He relied on stealth and control, his victims taken by surprise and then restrained. Fronto was neither of those things, so it should hardly be a challenge.

Moving around the wooden floor, he positioned himself a little way back from the head of the stairs, gladius in hand and ready for the fight. With a smile of satisfaction he waited. A long moment later - a moment filled with that eerie 'drag - thump' - the smashed, glistening, crimson head of the wounded ghoul appeared over the edge of the stairs, the misshapen eye swivelling in an attempt to join its partner as the Monster of Vipsul locked his gaze on Fronto.

'Caaaaan't kiiiiillllll meeeeee forrrr iiiiii kiiiiill yoooouuuuu' it hissed as it limped up the last step.

'I beg to differ' snarled Fronto flexing the knuckles of his free hand.

With that horrible dead thing grin, Tulchulchur limped forward, straight at him.

Fronto frowned. It was simply *too easy*. Something must be going on that he was not yet aware of? A quick scan revealed nothing else, though - the sounds of Berengarus' footsteps put him two rooms away yet at least. With a strange feeling of uncertainty, he put his weight onto the ball of his right foot and lunged forward. The wraith didn't even raise his knife to try and block the blow. Fronto's gladius sank into the flapping tattered robes and he felt it bite into something resistant. When he yanked the blade back out there was no blood. Fronto stared in confusion.

The ghoul grinned and simply let go of the knife, allowing it to fall away to the floor. Reaching into his tattered clothing, his hands closed on something. As the woollen shreds were swept aside, Fronto noted the bull hide chest piece that had protected the thing and realised that his blow had merely penetrated the armour and likely only grazed the ribs of the man beneath at best.

But it was not the bull hide to which Tulchulchur's hands had gone. They came out balled into fists and pressed tightly together in an almost penitent fashion. Fronto frowned as he took a pace backward. Whatever the lunatic had in those closed hands, it could hardly stand up against a gladius. The former legate's sword arm lanced out again, this time for the thing's maimed skull. The monster tried to tip his head to one side out of the way. He was surprisingly fast, but these days Fronto was faster. The sword's edge ripped through Tulchulchur's cheek, actually severing the connector for the lower jaw and then slicing his ear in half, grating against skull.

The wraith's jaw unhinged and hung in a horrible lopsided grin. Still the thing came on. Fronto tried to take another step back, but slammed up against the wall.

Tulchulchur gave a strange, keening giggle that bubbled the open maw with blood and leapt at him.

Again, Fronto lashed out with his gladius and this time the blade bit deep into the ghoul's chest, meeting resistance at the bull hide before piercing it and pushing through between the ribs and into the centre of the body. There was a momentary flicker of pain - or possibly irritation? - in the creature's strange gaze, and yet still it came on as though the wound were a mere scratch as if to embrace him in death.

In that moment Fronto found the hilt of his own gladius pressed up against him, still in his enemy's chest as the thing grabbed for his head. The monster was on him then, the smell of stale sweat, poison breath and mildewed decay mixed with fresh blood all about it. Even as the life was clearly fleeing the maimed, unpleasant thing, its hands suddenly flicked out and up.

Fronto's eyes widened as the throttling cord looped around his neck and the hands pulled tight. Tulchulchur still had a surprising amount of strength, yet it was clearly ebbing. Fronto could see the life departing the man's eyes in mere heartbeats as his own hands came up, abandoning his sword hilt in the desperate attempt to alleviate the choking pressure of the cord. With relief, he managed to hook two fingers inside the loop and prevent it from slicing into his windpipe.

'Weeee gooooo togetttttthhhhhheerrrrr' the thing hissed in his face, spitting blood and bile.

The wraith was dying but, with the ends of the garrotte looped and tied around his wrists, the falling weight of the slumping killer was simply adding all the more pressure to the garrotte. Fronto felt the first rising of panic. For all his skill with blades and his strength, he was in real trouble. With one hand trapped holding the cord a hair's breadth from killing him, he was left only with one hand. He could do nothing to untangle the cord from the wraith's wrists. The only option available was to sink to the floor with the dying thing, try to disentangle himself and retrieve his precious gladius from the body.

But he was too late for that.

Berengarus stepped into the room, swinging his long blade experimentally. The big German was grinning.

'Go on, then' Fronto snarled. 'Gloat. You appear to have me trapped.'

Desperately, his free hand was trying to disentangle the cord from his neck even as the rattle of death rose in Tulchulchur's throat. He needed to buy himself time to get free and retrieve his gladius.

Berengarus, however, simply swung his own sword once more as he stepped forward. He had no intention of dragging this out. Fronto stared as the huge barbarian grinned and shifted his grip on his sword.

And then the colossus suddenly straightened and spasmed, his head jerking. His eyes widened and bulged. Frowning in incomprehension, the big barbarian took a laboured step forward, but his body seemed not to respond as he expected and instead of closing on Fronto for the kill, he dropped to his knees like a sack of grain.

With only a simple blinking look of disbelief, the huge man fell forward onto his face.

Fronto's gaze moved to the large kitchen blade jutting from the man's spine halfway up his back - well placed to sever the nerves and paralyse, if not to kill. Even as he accepted the fact that he was saved, he looked up beyond the hilt to the form of his saviour in the doorway.

Lucilia looked shockingly calm.

'She was my mother you *shit*!'

Berengarus was not dead, his body shaking slightly as he tried desperately to rise despite the fact that his body was no longer obeying his own commands. His twitching hand was trying to reach round behind him to pluck the blade from his spine, but only his fingers seemed to respond.

423

Lucilia ignored him entirely as she stepped over the body and crossed the room to help Fronto remove the cord and stand. An angry red welt ran around Fronto's neck, making him look like the victim of a failed hanging.

'Come on.'

With Lucilia's support, he waited until his legs felt stronger and rose to his full height. He peered for a moment at the two bodies in the room. Tulchulchur was gone completely and there was no way he was going to waste even a copper '*as*' under the tongue of that thing. Berengarus was clearly alive and trying to communicate and to move, but remained twitching and immobile like some insect pinned to a board. Fronto knew that back wound. Even if the blade were removed, he would never walk again. There would be no movement in his lower half, but more than that, he appeared to be having trouble with the rest of his body too. *Good* Fronto thought. He would hopefully live a long, painful and extremely miserable life for what he had done. There was no carcer in Puteoli, but there were some lovely cave systems in the cliffs.

Slowly, rubbing his neck and clutching Lucilia as though he might collapse, he made for the stairs with a last look at Berengarus, whose mouth was opening and closing in some kind of plaintive whisper.

Let the bastard suffer.

'You shouldn't have come back. It was foolhardy.'

Lucilia raised an eyebrow. 'Think where you'd be if I hadn't, beloved husband.'

'True. But still…'

His wife's eyebrow simply stayed quizzically raised. 'What makes you think I came back for you?'

'What?'

'I needed to cut my bonds. The knives are in the kitchen.'

Fronto blinked and Lucilia simply laughed. 'Come on. Let's get some air. It smells in here.'

'You are a bloody marvel, woman. You know that?'

'Of course I do, dear. Now come on.'

Epilogue

Fronto stood in the courtyard garden of the villa, rubbing his red sore neck and enjoying the chill of the evening with the faint damp that threatened rain during the night to come. The events of the previous few days, and indeed much of the year, had been distilled in his mind in the solitude of the peaceful garden into a simple fact: nowhere was safe in these times. For so long he had spent two thirds of each year tramping around foreign soil with the legions, bringing the light of civilisation to the backward and extending the power and the influence of the republic, and the remaining third generally in some cheap cesspit of a tavern in Tarraco or Barcino gambling and drinking away the winter months.

And then he had broken his own personal rule and returned to Rome and to the bosom of his family and the last three years had proved that Rome and Italia were every bit as dangerous and troublesome as Hispania or Gaul, but with the added peril of having other people relying upon him there. That was the great change, of course. In bringing his troubles back home, he had involved the family and his close friends and imperilled them, and that was near unforgivable. His father would be appalled.

Simply: he could not realistically see himself living in Rome or even Puteoli. If he could not spend his days as the gods had clearly intended, knee deep in mud and entrails destroying the enemies of Rome, then it was time to start thinking of others instead of himself. Balbus had already stated his intention to leave a capital which seethed with discontent and violence and return to his estate above Massilia. Though he'd not said as much at the time, Fronto had made his decision exactly then. For the safety of his family he and Lucilia would leave Italia and move into the villa that Balbus had thoughtfully built for his daughter and son in law. While he dreaded a long future stretching out in front of him filled with nothing but vines and horticulture and horse rearing and dinner parties, it would be a comfort to be living only a few hundred paces from the older man, and it would be perfect for Lucilia.

Yes. Massilia it was. Sooner or later the republic would consume the port that still retained its Greek culture and nominal independence, and it would become part of Narbonensis, and then

425

who knew? Perhaps Massilia might get an arena and a hippodrome? That would be a comfort - something to distract him from the endless monotony of the farmer's life.

In a few more moments he would have to go back inside. Lucilia was preparing a hearty meal for them all and the men would be wondering where he had got to. It seemed they had come away remarkably lightly given the dangers they had faced. Fronto had acquired a sore throat and a huskiness to his voice from the near strangulation; Palmatus was limping but his leg would heal, as would Galronus' arm. Masgava was still pale and bed-ridden but seemed in good spirits and was convinced he would pull through. Fronto was glad it hadn't been him who'd had to help seal the man's stomach wound. Balbus had still looked pale and panicked from the experience by the time they arrived back at the villa with the big Numidian carried on a shield. The poor bastards who'd been locked in the steam room had been too far gone to save by the time the door was jemmied open, and the two with the sling and bow had been swiftly dealt with, but it could have been so much worse.

A few more moments. The night air was so peaceful.

A clatter of hooves.

Horsemen?

He heard the noise of the hooves on the gravelled path before the party crested the rise and began to approach the villa. He frowned. There were perhaps two dozen of them and even in the low evening light with the sun already disappeared behind the Misenum headland he could make out enough details. Soldiers. Many of them bore plumed helms and some wore cloaks.

What was this? Some new threat? Was Pompey really so stupid and bloody-minded that he would send soldiers in case of the failure of his pet murderers. News of their failure would not reach Rome for days, if at all. That depended on whether the sole survivor - a man called Acrab apparently - felt inclined to return to Rome and Pompey. Seemed unlikely.

Slowly, Fronto took a step backward. If they were professionals and the cavalry were accurate with their spears there was every possibility they could skewer him before he made it through the door and into the villa. He could hardly run, nor could he yell the alarm in case it just brought spears his way. And so he crept slowly backward, hopefully unnoticed by the riders, keeping his eyes locked on them.

Definitely around twenty of them. Half a dozen men in extremely high quality tunics and cloaks, their boots brocaded and decorated with embossed lions, their cloaks as glittering as the godsawful thing Faleria had made him years ago and that he'd lost not long after in Gaul. Behind those six officers, the rest resembled the Praetorian guard of a powerful general. And yet, he could not place the man at the fore.

He was not Pompey, Caesar or Crassus - Fronto knew all three by sight. Of course there were perhaps a dozen other men in Rome who rated such escort and spectacle in military style, but to Fronto's knowledge none of those were brave enough to pomp themselves up in a world where that could be seen as setting themselves in opposition to the triumvirate of greats.

The man was not thin, but his bulk was muscular and strong, not fat. His handsome face was wide and displayed both the lines of a man given to laughter and the complexion of a man given to drink. His hair was dark and short, yet uncontrollably curly. He seemed extremely at ease with himself, a fact that only put Fronto all the more on guard.

Back-pacing, Fronto had almost reached the door when the party pulled up just outside the gate and the leader slid easily from his saddle and stretched like a man returning home from a long day's work. His eyes met Fronto's and he smiled.

It was as though the tension had been exploded with a look. Something in the man's genuine friendly expression immediately discounted the possibility of violence or trouble. With an easy grace that reminded him of Caesar, the man strode through the gate into the courtyard garden, pausing at the entrance to bend over a rose bush and inhale deeply of its scent.

'Roses. Always a personal favourite, especially after a day's riding that leaves ones nostrils filled with sweat and manure' the man smiled.

'Erm...'

'Marcus Falerius Fronto?' The man grinned and nodded. 'You would have to be. Even allowing for the bias and invective in the description I was given, you are quite unmistakable.'

Fronto frowned. Still, something about the man's easy manner kept him relaxed and at ease in himself. Yet he was on the back-foot. Failing to react perhaps because he had no idea what he was reacting to.

427

'I'm he. May I ask who *you* are?'

The man's smile widened - something that should be impossible without splitting his head in half. 'I am Marcus Antonius and I'm tired and parched. Is there anywhere we can go and sample the delights of your vineyard while we talk?'

Fronto found that he also was smiling. He'd never met Antonius, though Caesar had spoken fondly of him at times over the years. A distant cousin but also a friend, Antonius had been busy out in the deserts of Syria and Judea while Caesar fought across Gaul, and Fronto had often wondered why he had not accepted a commission in the general's army.

Fronto gestured toward the door.

'What brings you to our house?'

'You, you fool. Well, you and your friend the former commander of the Eighth.'

Fronto's brow wrinkled as he stepped into the warmer brightness of the entrance hall.

'You're here on *his* behalf? Caesar is not one to change his mind or forget a slight. I cannot imagine him sending such an august person just for us after the trouble I've caused him.'

Antonius laughed - a rich, dark laugh like a glass of mulsum on a warm night.

'Beloved Bacchus, no. Caesar simply asked me to gather the best officers Rome had to offer and I intend to do that whatever his personal whims. When I take on a task, I do it to the best of my ability.' He winked. 'Sometimes Caesar needs a guiding hand, as I understand you are well aware.'

'How did you know where to find me?'

The irascible Clodius told me where I might find both you and Quintus Lucilius Balbus. He was adamant that you would not accept -. However, Caesar has spoken to me of you in the past and I suspect that you and I are alike in many ways; and if I'm right, I think you are ready to take up command in his army once again. I go in a month to join his ranks in Gaul, as do the others out there. Think on my request while we find your wine cellar and peruse its contents.'

Fronto followed the man across the hall, gesturing toward the stores where the wine was kept. His head was spinning. Not an offer, as put to him by Clodius and Caesar months ago - as though they were doing him a favour - but a *request*. As though *he* would be doing *them* a favour by accepting. Marcus Antonius was clearly shrewd. Time to push further.

'You came all the way from Rome to Puteoli for two men?'

'Ha. Hardly, Fronto. You are an important figure in my search, but not the only one. We are bound for Paestum in search of the indefatigable Gaius Rufio, and then to Grumentum where I hear Publius Cornelius Sulla lives in semi-retirement on a sizeable estate. You and Balbus are conveniently on my way. If I am any judge of men, by the time my journey is complete and I pick up Caesar's trireme at Ostia I will have a dozen of the very best military minds in the republic at my side.'

Fronto digested this as he made his way into the store room. Antonius' eyebrows rose in admiration at the racks of amphorae.

'He will fight against having me back' Fronto said quietly.

Antonius shrugged.

'Briefly, perhaps. He respects my opinion, though, and he is short of effective officers. He will overcome his personal irritations sooner than you might think. If you know him as well as I think, you know that he will never let personal matters interfere with his work.' He chuckled. 'I take it from your words that you are willing to take up your command once more?'

Fronto pinched the bridge of his nose. He and Balbus again after years away? Serving together, back under the general? A year ago he had been so adamant that the general's service was not for him - that Caesar was not to be trusted and even not to be believed; that he was unscrupulous and cold and calculating. Comparing him to Pompey - the great pirate killer and general, the thrice triumphant commander and beloved of the senate - he came off as a villain.

It had taken close proximity and involvement with the great Pompey to see beneath the man's civilised veneer and to the raging anger and vicious streak within. After a year in the supposed civilised culture of the heart of Rome Fronto's viewpoint had changed somewhat. Yes, Caesar *was* cold and calculating. He was a single-minded politician and capable of acts that scraped along the baseline of acceptability. And yet it was now clear to Fronto that for all that, he was still the best commander and possibly even the best man for Rome. Pompey might tear Rome apart with his rage and Crassus would ruin it with his avarice. Caesar might seek to be something of a tyrant as Balbus feared, but he was strong. And as he strengthened so would Rome and all those who served the general.

Lucilia and Balbina and the servants could move to Massilia and live in the villas above the great port city and he and Balbus would be close to home when a season ended. It was almost too good to be true.

'I'll have an answer for you by morning. You *are* staying, yes?'

Antonius smiled and indicated the racks of amphorae. 'I *was* hoping you would offer me the night's accommodation. Thank you. And I look forward to your answer.'

An eerie howl echoed hollowly from somewhere outside, or perhaps even deep in the earth.

'I didn't know Puteoli had wild wolves?' Antonius quizzed, his brow furrowed.

Fronto tapped a foot on the flagged floor of the storeroom and smiled. 'Just another guest acquainting himself with his new accommodation. I fear the caves of Puteoli are somewhat different from his homeland.'

* * * * *

The druid rubbed his pained knee and peered across the flames to the man on the heavy wooden bench opposite. Not for the first time he wondered whether they were doing the right thing.

His people had been the heart and soul of the Celtic world since the earliest days - the lore keepers and even the king-makers. They had been the link between the world of men and the will of the gods. Their ways were secretive because without such secrecy power would dilute throughout the world and much of the important lore would be lost.

The man opposite was busy running his fingers through drooping moustaches and toying with the braid at his ear. He was broad and tall and chiselled-cheekbones handsome. He oozed confidence and power. Three years ago, when the druid had been a renowned figure among the Ambiani and his tribe had been under siege by the Romans he had met their commander Caesar and had recognised instantly the man's hunger, power and will. Caesar - he had known at that time - was not a man to stop short of total victory - a man who saw a new world with him at the head of it. Those same things the druid could see in the gaze of the Gaul opposite.

Esus.

It was not his name, of course.

The *real* Esus was no simple *man*. The *real* Esus was the blood-slicked lord of war - the battle god who with Toutates and Taranis constituted the very heart of all druidic rites. It was a measure of respect beyond reason to call this man Esus.

But there were good reasons for the pseudonym.

For over a year now the Romans had been delving into the druids' business. They had upturned every stone and caught half a dozen messengers, trying to prepare themselves for what they saw as a plot against them. It had become necessary to give this man a new identity so that the Romans could not use his real name to uncover anything truly important.

Also, if all went the way the druids planned, there was every chance that this man would become the very embodiment of Esus in the world of men. He was an accomplished warrior, hunter and leader of men. He was of a noble lineage and a man who claimed to respect the druids and the old ways. On the surface it was everything they could hope for. The entire council had given their consent, despite the reservations a number of them felt.

After all, the man's father had sought to rule Gaul himself and he had been only *half* the man that his son had become. Could they trust this warrior? If they went to all this trouble and he was truly his father's son, they could be denying the rule of all Gaul to Caesar only to replace the detached and cold Roman for a single powerful overlord who knew them all too well. No druid would submit to an overlord whether he be Roman or Gaul

He sighed. The council had decided and everything was in motion. There was simply no going back now. Soon the whole world would writhe in flames and only one power could come out in control. If placing their very future in the hands of a would-be king was the cost of being that one victor then so be it.

'The Eburones were stupid' he said quietly, poking the fire with a stick.

The big man stopped playing with his braid, raised a quizzical eyebrow and then picked up his long, heavy, decorative blade and began to run a whetstone along it.

'And the Nervii were idiotic to go along with them' the druid continued. 'They acted too soon. They sought to achieve the goal early and without our aid - to win the glory of a free Gaul for themselves. And now the Treveri are embroiled with Caesar's other man, probably expecting us to rush to his aid.'

431

'It is all to the good' the big man said without looking up from his blade.

'How so?' the druid asked irritably. Three of the biggest tribes in the north-east had jumped ahead of the plan and now they suffered the consequences, weakening the potential army the druids could count upon.

The big man continued to rasp along the keen edge with the stone.

'They tested the Romans and showed us what they could do. Until this winter we had only ever reacted to their attacks or dealt with them in small risings. Ambiorix and his allies showed us to some extent what is possible - they did destroy two legions, after all - and what clearly *not* to do. Add to that the likelihood that the Romans will see this rising of Belgae tribes as the culmination of what they have discovered rather than a symptom or side-effect, and we might find the Romans becoming a little more complacent in the coming year.'

'Possibly' the druid conceded with a nod of his head. 'But still it was a waste of men. I cannot see any potential benefit that outweighs the loss of potential forces.'

The whetstone stopped mid-stroke and the bright, emerald green eyes of the man they had dubbed Esus looked up at him.

'When you asked me to lead, you did so not because of my lineage - and *certainly* not because of my father - but because I can bring you a strategy that will win you all of Gaul and the destruction of the Romans. And when we have risen up like vengeful spirits and driven them from our lands, I will become a second Brennus, taking our warriors back into their own lands and to the city of Rome itself. We will free Gaul and then shake and burn Italia and reclaim all our ancient lands that have languished beneath the Roman boot for generations.'

He scraped the stone down the rest of the blade, admired his handiwork in the firelight and then slid the huge sword into its sheath.

'*You* look only at the immediate effects. *I* am looking ahead to the future. I know that you have spent two years building this plan and you have been surprisingly effective given your lack of experience or skill in the world of war or politics, but now it is time to relinquish your control. Now I and my companions will take the reins of this beast you have been rearing and prepare to ride it against

Caesar. But we are still a year or more away from our objective, so be patient and leave me to my task.'

'Do not disappoint us' the druid said simply.

'Have no fear' smiled Vercingetorix coldly as he rose to his feet, looming in the small hut. 'Caesar will soon rue the day he trod our sacred soil.'

END.

Author's Note

Where do I start? MM5 marks a turning point in the saga. I felt that there were too many threads hanging in Rome and too many doors that needed to be closed or opened, bearing in mind what the next few years will bring, and so it seemed prudent to set a considerable slice of the action there. This had become apparent during MM4 and even before that, during the third book, and is one of the main reasons for the departure of Fronto at the end of book 4. The other was the seeming repetition of rehashing the Britannia campaign two years running without some extra fun on the side.

And so Fronto was in Rome. There were tales to tell with his family and I hope that this volume has fleshed out something of the family history and brought the reader a tiny bit closer to understanding Marcus. Moreover, Fronto has been sliding from his prime for a few years and, with what is coming, it was something of a necessity to bring him to epiphany point and turn him around, strengthening and revitalizing him.

Hence the introduction of Masgava, who is one of my fave additions for a while. Despite their relative minor roles, I also enjoyed Palmatus and Elijah. Galronus, of course, has come to the fore a little more in terms of his social side. It's all about *character* in Rome this time. I suspect that the 'star medal for interesting creation' will go to the monster of Vipsul, though. Creepy.

A prime matter of import hiding behind the themes and plots in the book was bringing Fronto to face the necessity of returning to his role with the army while bringing Caesar's position to such a low point that the desperate need for officers of his calibre would overcome any rift and allow the reconciliation of the two - or something similar in lieu of direct agreement.

There are, as you'll have noted, a surprisingly high number of character deaths in this particular book of the series. Only some of this is my doing! History is my ultimate master, and 54BC saw some brutal events leading to the deaths of characters that have become somewhat central to events. Blame the fates, eh?

I have chosen to ignore or twist certain factors or events in the pursuit of a clear storyline or because I find them dubious in their authenticity or they fit the tale badly. A prime example is that Caesar's diary speaks of Mandubratius as Caesar's motive for being in Britannia but since it is thrown in almost as an afterthought, it sounds a great deal like Caesar later trying to justify a costly and only marginally successful escapade. His removal from the equation did give me a chance to build up Cassivellaunus to be the interesting character he turned out and to add another dimension to the great 'Gallic conspiracy' rather than making him yet another victim of Caesar's brilliance. I prefer to think that some of the Celtic commanders of the era would have been a match for the great general's intellect.

I moved the likely arrival of the news of Julia's death, which probably happened at the early stages of the Britannia campaign and kept them largely in the background as I do not believe those events would add to the story in any greater detail. The news of his mother and daughters' deaths were so intensely private to the general that he never even mentions them in his own text and so I prefer to see him locking away the feelings and ignoring it publically. It fits the general I have portrayed

Removing Caesar from the 'rush to the rescue' of Cicero and placing it in the hands of the survivors of the Fourteenth made literary sense and allowed for a heroic return of their eagle and its raising in battle. The complexity of the distribution of legions in late 54 cannot be 100% resolved without making intuitive leaps. It also occasioned a shuffling of officers.

The revolt of the Eburones is a notable turning point in Romano-Gallic tensions of the campaign. It is usually treated as very much a separate event as the great rising that was to follow, as have the ones that went before. Separate tribes causing trouble as circumstances and opportunity saw fit. I see it somewhat differently. I see it as a gradual increase in organisation and resistance and have thusly tied it all together with a druidic conspiracy. While there is no evidence of this, it adds to the general theme, I feel, and we know little enough about the druids to make this entirely feasible. And so the first major rising has become a 'jumping the gun' on the main revolt to follow.

In many ways this book was about two things: the exploration of character in depth, and closing and opening doors in advance of future events, preparing for the rise of a real enemy of Rome and then the troubles that Caesar will both face and create in the years that follow. Consequently, there are still threads hanging. For instance: the prophecy has been left not quite fulfilled. It does not take a deep understanding of the period to see how it will complete soon and what effects it has. The prophecy will resolve a little more next year

I originally envisaged the ending of the book to be more something of a Roman 'First Blood' with Fronto in the John Rambo role, but in late planning it developed in something of a different direction due largely to the fact that I felt Lucilia needed to have the last word in the fight. I hope the conclusion sat well.

Three books in a row have had increasing chunks based in Rome, but that comes to an end now for a while. The events of 53 and 52BC are so tumultuous that there will be little chance to look beyond the disaster that is Gaul. Those of you who prefer the military side and lament the increasing forays into the city, relax. Books VI & VII are solidly military campaign in their setting. After all, Fronto has nothing to go back to Rome for now.

So, looking forward I am champing at the bit to get into books VI & VII which deal with the great revolt and its architect Vercingetorix (who I have had brought to the cusp by the ever-troublesome druids). I also get to deal now with Marcus Antonius, who was one of the original character templates on whom Fronto was based and so the play between the two should be thoroughly entertaining.

Fronto is the strongest, fastest and fittest he has ever been.

He'll *need* to be with what comes next.

Simon Turney - May 2013

Full Glossary of Terms

Ad aciem: military command essentially equivalent to 'Battle stations!'.

Amphora (pl. Amphorae): A large pottery storage container, generally used for wine or olive oil.

Aquilifer: a specialised standard bearer that carried a legion's eagle standard.

Aurora: Roman Goddess of the dawn, sister of Sol and Luna.

Bacchanalia: the wild and often drunken festival of Bacchus.

Buccina: A curved horn-like musical instrument used primarily by the military for relaying signals, along with the cornu.

Capsarius: Legionary soldiers trained as combat medics, whose job was to patch men up in the field until they could reach a hospital.

Civitas: Latin name given to a certain class of civil settlement, often the capital of a tribal group or a former military base.

Cloaca Maxima: The great sewer of republican Rome that drained the forum into the Tiber.

Contubernium (pl. Contubernia): the smallest division of unit in the Roman legion, numbering eight men who shared a tent.

Cornu: A G-shaped horn-like musical instrument used primarily by the military for relaying signals, along with the buccina. A trumpeter was called a cornicen.

Corona: Lit: 'Crowns'. Awards given to military officers. The Corona Muralis and Castrensis were awards for storming enemy walls, while the Aurea was for an outstanding single combat.

Curia: the meeting place of the senate in the forum of Rome.

Cursus Honorum: The ladder of political and military positions a noble Roman is expected to ascend.

Decurion: 1) The civil council of a Roman town. 2) Lesser cavalry officer, serving under a cavalry prefect, with command of thirty two men.

Dolabra: entrenching tool, carried by a legionary, which served as a shovel, pick and axe combined.

Duplicarius: A soldier on double the basic pay.

Equestrian: The often wealthier, though less noble mercantile class, known as knights.

Foederati: non-Roman states who held treaties with Rome and gained some rights under Roman law.

Gaesatus: a spearman, usually a mercenary of Gallic origin.

Gladius: the Roman army's standard short, stabbing sword, originally based on a Spanish sword design.

Groma: the chief surveying instrument of a Roman military engineer, used for marking out straight lines and calculating angles.

Haruspex (pl. Haruspices): A religious official who confirms the will of the gods through signs and by inspecting the entrails of animals.

Immunes: legionary soldiers who possessed specialist skills and were consequently excused the more onerous duties.

Kalends: the first day of the Roman month, based on the new moon with the 'nones' being the half moon around the 5th-7th of the month and the 'ides' being the full moon around the 13th-15th.

Labrum: Large dish on a pedestal filled with fresh water in the hot room of a bath house.

Laconicum: the steam room or sauna in a Roman bath house.

Laqueus: a garrotte usually used by gladiators to restrain an opponent's arm, but also occasionally used to cause death by strangulation.

Legatus: Commander of a Roman legion

Lilia (Lit. 'Lilies'): defensive pits three feet deep with a sharpened stake at the bottom, disguised with undergrowth, to hamper attackers.

Mansio and **mutatio**: stopping places on the Roman road network for officials, military staff and couriers to stay or exchange horses if necessary.

Mare Nostrum: Latin name for the Mediterranean Sea (literally 'Our Sea')

Mars Gravidus: an aspect of the Roman war god, 'he who precedes the army in battle', was the God prayed to when an army went to war.

Miles: the Roman name for a soldier, from which we derive the words military and militia among others.

Octodurus: now Martigny in Switzerland, at the Northern end of the Great Saint Bernard Pass.

Optio: A legionary centurion's second in command.

Pilum (p: Pila) : the army's standard javelin, with a wooden stock and a long, heavy lead point.

Pilus Prior: The most senior centurion of a cohort and one of the more senior in a legion.

Praetor: a title granted to the commander of an army. cf the Praetorian Cohort.

Praetorian Cohort: personal bodyguard of a General.

Primus Pilus: The chief centurion of a legion. Essentially the second in command of a legion.

Pugio: the standard broad bladed dagger of the Roman military.

Quadriga: a chariot drawn by four horses, such as seen at the great races in the circus of Rome.

Samarobriva: oppidum on the Somme River, now called Amiens.

Scorpion, Ballista & Onager: Siege engines. The Scorpion was a large crossbow on a stand, the Ballista a giant missile throwing crossbow, and the Onager a stone hurling catapult.

Signifer: A century's standard bearer, also responsible for dealing with pay, burial club and much of a unit's bureaucracy.

Subura: a lower-class area of ancient Rome, close to the forum, that was home to the red-light district'.

Testudo: Lit- Tortoise. Military formation in which a century of men closes up in a rectangle and creates four walls and a roof for the unit with their shields.

Triclinium: The dining room of a Roman house or villa

Trierarch: Commander of a Trireme or other Roman military ship.

Turma: A small detachment of a cavalry ala consisting of thirty two men led by a decurion.

Vexillum (Pl. Vexilli): The standard or flag of a legion.

Vindunum: later the Roman Civitas Cenomanorum, and now Le Mans in France.

Vineae: moveable wattle and leather wheeled shelters that covered siege works and attacking soldiers from enemy missiles.

If you enjoyed the Marius' Mules series why not also try:

The Thief's Tale by S.J.A. Turney

Istanbul, 1481. The once great city of Constantine that now forms the heart of the Ottoman empire is a strange mix of Christian, Turk and Jew. Despite the benevolent reign of the Sultan Bayezid II, the conquest is still a recent memory, and emotions run high among the inhabitants, with danger never far beneath the surface. Skiouros and Lykaion, the sons of a Greek country farmer, are conscripted into the ranks of the famous Janissary guards and taken to Istanbul where they will play a pivotal, if unsung, role in the history of the new regime. As Skiouros escapes into the Greek quarter and vanishes among its streets to survive on his wits alone, Lykaion remains with the slave chain to fulfill his destiny and become an Islamic convert and a guard of the Imperial palace. Brothers they remain, though standing to either side of an unimaginable divide. On a fateful day in late autumn 1490, Skiouros picks the wrong pocket and begins to unravel a plot that reaches to the very highest peaks of Imperial power. He and his brother are about to be left with the most difficult decision faced by a conquered Greek: whether the rule of the Ottoman Sultan is worth saving.

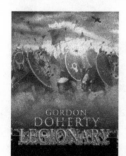

Legionary by Gordon Doherty

The Roman Empire is crumbling, and a shadow looms in the east. 376 AD: the Eastern Roman Empire is alone against the tide of barbarians swelling on her borders. Emperor Valens juggles the paltry border defences to stave off invasion from the Goths north of the Danube. Meanwhile, in Constantinople, a pact between faith and politics spawns a lethal plot that will bring the dark and massive hordes from the east crashing down on these struggling borders. The fates conspire to see Numerius Vitellius Pavo, enslaved as a boy after the death of his legionary father, thrust into the limitanei, the border legions, just before they are sent to recapture the long-lost eastern Kingdom of Bosporus. He is cast into the jaws of this plot, so twisted that the survival of the entire Roman world hangs in the balance.